CW00551482

CAGE OF TRAITORS

A TRIGGER MAN THRILLER

AIDEN BAILEY

INKUBATOR
BOOKS

Published by Inkubator Books
www.inkubatorbooks.com

Copyright © 2024 by Aiden Bailey

Aiden Bailey has asserted his right to be identified as the author of this work.

ISBN (eBook): 978-1-83756-416-3
ISBN (Paperback): 978-1-83756-417-0
ISBN (Hardback): 978-1-83756-418-7

CAGE OF TRAITORS is a work of fiction. People, places, events, and situations are the product of the author's imagination. Any resemblance to actual persons, living or dead is entirely coincidental.

No part of this book may be reproduced, stored in any retrieval system, or transmitted by any means without the prior written permission of the publisher.

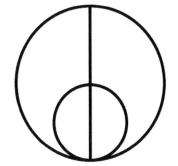

for Alyssa, with love

PART I

RETENTION

1

Rio de Janeiro, Brazil

The crack of three bullets, fired in quick succession, roused CIA operator Mark Pierce from his confusion.

Steam shot as a geyser from the bonnet of his sedan. The engine block lay crumpled against a brick wall. Humid air blown in through the shattered windscreen stank of diesel. People on the street in loose T-shirts, jeans and summer dresses ran both to and from his vehicle.

"Pierce!"

He turned his head at the sound of his name.

A late middle-aged man screamed from the passenger seat. He seemed sickly, like he'd suffered through a bout of chemotherapy. A shaved head, thin-framed glasses and a wiry goatee beard did nothing to improve his appearance. Ziplock ties secured his wrists around the passenger safety handle.

"Fuck, Pierce. You'll get us all killed!"

Pierce sat for a moment and focused on every single word the man had said.

He didn't know where he was.

He didn't know this man or understand why his car had crashed.

Every corner of his body ached, but no one part of his flesh hurt more than anywhere else. His mind felt like kneaded putty.

More bullets fired.

The rear window shattered.

A female screamed from the back seat.

Pierce ducked, then glanced over his shoulder. A young Latino woman in a yellow summer dress cowered low between the seats. Her smooth, light-brown skin shone with perspiration, and her face-framing bob converged in wet clumps. When he heard further shooting, she covered her head and screamed again.

"Pierce?"

Fighting his lethargic and aching muscles, he looked again at the older man. He didn't understand why he wasn't reacting to the violence erupting around him.

"Fucking shoot them, Pierce, before we're all killed!" The older man's eyes motioned to Pierce's belt, where a holstered 9mm semi-automatic pistol beckoned.

Suddenly finding his motivation to move, Pierce stepped out of the car as he gripped the Glock 19 sidearm in a shooter's grip, ready for lethal action.

Two men in light suits advanced. Spotting Pierce, both raised their FAMAE SAF submachine guns and fired. Spent .40 S&W casings flew from the noisy weapons. Flames licked from the barrels as bullets burrowed into the sedan.

Pierce ducked behind his wrecked vehicle and waited for the inevitable lull between shooting and reloading. When silence descended, Pierce dropped low and fired under the car, hitting the men's feet. Both assailants dropped as they screamed.

Pierce crouched but kept himself behind the cover of his wrecked sedan. He didn't know this location or his purpose here. Somehow, he'd crashed the vehicle into a stone wall inside a dense Latin American metropolis. He couldn't remember why he was in Latin America. His last memory was... Africa? The Sahara? The Congo?

"Fuck you, asshole!" the first injured assailant shouted in Spanish as he wriggled on his back. He tried to stand but couldn't with his mangled foot.

Despite the shooting pain in his head that came on when Pierce pondered his problems, he forced his mind to focus. Streets were narrow and steep. Many footpaths disappeared up the hill, crammed between tightly constructed houses built on top of each other. He identified a convenience store with Portuguese signage. Overhead, a cable car traversed through the sky, the bright sun reflected off its clean viewing glass. Further beyond lay steep, jungle-clad peaks of rock.

This had to be Rio de Janeiro. He had operated here once, long ago. Not with his current employers, the CIA, but with the special forces of... No, that was not a memory that would serve him here. But why he was in Brazil's popular tourist spot today was a mystery.

The fallen men alternated between bellowing screams or swearing in Spanish. Pierce spoke that language well enough and understood what they said. Where had he learned Spanish? Mexico City, as a child? Portuguese was the local tongue in Rio de Janeiro and mostly unintelligible to him, and not the language of his pursuers, either.

Deciding this was an unwanted deadly situation that required a resolution, Pierce advanced.

One assailant reached for his fallen submachine gun.

Pierce shot him twice in the head.

The second assailant, witnessing his partner's violent ending, paused as if considering whether to shoot Pierce or beg for mercy, then figured he had nothing to lose and went for his weapon. Pierce executed this foe in the same manner.

The woman in the car kept screaming.

Pierce looked up. The streets had cleared. The few pedestrians still visible watched with trepidation from behind brick walls or through holes in wooden fences. He spotted a thin dog with pronounced stick-like legs that watched him for a moment, then moved on.

When Pierce felt certain no one else was pursuing them, he checked the bodies. Each carried cash comprising Brazilian reals, and plenty of spare magazines for their submachine guns, but no identification.

Professional killers.

Pierce returned to the wreckage and rubbed his forehead. Pain still racked his body, but it was ethereal, difficult to describe or understand. Similar to a combination of drunkenness and experiencing constant electric shocks.

Back at the sedan, he noticed neither occupant had moved from where he'd left them. Physically, the woman in the yellow dress appeared unharmed, but she couldn't control her fear and kept screaming. The bound man remained calm as he pulled at the cable tie securing him to the safety handle, then yanked hard, trying to snap it. When he saw Pierce, he stopped trying to escape, and snarled, "I thought you were a better driver."

"I just saved your life." Pierce felt his response was appropriate, but the bound man's returned expression was disagreement. Pierce touched his forehead and again worried he might have a head injury. The flesh felt tender, but nothing seemed broken or cut. His head still hurt like everything else.

"Get me out of here, Pierce. The police are on their way. I'm worth more to you alive. Remember?"

Pierce tried to recall their relationship. He must know this man, if he had him bound and secured in his car. Was the man his prisoner? Was he a fellow CIA operator he had just saved from a kidnapping attempt? Was Pierce rescuing him from the pursuing men?

"Who are you?"

The man paused. He stared at Pierce as realisation struck. Then a cruel smile etched across his face. "I'm your fucking superior officer, that's who."

"What's your name?"

The man didn't laugh. "What kind of question is that?"

Pierce's head hurt trying to focus. "Who is she?" He pointed to the woman. Her screams had become sobs.

The bound man rattled his restraining cable ties. "What the fuck are you talking about?"

"I don't know...? Where are we? What are we doing?"

The man grinned again and seemed to relax marginally. "I thought you banged your head pretty fucking hard. I'm surprised you're not unconscious. Or dead."

Sensing all was not right, Pierce raised his pistol and pressed it against the older man's forehead. "I have a concussion?"

"More than that. You've lost your memories."

"No. I'm Mark Pierce."

"Well, not all of them, it seems."

Pierce sought context, but nothing came to him. Pierce knew himself. He was CIA, a Special Activities Centre, Special Operations Group operator. SAC/SOG Ground Branch, trained and perfected to operate alone for long periods in the field, delivering third-option justice where American influences could not otherwise reach. Proficient at all forms of combat and tradecraft, and fluent in five — maybe more — languages, including Spanish. He was a skilled killer, able to dispatch enemies of the state without experiencing emotional turmoil... Or was that what others expected of him, and killing for a living had cost him emotionally and brought on his faulty memory?

And was this man really his superior?

"You with the CIA?"

"Yes, I am! I'm your case officer." He nodded to the woman in the back seat. "We're extracting her from danger, taking her to a safe house."

"Why?"

Police sirens sounded in the distance.

Pierce turned, tried to gauge the approach vector adopted by the local law enforcement authorities.

"We can fucking talk all day. Or we can get out of here."

Pierce nodded. The man's suggestion to leave now made sense regardless of whether he was a foe or friend. Pierce found a black 6x9 Ratnik KAMPO tactical knife in a sheath strapped to his forearm and used it to cut the cable ties. Then he stepped back and kept his pistol trained on his supposed superior.

"Pierce, what the fuck are you doing?"

"Someone once told me, question everything? Was that you?"

The goateed man grinned. "You are one slippery asshole, Pierce. If you've forgotten everything, remember this: there is a good reason you're keeping me alive, and your own life depends on it." He stepped forward, staggered for a second, then thrust his arm towards Pierce.

Pierce instantly spotted the glint of a steel blade. Instincts and training took over, and he easily parried the strike, twisted the man's arm, bent him over until the limb almost snapped, and forced the older man to drop the weapon.

Pierce said, "You're a liar."

The man kicked out, caught Pierce behind the knee, and sent him rolling onto the cracked pavements.

Despite his groggy head and the generalised pain resulting from the car crash, Pierce staggered to his feet, ready to fight again. But the man was sprinting up one of the steep flights of steps and had a good dozen metres on Pierce already.

Pierce thought to give chase, but his head pounded like there were hammers beating at his skull. He didn't have the energy to pursue, thanks to his unspecified injuries and confused mind.

The sirens sounded louder.

The woman crawled from the car, then fell onto the cobbled pavement. She kept low so as not to be seen. Or shot.

Pierce walked to her. "I can't remember who you are, but I guess you know who I am?" When she didn't seem to understand him, Pierce switched to Spanish and asked the question again.

Timidly, she nodded.

"Two choices. Come with me, and I'll protect you, or stay here alone and wait for the police."

She held out her hand for Pierce to take. "I'll come with you."

She spoke Spanish. Another foreigner.

"Then let's move."

2

The favela, or urban slum, that Pierce and the nameless woman traversed comprised tightly packed houses forged from old wood, concrete bricks, plastic and rusted iron sheets. Each proceeding dwelling stacked upon the previous as they ascended the steep hill, and formed a haphazard collection of compacted multicoloured buildings. Overhead electrical wires ran like spiderwebs, and open drains stank of sewage. Murals of weeping women in prayer and snarling men threatening with pistols decorated blank walls. Pierce knew enough Portuguese to read graffiti that told the police to "fuck themselves!"

Later, Pierce realised they had climbed the narrow stairs for some time. He followed the shapely young woman in a yellow summer dress and ankle-high boots. He couldn't see her face because she walked in front.

"What are we doing?"

She turned his way. Her smooth skin was light brown, and her large bright eyes were a similar colour. Pierce guessed her age to be about twenty-five. Slim and of medium height, her poise and movement projected an alluring sex appeal. He also sensed she wasn't interested in him that way.

"Speak Spanish. My English is not good."

Pierce nodded and looked around. He heard distance sirens down the hill.

She said, "We're escaping the police?" When he didn't answer, she tucked a loose strand of her wet hair behind her ear. "You're saving my life. Both our lives. Not that I wanted or asked you to."

Memories of a car crash returned, and of a man claiming to be Pierce's superior, and that man's attempt to stab Pierce. Then memories returned of Spanish-speaking assassins pinning them with bullets fired from compact submachine guns.

"This is Rio de Janeiro, right?"

She nodded.

He saw the rise and fall of her chest. The steep climb in the humid conditions had already drained her stamina. In comparison, the ascent barely bothered him, but aching muscles and a sharp headache did.

Pierce heard a mosquito buzz past his ear. Awareness returned of the many red bite marks on his arms and face that itched.

She stood watching him, her face perspiring, her jaw muscles tensed.

He tightened his trembling fists. "You don't like me?"

"I don't like what you stand for. You're no better than the other man in the car."

A long paused followed without her completing her sentence. Eventually Pierce asked, "The other man in the car, who is he?"

"I don't know his name. All I know is that he kidnapped me off the streets. Then a few minutes later you kidnapped both of us and drove us into the favela, convinced someone was following us."

"Someone was," Pierce answered. "The men, remember, shooting at us after we crashed?"

She rolled her eyes. "Then everyone wants me, but none of you care what I want."

Pierce didn't answer, as his mind tried to piece together the events before the car crash, but nothing came to him.

"Not that I should care, Mark, but you don't look well."

"I'll be fine." He tried to remember when he had told her his name and guessed it could have been before the car accident, a time he could not remember.

Pierce tried to understand why they were heading up and through these labyrinthine passages. Then he remembered the sirens and figured they'd fled the police. Narrow streets provided both concealment from aerial helicopter surveillance and a network of passages from which to befuddle any ground-based pursuers. Any police coming for them could only do so on foot. He doubted any would, as favelas were dangerous neighbourhoods for uniformed officers. Local criminal groups and gangs would target cops with concentrated violence until they fled again.

Pierce gestured for her to keep walking, not allowing her a moment to catch her breath on the steep climb.

"Where are we headed, Mark?"

"Up."

"You know this favela?"

"No."

"Why am I your prisoner?"

Pierce paused when he realised he didn't have an answer

to that particular question. Conversely, the answers he needed from her were many, but now was not the time to press her. He didn't wish her to know that he had lost his short-term memory, fearful she could use this against him if she knew.

"Why should I trust you?"

Pierce almost said she shouldn't. "I'm the only person in the last fifteen minutes who hasn't tried to kill you."

She huffed, turned, and kept walking. Pierce noticed she didn't flee from him, and he wondered why.

As they climbed, his headache still felt like nails being pounded into his head. His awareness grew of the bruises spreading across all his muscles. Every part of him ached, his nerves responding as if they were both on fire and bathed in ice.

When he tried to remember his recent past, there was almost no recall.

Perversely, long-term memories were easy. He was Mark Pierce, code name the Trigger Man. A paramilitary officer with the CIA. Mackenzie Summerfield was his case officer, and soon he'd report in. Now that he remembered his only friend inside the Central Intelligence Agency, he recalled there was an important reason to make contact, and to do so urgently, but the purpose of the call he had forgotten.

His mind turned to recent operations in Mali in West Africa and Yemen in the Arabian Peninsula. He'd partaken in extensive missions in each war-ravaged country, but details remained elusive. Were these locations important?

Why was he in South America? Why was he running with this young woman who didn't trust him? Who was the man who'd tried to gut him with a knife?

For all these questions, Pierce had no answers.

Thinking hurt his head and fogged his mind.

Then from nowhere, a vivid image assaulted his mind's eye.

A naked woman...

Tied to a chair...

Her face bruised and cut from a prolonged beating...

Pierce couldn't be certain, but he imagined the naked and tied woman was the same woman who joined him now on their ascent...

Pierce shuddered and pushed the image aside.

As they climbed, he checked the many doors to see if any were open. None were. Thin people appeared everywhere on the narrow streets, and many were children. Two men tried to rob them at knifepoint. Pierce scared them off with his pistol, giving them to the count of three to scram before he stopped playing nice. They didn't argue and vanished.

Pierce and his companion eventually reached the green rainforest that grew to the slum's edge. Thick foliage comprised vines and creepers that strangled the many tree branches. He glanced back, marvelled at a commanding view of Rio de Janeiro, with its famous white sand beaches, expensive and well-organised suburbs further down the slopes, dramatic coastline, mountainous peaks, and cable cars.

But now was not the time to play tourist. Pierce was obviously in the middle of an operation, so he turned back to the dirt jungle trail and kept trudging, hoping at least one recent memory would return to him soon.

They followed the path that led them over the peak separating this favela from the next. Common garbage and the occasional pile of excrement littered the trail. Nearby towered a pylon supporting the cable cars that crossed above.

He no longer heard sirens, and felt the police no longer pursued them, so he relaxed slightly.

Descending now, with gravity working with and not against them, they soon increased their pace.

He examined the woman again. Judging by the cut of her clothes, she wasn't from the slums, but from a middle-class upbringing. She certainly had Latino blood in her. "Who are you?"

"I told you who I am."

"Please tell me again."

"For God's sake, you knew exactly who I was when you kidnapped me!" When he said nothing and refused to look away, her face softened, and she said, "Are you having memory problems? You hit your head hard back there."

"Let's just say the last few hours are lost to me." This wasn't strictly true, he'd lost far more time than that, but perhaps it was enough to get her to tell him information that should already have been obvious to them both.

"Very well. You'll find out soon enough without me, I suspect, so I'll tell you. I'm Amelia Reyes."

Pierce tried to remember if that name meant anything to him, but nothing solidified in his hazy memory.

"Why are we speaking Spanish and not Portuguese?"

She nodded. "I'm from Caracas, Venezuela. I had been hiding out here in Rio, away from the secret police of my country. But you two men changed all that when you turned up out of nowhere and kidnapped me."

"Why are we together?"

The woman stopped walking, which forced Pierce to halt with her. She turned towards him. One leg poised in front of the other, and her hands rested on her hips. "You're unbelievable!"

"What do you mean?"

Amelia sighed. "I'm your prisoner. I really don't like men who use force to get what they want. Little wonder I don't respect you."

Pierce looked around. "Go, then."

"What?"

"Leave. I don't know why you are my prisoner. I'll make you free again."

She stared for a long moment. His eyes were drawn to the nakedness of her shoulders in the dress she wore.

Naked...

Bound...

Beaten...

"What's wrong?" he asked, when she wouldn't stop looking at him.

Her eyebrows pinched together as she pursed her lips. "I really don't understand you!"

Pierce laughed. "Sometimes, I don't understand me either."

"This isn't funny. This is serious. While you might have saved me from my kidnapper, you are just like your friend. A murderer. I don't respect killers. In fact, I detest them. I detest you!"

Her statement confused him. "He was my friend?"

Amelia both laughed and sneered. "I wouldn't think so."

"Why did you say we were?"

"I was being sarcastic." When that comment didn't provoke a response, she said, "He tried to kill you too, multiple times. You tried to return the favour, also multiple times. He hates you, and you hate him. You are the extreme opposite of friends."

Pierce tried to recall the identity of the goateed man.

No memories came to him, and it hurt just trying to think on this problem. Pierce rubbed his forehead in an effort to alleviate the physical pain that came with the elusive thoughts.

She reached out and touched him on the shoulder. "Despite what you stand for, Mark, I'll tell you this much for free. You do have a head injury, and a bad one at that, even if there are no physical signs on your head. You're not retaining short-term memories, and for a period far longer than a few hours."

"It's obvious?"

She chuckled, but her joviality remained laced with anger. "Yes, it is." She paused to catch her breath. "Why was the goateed man trying to kill you?"

He shrugged. "I don't know, Amelia."

"Or more accurately, you did know, but now you've forgotten why." She suddenly lost the hardness in her face, then held his jaw in her soft hands. "It's okay, Mark. You hit your head, remember? Maybe you're not as bad as the others. Maybe when you are healed, you'll show me your nice side, and I'll forgive you."

"'As bad'? 'Nice side'? What do you mean?"

"I told you. You are a killer. A murderer. The type of person I've stood against my entire life. It is men like you who destroyed my family, my home, and my whole world."

Pierce nodded. He empathised with her point of view, but he had come to terms with the dark side of his profession long ago, accepted who he was and what he did. It was about balancing the equations. Every bad actor he termi-

19

nated potentially saved the lives of many more innocent people that same bad actor might have killed in the future, should he have allowed them to live. Few individuals appreciated or understood his clinical perspective, including the woman standing before him, so he rarely expressed his point of view.

"I'm surprised you weren't more seriously hurt in that crash. But give yourself time, and rest, your mind will heal, and you'll remember exactly what kind of man you are."

Thinking caused him sharp headaches, but he tried to fathom his current predicament anyway. The woman presented as trustworthy, but duplicitous individuals had betrayed Pierce in his past. Until he recovered from his short-term memory loss — if he recovered his memory — he must watch her closely. If she were acting against him, and her compassion was a ruse, then she would bring his enemies straight to him. His vulnerable mental state presented the ideal circumstance to trick him, or allow her to flee. Was it better to keep her close, observe her until he knew more, or cut her loose?

"Seriously, you don't look well. You want to rest for a bit?"

He shook his head.

"Savannah will worry about me. We need to contact her."

"Who?"

"Savannah? She's my girlfriend? Don't you secret police types keep files on everyone you intend on kidnapping?"

Pierce nodded. What else could he do? Every thought turned to fog. Every investigation in the locked corners of his mind only brought on unbearable physical pain.

"Mark?"

Now it was he who paused before he spoke. "Let me ask

you a question, Amelia. Was I trying to kidnap you or save you from the other man?"

Amelia Reyes didn't answer him, but Pierce could see in her micro-expressions as she stared off towards the horizon that this scenario was plausible now that she had properly considered it. This gave him hope that she was not the enemy, and that his current predicament might not be as precarious as he had earlier feared.

"Are you saying you're a noble man, and this is a rescue mission?"

Pierce shrugged. "Aren't you rescued already?"

Again, she considered what he said, until her face hardened once more. "Then you are going to let me go?"

"If you want to go off by yourself, do so."

She didn't move. Only stared at him.

"Then stick with me. My plan is we keep moving in this direction. Then we'll find a hotel and decide our next steps from there. You okay with that?"

She didn't answer, so he kept walking, and she followed him.

3

Once Pierce and Amelia had descended the other side of the mountain, they entered another favela and trekked through its narrow streets until they reached a road. He checked that he had money in his pockets, then hailed a taxi and requested they be taken to Barra da Tijuca, an upper-class neighbourhood of Rio de Janeiro near the beach.

When they arrived, they stepped out of the taxi together, and she walked with him. This required no coercion, which surprised Pierce after her earlier assertion that he had kidnapped her. But she was cooperating, so Pierce went with that.

The establishment Pierce had brought them to was a mid-price hotel overlooking the sandy Praia do Pepe beach. After paying with cash and checking in under false names, the porter took them to a clean seventh-floor room that featured two beds, a spacious bathroom and a lounge area. All surfaces were white and polished.

"Thank you." Pierce gave a generous tip, but not enough to be memorable. The porter promptly disappeared.

While Amelia explored the cupboards and minibar, then disappeared into the bathroom, Pierce checked his possessions. A passport in his money belt said he was Irish, and his name was Calum Reed. No doubt a forgery, but Pierce couldn't spot any imperfections. A professional job? Had he arranged for it through underworld contacts, or had the CIA prepared it? The problem was, he had answers to none of these questions, and the truth about their origins could be the difference between them working only as casually glanced at identification papers, or ones that would get him safely through the most advanced airport customs security systems. He had to assume the former until he learnt or remembered more.

He listened as Amelia returned from the bathroom and sat on the bed opposite him. He remembered she had run the basin tap for some time. How long had she stayed in there? He couldn't remember and wondered if this was another downside of his head injury.

"What now? Mr Killer?"

He sensed hostility, yet she had followed him willingly. What did she fear more than she feared in him, if sticking with him was the safer option?

"How long have we known each other?"

"We only met this morning. We'd never met before then." She clasped her hands together and sat next to him on the double bed, then shuddered. "There were moments in the favela when I thought we would both die."

Pierce nodded. It infuriated him that nothing from before the car crash was coming back to him, and the dull ache in his body had grown into generalised stabbing pains he couldn't define. "Do you know the man who was with us, and why he wants us dead?"

She smiled, then cast her eyes downward. "We didn't really get to speak. You were mostly arguing with each other."

He shook his head, looked downwards like her, and rested his elbows on his knees. "I'm sorry."

She turned and looked at him with wide eyes, then wiped away the tears gathering there. Then she touched his arm. "I don't like you, Mark, but you saved my life. So don't be sorry. It's not your fault what happened."

"No. I'm sorry for what I'm about to do." Getting up from the bed, he found an iron in the cupboard, then tore out the power cord. "I'm going to tie you up."

"What?" Tense now, she shuffled away from him. The fear in her eyes was unmistakable. "You're unbelievable."

"Until I know more, I'm sorry. I can't trust you. When I must operate alone or need to sleep, this is how it has to be."

She stood and recoiled further from him. "God have mercy on me! I take it back. You're as bad as the other men."

He didn't move, waited until her breathing returned to a normal pace and she sat again on the bed. "You're scaring me, Mark." Her voice became a whisper. "Do you know how long I've lived in fear?"

"No?"

"My entire life! And now you, who is supposedly my saviour, want to terrify me again."

"I know, and I'm sorry."

"Do I have a choice?"

Pierce shook his head.

"What about my girlfriend? Savannah? She's worrying to

death about me. She was there when the other man kidnapped me off the street."

Pierce considered her request. No memories came of a second woman. "When I return, we'll discuss your friend Savannah and reunite you both. Now, are you ready?"

To his surprise, she allowed him to tie her with the cord and gag her with a torn-up pillowcase; then he secured her to the bed. She cried as he tightened the knots and checked them twice. As she lay sprawled on the sheets, trembling, he said, "I'll be less than one hour. I've ordered room service to arrive in two. If I'm not back by then, I'm dead or captured, and never coming back. Do what you have to do to look after yourself."

The young woman nodded and stared up at him with wide eyes, moisture gathering in her tear ducts. He suspected her anguish was not because he'd restrained her, but from the past traumas Pierce's actions had dredged from her suppressed memories. Pierce hated himself in that moment, but he saw no alternative.

Then the same image flashed in his mind he had seen while they had been walking.

A woman, tied naked to a chair, her face bloody and cut from multiple beatings...

This woman...

A second image filled his mind.

Him, also tied naked to a chair. Beaten and cut, inflicted with similar wounds...

He found he couldn't face the emotions these images stirred in him, because when he tried to focus on them, the stabbing pain in his head worsened.

Suppressing these memories by focusing on action, he headed into the lobby and out onto the streets. The Barra he remembered from an earlier mission during the Rio Olympics was like the Barra he immersed in now. It must be why he chose this district to hide, for he knew its many streets, and the Barra was popular with tourists, allowing him to blend in. He passed elegant restaurants expunging a variety of scents, most of them derived from grilled meats. Couples and groups drank beers and cocktails while a street corner band played salsa music. Colourful umbrellas shielded outdoor table settings from the burning sun.

Fighting his crippling headache and the pain surging through every muscle, Pierce forced himself to walk with purpose until he could watch a young man in jeans and a red T-shirt, scruffy hair and a close-cropped beard unlock his phone and check his messages. Pierce caught the PIN. When the man finished the call and returned the phone to his pocket, Pierce knocked into him and simultaneously apologised for his clumsiness while pocketing the phone. The man grumbled and walked off, and soon Pierce was on his way too, the incident forgotten. A few minutes later at a quiet corner of the street with the hotel still in visible range, Pierce used the lifted phone to dial a secure number, gaining him access to the second most secretive department inside the CIA.

"Code in, please?" The voice was American. Male.

"Three, one, Delta, one, Echo, nine, Bravo."

For a moment, the line was silent.

"Is there a problem?" Pierce asked.

"That's a deactivated code. You want to try that again?"

4

Pierce paused. How had his code expired? How much time had he lost?

"Check again."

"Your ID expired," said the CIA officer. "What is your code name?"

"Trigger Man."

"Actual name?"

Pierce studied the many faces walking the streets, expecting a surveillance team to track him here and now. "Not over this line."

"Very well. Response words protocols. I say 'November'?"

He closed his eyes and concentrated, but the more he focused, the worse his headache felt.

"Trigger Man?"

"Nocturne."

"Correct. I say 'kangaroo'?"

"Katana."

"One more. I say 'chessboard'?"

Pierce pressed his thumb and fingers into his forehead and tightened his eyes shut against the pain.

He didn't know this response.

"Sir?"

"I..."

"Sir, I say 'chessboard'? Last chance."

Pierce knew he knew this code, but he couldn't remember what it was.

"I'm afraid I can't—"

The speaker cut off, but the line remained connected.

He focused again, listened for sounds from CIA headquarters in distant Langley, Virginia.

"Trigger Man?"

A woman's voice, educated, intense, and from the Deep South based on her accent. Certainly not a voice he recognised.

"Yes, ma'am?" Sweat poured off Pierce's head. Bright sparks burned in his eyes even when he closed them.

"This is a first, a call from a corpse."

He shuddered. Not the news he expected.

"Why are you back from the dead, Trigger Man?"

Pierce killed the call. He pulled the phone apart, snapped the SIM card and dropped the pieces into a drain. He raced to the hotel.

Dead.

What the hell had happened?

He needed to reach Mackenzie Summerfield, his case officer. He only trusted her. Theirs was a mutual and earned respect. Grown through integrity, competence and a faith in each other's abilities, even under the most trying of circumstances. Pierce had never lost his memories before. Never felt this crippled in the field. She would help him.

Instead of Mackenzie, another woman from the CIA had informed him he was supposedly a corpse.

How had that happened?

He could think of only one answer.

Pierce had faked his death and gone dark.

Calling the CIA had been a mistake.

Langley assets would converge on him even now. Kill or capture. It didn't matter their mission objective, he couldn't let them take him.

Pierce staggered into the hotel. His hands and legs shaking, his headache almost blinding, and his muscles on fire. His body told him to sleep, recover, but that would be a mistake. Physical injuries stung, but it was the thinking that hurt more. Planning, strategising, remembering...

Amelia Reyes in the yellow summer dress filled his thoughts...

Was she the woman he kept remembering?

Bound and naked and beaten?

Was that why he'd rescued her?

She was not beaten and bruised in this moment of time, and she had claimed today was the first time they had met.

Taking the stairs, Pierce burst into the room, finding Amelia still tied to the bed. He undid her bindings, then guzzled a water bottle from the minibar and splashed cold water from the bathroom tap onto his face.

The young woman sat on the bed. She looked exhausted, and her eyes were red, but not beaten or cut. Maybe he'd seen a video of her from an earlier interrogation session. Months or weeks earlier perhaps.

She rubbed her hands and wrists against the redness brought on by abrasion. "God forgive you. You're unbelievable, Mark! I just can't work you out."

At a mirror, he forced himself to stare into his own eyes. His reflection stared accusingly back at him. He had never looked at himself with so much loathing before, or at least he had no memory that he had. What had he done that was so awful that he didn't like himself?

"Seriously, Mark, are you okay?"

Water dripped off Pierce's chin and nose. How many times had she spoken his name, and he'd not realised this was telling him something? He would have normally used an alias, or not told her any name at all until he trusted her. Had the other operative told Amelia who he really was?

"Mark?"

"Who is Amelia Reyes? Why are you important?"

Her teary red eyes looked away.

"Amelia!"

"I'm an activist, okay? I protest against my corrupt government, a voice for the hundreds of thousands of people Venezuela's secret police — the SEBIN and FAES — torture and murder every year. Speaking out against the Venezuelan regime makes me a target. There are rewards on my head, so I'd say that is reason enough for someone to want to kidnap me! Tell me, Mark, is this what you wanted to hear?"

There was anger in her voice, but also passion and a fierceness Pierce could respect. He didn't hear any lie in her words, and for the moment while they faced more pressing problems, her statement was good enough for him. "We need to leave. We're in danger." He stepped into the bedroom and scanned for anything he might have missed. Nothing struck him as important, so he turned his attention back to her.

Her wet eyes grew large. "Mark, you're sweating. Your entire body is shaking."

He looked at his hands. Tremors gripped his fingers and wrists. His legs shook like tree branches ravaged by a powerful storm. Where had these tremors come from? The car accident?

"Mark?"

He remembered the CIA was closing in. They would have triangulated the GPS location of his cell phone. An in-country team would soon prep and close their net around him. If they caught him, interrogations would follow, and he might possess secrets he couldn't let them know. Why had he faked his death and gone rogue, becoming a nomad in the world? No answer he imagined presented a positive solution to this mystery.

He glanced at Amelia, who seemed to both loathe and trust him. Was she expertly playing him? She must have answers, so he must keep her close. "We can't stay. Kill teams are coming for us, even now—"

"How do you know?"

He pulled her to her feet. "You've got sixty seconds. Grab what you need."

She disappeared into the bathroom while Pierce checked over his Glock 19 semi-automatic 9mm pistol, his small arm of choice with three spare magazines in his jacket pocket. He'd concealed a favoured KAMPO tactical knife in an arm sheath. Besides his money and false identification papers and credit cards, other equipment included lock picks, a Maglite, matches, a packet of untouched Marlboro cigarettes and tiny wire cutters. Whatever Pierce had been up to before the accident, he had prepared. This suggested he wasn't running, but executing a mission.

And since he no longer reported to the CIA, this must be a mission of his own devising.

"You look ready to pass out."

She stood in the doorway. The bathroom light created a halo around her shapely figure, visible through her yellow summer dress. He guessed her age to be mid-twenties. Too young to be caught up in his violent world. But Pierce had entered his profession much younger, as a teenager, and he too was soon caught in a world of murder and deceit that no one had prepared him for.

Exactly how he felt right now.

"Let's go."

5

Langley, Virginia, United States

As a senior operations officer of America's Central Intelligence Agency, Patricia Knight was a busy woman. Every minute in her fourteen-hour workday felt precious because every minute she did important work that ultimately saved American lives.

So why did she suddenly feel that she had screwed up?

She supposed an impromptu meeting with the CIA chief of the Special Operations Group, or C/SOG as everyone called him, was an opportunity. A sign perhaps that she was doing well, and her efforts had come to the C/SOG's attention. But with the news she'd just learned regarding the supposedly deceased Trigger Man not being dead after all, their meeting now seemed another obstacle in getting the job done.

Knight ignored the chief's assistant, making a face as she pushed past him into the chief's plush office with a seventh-floor window view. She sneezed as she passed, then blew her nose into a tissue she kept in her pocket for such occasions, hating that her allergies were getting the better of her.

The executive officer of the CIA stood waiting, as if expecting her.

Knight admitted he looked the part.

With thick dark hair and beard, Abdul Ibrahim wore only grey suits, but he always wore them well. Today his three-piece design looked to have cost a week's wages, perhaps worn for an earlier meeting at the White House. His black shoes were always shiny, and his silk tie was a perfect Windsor knot. Knight asked herself — and not for the first time — if the man enjoyed a loving and respectful married relationship with a woman who supported him. She had no one in her life, and he was exactly her type.

Ibrahim met her stare and smiled, projecting his signature endearing manner he must have perfected decades ago, which always made other people feel at ease. His rigid posture no doubt drilled into him during his days as an officer with the Office of Naval Intelligence, which also made him gentleman-like. But Ibrahim was as ruthless and cunning as any operative in Langley, who doggedly got the job done whatever the cost to other people's careers or lives, to ensure they always advanced America's foreign interests.

"Ah, Patricia, good to see you."

"Yes, sir. It's been a while."

"We first met at a Senate committee, if I remember correctly?"

"You do, sir." That committee had centred on a black-budget operation in the Himalayas, and Knight had done her best to obscure the truth with "risks to active operations" responses to every question. Her role that day had been to protect Ibrahim's reputation regarding morally questionable decisions he'd made, and he had never thanked her for doing so. She could have lost her job if the truth had come out, and her career in intelligence would have come to a sudden and abrupt end. "You wanted to see me urgently?"

He nodded, then looked to his computer. "Just received news concerning the Trigger Man. Seems he's not dead, as you reported three months ago."

Straight to the point. But Patricia Knight had already guessed this was the subject of today's meeting. She wondered what Ibrahim's interest in the Trigger Man was, because nothing before in her investigations or operations had prompted his direct engagement with her. His under-lings had performed that duty well enough until now.

Ibrahim's eyes narrowed. "Didn't your operative shoot Trigger Man dead, off the coast of Angola?"

Knight had already examined her feelings around this sudden revelation. Less than twenty minutes ago she had spoken to the Trigger Man personally, in a brief but disjointed conversation. Voice analysis confirmed it was Mark Pierce. Trigger Man's "alive" status worried her as much as it did Abdul Ibrahim.

"So I was told."

Knight remembered the after-action report and briefing from her top operative, whose mission was to turn Pierce into an off-the-books asset. Instead, the operative put a bullet through his chest and dropped his body into the churning Atlantic Ocean. Knight had watched the live drone footage as events unfolded and had believed it herself. They never found Trigger Man's body in the dangerous ocean currents that evening. Never expected to.

"The operative who told you this is Rachel Zang?"

Knight nodded. She considered how much Ibrahim knew, and how much of this conversation was a test. Zang had either lied or misjudged the situation. Either way, that didn't bode well for Zang's ongoing operational future with the CIA. And Zang was Knight's best operator, so losing her would damage Knight's long planned and implemented objectives and missions significantly.

"I don't know what to say, sir. Until twenty minutes ago, Pierce *was* a corpse. Fish food for bottom feeders."

Ibrahim gestured she should take a seat. "What happened?"

She obeyed, and he sat opposite at his polished oak desk. She noticed the Qur'an on a pedestal on his shelves, next to a large print of the American flag. Ibrahim was something of an anomaly, being the only Muslim to reach a senior position within the CIA.

"Twenty minutes ago, Trigger Man coded in from Barra da Tijuca. That's Rio de Janeiro," Knight said, pre-empting the chief's next question. "A contract team is moving in to take him out as we speak."

Ibrahim raised an eyebrow. "Not our own people?"

"No."

"They equipped to neutralise a man with Pierce's capabilities?"

"No."

Ibrahim raised his eyebrow higher and leaned forward. "I think you need to explain yourself, Patricia."

Knight nodded and leaned forward herself. When she spoke, it was close to a whisper. "Ten months ago, Pierce disappeared in Morocco. A short time later, we uncovered his many attempts to buy and use nuclear waste for a dirty bomb. That made him a terrorist. But just before he faked his death, Zang identified that a corrupt senior CIA operative had framed Pierce for those crimes. The Trigger Man was innocent. Always has been."

"Then why do you want him dead?"

"I don't."

A long silence grew between them.

"Sir," she said, realising that Ibrahim was several reporting lines above her, highly influential inside the CIA and deserved an explanation as to her convoluted strategies. "I'm running a very delicate operation. One I can't talk to you about here, as there are security risks. And now that I know Pierce is back on the scene again, I'm fast-tracking to get my old plan for him up and running again."

That comment caused another eyebrow raise since the CIA headquarters were supposedly one of the most secure buildings in all the United States.

"Sir, I need an operative who — as far as it concerns the rest of the world — has turned dirty, but in reality hasn't, who can operate as an asset within a rather dangerous organisation my team is trying to infiltrate. I have been looking for an alternative candidate, but now..." She paused as she gathered her thoughts. "Now he's back, Pierce is still perfect for the role."

Ibrahim made a cage with his fingers and leaned back in his chair. "Why is this the first I'm hearing about it?"

Knight recalled that before taking on the C/SOG role, Abdul Ibrahim had been the head of Operations, Russia. She had believed, despite his faith and cultural background, that he'd lacked interest in Middle East operations, which was her mandate, not his. But now it seemed he had become overtly interested in her and her missions, which had of late been focused on that troublesome corner of the world. "I can brief you, sir. But not here."

He frowned. "You think someone has bugged my office?"

"Unlikely, but I'm potentially compromising my long game if it is. I might already have, with the little I've now told you. If I'm to get my old planning operational again, the world needs to believe Pierce is a rogue agent. That's why I'm sending incompetent contractors. Bring authenticity to the ruse, because the Trigger Man *will* kill them all without breaking a sweat, and this allows him a simple escape."

"You're okay with sending those contractors to their deaths?"

Knight nodded and cast her eyes downwards. "I know what you're saying. But this team, they accept questionable contracts from local narco gangs such as Red Command who rule various favelas. They kidnap politicians', prosecutors' and police officers' wives and children for ransom. They are scumbags, so no substantial loss. Sending this team, however, sends a message to Pierce and the intelligence community that the CIA still hunts their former operative." She watched Ibrahim balance the moral dimensions and question how much she was selling this story by potentially sharing only the facts she wanted him to hear. She *was* holding back, but what she had revealed *was* the truth. These people were scum.

"Pierce was dead in your mind only twenty minutes ago?"

"I know." Knight licked her lips and tried not to sneeze again. "It's an opportunity I have to take."

Ibrahim spent a long moment mulling over what she had

said. "Fine. Where is Rachel Zang? The operative who claimed to shoot Pierce?"

"Port-au-Prince. Haiti."

His eyebrows pinched as his stare intensified. "In the field? On a mission?"

"Yes, sir."

"What about Mackenzie Summerfield, Pierce's former case officer? Where is she?"

Knight shrugged. Ibrahim knew far more about Pierce than she had given him credit for. "Disappeared in England three months ago. We had her under observation, but she gave us the slip."

"Speculations?"

Knight shrugged. "Considering she's Trigger Man's primary contact, Summerfield is likely in hiding with Pierce. She ran him for two and a half years, in Yemen and Niger, and they were, or still are, close friends."

"Something else is bothering you. I see it in your eyes."

She licked her dry lips. "Perhaps it's a coincidence, sir, and perhaps not. I should point out Zang was the last known contact with Summerfield. And, incidentally, Pierce too."

Ibrahim rose out of his chair, showed Knight to the door. "Bring Zang in. If we've lost Summerfield and she's not around to help us, I'm presuming Zang knows better than anyone the mind of the Trigger Man. I want to speak to Zang personally, and you too, as soon as she is stateside."

"Yes, sir."

"We can do this outside Langley if need be. But first I must know what's going on. Really going on. We'll speak again before the day is out."

Knight stood and followed him to the door and fought her sniffles. "Yes, sir."

Once outside the C/SOG's office, her cell phone red-flashed.

In Rio, a team of Venezuelan intelligence and paramilitary officers were moving in for a kill, and their target was Mark Pierce.

6

Rio de Janeiro, Brazil

Knowing that they had delayed long enough, Pierce and Amelia stepped out into the hall linking the many hotel rooms upon the seventh floor.

The elevator door opened before they reached the stairwell. A woman and a man stepped out laughing. A handsome couple, in their thirties, in ironed slacks, collared shirts and jackets as if ready to head out to a party with friends. The dark-haired woman hung off the man's arm, smiling with excitement. He too featured dark hair, cut short and adhered to his scalp with mousse. They talked in Spanish, of a friend who had a boat... who was throwing a party...

Everything about the scene was wrong.

The couple sensed Pierce's unease in the same instant he did.

The pretence vanished one second later as the two operators drew pistols.

The man was closer, so Pierce rammed into him, knocked him into the woman, which sent them both crashing into the wall.

A gun fired.

The woman dropped.

A pool of blood poured from her heart.

The man's face tightened with rage. He came at Pierce with every muscle flexed like cables of steel. With his pistol lost in the earlier melee, the man pulled a knife from an arm sheath and thrust the sharp end at Pierce.

Pierce feinted, dropped low to confuse the attacker, and swept out his leg, which toppled the man and sent him crashing onto his back. The low kung fu roundhouse kick did its trick.

As the man flailed on the carpet, Pierce reached for his pistol. He figured with one gunshot fired already, another would make no difference. But as he drew the weapon, the man flipped onto his feet and kicked the sidearm from Pierce's grip. The pistol smashed against the wall and dropped.

The attacker's eyes darkened. His mouth snarled. He advanced with controlled jabs and sweeping kicks.

Pierce blocked and parried, searched for and found an opening in the man's technique, then hit him with force in the stomach using another kung fu jab.

Up close and in each other's face, wrestling for control, Pierce rammed his snarling foe into the stairwell, curled an arm around the attacker's thigh and tipped him over the railing.

The assailant expressed surprise as he fell past seven floors, his body colliding with the metal railing several times before he crumpled on the last floor.

Even from this height, Pierce heard many bones break.

Returning to the corridor, Pierce collected the fallen pistols and checked the female assassin. No pulse. No breath.

During the melee, Amelia had crawled into a door alcove and clawed at the wooden frame. Tears streamed down her face. Her mouth lay open in a silent scream.

Pierce helped her to her feet as he reflected upon his instincts that a kill team was coming for him had proved correct. "Come on. I'll get us out of here."

In the stairwell Pierce noticed a second man in a black shirt and blue jeans with an old Uzi 9mm submachine gun advancing upwards three steps at a time, out of breath and making much noise.

In a single fluid motion that lasted only a second, Pierce leaned over the rail, lined up the target and blew a hole out the back of his head. Blood splattered across the concrete wall like paint from a spray can.

Pierce frowned. This assailant seemed amateurish compared to the man and woman he'd fought less than a minute earlier.

Amelia vomited.

Pierce kept her moving and pushed past the corpses.

She threw up twice more before they reached the ground floor and stepped over the corpse of the fallen man, his arm jutting outwards at an impossible angle for a living body. When she headed towards the lobby entrance, he stopped her, and they moved instead through the kitchen and out the back.

He expected another assailant, and there he was, agitated in the alley. Bright shirt, shorts, a Browning semi-automatic pistol held out, with which he made wide theatrical sweeps, so Pierce could see it easily. He carried a nervous twitch in his stance.

Pierce readied his pistol.

Then the man's chest erupted as a star pattern of gore. He fell dead in a puddle of fetid water.

Pierce hadn't shot him.

He ducked inside, pulled Amelia close, forcing her to follow him, knowing a sniper kill when he saw one. Were two kill teams converging on him, getting in each other's way?

Despite her terror, Amelia remained placid. She must have been in shock, for she allowed him to lead her through the carnage and chaos without resistance. Mentally, she might not cope with the violence erupting around her, but he'd deal with that later. Physically, she was intact, so that counted for something.

Returning to the kitchen, he pushed past a chef and threw oil on a gas stove top, igniting a fire. Chaos erupted as the staff verbally abused him and threatened him with fists until he aimed the pistol in their direction. They backed off.

The flames grew, and soon a raging fire burned.

Pierce and his companion exited the kitchen, but not before he triggered the fire alarm. Sprinklers erupted from the ceiling, wetting everything. Klaxons drowned out all other noises. Soon, staff and guests fled the building, providing a cover of panicked bodies.

In the confusion, Pierce snatched a cap from a young man and took a jacket from a table where another couple had shared drinks. He slipped on the cap and wrapped the jacket around his companion, then ran with the flood of bodies escaping through the main door.

"Keep your head down," Pierce whispered into Amelia's ear.

Outside, they moved with the throngs of business travellers and vacationers.

Gunfire sounded, and the crowd panicked, ran in every direction and into the oncoming traffic on the road outside. Brakes squealed as cars and mopeds skidded to a sudden halt. A cyclist hit a four-wheel drive and catapulted over its bonnet. A taxi ran into the back of an SUV.

Another gunshot and a man next to Amelia fell dead upon the pavement.

Pierce pulled her as they sprinted across the street into a Thai restaurant. The powerful scents of lemongrass and ginger hit his nostrils as they knocked over diners and tables and forced their way through the kitchen and out the back.

Another alley beckoned. Skinny cats hissed at them. Vines grew along the walls of the buildings, providing meagre cover from the sniper, no doubt searching for them from a higher, more advantageous position.

"Keep moving!"

She didn't resist. She let him drag her wherever he wished to go.

Pierce imagined scenarios where two teams might want to kill them, but were they after him or her? Or both?

Sticking close to the walls and out of sight of any likely sniper points, they followed the alley to another crowded street. Buildings were mostly two stories and of modern architecture with balustrades and balconies, painted in light blues and soft yellows. Trees decorated the urban landscape. The air felt damp, and the daytime heat was electric in its intensity.

A small, lime green hatchback 1.3-litre Ford Ka screeched

to a halt less than a metre from where Pierce and Amelia stood. The passenger door flung open.

"Get in!" said the driver.

It was another young woman in a singlet top and jean shorts and one side of her head shaved close to her scalp. The rest of her hair she'd dyed jet black, streaked with three lines of purple. Silver studs decorated her nose and ears.

"Are you crazy? Get in!"

Pierce felt his headache again, like a stabbing pain in his temples. He turned to his companion. "You know her?"

"Yes!" Amelia emerged from her daze. She had already lost the jacket. "My girlfriend. This is Savannah." She pushed Pierce into the front seat as she threw herself in the back.

Savannah spun the wheels again as they took off. She was a nimble driver and expertly zipped around mopeds, pedestrians and larger vehicles and in minutes had them on the three-lane Avenue Ayrton Senna, headed north.

Pierce glanced behind them but spotted no tail. Had they escaped the shoot-out that easily? Only time would tell.

He turned to Savannah. "How did you know where to find us?"

"How did I know?" She turned to him and grinned. "She told me."

Pierce glanced at Amelia in the back. The women were the same age, but Savannah was taller and more muscular compared to her friend. "When did you call her?"

Amelia shrugged. "Just before you tied me up. When I was in the bathroom. I used the hotel phone, the one in the bathroom."

Pierce remembered the tap running for a time, no doubt to cover the noise of her phone conversation. He'd wondered why he had missed that detail and why he hadn't acted on it, but could only put it down to his pounding headache and disorientated state.

"Tied you up, did he, Amelia? Lover, I didn't know you were into that kind of thing?"

Amelia blushed, then retched again. Nothing came up but spit from her mouth and tears from her eyes.

"I've been driving around this block for ages, wondering when you would show. I was worried sick."

Pierce tried to answer but found he couldn't speak. The pain in his head grew acute, and for a minute he thought he was about to pass out.

"He can't answer because he hit his head," said Amelia. "Mark's lost his short-term memory, so everything is a bit confusing for him right now..."

Pierce accepted he had a memory problem, but his situational awareness remained top form. He looked behind them, sensing danger, and recognised a tail when he saw one. Two black Troller T4 four-wheel drives, each with two men in the front cabin, one driving and the other packing a submachine gun, sped through the traffic to catch them.

They had not gotten away so easily.

"Right, ladies, new plan."

7

Langley, Virginia, United States

Patricia Knight wasted no time storming into the CIA third-floor operations room, assigned to her team now monitoring a gun battle raging in the streets of Rio de Janeiro's Barra district. A hotel under siege with multiple shooters and multiple targets, and the Trigger Man at the heart of the chaos. According to CNN, the body count was at least nine people. On Fox News, it was twenty.

"What coverage do we have?" Knight asked the team working in the dark room with its many flashy monitors and a wall of multiple LED screens displaying dossier images of Mark Pierce, surveillance footage secured from the scant active CCTV cameras in Rio, and text feeds from the Rio Civil Police's online crime response database.

"We had satellite footage, ma'am," reported Kashif Hussain, Knight's senior intelligence analyst and artificial intelligence expert, who regularly and expertly applied his pattern-recognition software to draw connections that human minds could not achieve in active scenarios like the one that confronted them now. Knight hoped Hussain's skills lived up to their reputation today. "It's beyond range now, ma'am, but what we recorded is actionable."

"Show me."

An image on the wall screen flickered and changed. An elevated view of Pierce leading a woman in a yellow dress and denim jacket through a panicked street. Hair in disarray hid the woman's identity. He wore a cap covering part of his face, but he'd turned in this still image, presumably responding to a taxi and an SUV colliding.

"Facial recognition places the target as an eighty-three per cent match to Mark Pierce. Gait analysis at ninety-two per cent. I thought he was dead?"

"That's our man! And he's not, as you can see." Knight recognised Pierce from file images she had pored over often these last months. "We still tracking him?"

The room was silent.

"I'll take that is a no?"

"Yes, ma'am. I mean, no, ma'am, we're not tracking him now." Hussain's fingers flicked across his keyboard as he pulled up further files for them all to peruse. "We lost Trigger Man eight minutes ago. We suspect he moved through this Thai restaurant, then escaped in a car here. Because of the building angle at this position, we couldn't secure imagery on which car collected him. So far, I've narrowed it down to seventy-seven possible escape vehicles—"

"And we don't have the resources to track them all," Knight said as she finished Hussain's sentence for him while her shoulders slumped.

"I'm running scenarios now, ma'am. I should narrow the possibilities to a dozen cars shortly."

Knight shook her head. Twelve cars were still too many. "Any ideas? Anyone?"

Pierce had escaped the kill team as she'd planned, but she hadn't planned on losing him entirely. Satellite imagery should have kept him in their sights easily enough, but no, the Trigger Man had evaded invisible surveillance tech he shouldn't have known was tracking him. She made a mental note not to underestimate his capabilities again.

"Come on, team! If the answer's no, have the balls to say so."

"No, ma'am," said her signals intelligence, or SIGINT, technician Rachel Howman.

Hussain's fingers again flickered fast across his keyboard. "We are, however, compiling IDs on the two kill teams."

Knight raised an eyebrow. "Two?"

"Yes. The first is… was… our narco contract team. They're all now on the permanent inactive list."

Knight waved her hand dismissively. "I know about them. I sent them in."

Howman transferred an image to the wall screen. "The other team comprised at least six individuals. We caught a clean satellite imagery of one sniper."

Knight studied the image of a muscular man with close-cropped dark hair positioned in a shooter's stance on a nearby rooftop. A Steyr SSG 69 sniper rifle in his grip aimed at the crowded streets below.

Hussain said, "That's a ninety-seven per cent match to Maceo Parra. A known FAES paramilitary operator and free-lance assassin for hire. Clients include the Chinese, Cubans and various Colombian narco groups."

Knight frowned. "I know him. I thought he transferred to SEBIN? The Bolivarian National Intelligence Service?"

Howman said, "Unclear, ma'am. Tactics we've observed today, however, suggest this is a FAES team."

Knight nodded. "So he regularly switches between both?"

No one answered her.

Knight reflected upon her own knowledge. SEBIN was Venezuela's intelligence organisation and political police force loyal to the current regime, tasked with destroying that country from within while securing the power base of the kleptomaniac ruling party, and infiltrated by Cuban intelligence. Their role in the corrupt dictatorship was simple enough to understand: suppress, intimidate, torture, and murder anyone who opposed the Venezuelan president's position of power, and maintain the failed socialist government. The perfect organisation for a man with Parra's sadistic tendencies.

Knight had a particular dislike for SEBIN, who held captive tens of thousands of political prisoners in inhumane conditions and murdered scores of civilians across the country every day. A particular torture they regularly practised was "white room sensory deprivation". Political opponents of the regime were incarcerated in soundproof cells lit with bright lights to dismiss all shadows, and endured in these isolating conditions for months on end. Silence and nothing to look at drove most prisoners to madness.

SEBIN's affiliates weren't any better and included Russian, Chinese and Cuban military advisors, narcotic traffickers and left-wing guerrillas hiding out in the Amazonian rainforests. There was nothing nice to be said about this organisation, which, in Knight's mind, equated to Stalin's secret police of the 1950s. She had no hesitation in ordering the execution of the SEBIN team, but that would require an operator on the ground with the skills and resources to take them out.

Someone like the Trigger Man.

Why was Mark Pierce not already on her team and answering to her? And why had he faked his death in the first place?

What Knight also couldn't understand was what SEBIN wanted with Pierce. Much of the rogue operative's operational history was a redacted and secret file she did not have access to. But she knew his history from the last four years when Pierce "officially" worked for the CIA, and he had never once operated in South America in that time. If this were a revenge mission for past actions against SEBIN, it was from Pierce's "before" period, and SEBIN had taken their sweet time coming after him. That made no sense.

No, it wasn't Pierce they were after. SEBIN's objective was the woman at Pierce's side, in the bright yellow summer dress. Who was she?

"What do we know about his companion?" Knight asked the room.

No one answered.

"For God's sake, team, find out!"

She lifted a handset on the desk next to her and dialled a burner phone in Haiti.

The call rang out for the tenth time today. She mumbled under her breath, frustrated that her top operator, Rachel Zang, hadn't checked in for over twenty-four hours.

The secure door to the operations room sprang open. No one entered, but Knight saw Abdul Ibrahim standing outside, hands in his pockets and his eyes bearing down on her.

Knight turned to her team. "Come on, everyone! Full workups on all participants. Live targets first. Reports on my desk within the hour and every hour after that, with updates. And find Pierce. And find out what he's been up to these last three months!" She turned and exited, expelling an audible huff so they all knew she wasn't happy with their performance.

The C/SOG had no smiles for her either.

"I know what you will say, sir."

Ibrahim shrugged. "That you should contain the situation? I don't think that's your objective. I think you want 'uncontained'."

She raised an eyebrow. "That's an unexpected response?"

He grinned. "I know you want to talk outside these walls, but time is against us."

Ibrahim gestured she should follow. He led her to a secure conference room fitted out as a SCIF, a sensitive compartmented information facility. This room was impenetrable to all forms of surveillance, with no means of communications in or out. When the doors sealed behind them, she moved to a seat, ready to fall into it, then watched Ibrahim walk to a wall and press his finger against a corner in a panel. The panel sprang open, revealing a second SCIF within.

"Precautions within precautions, Knight. I now understand you are the nineteenth person on this planet to know of this room's existence."

Knight was impressed. She followed him in.

This SCIF was classier, with a bar and lounge chairs. Ibrahim took a bottle of tonic water and poured it into a glass. "I don't drink alcohol, of course. But I'm happy to mix you something."

"Thank you. A bourbon on ice?"

For a moment she considered her request for hard liquor too bold, but he mixed her drink without question, then sat on the sofa opposite Knight. "This is as secure as you'll ever get, Knight, so tell me everything."

8

Rio de Janeiro, Brazil

P ierce knew Savannah had done well to get her Ford Ka onto Avenue Governador Carlos Lacerda, a highway speeding their passage through crowded Rio de Janeiro. This route cut through the mountainous jungle-clad and cliff-edged Parque Nacional da Tijuca, separating two of Rio's major urban sprawls, and in its centre was a one-kilometre-long, poorly lit tunnel they would soon enter. A path that provided both risks and opportunities.

Savannah expertly dodged between slower traffic, but she couldn't build speed quickly because of the car's tiny engine. Pierce watched the traffic, expecting pursuit at any moment, but so far, they were in the clear.

Amelia asked from the back seat, "What's the plan?"

Pierce said, "A surveillance-detection route. We need to shake whoever it is that is tracking us." He turned to Savannah. "I need you to follow my instructions to the letter.

There will be doubling back, switches, speeding up and slowing down. You okay with that?"

Savannah nodded and kept her eyes on the road, skilfully ducking between two cars driving more slowly than anyone else ahead of them, slowing the traffic behind them.

He glanced back and now noticed two Troller T4s tailing their Ford Ka. With their more powerful engines, they could easily keep pace with the tiny hatchback.

He gripped his Glock 19, checked the magazine, ensured fifteen 9mm bullets remained available for lethal action, then pulled back on the slide, ensuring a round slotted into the firing chamber.

"What are you doing, Mark?" asked Amelia, rising panic in her voice now. "Killing again? Do you ever stop?"

Ignoring the imaginary nails of pain pounding into his skull and the fog hovering over his mind, Pierce glanced again at the rear-view mirror. The Trollers weren't getting any closer, yet, but they were certainly tailing them and didn't seem bothered that this would be obvious to Pierce and his companions.

"Mark?"

Pierce gritted his teeth. "Two black four-wheel drives, a man in each packing FAMAE SAF submachine guns. Tell me, are they here for me, or are they here for you?"

The two women glanced back. Amelia paled when she saw the Trollers and the armed killers, and her breathing suddenly became more rapid. "They're coming for me."

"Who are they?"

"I suspect they are SEBIN."

Pierce nodded, knowing that SEBIN were Venezuela's secret police, with a reputation for murder, torture and brutality. This made sense if what Amelia had told him was true, about her being an activist against the corrupt Venezuelan government. He realised there was no way they could outrun them, so he needed to devise an alternative strategy. "There!" Pierce said to Savannah, who had three purple-streaked jet-black hair strands fluttering in the wind blowing through their open windows. "Get in front of that truck."

Savannah sped the lime green Ford Ka onto the slow lane ahead of a triaxial truck that must have weighed in at over thirty tons.

"Keep the distance between you and the truck to a minimum," Pierce said, figuring the tactic at least prevented the Troller T4s from ramming them from behind. They might still try to run the Ford Ka off the road with a side-sweep, and Pierce had no tactic to prevent that... yet. What he needed was an exit lane off the freeway, but suspected with Parque Nacional da Tijuca looming on the horizon, that opportunity was long gone. He needed another plan, and fast.

A long dark tunnel beckoned ahead, taking them beneath it.

Parque Nacional da Tijuca?

Savannah glanced again at Pierce. "You know we don't have anywhere near enough power to outrun them?"

Pierce nodded. "I have other plans."

"Want to share?"

"In a minute."

So far, the two pursuing vehicles had hung back. Pierce suspected they did this so as not to cause a scene until they reached a more private section of the freeway, like inside the dark tunnels where there would be fewer witnesses to their impending assault. Pierce had no intention of waiting that long.

He remembered the expressway from a previous and distant mission. This was a well-maintained road with concrete barriers and lush vegetation grown right to the kerbs. Ahead loomed the urban park, within the heart of Rio. Its rocky peaks, shrouded in a rainforest ecosystem, reached almost a kilometre into the skies. The Avenida passed beneath and alongside the rocky protrusions through a series of tunnels and engineered cliffs. Soon the expressway dipped into rock-cut edges and tall evergreen trees, and now the road felt claustrophobic. Signs denoted a speed limit of one hundred kilometres per hour. Not that their pursuers would respect local traffic laws.

Pierce glanced at his side mirror. The two black four-wheel drives kept on their tail. The men inside were in no hurry. Cars and motorcycles of all makes and models zipped past and around their three vehicles and the truck behind them.

"See that tunnel." Pierce pointed to the first circular cut in the expressway ahead. "When you cross inside, speed up."

The purple-haired driver laughed. "I'll do my best. My foot is already all the way down."

Pierce noted she seemed more at ease in this stressful situation than her girlfriend. Not that Pierce minded; he needed a competent driver and was thankful their seating arrangement weren't reversed. He squinted his eyes, so they almost closed, reducing the amount of sunlight reaching his pupils.

They hit the tunnel. Despite her complaints and a few

gear crunches, Savannah pushed their speed up from one hundred to one hundred and twenty kilometres per hour.

Pierce looked back. Their action had the desired effect. The two four-wheel drives sped up, closing the distance between them.

The first tunnel proved short and soon opened into a gully surrounded by further engineered rock faces beneath jungle-clad peaks.

Another tunnel loomed ahead.

"Again!" Pierce said as they hit the next rocky underground road, while keeping his eyes squinted. "Accelerate!"

The driver complied. Somehow, she had them racing at one hundred and thirty-five kilometres per hour, zipping past trucks and sedans maintaining the legal speed limit. This had to be the fastest their Ford Ka could go, especially while climbing against gravity. Their pursuers, however, barely spent any effort to keep pace.

While strings of yellow lights illuminated the interior of the rock-cut tunnel, it was still much darker than outside, and everyone's pupils needed time to adjust to the dim light. Except for Pierce, squinting had opened his pupils and prepared his eyes for low-light action.

"I'm about to do something crazy. Just keep driving."

Savannah nodded.

Pierce gripped his seat as he opened his door and leaned out. The four-wheel drives were close, as he hoped they would be. He opened fire, emptying an entire clip into the driver's side wheel of the first vehicle. The noise became near deafening inside this echoing chamber, and the muzzle flashes were bright. His aim, however, remained true, and the front wheel burst into a volley of shredded rubber.

In a jarring instant, the damaged Troller T4 turned

sharply and flipped, then smashed into the second pursuer. As an entangled mess of jagged metal, both vehicles crashed and rolled, then crashed with devastating force into the rocky tunnel walls and crumpled, while thankfully not taking out any other vehicles in the process. Pierce doubted anyone inside would walk away with only minor injuries. Or walk away at all.

"Fuck!" shouted Savannah as Pierce clambered back inside and shut the door.

"Keep driving," he said, noticing his hands shook violently. Was this new infliction a symptom of his recent head injury?

From the deep recesses of his mind came the answer "no." The shakes had been with him for far longer than today, and he should be careful to control them.

He noticed Savannah's trembling limbs. She gritted her teeth and looked ready to burst into tears.

"You're doing fine," he said, ejecting the first magazine from his Glock and loading a fresh one.

She nodded and kept driving.

He looked back at Amelia, who expressed more tears, which streamed down her cheeks. "Mark, how many people did you kill just then?"

"Four. Hopefully."

"You didn't?"

He shrugged. "It was us or them. I'll always choose them."

The tunnel opened again, and Pierce identified suburbia to his left and jungle to his right. Ahead would be further tunnels, shrouded in darkness, where it would again be increasingly difficult to spot them and make their escape easier.

And so far, no police had pursued them. With luck, they had gotten away without drawing the attention of law enforcement.

But that didn't mean Pierce believed they were safe and away.

Far from it.

9

Langley, Virginia, United States

K night composed her thoughts while sipping bourbon, which tasted rather oaky. She returned her attention to the chief, Special Operations Group, seated opposite her. The SCIF they occupied felt cosy, comforting her with luxurious furnishings and soft architectural finishes. Perhaps that was the point. Perhaps the C/SOG wanted her to relax so she'd talk freely.

"It's about oil, sir."

Abdul Ibrahim nodded as he undid his suit jacket buttons. "Oil is the backbone of the global economy. What are we discussing, specifically?"

"You've been read in on Kozan Petroleum?"

His nod was slight, but his eyes betrayed this was a corporation not on his personal radar. "Private Turkish enterprise?"

"Yes. No shareholdings other than those held by the

founder, Morat Kozan. Today worth three point eight billion US dollars. Entered the market in the early nineteen nineties when they successfully capped burning Kuwaiti oil wells during the Gulf War. You'll remember Saddam Hussein's failed military occupation of the Gulf State and his departing gifts of fiery hell as our Coalition Forces liberated the country?"

"Of course. I was in Baghdad at the time, as a teenager. My parents supported the Coalition Forces, and that ultimately bought me, my siblings and my parents' citizenship in the United States."

"Well, with the money he made in Kuwait, Kozan then developed profitable oil wells in Iraq, South Sudan, Nigeria and Libya. Exploration and production in countries embroiled in or coming out of prolonged conflicts."

"What do you suspect, specifically?"

Knight noticed Ibrahim had a particular skill at maintaining constant eye contact. He never looked away and rarely blinked. This unnerved her, so she cleared her throat before she spoke.

"Kozan can extract oil from countries where knowing who to pay for protection is not just the difference between making a profit or a loss, but coming out of the deal alive. For example, in Nigeria, insurgents and criminals bunker many of the Niger Delta oil fields and pipelines—"

"Bunker?"

"Oil and gas jargon. Illegal tapping of supply lines to siphon off the petroleum products they carry. The Niger Delta is a messy war zone and an environmental disaster. Oil companies there lose much of their production before it reaches tankers ready for shipping to overseas markets. Every day, paramilitary groups and insurgents drain pipelines everywhere, and many ruptured lines pollute the rivers or are permanently on fire. Unlike the rest of the world, it's more cost effective for foreign companies in the Delta to drill oil offshore where insurgents can't easily compromise them."

"You're telling me Kozan Petroleum can operate in parts of the Niger Delta where no one else can? Local insurgents and criminals leave them alone?"

"Yes, sir. Morat Kozan makes his fortune on-selling oil that only he can safely reach and protect back to multinational companies who often purchased the original rights to those fields."

"I see."

"An example is the Trident Pipeline the Texans were building in Kurdish Iraq after the fall of Islamic State. Were you read in on that incident?"

Ibrahim nodded. "Pipeline destroyed by forces loyal to the Syrian president, if I remember correctly?"

"You remember correctly. Conveniently, Kozan was ready to step in with its own pipeline once the Texas company had to withdraw. Too many kidnappings and beheadings of Trident employees. Since his pipeline started flowing with dinosaur juice, Kozan has operated there safely for five years now, free of insurgent interference, and selling the same oil back to the Texans at a premium."

Ibrahim drank the last of his tonic water, then tapped his forefinger gently against his temple. "I'm guessing you're trying to determine how he does it, and who is providing him intelligence capabilities, and what powers of intimidation they actually wield?"

"Yes..." Knight was ready to say more, but her nerves stopped her.

Ibrahim shifted in his seat. "Patricia, this is the point in our conversation where you'll tell me the secret you don't want anyone to know. Including me."

Knight nodded. There was a possibility Abdul Ibrahim might be on Kozan's payroll, for someone inside the CIA regularly passed on classified intel regarding her operations against the oil entrepreneur. If Ibrahim were the traitor, once she told him what she knew and feared, her career, and potentially her very life, would be at an end.

However, no opportunity was without risk, and she needed to move forward with her schemes. If, conversely, Ibrahim was truly on her side, he could provide resources and funding that until now the CIA had denied her, and she needed.

"I've been actively investigating Kozan for twelve months. During that time, I've lost four good operatives."

The C/SOG nodded. "There are risks in what we do."

"Except all four operatives died here, in the United States. One in a car accident. Another from a heart attack. One from a mugging in Baltimore, and the last while on vacation. He slipped off a cliff while hiking through the Appalachians."

Ibrahim took a long, thoughtful breath.

Knight watched and judged his reaction. His expression carried as much shock as when Knight had first realised the unusual deaths were more than coincidences.

"Rachel Zang remains my only living senior operative. I keep her on the move and never in the United States unless absolutely necessary. So far, that tactic has kept her alive."

"You believe a double agent operates inside the CIA, reporting your activities to Morat Kozan? And this agent is coordinating assassinations of our operatives before they get close to penetrating his organisation? That's a serious accusation, Patricia."

"I believe this is the truth, but it's more than that. As you said, and what I have long believed, is that Kozan Petroleum is not doing this themselves, but has connections to a vast network of highly competent and sophisticated intelligence personnel operating on a global scale, aiding his company in remaining one step ahead of all the competition. Intel that keeps their business interests secure in countries where they have no right to be operating safely in. It seems logical that if a double agent operates inside the CIA, this 'intelligence organisation' is behind that penetration. Kozan is only the tip of the iceberg."

Ibrahim tugged at his collar, as if his Windsor knot were too tight. His openly expressed worry gave Knight confidence he was the right superior to confide in. Fears now shared would keep him awake at night, too. She wiped her nose, sensing that it was runny again, and her allergies were bothering her.

"Sir, at this very moment in Port-au-Prince, Haiti, Zang and her team have a potential Kozan-connected intelligence target under surveillance, ready for extreme rendition," she said, referring to the tiny Caribbean nation where her people had operated for the last few weeks. "However, only Zang knows the real reason why we are after this man."

"How so?"

"The target recently returned from the Niger Delta, where he regularly engages with insurgent groups protecting Kozan's pipelines. We believe this target is a senior player in either Kozan Petroleum or the intelligence organisation we know nothing about. We should know more when Zang delivers this man to our detention camp in Guantánamo Bay, Cuba, ready for interrogation."

"And Mark Pierce? The Trigger Man? How does he fit into all of this? Why is he back from the dead, and why is he in South America?"

"That," said Knight, feeling a chill in her heart, "is where it gets really interesting, and not in a good way."

10

K night motioned to the bar. Ibrahim nodded, so she stood and made them fresh drinks. Tonic water for him and lemonade for her. She needed a sugar hit more than alcohol after operating for so long without much sleep since sending her team into Haiti, but then she never slept much even when situations were calm and uneventful.

Knight noticed Ibrahim's precise and controlled movements. He projected a quiet power, and she could not help feeling attracted to him. Not that she would act on impulses. She was too sophisticated to debase herself by allowing emotions to control her life, plus she didn't completely trust her superior even though he seemed on her side at this juncture.

She handed Ibrahim his glass, then returned to her seat. "Trigger Man has no connection to Kozan Petroleum. None."

"Explain?"

"I tasked Zang with recruiting Pierce, but in a manner we could present him as a rogue operative, ready for insertion inside Kozan's organisation as a double agent. Pierce knows nothing about this, because Zang never brought him in so we could properly brief him."

"Let me clarify, Patricia. The shoot-out in Rio, FAES's and SEBIN's involvement, has no discernible link with your Kozan operation, and yet you say this is the crux of what all this is about?"

Knight hesitated, for she was about to reveal compromising information that would not present her or her team in a positive light. She'd known this moment loomed, and like a Band-Aid that had long healed the wound beneath it, she needed to rip it off. She might as well do so now and face whatever fate awaited her. "On the surface, it looks that way. That there is no connection."

"You're being cryptic again, Patricia."

She cleared her throat. "Well... the connection is that Morat Kozan is actively pursuing business opportunities in Venezuela."

Ibrahim tensed, then said, "I don't like where this is going."

She swallowed and asked herself why he could call her by her first name, and she had to call him "sir." Suddenly the C/SOG wasn't attractive anymore. "Neither do I, sir."

"You must have an idea. What connects Kozan Petroleum, the Trigger Man, FAES and SEBIN?"

She cleared her throat and sniffled. "There is only one connection I can logically make."

"And that is?"

"The man who framed Pierce as a nuclear terrorist, who forced the Trigger Man to run. I'm talking about a former and very senior CIA operator."

Ibrahim raised an eyebrow. "You're talking about Idris Walsh?"

"Yes." Knight cleared her throat, realising the C/SOG knew far more than she gave him credit for concerning Trigger Man's prior history. "Walsh ran the task force that hunted Mark Pierce until Walsh himself disappeared when his deceit came to light. He *was* the culprit buying and selling nuclear materials while framing Pierce for those same crimes. Former CIA head of Special Operations, North Africa, Walsh had a history of murky operations in Africa, Türkiye, the Middle East, Central Asia, Russia, *and* South America. It's hard to tell the truth from the lies with Walsh. Vanished the same time Pierce did."

"Three months ago, yes."

"That was when I realised Pierce was not the enemy, when Zang exposed Walsh as the bad actor he is, and I saw the potential to recruit Pierce as a double agent. Walsh almost secured what would have amounted to nearly ninety million in liquid assets through his nuclear dealings, and God knows what he would have used that money for. Further acts of terrorism, no doubt. Pierce was... is... hell-bent on destroying Walsh for what the man did to him. Walsh tortured and incarcerated Pierce for seven months in a remote jungle paramilitary camp in Central Africa. I'm talking electrocution, waterboarding, stress positions, you name it."

Ibrahim tensed. His frown creased the age lines around his eyes. "You're still not making yourself clear here, Patricia. Spell it out."

Knight felt the butterflies rise in her stomach. She was about to reveal how incompetent she might be, expose an embarrassing secret she had hidden well enough until now.

But if she didn't bring her failure to light soon, someone else surely would. Better to be upfront now, hoping her honesty saved her career. "Recently, after examining various elements of circumstantial evidence we've put together, we now believe that before Walsh disappeared, he stole a motherlode of CIA intelligence."

"*WHAT?*"

Knight felt her muscles contract and her body shrink. She had never before witnessed Ibrahim lose himself to anger as he had in this moment. "Sir, much of the stolen intel featured our operations against Kozan Petroleum. We suspect Walsh found something in our data that is of value to the Venezuelans, that they will pay a lot of money for."

"Connected to Kozan?"

"Yes."

She watched as Ibrahim's eyes darkened as he sucked in air through his nostrils and held it. "You realise how serious this is?"

She shuddered, unable to suppress her body's natural stress response to Ibrahim's accusation. "I do, sir."

He leaned forward and maintained his piercing stare. "I don't think you do, Knight. You're saying you compromised a motherlode of intelligence some time back, and I'm only hearing about it now?"

"To be fair, this failing only just came to light," she lied.

"Knight, this is compromised intelligence that you can't quantify. Intelligence that might threaten the lives of hundreds of active and undercover operatives and assets across the globe, that has left them exposed for months! I could fire you right now for that level of incompetence. I could even bring criminal prosecutions against you."

Knight felt her throat tighten. She'd always appreciated

the gravity of her blunder, hence her strategy to come clean now, when her actions would resemble a lack of judgement rather than a deliberate attempt to hide a serious security breach. Although Knight had suspected Walsh's theft for some time, she'd recently discussed the possibility with Zang to cover her tracks now when she was ready to reveal it, allowing Zang to draw similar recent conclusions regarding the breach. Two women exposing a failure together looked better than one woman hiding it.

"The only reason Zang and I haven't come forward until now — which is what I am doing here — is because this is all very new, and because of the potential Kozan mole inside my team. Whoever this individual is, they might have been the culprit providing Walsh with the intelligence. And if I told the wrong person..."

For the count of five seconds, Ibrahim said nothing and barely moved. She watched as his mind calculated, assessed what she had told him and how it all fit into the larger puzzle they called the game of spying. "Where is Walsh now?"

"That, sir, no one knows..."

He leaned forward, unblinking, and held her stare like a snake does before it strikes at its prey, injecting it with lethal venom. "You have an idea though, don't you, Knight?"

She shrugged. "Why would Pierce travel to South America in the first place? Only one reason I can think of. He's found Walsh in Rio de Janeiro, and now he plans on killing him. This is how it all connects."

11

Rio de Janeiro, Brazil

Once on the other side of the tunnels and with Parque Nacional da Tijuca far behind them, Savannah followed the freeway for some distance as they re-entered the metropolitan neighbourhoods of the city. Pierce had earlier considered getting them off the freeway because this route was an easy location for their enemies to find them again, but if they turned off into the high-density metropolitan streets, their ability to move quickly would be significantly reduced. There were no good choices, and calculated distance gains rather than confusion was better at this stage considering the wreckage they had caused on the freeway earlier.

Seemingly from nowhere, a police vehicle passed them fast, coming the other way.

Pierce, Savannah, and Amelia held their collective breaths for several seconds after it sped on and disappeared into the traffic behind them.

"Did they see us?" Amelia asked.

Pierce thought the driver had watched them closely as they had passed. "We should assume they have."

"What now, Mark?" asked Savannah, as they took Avenue Maracanã, passing under chaotically arranged power lines, established kerb-side trees and multi-storey apartment blocks. "We've been following this route for some time, and it's out in the open and exposed. Shouldn't we disappear into the narrower streets?"

Pierce nodded while quietly making a note of Savannah's astuteness. "Yes. You're right; we've risked this route for too long."

They were passing Maracanã Stadium on their left, the massive football stadium that in its time had hosted FIFA World Cup events, and in its heyday could seat two hundred thousand spectators. "Go left around here; then take side streets at random."

Then Pierce noticed two more black Troller T4s crossing over the traffic, moving with speed so they would be directly in front of the Ford Ka in seconds, forcing them to brake suddenly and come to a halt.

Pierce guessed at the trap and pulled hard on Savannah's steering wheel, turning the car left suddenly and sending them crashing over the kerb onto a wide paved area. The alternative had been to crash into the four-wheel drives.

Savannah screeched as the Trollers sped behind them, dodging oncoming traffic coming the other way now that their quarry had bypassed their trap. Then Pierce saw they were careening straight into a series of market stalls selling football T-shirts and other paraphernalia. Savannah turned fast enough not to hit any pedestrians while at the same time Pierce honked the horn, sending people fleeing out of their way.

But the action wasn't fast enough to save their Ford Ka, as they drove through a line of palm trees and straight into the locked gated entry into Maracanã Stadium. The car jolted to a sudden stop, and the force of Pierce's seat belt compressing his chest inflamed the pain already surging through his battered body.

As steam erupted from the engine block, Pierce stared through the spiderwebbed windscreen until he could orientate himself, and realised that he wasn't badly hurt. The crash, however, had crumpled the iron fence gate that had otherwise prevented access to the stadium, providing a narrow path inside.

Pierce turned to the two women. "Are you both okay?"

Savannah nodded. "I'm good." She touched a trail of blood coming from her hairline but didn't seem bothered by her minor wound.

Amelia said, "I'm not!"

Pierce looked her over, noticing that she was scrambling to unbuckle her seat belt, and all her limbs seemed to be moving fine. "But physically you're okay?"

"Maybe? But what's that got to do with anything?"

"Everything."

Pierce was soon outside the wrecked Ford Ka, and so was Savannah. He then dragged Amelia out and onto her feet as he noticed the two Trollers were now up on the kerb also. Six men in dark clothes clambered out of those cars, equipped with more FAMAE SAF submachine guns.

"Run!" Pierce yelled as he drew his Glock and fired in the assault teams' general direction, in a hope to pin them down. "Into the stadium, now!"

Savannah and Amelia were already sprinting ahead, down the long, wide entrance hall leading into the stadium.

Once Pierce was behind the wrecked gate, he knew he needed to hold off the team of at least six heavily armed men pursuing them, because the corridor ahead was wide with no cover. So he fired his Glock at where he knew the Ford Ka's fuel tank would be. Three shots, and it exploded in a fireball, blocking the path through the wrecked gate Pierce and his companions had taken. Two men were caught in the blast radius and incinerated instantly. As for the remaining four attackers, it wouldn't slow them for long, but hopefully long enough for Pierce, Savannah and Amelia to get away.

As Pierce ran after the sprinting women, he wondered how this assault team had found them so fast.

Once at the other end of the empty, one-hundred-metre-long corridor, Pierce heard the assault team pounding the ground behind him. He looked ahead and saw Savannah and Amelia had reached the stadium's outer ring and had taken a stairwell upwards, towards where the highest spectator seats would be.

Too late to offer an alternative route suggestion, Pierce pursued them and tried to pretend his head didn't still feel like a thousand hammers were constantly bashing at it.

12

Pierce sprinted up several levels before bullets tore up the air around him, chipped concrete walls and shattered fluorescent strip lighting. He fired blindly back down the stairwell, hoping to convince his attackers that advancing on him was not in their best interest. He also presumed the team of four would have split, and others would be coming for them via other stairwells.

In response to his shooting, full, automatic bursts from submachine guns fired upwards through the stairwell, but they were more covering fire and not well aimed, so they all missed him. Instinctively, Pierce switched out the empty magazine and slotted in his last magazine of fifteen 9mm rounds of lethality. Pulling back the slide, chambering the first bullet, he fired three times down the stairwell, pinning whoever engaged him.

Pierce looked back and up the stairwell. Amelia with her choppy bob and blood-splattered yellow summer dress, and Savannah in her singlet and jean shorts with raven hair shaved close on one side and the other with streaks of purple, stared back at him. Perspiration saturated their skin and clothes. Their wide-eyed and open-mouthed fear was unmistakable.

"Keep moving!" Pierce fired again. "MOVE! NOW!"

He took off up the stairs, pushed the two women onwards. Submachine-gun fire followed them.

He herded the women, forced them to move faster.

Pierce fired again down the stairwell. He would deplete his bullets at any moment.

The stairs ran out, so they opened the exit door onto the vast outer rim of the sporting stadium.

A quick scan identified barrel-sized concrete planter pots with metre-high palms. With strength Pierce didn't know he possessed, he tore one from its corner and bounced it down the stairwell. As it smashed across the steps like a loose cannonball on a pitching ship, Pierce followed in a sprint.

A level down, the potted projectile collected one enemy target, catapulting him backwards.

A second opponent stepped back and avoided serious injury, but his distracted focus on the palm barrelling past, and not on Pierce, cost him. His FAMAE SAF submachine gun pointed upwards, not positioned for effective shooting, and left him vulnerable.

Pierce used that moment to shoot him twice in the chest.

The man staggered backward, but didn't drop dead as Pierce had expected.

Pierce saw why. The opponent wore body armour.

Pierce didn't hesitate as he aimed again at the stunned opponent and drilled a bullet through his forehead. Eyes rolled upwards and turned white as the back of the man's skull exploded outwards with gore smearing the concrete behind him red.

Pierce turned and aimed down the stairwell.

The palm in its severely cracked and chipped pot now sat upon the second foe's shoulders, where it had pulverised his head. The man's limbs spread at unnatural and unmoving angles.

Pierce checked his pistol. One bullet remained, so he grabbed a fallen submachine gun and secured four spare magazines from the corpses, then raced back up the stairs. There were two foes still unaccounted for, but that only presumed reinforcements weren't on their way or already here.

He heard screaming, then gunfire.

Emerging into the outer rim of the sporting stadium, Pierce looked for the women. But they had vanished.

Then he heard more screaming and additional gunfire bursts.

Pierce sprinted to a corridor opening onto the vast and empty football arena of Maracanã Stadium. He'd visited this facility during the Rio Olympics on another mission, when the scene before him had featured thousands of cheering fans, and a football match between competing nations had been a spectacle to behold.

Today Maracanã Stadium was empty, decrepit, defaced with graffiti, and stadium chairs were missing in their thousands. Rio's city council had allowed this once grand stadium to deteriorate and become unusable. A graveyard of sorts, vast but absent of fans and players, and no caretakers.

Pierce scanned the gigantic sports ground with overgrown grass, its wildness defacing the playing field. He spotted movement, then heard gunfire further down in the isles. It took Pierce a second to realise that bullets were aimed at him.

He dived onto faded seats, then sprinted between their rows as metal rounds pinged off concrete steps and shattered plastic backrests. He covered an entire row before he glanced up to spot an armed combatant advancing up the stairs with his submachine gun raised and his eyes focused along the barrel. When he spotted Pierce, he fired again. Pierce ducked down just fast enough to avoid losing the top of his skull.

A woman cried out.

Pierce heard further commotion and the man swearing in Spanish.

He rolled through a gap in the seats, then emerged with his FAMAE SAF aimed and ready.

The combatant, no less than fifteen metres from Pierce, had Amelia in his grip, pulled her to her feet and held her close as a human shield. She resisted his hold and screamed again, struggling violently so he couldn't secure a firm grip.

When she pulled away, Pierce used the opportunity to fire a quick burst of bullets that tore open the foe's thigh. He grunted and dropped to his knees, then toppled over. The flow of red was torrential, and Pierce knew he'd ruptured the man's femoral artery. Only a tourniquet applied immediately would prevent him from bleeding to death in the next minute, and even then, his odds of survival weren't good.

As the man screamed, Pierce moved position. "Get down!"

Amelia in her shock responded by turning in a circle and remaining upright.

"Drop! Get down."

"Mark?" she called out, and staggered towards him. Her red eyes ran with tears. "They took Savannah!"

Pierce didn't answer, and when she was close, he pulled her down so the chairs shielded her.

Amelia's tears became sobs. "My girlfriend, he has her. And he's going to kill her."

"Who?" Pierce asked.

But he didn't need an answer. He knew who had her. The last man alive who had pursued them across Rio de Janeiro on this very long and dangerous day.

13

"We'll save her," Pierce said, although he felt uncertain how he would rescue the captive girlfriend. The more he tried strategising, the more his mind fogged, and the more his headache intensified. Then he remembered: the woman with him had no head injury. She could do the thinking for him. He only needed to ask her the right questions. "How many gunmen?"

"What?"

"Numbers. How many?"

She shuddered. "I think... just one. But he has Savannah, as I said."

"Weapons?"

The woman glanced at Pierce's submachine gun, indicating that their armaments were the same.

They heard Savannah scream again.

Pierce peered over the broken chairs and down the stadium towards the grass playing field. The final opponent stood tall at ground level, with his close-cropped black hair, an olive-green jacket, and denim jeans. His eyes focused on

Pierce, for he had always known their position. He held Savannah in front as a shield. One arm wrapped around her neck held her immobile, the other pointed a high-calibre revolver at her forehead. The weapon wouldn't just kill her but disintegrate her skull and everything inside and around it.

"American, listen to me!" the foe yelled across the empty stadium in English with a Colombian or Venezuelan accent. "I will kill this woman unless you deliver the other woman to me."

"Mark!" Tears gushed down Amelia's face as she gripped his shoulder. He saw how much blood stained her once yellow dress. "She can't die. I couldn't live with myself if something happened to her. Savannah's... all I have left..."

Pierce nodded. Normally he could devise a plan in these scenarios, but his mind refused to cooperate. For the first time since his parents' death when he was sixteen, he felt powerless.

He also struggled to understand why he was helping these women. He knew nothing about them and could still not recall anything from before the favela car crash, nor did he have any understanding as to why he was in South America in the first place. But he also guessed those questions could be answered later, when, or if, they got out of this predicament alive.

Amelia wiped tears off her cheeks. Then her face lit up as an idea took hold. "Mark, that man wants *me* alive, not dead—"

The foe's yells interrupted. "American, I'm counting to ten. When I reach ten, I blow her brains out. Comprehend? One..."

Amelia shuddered. "Mark, point your gun at my head.

Threaten to kill me. Make me your hostage. That will get you close to him, and…"

"Two…"

Pierce nodded. It wasn't much of a plan, but it was better than anything he had come up with, which was nothing. He checked his Glock, discovering a single round in the chamber and the magazine empty, and no spare magazines on his person. Pierce could use the FAMAE SAF submachine gun to hold this woman at gunpoint, but to swing it against his foe would prove cumbersome compared to a pistol. The submachine gun he would sling over his shoulder, there if needed, but the reality was he had to make sure that the single 9mm bullet counted.

"Three…"

Pierce nodded, pressed his Glock against Amelia's head and held her arm twisted behind her back, allowing him freedom of movement when he needed to release her in a hurry.

"I'm coming down." Pierce's voice carried through the ghostly stadium.

The sun, finding a break in the clouds, made it difficult not to squint. Pierce recognised his foe had positioned himself so the sun was behind him and shone directly into Pierce's eyes. A man who planned the minutest of details was not a killer to be underestimated.

Pierce marched his captive down the stained concrete steps until they stood eight metres from the killer and his hostage. Make-up streaks on Savannah's face ran as black lines down her cheeks. Her wide eyes stared at Pierce, and he saw in her the unmistakable fear that came from knowing she could be dead in seconds.

The killer sized up Pierce, and Pierce did the same. The

two men were similar in physique. Both tall, slim and muscular. Each moved using only precise movements, and each noticed every aspect of their environment. The women were shields, and the men's weapons pointed not at each other, but at their hostages.

They were the same.

"How do you expect this to play out?" Pierce asked.

They heard distant police sirens.

With the earlier shooting and the trail of corpses spread far across Rio de Janeiro, it was only a matter of time before law enforcement showed up.

Pierce judged whether he could achieve a clean shot without injuring Savannah, but he didn't think so. The killer seemed too precise, too situationally aware. He'd react with the same speed and precision, which would only result in both men murdering each other and the women too.

Except he only had a single bullet.

"We're just going to stand here and wait for the police to kill us both?"

The foe said nothing.

The sirens grew louder.

"I don't think you want to end up in a Brazilian prison any more than I do."

Pierce knew that once incarcerated, it wouldn't be long before the CIA found and extracted him. If Pierce had gone dark for a reason, and his reasons opposed CIA objectives, a lifetime sentence in an Asian or Middle Eastern CIA black prison might be his ultimate fate, and that would be worse than imprisonment in Latin America for crimes of murder.

He didn't know why, but he felt he owed it to Amelia and Savannah to keep them alive, and that objective was more important than securing his personal freedom. Unfortunately, the best means of keeping them alive was to wait for the police to arrest them all. But that decision was behind them now. Neither Pierce nor his foe could flee without the other gaining the advantage and shooting to kill.

"No chitchat?"

The killer grinned.

When Savannah struggled, the foe pressed his .44 Magnum revolver against her temple until she complied and stood placid in his iron-like embrace.

"Mark?" whispered Amelia. She had expected Pierce to act by now, but with the fog and pain racking his body, he couldn't think straight. He didn't know who anyone was, their allegiances or motives, or even why he was involved with any of them. He also didn't believe, in this situation, violent action could effect a desirable outcome.

They heard the police cars screech to a stop outside. Then they heard boots pounding concrete as uniformed officers with assault rifles, body armour and helmets filled the stadium.

In that moment, Pierce recognised that their predicament didn't bother the killer, and he soon saw why. When two dozen riot officers surrounded them, twenty-four barrels pointed at Pierce and none at the killer.

It had been the police car passing them on the freeway that had tipped off this killer as to where they were.

Recognising his defeat, Pierce released Amelia, held up his Glock in a non-threatening pose, dropped it at his feet, then allowed the submachine gun to slip off his shoulder and fall to the concrete with his pistol.

One officer yelled Portuguese words at Pierce. He got the gist of the command, so dropped to his knees and laced his fingers together behind his head.

Amelia looked at Pierce, expressing shock and betrayal.

Naked...

Bound...

Beaten...

"I'm sorry," Pierce said to Amelia and Savannah as an officer took both women and cuffed them while another officer cuffed him. They left him on his knees.

Pierce watched as the police conversed with the killer. He couldn't hear what they were saying, but the conversation presented as friendly. Then Pierce watched the killer pass over several rolls of one-hundred-US-dollar bills.

Both women, now cuffed, sat upon the concrete with police officers behind them, guns pointed at their heads.

The killer approached Pierce, his pistol in his hand. The muzzle he pressed against Pierce's forehead felt hot from all the bullets it had already expelled. "I planned better."

"You don't say much."

"Neither will you, in a minute."

His weapon was a Taurus Raging Bull 454 revolver. Its high-calibre, high-speed bullet would make a mess of his face. Nothing discernible would remain to identify him.

"You're too dangerous to keep alive." The killer pulled back the hammer, and the long silver barrel was all Pierce could focus on.

Even if he fought now, the police would still gun him down.

The killer's cell phone rang.

The man glanced at the number, frowned, then gestured to two officers to watch over Pierce as he answered. "Yes... Yes..."

Pierce followed the killer's component of the conversation, because they spoke Spanish.

"I have Songbird... And her friend..."

Songbird. This sounded like a code word to Pierce, a name this man and his team had assigned Amelia Reyes, giving evidence that Amelia's supposition that this kill team was from SEBIN.

The killer kept talking on his cell phone. "Yes... the American assassin is with me now... Yes... What...? Ten million...? You're joking...? No, I don't think this is a joke... Okay... I understand."

With the call ended, the killer holstered his weapon. "It seems, American, this is your lucky day." He took a cigarette-sized case from his pocket, opened it, and Pierce saw a syringe and several vials inside. "What is your body mass?"

"Sixty kilograms."

The man laughed. "You're lying. Your mass is significantly more, with all that muscle." He drew a liquid substance into the syringe, then gently pressed the plunger and tapped the needle so no air remained inside. "Don't resist if you want to wake again."

Pierce knew he had no choice. He might or might not wake from whatever drug the killer would inject into him, but he wouldn't survive a volley of bullets if he made any feeble attempt now to escape. And if he lived beyond this moment, he might still find a means to save these two women who depended on him. In death, he could achieve nothing.

The syringe penetrated his neck.

Clear fluid flowed into him.

The world turned blurry, then dark, and then became nothing.

14

Port-au-Prince, Haiti

Port-au-Prince was a city of slopes, frantic traffic, four-wheel drives and motorcycles, rubbish-strewn streets, palm and banana trees and thick tropical vegetation, and densely packed housing with high walls and armoured gates.

All faces were black, but no one bothered Rachel Zang as she walked the streets in Petion-Ville, the upper-class neighbourhood of the Haitian capital with a view over the city and the Caribbean Sea. She stood out, but this was the quarter where all the foreign aid workers lived and operated from, and many of the commercial buildings here functioned as offices for the various Christian and secular non-government organisations still aiding Haiti's recovery after the devastation of the 2010 earthquake, which had killed at least one hundred thousand Haitians and had destroyed much of the already decrepit infrastructure of the city.

She passed street vendors hawking mangos and bananas,

women in colourful dresses or tight jeans, billboards of presidents who had joined the long list of politicians who had been assassinated at one point or another in Haiti's turbulent and violent history, and watched the long queue of cars and motorcycles parked at a gas station, waiting to pay the exorbitant prices for fuel.

For Rachel Zang, these vibrant impressions of Petion-Ville constantly bombarded her senses. This was a city alive with people, and many of them remained trapped within cycles of crippling poverty. She mused that it would be good if her mission here could accomplish some relief for these people, but it wasn't. She was distracted by a potcake dog crossing her path. The dog looked cute, with its smooth coat, cocked ears, and long face, but Zang knew many canines here carried the rabies virus, and she didn't need a potentially fatal bite affecting her operation at this moment.

"Target in range in five seconds," a voice radioed in her ear. "Turning west on Rue Darguin in three... two... one..."

Zang spotted Alpha Mansaray in the flesh for the first time, wearing a soft brown cotton jacket. He proved taller and broader than his CIA photos projected. His rippling muscles seemed eager to shred his clean and neatly ironed yellow shirt off his chest and shoulders. His shaved head, as a disguise against early baldness, reflected the hot midday sun back at her. Face etched with a permanent snarl, Mansaray paid her no notice, so she followed.

"Remember, this is a lethal target." Jarrad Felton spoke again in her ear, her technical operations officer hidden in the surveillance van several blocks distant near the target's expected destination. "Just got word from Langley. It *was* Mansaray who slaughtered three men in the Niger Delta last week."

Zang clenched her teeth. Felton was being all masculine and protective. In hand-to-hand combat she could take him down in seconds despite the hours he spent in the gym building his physique. In all the psychological and physical tests that the CIA subjected them to, she'd scored better than Felton in every category. Zang was the seasoned field operative here, and even if she wasn't physically and intellectually superior to Felton — which she was — she remained the senior operative and mission leader. A fact Felton didn't seem able to grasp.

"Jarrad, do I look worried?"

"You should be worried."

"And you should cut the chatter. Focus on the mission. Identify who Mansaray meets, because he'll reach your position shortly." She felt sweat run down her face, and not just from the tropical heat of the Caribbean.

"Yes, ma'am."

Mansaray pushed through the crowds and moved with purpose. She watched him clench his fists tight until veins bulged in his hands. Zang knew uncontrolled rage when she saw it, for Mansaray seemed close to losing his cool and ready to initiate a fight, and she wondered why. So as not to antagonise him, she waited until he passed and had walked some distance before she picked up the pace and followed.

In the next block, Mansaray ducked across the street, to bypass honking motorbikes and a truck overloaded with rice sacks that sped past. Then he cut through an earthen cemetery with hundreds of graves marked only with wooden crosses and wilting flowers.

"Who's with you, Jarrad?" Zang whispered, should her voice carry and their target overhear them.

"Peter is tailing you, ma'am, ready to take over when you need to drop back."

"That's because of my beautiful black face." Peter Jeffers on the radio used an over-the-top Jamaican accent that almost caused Zang to laugh out loud. Earlier they'd practised accents, and Felton couldn't understand that his Caribbean impersonation sounded South African, much to the amusement of the rest of the team. This was a playful dig at Jarrad Felton, who seemed not to understand banter or humour, much to the ire of the rest of the team.

Peter Jeffers's expertise lay in hacking and IT security, but like every member of the team, he was multi-talented and today best suited for boots-on-the-ground surveillance. As an African American, no one gave him a second glance in the streets of Port-au-Prince. Zang trusted he had her back.

"And Olivia?"

"I'm with Jarrad, in the van," answered Olivia Sharp, their intelligence analyst. "Although I'd rather be outside, with Felton's farting. Diesel fumes never smelled so good."

"Fuck you, Olivia! If I remember, *you* volunteered to work with me because you can't get enough of my manly physique."

"In your dreams."

"I am, unfortunately, every night."

Zang smiled, liked how her team could joke and give each other a hard time — except for Felton, who could never just be playful with the rest of them. But Alpha Mansaray was a serious opponent and required their full attention. Time to convey the real dangers they faced and return their focus to the mission. "Okay, it's serious time, team. It's game on."

"Roger that!"

They responded one after the other and, in an instant, shelved their jokes, which could wait until the operation ended.

Mansaray kept up his pace as they entered a retail district. He ignored mango sellers and temporary stalls hawking bright cloths and sandshoes, stepped over a faded Pepsi sign fallen across the footpath, and still he had not glanced back. The man was too confident, and Zang didn't like it. It was like he knew they had him under surveillance and didn't care.

Formerly a detective sergeant with the Nigeria Police Force's Criminal Investigation Department, five years ago Alpha Mansaray had made the more profitable transition to mercenary. Zang's interest was his suspected links to Kozan Petroleum, which today's meet should soon confirm and provide them with a new target to place under surveillance. Why Kozan Petroleum was in Haiti was unknown to Zang and her team, as Haiti produced no oil and gas of its own and imported most of its oil from Venezuela. After the meet, they would then bag Mansaray and extract him to a CIA black site for prolonged interrogation. The syringe loaded with a CIA-manufactured incapacitation drug was ready in her hand.

The latest intel was that Mansaray's yet-to-be-identified contact waited inside the Outlandos D'Amour bar, a few blocks from her current location.

Felton and Sharp hid in the van parked across the road. They had already planted multiple bugging devices inside the establishment. While background noises in any social venue were always a problem, Sharp expressed confidence that if Mansaray stood close to one of her audio surveillance devices, they'd hear everything he and his contact had to say.

Feeling the growing sweat on her body, Zang pushed on.

Mansaray soon reached the bar, but in the last moment when she thought he would step inside, he turned and picked up speed.

He advanced on Felton and Sharp's van.

"Shit!"

"What's the problem?" asked Sharp.

"Jarrad! Olivia! He'll be on you in seconds—"

Gunshots.

Passersby panicked and fled. Many screamed.

Zang counted off the bullets fired. Eight, all placed into the surveillance van's centre of mass.

"Team...?"

All she heard over the screams of the panicked crowd was radio silence.

Mansaray pried open the van's gas bowser with a tiny crowbar produced from his jacket, then tore off the lid. He stepped back, fired his pistol several more times, until a bullet entered the nozzle. The proceeding explosion proved louder than the bullets, like a thousand sheets of corrugated iron crashing down around her. The hot-red blast blown out from the fuel nozzle was like a flamethrower. Then as the tank ignited and ripped open the chassis underneath, the van leaped into the sky, turned over and crashed on its roof, and soon became engulfed in intense licks of brilliant red and orange.

The crowd had already fled. Mark and Olivia were the only casualties.

Alpha Mansaray looked up at Zang, grinned and showed his teeth.

He had always known she was there.

He switched out the magazine in his pistol and raced towards her.

15

R achel Zang could have run with the crowd, but she stood her ground, pulled her SIG Sauer P227 semi-automatic pistol from where she'd tucked it in her pants, and fired three close shots at Mansaray.

The muscular man expressed surprise that she had engaged rather than fled, and ceased advancing. Her shots had missed, but they'd pinned him down, forcing him to duck behind a parked Jeep.

Zang kept firing, counting down the shots until one remained in the chamber and two in the magazine. Mansaray wouldn't lift his head and shoot back while she maintained her superior firing position, and she hoped he didn't count bullets.

When he thought she was empty, he raised his head above the engine block.

Zang was ready. A single bullet pinged off the bonnet and grazed his skull.

To her surprise, he seemed not to notice his injury and returned fire.

He missed.

Then blood trickled into his eyes, blinding him.

With only two bullets remaining, and despite her earlier lucky shot, the distance between them seemed too great to assure an accurate mark. Zang turned and fled down a side street, darted across crumbling paved roads, bypassing motorbikes, taxis and four-wheel drives that were the vehicles of choice for the wealthy in Haiti. Moving through the Petion-Ville streets, passing restaurants and gyms, she switched magazines as she moved with speed, and wondered at Peter's fate. He wasn't checking in.

Police sirens sounded.

As she sprinted, Zang kept glancing back, half expecting Mansaray to be upon her.

He was nowhere to be seen.

Sensing that she was alone, Zang slowed her pace and spoke into her mic. "Peter, you copy?"

"Yes, ma'am," Jeffers sounded in her ear. "You okay, I thought you'd taken a bullet?"

"I'm a lucky girl." Zang got her breathing under control. "Olivia and Jarrad didn't make it, though."

She heard him swallow, then detected the croak in his voice. "I saw."

"Get to the safe house. Prepare for immediate evacuation."

"Yes, ma'am."

She turned a corner.

Peter came the other way.

At first, he expressed fear when he spotted her pistol, then joy when he recognised her as friendly.

Then the top of his skull exploded outwards. Bloody mist and vaporised brain matter filled the damp air. His corpse dropped as an inanimate heap of flesh and bone into the mud.

Alpha Mansaray waited behind where Peter had stood, half his face caked in fresh blood. He turned his pistol at her and squeezed the trigger.

The gun jammed or was empty, but Zang flinched like she had taken a bullet.

She should have drawn her pistol, but shock numbed her reflexes.

Mansaray, however, was ready for the melee and moved like a piston, fists pounding towards her.

Only her nimbleness saved her from a killing blow. Suddenly alert, Zang ducked, twisted away from his powerful strikes, which deflected past her, and he stumbled.

She ran up onto his back, locked her legs around his neck, and twisted him so he fell with her. The drop should have snapped his neck. But Mansaray was ready and twisted her at the last moment so she lost her grip and fell hard on the muddy road.

The impact winded her, but she still rolled properly, breaking nothing, and was back on her feet in seconds. She went for her pistol, but had lost it in her struggle to survive.

Mansaray's shirt had torn beneath his jacket, exposing the taut muscles lining his chest and abdomen.

It was in that moment she spied the symbol tattooed on his left pectoral.

For three seconds she didn't breathe—

A symbol she'd first witnessed fifteen long years ago, but one burned into her memory and as familiar to her as her own face in a mirror.

A circle within a circle, both dissected through their middles with a straight line.

Blood from Mansaray's superficial head wound had dribbled down and across it—

Mansaray came at her, fuelled by rage and ready to pummel her into a corpse, until a police car screamed to a halt between them.

Zang and Mansaray split and raced in opposite directions.

After sprinting five blocks, Zang found herself in a suburb catering to businesses and hotels. She hailed a taxi, paid the agreed fare in advance, and asked to be taken to Toussaint Louverture International Airport.

As her taxi blared its horn at the meandering traffic to get it moving, Zang sat for a moment and considered what she had learned, and what she had lost. Too little of the first and everything of the second.

Alpha Mansaray had known from the onset she and her team had tailed him. The symbol confirmed he was a member of the clandestine organisation she'd spent half her life trying to understand and destroy, so that was one piece of useful intelligence she'd gained today. His actions evidenced Patricia Knight's supposition that a double agent had infiltrated the CIA. But who was it? Too many of their team were dead because of this mole, and now Olivia Sharp, Jarrad Felton and Peter Jeffers counted amongst their losses. Three more anonymous stars for the honour walls of Langley.

She pressed her fist against her forehead and fought the urge not to violently punch the passenger seat in front of her.

Zang's cell phone rang.

A US number.

Zang had missed over a dozen previous calls from this caller.

"Yes?" She spoke Russian because Patricia Knight was fluent, and the likelihood of the taxi driver understanding her was remote.

"You're not taking my calls, Zang?" Knight also spoke Russian.

"My... team..." Zang could barely speak. "They're... all dead."

"What? How?"

"Our target... He knew we were coming."

There was a pause, then sniffles, which suggested Patricia struggled to contain her emotions. She had known and respected Zang's team as much as Zang had. "Where are you now?"

"Exfiltrating myself from Port-au-Prince."

"You require assistance?"

"No," Zang said through her clenched jaw. "I'll call when I'm secure."

"Get yourself to the States. Miami. We need to talk. There have been some other... unexpected developments."

Zang was about to ask what Knight meant, but the call had already ended.

PART II

REACTION

16

Venezuelan Airspace

T hin air. Clear blue skies. Snowcapped mountains with sheer cliff edges. A vast concrete dam a kilometre wide. Massive, spinning, hydroelectric generators—

Pierce set the explosive's timer for eight minutes—

His eyes fluttered.

A pain similar to a boot pressed into his face gripped his skull.

Internal pain from an earlier injury.

He felt a shudder, recognised it as turbulence. The air in his nostrils and mouth felt dry and recycled. Awareness grew as the dream faded. He realised wires constrained him to a passenger seat fixed inside an airborne commercial jet.

Opening his eyes, Pierce spied the beige and brown colours of an older model Hawker 800 aircraft.

Amelia sat opposite him. Her face was a collection of

purple bruises, and her hands, immobilised with cable ties, rested on her lap. Pierce remembered the blood on her dress wasn't hers.

Next to her sat Savannah. Someone had beaten her too, leaving her eyes dark, and on one side of her forehead, a bright purple bruise swelled. A split lip had bled down to her chin and dried as crusty, rust-coloured flakes. Tight cable ties around her wrists left her hands red and puffy.

Despite his painful headache, Pierce gritted his teeth and vowed he would hunt down and kill whoever had tortured these two young women.

"You're awake."

He glanced backwards, towards the rear of the aircraft. The lean muscular killer with close-cropped hair sat in one beige seat, sketching on an artist's pad. He wore a black shirt and matching chino pants, a change of clothes since their last encounter. A shoulder holster on prominent display slung a Raging Bull 454 revolver. Its .44 Magnum rounds would rapidly depressurise the cabin should he use it, so a useless weapon unless they all wished to die together. Then Pierce noticed the Taser swinging from his belt. Sitting near the killer were two men in flashy polo-neck shirts, also with shoulder holsters packing a Glock 32 .357 semi-automatic pistol for the first thug and a tan-coloured Beretta M9A3 9mm pistol for the second.

Pierce tested his bindings, to find his arms pulled behind his back and constrained with what felt to be coiled metal wire. The same wire immobilised his ankles and neck, and all five points presumably collected at a point behind his chair at the small of his back.

"You think I'm too elaborate with my restraints?" The killer spoke English with either a Venezuelan or Colombian accent, but his words were precise and clearly enunciated with no hint that he had any problem with the language.

Pierce gave a slight nod, as he recognised this foe was a meticulous planner. "I think you've overestimated my abilities."

The killer grinned. "Oh, I don't think so." He advanced and sat in the seat on Pierce's left. The sketch he'd worked on hung loose in his left hand. Pierce noticed that the comic-book-style drawing was of the killer himself firing his pistol into Pierce's head, and Pierce's skull shattering and opening with blood, gore and brain matter spraying across the page. The resemblance to both men was commendable.

"You like?"

Pierce shrugged. "I think you've wasted your talents."

"On art?"

"No. On killing."

The man grinned and seemed to relax, but Pierce detected no reduction in his situational awareness. "A man can excel in many talents."

Pierce glanced at his opponent's bruised knuckles. "Including beating women?"

He nodded again. "These two are not as innocent as you might think... Mark."

He studied Pierce closely for a moment, but then Pierce realised, as an artist, he would. But he'd also study Pierce to gain a measure of him and understand what kind of foe he was dealing with. Pierce also noted this man knew his name, or first name at least, but that could have been because he'd overheard Amelia calling him this in Maracanã Stadium.

"I'd planned on killing you in the stadium. A man like you is too dangerous to keep alive."

"Then why didn't you?"

He shrugged. "Because my boss ordered me not to."

Pierce shrugged too, but that only caused the wire around his neck to tighten. Since waking, he'd schemed how to escape his bonds, but no solution had yet presented as a viable option. The man before him had been careful to ensure Pierce had no means of escape. He would expect Pierce to attempt to fight for his freedom should a situation present itself to do so. The killer was not wrong.

"I'll bite. Why does this mysterious boss of yours want me alive?"

"Apparently, the Chinese are very interested in you. Yet weirdly, they know nothing about you. Not your name, nationality or history — unfortunately — except that you are a top enemy of their state, and they detest you very much. They will pay ten million US dollars if SEBIN deliver you to them alive."

SEBIN? This man must represent Venezuela's secret police and their interests abroad. So what Amelia had told him was the truth, which gave him confidence that his instincts to help these two women in their battles with this group was not misplaced.

"And dead?"

The killer closed his sketchbook and tucked it down the side of his seat. "Only half a million. And only if we bring them your corpse."

"That must be a dilemma for you. Is that why you drew a sketch of me first, as proof that when you first captured me, I was alive?"

The SEBIN operative kept his face impassive. "No. Sketching is a hobby. I like comics, especially violent ones like *Akira*, *Hard Boiled*, and *Lone Sloane*."

Pierce had only heard of the first one and then only knew it through the movie. "That must be nice for you." He glanced at the two women, both tense with fear. They kept their eyes cast downward, and each barely moved. Then Savannah caught his eye and glanced at her clenched fist in her lap so only he saw. She had a plan and wanted Pierce to know.

The SEBIN killer sensed their exchange, and although he had not witnessed the eye contact, looked back and forth between them both. He rose out of his chair and walked behind Savannah, then pulled at her hair, yanking her head up and exposing her neck. With his other hand, he pressed a matt black tactical knife against her throat. "Shall I slit her open, Mark, since she serves no purpose?"

Pierce swallowed against the itch rising in his throat and decided to bluff. "I don't know who she is."

The man held the knife close as tears flooded from the eyes of both women. "Yes, that makes sense. Amelia and Savannah both told me you have short-term memory loss." He nodded to each woman as he spoke their names. "That yesterday you hit your head pretty hard. So of course you don't know if these women hold value to you or not. I wonder if that is going to be a problem."

Pierce closed his eyes as a memory came to him suddenly.

A naked woman, bound and beaten, pleading with her eyes for Pierce to find and rescue her...

That naked woman was neither Amelia nor Savannah.

He saw himself staring into a mirror, and his reflection detesting his chosen identity. The paths he had taken... The decisions he had made...

He opened his eyes.

Knife still pressed against Savannah's neck, the killer watched Pierce with distracted interest. "Or maybe not. It looks like you are remembering a past incident? Something that is painful for you to recall?"

17

P ierce's thoughts turned bleak, for he had no viable plan for how to escape this predicament. His mind still felt foggy, and any attempt at clear thought only proved to confuse him further.

He tested the wire bindings around his wrists, and as he suspected, if he pulled on them, the wire around his throat constricted. The killer was proficient down to the minutest details. His tradecraft was amongst the best Pierce had ever encountered in a foe.

Even if Pierce could escape his bindings, which he doubted, he'd still face three armed targets and their leader, the latter a skilled and cunning operator. His only hope lay with Savannah, still with the killer's knife at her throat. Pierce felt certain she had signalled earlier that she had a plan, which left Pierce questioning who she might be, other than Amelia's girlfriend, and where her allegiances really lay, yet he sensed she might also present a solution to escape the wire contraption. Therefore, Pierce's best course of action was to talk, distract his enemy so she could act.

"I wiped out your entire team." When the killer remained unresponsive, Pierce added, "Doesn't that piss you off?"

The killer shrugged, pressed the blade against Savannah's neck until a prick of blood dribbled down her throat.

"You have a name?"

The man smiled again, returned his knife to the sheath on his arm, and released Savannah's hair. The cut was superficial and non-life-threatening. "If I told you, you'd just forget."

"His name is Maceo Parra."

Pierce and the killer both turned to Amelia. Her dark, bloodshot eyes focused on the man who had tortured and beaten her. She carried a distant gaze, suggestive she'd shut down any feelings she'd once possessed, because past traumas had made her a stranger to her every emotion.

Parra turned his attention to Amelia. "You've held out on us both, haven't you, little one?"

The young woman sneered. "Sergeant Maceo Parra. The legendary sociopathic FAES special forces sniper who runs with covert SEBIN death squads. The 'Comic Book Killer' they call you. I know all about you, Maceo. I know every intimate detail there is to know about you, and do you know why?"

Parra made a chuckling sound at the back of his throat. "Why don't you tell me?"

"It's because you murdered my mother."

The cabin fell silent.

If Parra felt any remorse about this revelation, he hid it behind an icy stare. Perhaps he had killed too many women in his past to remember her.

"You drew a picture of it too and mailed it to me. What kind of sick individual does that?"

Pierce noticed a charismatic strength in Amelia. He knew she could command any conversation and could always convincingly articulate her point of view. Suddenly, this realisation suggested his memories of her had improved... but not everything that was important about her returned to his mind. If he just reached out, he felt he could grasp those evasive thoughts and make them solid... Remember who she really was...

"Maceo. Parra." Pierce spoke the name out loud, questioned if he knew this man, if they had crossed paths before the shoot-out in Maracanã Stadium.

Nothing came to him.

He tried strategising instead, only for his mind to fog, and a migraine-like pain in his head drained him of what mental strength he still possessed.

Amelia, perhaps sensing his distress, caught his attention. "Mark, look at me!"

He did as she commanded.

"Mark, Parra is returning me to Venezuela so the president can humiliate me."

"Why?"

Parra chuckled. "You still don't know, or still can't remember, who Amelia Reyes is!"

She had told him she was an activist against the Venezuelan or Bolivarian regime, as they were also known by.

Then he remembered she was famous, a celebrity, but what for?

Parra's chuckles became laughter. "You should see yourself, Mark. The confusion, the pain you are feeling, you really did do a number on your head."

Pierce pushed through the pain.

She wasn't the naked and beaten woman pleading for his help...

Amelia had a YouTube channel, with billions of views and five hundred million likes.

Amelia Reyes, as a child...

A collage of one-second-long videos, each snapshot a day in her life, growing up in the violence and poverty of a decimated Venezuela. A transition from a happy, vibrant child into a terrified teenager. Over thousands of video grabs, her smiles and joyfulness had transitioned into fear and catatonia. Pierce remembered her haunting expressions and disconnection from the people who loved her. The same woman sat across from him now, and she still looked just as haunted and emotionally empty.

Millions of supporters had resonated with the emotions the video had portrayed so well. It was not a surprise, then, that Amelia Reyes became the public face that represented the fear and horror that millions of Venezuelans experienced every day. She was a powerful, unspoken voice for the silenced men, women and children who had vanished, and those kidnapped, tortured and murdered by the Bolivarian secret police.

SEBIN.

And somehow Pierce had found Amelia in Rio de Janeiro, or she had found him.

Why could he remember this, yet nothing from the last few months had come back to him? Or were his memories returning to him only bit by bit as the injuries to his head slowly healed, and was this a normal process? Then he recalled head injuries were always complicated. He had seen the effects in soldiers he had fought with in the past, and no two victims ever suffered identical mental symptoms. But what he did know from prior experience was, if his memories didn't come back to him in the coming days or weeks, they would likely never come back at all. Was this memory, then, of Amelia Reyes as a YouTube sensation a sign that he was on the mend?

He hoped so.

Pierce was clinical when he nodded to Parra while he looked at the young activist in her still bloodstained yellow dress. "This man, Amelia, he murdered your mother?"

Amelia Reyes glanced at Parra, then nodded as tears gushed from her eyes.

"I promise you I will kill him... and soon."

Pierce failed to see Parra's fist before it hit him, which rattled his jaw and brought bloody spit to his mouth. Bright lines of light filled Pierce's vision, and his eyes lost focus. The pain was shocking, but no worse than the imaginary nails biting at his skull or the wire tightening around his throat. For a few seconds, he thought he would pass into unconsciousness, but he fought his pain and tenuously maintained his grip on reality.

"You'll never have the chance to kill me," said Parra. "The Chinese will execute you first, days or weeks from now, but not before they torture you for whatever purpose you—"

Savannah convulsed, fell forward from her chair into Pierce's lap, vomited over him, and shook like she was experiencing a fit. Pierce suspected a ruse, and if it was, it was convincing.

Parra pulled Savannah backwards and threw her to the cabin floor. Ignoring the vomit, he checked Pierce's lap and reached down between the folds of his pants, not caring that he touched Pierce's groin. He soon found what he was searching for, a paperclip. In the hands of a skilled operator like Pierce, a paperclip was a useful weapon or a tool to escape handcuffs and other means of incarceration.

Parra had trained and perfected the same skills and had guessed Savannah's ruse. He pulled the woman with the purple streaks to her feet and punched her hard in the skull, sending her toppling back onto and over her seat to crash hard against the cabin floor.

She didn't get up, and she didn't move.

Parra took a water bottle and washed the vomit off his hands. "You didn't tell me she was on your team, Mark."

Pierce hadn't considered this possibility, but now he did. Because along with the paperclip, during the ruse, she had also slipped a tiny pair of wire cutters into Pierce's right hand.

18

Caracas, Venezuela

Five armour-plated Toyota Prados sped through the streets of Caracas. The convoy's route took them through the Upper East Side, home to Venezuela's few remaining wealthy citizens, but even here, queues of malnourished, skinny men and women lined up in their hundreds outside grocery stores stocking only empty shelves. A few street vendors sold roasted chickens or pigeons. Burger King and McDonald's restaurants stayed open but served no one because of their exorbitantly priced meals. A full tank of gas might only cost a few US cents, but a single roll of toilet paper cost more than what ninety per cent of the population earned in a month. Bananas were the only plentiful and affordable food, and most were green and unripe. Across Venezuela, the only people making real money had joined a criminal gang or had joined the regime. Everyone else slowly starved to death.

SEBIN's director, Juan Garcia, watched from behind the

mirrored windows of the fourth Prado and recognised a city verging on collapse. It was his mandate to ensure descent never occurred.

But SEBIN weren't here to protect the people, rather to prop up the Bolivarian government of Venezuela, and his only means of achieving this goal was through violence and terror. If that meant executing problematic dissidents, funding *Colectivo* paramilitary gangs for their extrajudicial killing skills, suppressing street protestors with rubber bullets and tear gas, and making anyone who spoke up against the regime disappear, then that was what SEBIN would do, and they would do it well. It seemed likely Garcia would soon need to execute one or more of those strategies today, when he faced his newest problem looming ahead of him.

Earlier, he'd dealt with the crisis concerning Sergeant Parra and Amelia Reyes in Rio de Janeiro, and the slaughter of some of his best operatives by an unknown assassin who had appeared from nowhere. That problem was far from resolved, but right now, he faced a far worse dilemma. Parra and Amelia — whom he had given the code name Songbird so no one outside of SEBIN got a whiff of what he was up to — would have to wait. At least they were on a flight destined for Caracas now, and Garcia could deal with them both when they touched down.

Garcia's cell phone rang, distracting him from his worrying thoughts. He recognised the number immediately. He didn't wish to speak with his wife, but putting it off would only worsen Marcela's always simmering passive-aggressive- ness. He answered.

"Darling, got a moment?"

His forty-three-year-old wife's sweet lyrical tone always

left Garcia imagining her spending vast quantities of the money he earned.

"Juan, you there?"

He glanced at his Omega Seamaster watch and examined the sweep of the second hand. "Yes, I'm free. I have at least five minutes to talk."

"That's lovely, darling. It's about the ladies from the tennis club. You know how I said it was soon my turn to host a tea party? Well, soon is now. That won't be a problem, will it, if I organise it at our home next Tuesday?"

Marcela's social life was of no interest to Garcia except where it might affect their personal security and in protecting their only child, Sofia. Then, as his thoughts focused on his fifteen-year-old daughter, he frowned and glanced again at his watch, processing what time it actually was. "I can't hear the piano. Is Sofia not practising, as per her schedule?"

Marcela sighed. "Sofia really doesn't like piano, darling. Hasn't for years."

Garcia tensed his jaw and took in a slow breath. "I don't care, Marcela. I pay good money for her lessons. Sofia will just have to learn to enjoy them."

Marcela sighed again and gave no response.

"Get her on the piano, now! When you do, I'll give you an answer concerning your precious tea party."

"It's so boring, Juan, having to run everything past you all the—"

"I make the money, *darling*! I have the last word on everything. Besides, it's for both your protection!"

"How do piano lessons make our daughter any more protected?"

He growled, not wishing to be drawn into an argument

he didn't care to partake in. "You know what my role involves and the risks we face, Marcela. But you also don't mind the money I make risking my life every day supporting the high life you have become so accustomed to. So get Sofia back on the piano, appreciate my money, and stop fighting me on details that are important to me."

Garcia noticed his heart rate and breathing had increased despite his attempts to control both. He counted to five in his mind before Marcela answered with the response he hoped to hear; otherwise the conversation would have turned far nastier as he lost his cool.

"Yes, darling," she answered in a demure tone. "You are correct, as usual. I'll call you back shortly. Sofia—?"

She ended the call.

He threw his phone down on the upholstered seat and fumed. Thank God for his mistress and her calming influence; otherwise he would have strangled Marcela to death years ago.

Up ahead, they had reached their destination in an industrial sector of the city, and behind it up on a hill sprawled one of the city's many barrios, or slums, which cast a shadow on the ominous scene before them. He identified three VN-4 Rhinoceros armoured personnel carriers of the Guardia Nacional Bolivariana de Venezuela, or the Bolivarian National Guard of Venezuela, or simply the GNB. Dozens of foot soldiers in maroon berets, riot gear and slinging Russian AK-103 assault rifles secured a large warehouse surrounded by three-metre-high security fences. All faces were pale and sombre, and some men looked ready to piss their pants, if they had not done so already.

Something inside the warehouse had spooked them all.

The Toyota Prados came to a halt as Garcia's FAES security detail fanned out, weapons ready. Only then did Garcia step out and feel the heat and humidity that always lingered along with the city's ever-present smog and diesel fumes. Today he wore white cotton pants and shirt, and his dark hair he held flattened against his scalp with styling gel. It wouldn't take long before his clothes stained, absorbing the pollution thick in the air. He should have chosen a different wardrobe today, but it was too late to regret such decisions now.

A moustached colonel of the GNB, with a slight paunch, approached. Garcia recognised him immediately as Jesus Alvarez, responsible for maintaining greater Caracas's internal security and public order. The high-ranking officer saluted as his posture turned rigid.

"This'd better be worth my while, Colonel," Garcia said as he slipped on his white Panama hat to protect his slick hair from the burning sun.

"It's not good, sir."

Then the stench hit Garcia's nostrils with the force of a hammer blow. The reek of death, of rotting corpses, and shit and bile was overwhelming. He heard the buzzing of flies, and along with the odours, they originated from within the warehouse.

"It's happened again?" Garcia asked with a snarl.

"Yes, Director."

He wrapped a scarf around his nose and mouth. "Well, let's get this over with."

19

As Garcia and Colonel Alvarez approached the warehouse, they gagged. Soon their eyes watered from the stench wafting into the outside air. Garcia felt bile rising in his throat.

The warehouse interior was exactly the same as the previous three incidents Garcia had witnessed these last weeks. Dozens of dead soldiers, in this case the rank and file of the Army, lay chained to the walls. Physically, none of them seemed to display any external signs of trauma from infections that could explain their demises. Many of the men had shit themselves, which was obvious from the stench, but any man chained for a period of time did that. Flies buzzed everywhere, and Garcia saw maggots crawling inside one dead soldier's open eyelids and mouth, but again, this was a post-death outcome and didn't explain what had killed them.

The SEBIN director clenched his fists tight. As with the previous attacks, whoever was behind this insurrection had brought the soldiers in alive, then chained them to the walls before subjecting them to some yet unidentified chemical or biological weapon. Garcia had witnessed his share of horrific deaths in his career, but nothing terrified him like the expressions of fear and pain etched on the faces of these corpses. They had died slowly over many days, he could tell that much, and their passing had been in excruciating pain. He would prefer almost any other death than this one.

"Fuck!" exclaimed Garcia. He turned and marched from the scene before he barfed.

Colonel Alvarez followed him, tears streaming from his red eyes. "They're soldiers from a local infantry division. Disappeared two weeks ago during a training exercise in the Coastal Range."

"How many 'disappearances' now, Colonel?"

The GNB officer swallowed, then coughed. "Seven, sir. Army, Navy and Air Force."

"We've had three groups that previously disappeared turn up like this now. Hidden in warehouses and murdered with chemical weapons. And all showing up within fifty kilometres of Caracas?"

"Yes, sir."

"You'd better find out who's behind this, Colonel, and soon."

Alvarez's body tensed as he motioned to say more, then changed his mind. He didn't have to, because his words would only be to articulate the same fear they all shared. If word spread amongst the enlisted soldiers regarding this existential threat they now faced, it might spark riots and bring retribution upon the officer class. Whoever was behind these attacks, it seemed likely this was their intention, to deliberately provoke the collapse of the entire Venezuelan military machine. Garcia could not let that happen because, if for no other reason, his own existence and that of his family would come under threat. The president never tolerated failure, but the president wouldn't be his only problem.

"If we don't fix this, Colonel, neither you nor I will survive this."

"Yes, sir."

"Stop fucking saying 'yes, sir' and tell me something I can use."

A bead of sweat ran from Colonel Alvarez's cap along his forehead, then across his nose before finally collecting in his already damp moustache. "Director, whoever is behind this, they are professionals. They leave no evidence."

"There must be something. What about blood samples? Take some and do tests. I want to know what it is we are dealing with."

"We have samples, sir. We are running tests, but..."

Garcia knew what the colonel implied in his unfinished sentence. With the various economic and military sanctions imposed upon Venezuela by the rest of the world, medical and pathological resources were scarce. No one in the country had the labour or technology to perform the required clinical investigations to tell them what they were up against. Collecting blood samples was a waste of time.

"Director, there is something else."

"What the fuck is it now?"

"When we arrived here, one soldier was still alive. But... he wasn't rational. He was hyperactive, kept talking about ghosts and the like that weren't there. But weirder still, we offered him water to drink, and that freaked him out."

For a moment, Garcia reflected on what this could mean, and wondered if the hallucinating soldier had infected the first soldiers on the scene with this mysterious disease being used as a weapon of war against him. "What did you do with this man?"

"I had to shoot him." Alvarez pointed back towards the warehouse. "His body is still in there, with the others."

Garcia nodded. The threat of a biological or chemical weapon attack terrified him, not that he would ever express such fears. He had to be strong and in control at all times. If he ever appeared weak, even once, he would lose his power and authority as others challenged him for his position.

"You made the right choice, Colonel. Now burn down this warehouse, like the others. Incinerate all the bodies. We can't have this getting out."

"Yes, sir."

"And then fucking find out who in sweet fucking Mother of Mary is behind this!"

Five minutes later, the warehouse lit up as an inferno, incinerating any evidence that Venezuela's military was under threat. But Garcia knew this was a superficial cover-up at best.

Garcia was back inside his Toyota Prado, now third in the convoy, returning to SEBIN headquarters, trying not to think about the threat he faced, when his cell phone rang again.

He checked the number. It was Marcela.

"What do you want now?" He couldn't hear Sofia on the piano in the background as he'd hoped.

"Hello, Mr Garcia."

The SEBIN director tensed. It wasn't his wife who answered, but a man with an Italian accent. "What the fuck—!"

"You should listen to me carefully, Mr Garcia." The stranger spoke English in precise and clipped tones. "Ten minutes ago, I know you witnessed the terror inside that warehouse, and you've seen similar terror in other warehouses. I know you know what the implications are if this situation gets out of control... And I will ensure it gets out of control unless..."

Garcia growled, then screamed down the phone line, "Whoever the fuck you are, you're dead! You hear me? I'm coming for you, and when I find you, I will cut off your limbs and balls, one by one, with a chainsaw—"

The Italian man laughed. He expressed not even a hint of fear. "No, you won't, Mr Garcia. If you take a moment and think about it, you'll realise I am the only man on Earth who can stop a similar chainsaw fate befalling you. Your president won't be happy if he learns what you are covering up..."

Despite the rage consuming him, Garcia didn't answer. The stranger hijacking his wife's cell phone number might just have a point. He might even have her physical phone, and he would check to ensure he did not as soon as this call ended.

"You and I should meet, Mr Garcia, and soon. I have a proposition you won't want to resist."

"When? Where?" Garcia asked, knowing that he really didn't have a choice here.

"In Mexico City, later this night. There is a ticket waiting for you at the Copa Airlines desk at Simón Bolívar International Airport. Hurry, you don't want to be late."

20

Venezuelan Airspace

"Check her!" Parra barked his order to the thug with the Glock.

The sweaty underling nodded, then shuffled between Pierce and Parra to reach the unconscious Savannah as their jet flew on, headed north judging by the angle of the sunlight streaming through the window. Other than when the thug passed between them, Parra maintained constant eye contact with Pierce. Pierce used the momentary opportunity with the blind spot to snip the wire from his right wrist, and immediately, the tension released from around his throat.

Even with his clinical hyperawareness, Parra didn't seem to have noticed the loosened wiring.

Behind Parra, Pierce heard Savannah groan as the thug manhandled her. Her moans sounded fake to Pierce's ears, which gave him hope.

Knowing that opportunities for escape remained limited, Pierce readied himself to cut another strand of the wire. He waited for Parra to glance away and assess the situation with the downed woman. She was providing Pierce with every opportunity to make his escape, but Parra's eyes never left Pierce.

Groaning, Pierce realised there were no opportunities with this killer. The man had never once dropped his guard.

"You know, I can do this all day?" Pierce said. "I'm not going anywhere."

As if the forces of nature themselves chose Pierce's side in that moment, the aircraft hit turbulence, and everyone jolted in their seats, or stumbled if standing. Parra, too, tripped on his feet and glanced away.

Pierce leveraged his second opportunity and cut the wire from his left wrist. Then with lightning motions, he impaled the resulting length of cut wire into Parra's left forearm.

The wound took Parra by surprise. He looked away again only for a second to understand the injury. Then as their eyes locked once more, and with only touch to guide him, Parra felt around his flesh where the wire protruded. No blood seeped from the wound, and Parra didn't pull it free as Pierce hoped he would, offering a third opportunity to act.

Not willing to lose his gains, in full view of Parra, Pierce snipped the wire constraining him around his neck. No time remained to cut his still bound feet because Parra was already upon him.

The FAES operative's tense fingers tightened around Pierce's throat. He ignored the wire protruding from his arm as he pushed his weight down upon Pierce, crushing his windpipe.

Pierce struggled from his limited position, felt his throat constrict while he simultaneously failed to manoeuvre from under Parra's powerful grip. He yanked the wire from his foe's arm and again stabbed the man in the shoulder, but to no further effect. Parra expertly ignored the pain.

Knowing he was running short on options, and that he would soon pass into unconsciousness if he didn't soon lessen the pressure on his windpipe, Pierce felt his face redden and his tongue grow large in his mouth. He could no longer draw breath. He must break Parra's grip, or he'd soon be a dead man. But how? Whatever strength or skill he'd once possessed, his head injury had diminished his abilities to a point where he could not act in this scenario of death.

Appearing from nowhere, Amelia rushed Parra from behind, wrapped her bound wrists against his neck and throttled him.

Parra fell backwards as he fought her off.

With the pressure released from Pierce's throat, he sucked in oxygen.

The aircraft rocked as they hit further turbulence.

Parra and Amelia, now on their feet and wrestling, toppled and rolled backwards.

The second thug rushed Pierce.

Realising he still gripped the wire torn from Parra's shoulder, Pierce turned the makeshift weapon and impaled it through the advancing thug's throat.

The foe stumbled, at first uncertain of what had happened. Then as his eyes lost their focus, spurts of sticky crimson fired from a ruptured jugular. In a last-ditch attempt in exacting revenge for his now impending death, the thug pulled his Beretta M9A3 and fired randomly.

Pierce shrank into his chair as bullets pinged around him and throughout the cabin. He heard windows shatter, then sudden wind rushing around them with hurricane ferocity.

The dead thug slipped to his knees before the strong draft caught him and pinned his corpse against one broken window, slowing the rate of airflow as it escaped the cabin. The body bent at an unnatural angle as the violent pressure tried to suck him outside.

The aircraft pitched and fell into a dive.

Parra, Amelia, Savannah and the first thug couldn't keep their balance and rolled downwards towards the cockpit at the front of the Hawker as the pull of gravity disappeared.

Still holding the wire cutters, and because his seat belt held him immobile, Pierce could now snip the last constraining wires from his ankles. Then, as the aircraft steadied, he unclasped his seat belt.

Then the aircraft lurched and rolled again.

With the cabin air pressure thinned out, the dead thug dropped from the window and rolled across the interior and into Pierce, and they both tumbled with the rest of the passengers.

By now Amelia and Savannah were free of their captors, and with the chaos erupting around them, they both lunged for seat belts hung from upside-down chairs and held on as the aircraft shuddered.

The second thug with the Glock, with nothing within reach to grab onto, dropped as external forces fired him into the cockpit, where he crashed into the back of the pilot. An instant later the pilot smashed his head into the flight console, and both men were out cold.

The engine fired up, and the aircraft rolled again with greater angular momentum than before.

Soon they were spinning in turning circles.

Pierce found himself running around the cabin like a mouse on a spinning wheel. The perception of gravity kept shifting. The pilot or pilots, either dead or unconscious, had lost all control of the aircraft.

As Pierce struggled to remain on his feet, Parra leaped at him, fired a fist like a piston aimed for Pierce's head, but missed when the aircraft lurched again.

They grappled with each other as they rolled across the cabin roof, then toppled over the shattered windows and tumbled down to the seating area again. With their bodies pressed hard against each other, both men found it impossible to land a punch, so they wrestled instead.

As the thin outside air filled the cabin, it brought with it an icy chill. After a minute of close in-fighting, the men gasped for breath, each unable to oxygenate their muscles enough to deliver a striking blow.

Pierce guessed they were falling to their death and would soon hit the earth at a velocity of well over a thousand kilometres per hour. There was nothing either man could do to avoid this fate, but to restrain the other's grip, to stop each other from delivering a now pointless killing blow.

They would die together.

Then the plane levelled out.

And the air didn't taste so thin anymore, suggestive they had descended significantly since depressurisation.

With renewed energy from the reoxygenated air, Parra reacted first, punched Pierce hard in the kidney, and then a second time.

Pierce tried to fight back, but his foggy mind betrayed him and left him paralysed and placid.

Parra clobbered Pierce in his cranium, almost rendering

him unconscious. As his head swam, and black shadows danced on the edge of his conscious mind, Pierce asked himself, how was it possible to lose so much of his once honed and perfected fighting techniques? Had his earlier head injury affected him worse than he'd expected or hoped for?

That question might soon be moot.

Now the aircraft eased into a steady path.

Despite the punches Parra continued to lay into Pierce, the American remained aware enough to presume Savannah was a competent pilot and had commandeered the cockpit, attempting to bring the Hawker back under control.

This prompted far more questions than it answered.

But answers must wait. They might not crash after all, so he had to fight.

He drew upon the last of his mental reserves and kicked Parra in the chest.

Caught off guard, the Venezuelan tumbled backwards, and the men separated.

As Pierce tried to climb onto his feet, the imaginary hammering nails in his head returned, and his mind threatened to blank again.

He spotted Parra slipping on a parachute; then he forced one on Amelia, where she cowered in a seat. She was as battered and bruised as the rest of them.

Pierce rushed Parra, only to have his foe fire his Taser. Two electrodes impaled Pierce's chest, and the attached wires forced fifty thousand volts of electricity through every muscle in Pierce's body. He convulsed, lost control of his nervous system, and collapsed onto the unsteady floor of the shaking aircraft.

The next moments lost all clarity and logic.

He remembered the cabin door flinging open.

He remembered Amelia and Parra jumping from the falling aircraft...

He remembered Parra shooting up the cockpit...

The order wasn't right. But then, he wasn't right either.

21

"**W**ake up!"

Pierce convulsed, brought up phlegm and blood in his mouth, which he coughed out. His body felt beaten and abused. Too much pain. If he just closed his eyes... it would go away... forever...

"Mark! Wake up!"

He forced his eyes open.

Savannah, her face a mess of cuts and bruises, with trickles of blood staining her left cheek and her black and purple streaked hair a tangled mess, shook him. Pierce had enough wits about him to notice she wore a parachute. And that the falling aircraft still rattled around them.

"Parra shot up the controls. We're over jungle, and we're going to crash."

"Para... chute?" He struggled to speak.

"Only one left!" She hauled him to his feet. They stumbled as the decimated cabin lurched again. "Trust me!"

Together, they clambered over the corpses of the dead thug he had impaled earlier, and glanced into the cockpit, where the second thug had collided with the pilot and knocked them both out cold, if not killed them. At the open door, Pierce glanced at a carpet of green foliage with wisps of clouds floating much higher in the air. The world seemed to turn, and gravity soon orientated towards the cabin, pulling them back in.

They stumbled to the door, fought the forces drawing them backwards, as Savannah pushed him out, and they careened through the sky.

The aircraft spun as Pierce's perspective flipped from green to blue and back again, over and over.

Then he had enough sense to remember what they were attempting.

Savannah dived with him.

Pierce flattened himself to slow his descent. It was impossible to tell how far above the jungle they were, if they had only minutes or seconds of freefall to spare.

He tried to grab her outstretched hands once, then twice.

They both turned fast and out of control. They couldn't reach each other.

With the air rushing around him pressing his face out of shape, there were only so many attempts Pierce could make before she gave up and pulled her ripcord.

He lunged out and gripped her.

She grasped him, and he pulled her close, wrapped his arms around her and dug them in behind the harness belts of her parachute.

Savannah pulled the ripcord.

The jolt was more jarring than Pierce remembered from his last time parachuting. He almost slipped and lost his grip. But one hand stayed locked in, and he held.

Their descent slowed, but still the jungle canopy raced up fast.

They hit the green foliage with speed.

Pierce tore from Savannah's grip, slipped through the branches, and bounced on bending branches too thin to support his weight. One snapped, and he dropped through more leaves before a vine caught him around an ankle.

He swung upside down, spun in a wide circle beneath the canopy where the underside of the jungle opened, and the world darkened.

The vine snapped, and Pierce plummeted three metres into a large puddle of mud.

Coming up for air, he rolled and contorted as pain racked every centimetre of his body. How much abuse could he endure before one more injury broke him completely and cost him his life?

But he was alive now. Pierce rolled onto his back, turned and twisted his arms and legs, and felt all over for major cuts, broken bones and impaling injuries, but discovered none.

He dragged himself from the mud until he fell on a mound of damp leaves, and just lay there, breathing fast and shallow, trying to accept the pain that stung every corner of his complaining body.

Savannah shimmied down a vine, then staggered towards him. Covered in bruises, she collapsed by his side, panting hard. She lay on her back and squirmed against her own bodily agonies.

"You okay?" she said through rapid breaths.

"I'll survive. You?"

"About the same."

The intensity of multiple pain sensations was too much, and he passed into unconsciousness.

And he dreamed of a woman tied naked to a chair and beaten horrifically.

She told Pierce he was running out of time.

22

Rio de Janeiro, Brazil

I dris Walsh saw himself as a dirty rat caught in a trap, waiting for the trap master to decide his fate.

The men who'd snatched him from the Rio streets, while he'd been out shopping for provisions, had cuffed and bagged him expertly. Then they had brought him to a dingy house that stank of sweet-scented garbage and featured bugs of all varieties that crawled on the water-stained concrete floor and mouldy wooden rafters.

After stripping Walsh naked, they tied his hands behind his back, then looped a noose around his neck. The noose went up around the rafters, and Walsh had imagined this was his end. Instead, they only lifted him high enough to hurt, arranged so he had to stand on the tips of his toes to not strangle himself. His wrists they tied to another rope looped over another rafter. This rope they tightened to lift his arms up high and at an angle that forced him to bend forward. His captors then left him in this position for hours.

The irony of Walsh's predicament remained forefront in his mind. He'd tortured dozens of his own enemies with similar techniques, including Mark Pierce, the troublesome ex-CIA operative who should be dead a dozen times over by now. During his hours of discomfort, Walsh had often wondered if it was the Trigger Man who had turned the tables here.

Despite the layers of sweat that ran off his body because of the heat, and the dryness in his mouth, Walsh didn't seriously believe it was Pierce who held him captive. Prolonged stress positions weren't Pierce's style, for his old enemy would have simply put a bullet in the back of Walsh's head. Neither man valued the other enough to allow them to live a second longer than they already had. Eventually, soon, one of them would be dead because the two could no longer cohabitate peacefully in the same universe.

Perhaps Walsh would no longer be Pierce's problem, and the feud would end today. Almost everyone Walsh had tortured in this manner had ended up a corpse when the victims finally gave up their secrets. Would Walsh's fate be any different?

After many hours in this position, Walsh's body spasmed, and not just from strained muscles and the rope burns around his neck and wrists. The old bullet wound in his gut, where Pierce had shot him in a Moroccan medina that had later resulted in a liver transplant, ached with a sharp, stabbing pain. That injury had aged Walsh a decade in a single year, and the pain now felt unbearable.

Walsh had thought to strangle himself many times in the last few hours. Just fall and die. But he could never bring himself to do so. He was a rat. No, he was the king of rats. He would fight to the very end and use every dirty trick in his arsenal to survive. The men who restrained him had reason to keep him amongst the living. When they believed they had broken him, they would return, and they would talk. It would be then that Walsh might find his path to freedom.

Time passed.

When a captor stepped into the torture room, Walsh found him unimpressive. His complexion was Mediterranean, and he was of slightly shorter stature compared to most men. His scalp and face he'd shaved down because of balding on top, so that his jaw, chin and the back of his head were speckled with thousands of black dots where the hair never had the chance to grow. He wore a black short-sleeve shirt, tight blue jeans and laced shoes.

But it wasn't the physical attributes of the man that lingered in Walsh's mind. It was how he moved. Controlled, precise steps. He wasn't physically imposing, but he commanded the room. The dark brown eyes took in everything.

Walsh maintained eye contact until the man walked behind him. Try as he might, there was no dignity in Walsh's plight, and no point pretending he controlled any power in this exchange, because Walsh didn't have the will in him to fake it. He sought a clever remark to speak, a statement that would present him as valuable. But he suspected this man was as professional as he was, and knew exactly what he wanted, and how he was going to get it.

"You are wondering" — the man spoke softly but powerfully in an Italian accent — "whether you are going to walk out of this room alive."

Walsh sniggered. "I'd already be dead if you believed I had nothing of value to offer."

The man stepped in front of Walsh again and smiled.

"This is true. What do you believe it is that you can offer me?"

Rolling his eyes, Walsh sneered. "I have no fucking idea."

The man shrugged, then walked around behind Walsh for a second time. He took the rope that held Walsh's wrist up high and pulled on it. This cause Walsh to trip on his feet and the noose to tighten. He couldn't breathe, and as he choked, his face reddened and his tongue swelled like a fat sausage inside his mouth.

Then the rope released, and Walsh staggered back up onto his aching toes. He breathed again and still believed this moment was not yet his end.

The man stepped before Walsh and halted. "Let's pretend for a moment, Mr Walsh, that you and I are civilised men, and that we can talk as civilised men do."

Walsh remained impassive for a moment, then nodded.

"Good. You understand that your actions over this last week have upset a very delicate operation my organisation is executing? Yes? No? An operation, I should say, that has the potential to make my people a lot of money and gain us much geopolitical leverage. You, Mr Walsh, threatened all this when you kidnapped Amelia Reyes, in your pathetic attempt to sell her off to SEBIN."

Walsh must have reacted to that statement with involuntary facial expressions, because the man expressed amusement and studied Walsh more closely. Earlier, Walsh had rated it as a high possibility this man was a representative of the Venezuelan secret police, but clearly, he wasn't.

"I can see your mind is trying to play catch-up."

Walsh nodded.

This brought a smile to the man's face. "Ms Reyes was exactly where we wanted her to be, a thorn in the side of the

Bolivarian government, spilling secrets the Venezuelans wanted kept secret and causing division amongst the president's inner circle. She embarrassed them to no end, from a protected and secure hideout in Rio. But now she has returned to her home country, forcibly, and her very life is at risk. Not ideal at all, and you were the fucker who handed her over to SEBIN."

With lightning speed, the man punched Walsh in the gut.

The pain was sudden and intense, causing Walsh to double over. But when he did, the ropes around his neck and wrists tightened, and he choked again. He made himself stand tall, fought against the agony exploding around the flesh where another man's liver lived, and tried not to vomit. If he vomited, nothing would save him.

The Italian took a handkerchief from his pocket and dabbed the beads of sweat building on his shaved scalp. "Luckily for you, Mr Walsh, two of my top operatives are in Venezuela even now, on a rescue mission to bring her back. Let's hope, for your sake, they do and return her unharmed. Damaged goods, as they say, are not the same as fully functional apparatuses. Damaged goods serve no purpose, and their only value is eradication. To be thrown out with the other trash."

When the coughing stopped, and the tears ceased flooding from his eyes, Walsh deemed to speak. The physical pain was near unbearable, and his nakedness was a psychological weapon used against him, but Walsh had not yet abandoned his dignity. "Is there a point to all this?"

The man paused, then chuckled casually. "Of course there is. As you will soon discover, Mr Walsh, I know all about you, like I know all about every man and woman who crosses my path or becomes a target of my interest. I know you are ex-CIA, and you spent decades obscuring your many past operations and accomplishments from even your superiors, because of the dirty corrupt games you liked to play for personal gains. And after your last fuck-up, the American government now has multiple off-the-book assets hunting you down. They have a single mission objective, which is your sudden and immediate death. The Venezuelans want you dead, too. I also know a secret about you that you think nobody knows, but I do."

Walsh shuddered. He held many secrets, and one in particular no living person should know of, and if revealed, might finally break him when nothing else ever had.

"Curious? Yes? No? I'm talking about what you did when you were a teenager, Mr Walsh. On Long Island? Do you remember?"

Every muscle in Walsh's body tightened. He knew what his captor was referring to. He remembered the despicable act he'd performed that day. That one tragic, horrific event defined everything that had made him the man he had become. Good and bad.

"We will not talk about that today, though. We will talk about what it is you can do for us — my organisation — to make up for your decades of so many terrible mistakes. Today, Mr Walsh, *is* your lucky day."

23

W alsh's captor again stepped behind him. The former CIA spymaster expected further torment against his bound and contorted form, but not the release of the rope holding his arms up high, so his bound wrists fell back against his bare backside. Then the Italian man released the tension in the rope around Walsh's neck, allowing him to stand normally on flat feet, despite the noose remaining in place. Walsh stayed bound and constrained, but the aches he had endured for hours no longer tortured his muscles.

The man then produced a bottle of pills from his pocket, which Walsh immediately recognised as his anti-rejection drugs. Without them, the cells in his body would recognise Walsh's liver transplant as a foreign invader and work to destroy it. He needed to take those pills every day if he wished to maintain any resemblance to a long and healthy life.

"Mr Walsh, I am going to use your medication against you. I will control their availability, allow you your daily swallow so long as you follow my instructions. If you betray me, the drugs disappear."

Walsh nodded, furious that he must capitulate to this smug man he knew nothing about. Then he considered, now was the time to bargain, to improve his situation further, for Walsh had always prided himself on being a consummate negotiator. "The man who snatched Amelia Reyes, his name is Mark Pierce. I know Pierce and his methods because he is also former CIA, and he once worked for me. I can find him and bring him to you. Dead or alive."

The man laughed until his belly shook. "You know nothing about anything."

Walsh stared. He felt confused and out of his depth. These were not feelings he enjoyed or ever wished to endure, but here he was, suffering the same indignity and pain he had inflicted on so many others in the past.

"Mr Pierce is not your problem. I have people dealing with him and Ms Reyes, and those same people have very clear mission objectives of their own. Mr Walsh, you need to learn humility and accept that you have to give up any notion of revenge against this individual you also know as the Trigger Man." Walsh must have expressed surprised, because the man grinned. "Yes, I know all about your CIA operator. If you go after Mr Pierce, you act against me and the organisation I represent. Such actions will not serve you. Do you understand what I am saying?"

Walsh nodded, but he didn't understand. Why did this man want Pierce alive and active in the world? Surely Pierce was a common enemy if he planned on rescuing Amelia from whoever threatened her harm. Dangerous men like Walsh and the thugs of SEBIN, and the man before him now and the mysterious group he represented.

"Good. Then let's get to business. My name is Mr Real. The organisation that I represent, while it remains unknown to you, you have already encountered several times in the past. Most recently in Baku, and before that, in Mali."

Walsh frowned and tried to recall who those individuals might be, but nothing came to him.

"It is not important that you remain confused. Understand only that we have people everywhere. We are far more pervasive than you might guess or even imagine. And now we are about to recruit you into our global organisation and, through you, extend our influence even further still. My gesture will offer you a level of protection that you don't currently enjoy. Which is to say, operating on your own as you have until now, barely surviving."

Mr Real clicked his fingers. The only door to this dank chamber opened, and a young woman stepped in, carrying a stool and a black satchel that resembled a doctor's bag. Attractive and slim, her features were those of a Japanese or Korean woman. She wore long pants and a loose blouse that were modern in style. She placed the stool next to Walsh, then opened the bag, which she rested on top of the stool.

"My colleague here will tattoo you with the mark of my organisation. A brand if you will, that designates ownership much as your people, and my people, once branded the slaves we stole out of Africa hundreds of years ago in both our histories. If you resist, she will beat you with the device she now holds in her hand."

Walsh looked again to the silent woman, saw that she held a two-foot-long length of bamboo in her right hand. He hadn't seen her carry it in and wondered where she had kept it. In the folds of her loose pants, perhaps? She swished it through the air as if swatting flies. Many decades ago, an

African warlord had once beaten Walsh with a similar bamboo stick, and Walsh did not wish to endure that pain again today. He had suffered too much already.

"Shall we begin?" asked Mr Real.

The former CIA spymaster nodded, knowing he had no choice.

The woman commenced her work, pricking the skin over Walsh's diminished left pectoral muscle. Because of the rope around his neck, he could not glance down to see what mark she branded him with. At least the pain was inconsequential to the earlier tortures he had endured, or the bite of her stick.

Mr Real stepped back, clasped his hands behind his waist and continued to monologue while he watched his underling prepare her art. "This is about oil, Mr Walsh, and my organisation's plans to control more of its global supply. As you will know, Venezuela is sitting on the world's largest untapped oil reserves. Over three hundred billion barrels. Almost a fifth of the world's supply, and the idiot Venezuelans can't exploit it because they've destroyed the critical infrastructure their country needs to extract it."

Walsh coughed as the ink needle pricked his skin. "Don't the Chinese effectively own Venezuela's oil? They've bailed out the country's corrupt president with plenty of loans, enough for the Chinese government to buy out the 'state-owned' oil company when the president defaults on his multi-billion-dollar debts?"

Mr Real grinned. "This is true, but even so, the oil still doesn't flow. The president put his military cronies in charge of the state-run oil company, and with no understanding of how to manage a corporation, those cronies ran all the refineries and supply pipelines into the ground. None of them now function. We, however, have a plan to take control of those refineries and pipelines and bring them back online, so that if the Chinese and the Venezuelans want access to that oil, they'll have to appease us to ensure its uninterrupted delivery."

Walsh flinched when a needle prick hit a sensitive nerve. The tattooist ignored his pain and continued with her inking.

Walsh said, "So you want me in Venezuela? What do you think I can do for you there, with SEBIN already hunting me down and ready to kill me?"

Mr Real laughed again. "We don't want you in Venezuela, Mr Walsh. In fact, we want you as far away from there as possible."

"Then where? And what do you think it is that I can do for you?"

"We want you in Haiti. What we want you to do for us in that impoverished Caribbean nation... we will explain in good time. Ah, I see a finished tattoo. Thank you, my dear, you can leave us now."

The woman took her stool, bamboo cane and bag, and departed.

Only then did Walsh strain against the noose about his neck and glance down at the red skin festering around his first tattoo.

A circle within a circle, both dissected by a straight line.

24

Amazonas, Venezuela

A dark medina street...
Police sirens. People shouting...
A knife. A gun. A man falling forward, holding his gut.

Pierce's palms shining in the streetlights, sticky with thick blood—

He opened his eyes, realised he lay on his back, and it was night. The only light shone from a crackling fire.

Pierce sat abruptly.

A woman in a bra and briefs dried her clothes by a campfire. He heard insects and other distant animals that might be bats and the dripping of water from above. There were no stars because the canopy was like a roof over the jungle.

A stabbing sensation gripped his head, and the aches and twinges he'd endured for two days stretched across every corner of his skin and muscles. He hurt, his body kept reminding him, but not as bad as he had yesterday. Similarly, his mind felt less foggy than before, but certainly not clear. It seemed, though, that he was on the mend.

Then he noticed dried mud caked his body.

"You'll want to clean yourself," Savannah said. The flickering flames cast sharp shadows over her toned, muscular body, which was also patterned with bruises and cuts like those decorating his own skin. He noticed this morning she had cut her hair short like that of a boy, her ear and nose studs were missing, and the purple streaks were gone. "Don't want any infected wounds. Not here, in the jungle."

Pierce nodded and, with stiff movements, shuffled over to her.

She pointed. "There is a stream about five metres in that direction."

"Yes, ma'am."

He stumbled through the darkness until his boots splashed in running water. Using only the sensations of touch, Pierce stripped, then splashed water over his body, washing away the grime. His injuries comprised more bruises than cuts, but they all hurt as he cleaned them. Then he washed his clothes.

Afterwards, he wrung his clothes free of excess water, then slipped on his boxer shorts. Refreshed and feeling revived, he drank the water, enjoying its clear taste as he rehydrated. When he returned to the campfire, he sat on a log Savannah had dragged to their makeshift camp. He held out his pants to dry.

"You're looking better."

"I feel like a habitual stoner who just got beat up by his drug dealer."

Savannah laughed. "I said better, not great."

They sat for several minutes, silently drying their clothes before Pierce asked, "What is our situation?"

"We have our clothes, a Glock 32 .357 semi-automatic with six bullets, and some cables I salvaged from the parachute. I also managed to grab a cell phone and some cash during the battle, but the latter won't go far."

"That good, hey?"

A mosquito buzzed past Pierce's ear. He noticed the bites on his skin. Malaria was a real possibility here in the jungle, with no medication or repellent to fight off the bloodsucking insects. How current his inoculations were, Pierce could not recall.

"It's not as bad as you might think. While we were in freefall, I noticed a river and township just north of here."

"You know which way is north?" Pierce asked, because he could not guess their orientation, and there was a real risk they could never find a path out of the vast Amazonian jungle if they headed off in the wrong direction. To the south lay thousands of kilometres of thick rainforest and nothing else, which they would never survive no matter their skills if they wandered in that direction.

"We have a stream. We follow it long enough, it should flow into the river I saw."

Pierce grinned, appreciating Savannah's logic. "Good. Then this is the point where I ask you who you really are."

She had been drying her singlet top and now slipped it over her head and across her taut body. She lifted her shorts and now held them out to dry. Steam poured from the fabric at the same rate it did from Pierce's pants. "I'm Colombian intelligence, DNI. Direccion Nacional de Inteligencia."

Pierce nodded. Her statement, at least, made sense. "Did Amelia know?"

The woman who went by the name Savannah — which Pierce now suspected wasn't her real name but rather a fabricated legend — shook her head. "No, I'm a 'honey trap', as you Americans like to call it. But I am a lesbian, so no faking was required. Not that you will believe me, but my emotional attachment to Amelia is real. You can't live for years as lovers and not develop a genuine, emotional connection." Pierce didn't respond, so she said, "It doesn't matter about me and my desires. All that matters is that Amelia is not the enemy."

Pierce wasn't certain which parts of her story he should or should not believe. "Want me to keep calling you Savannah?"

She chuckled again. "I don't see why not... Mark Pierce."

He nodded. She knew his name, or at least the name he had used for the last four years, which suggested she knew far more about him than he would have liked. More, perhaps, than he could remember himself.

"My legend is Savannah Fonseca. I inserted myself into Amelia's life partially to protect her, but mostly to feed her actionable intelligence provided by my DNI masters. For years, Amelia relayed my insights to the world through her YouTube videos, enabling her to accurately criticise the Venezuelan government and embarrass that cunt of a president and his horrific dictatorship. A long-term strategy to bring down the regime. One of many strategies the DNI employ against our hated neighbour."

Her story fit together nicely, a plausible strategy the DNI would realistically adopt. Most refugees fleeing impoverishment, starvation and police brutality in Venezuela ended up in Colombia, and the failed nation had brought much instability to Colombia it didn't need. But Pierce sensed there was much more to the tale than Savannah would reveal this night. He would come back to her story later, when he didn't hurt as much as he did, and his mind had cleared its perpetual fog.

"You don't believe me?"

Pierce shrugged. "Does it matter if I do or don't?"

She shrugged with him. "I guess not. Just know, if I wanted you dead, I could have killed you while you slept. I know you are formerly CIA and now a rogue operative. But I also know your self-imposed mission wasn't so much to rescue Amelia, but to kill the man who kidnapped her. Idris Walsh."

The name brought a spasmodic jolt to Pierce's neck and shoulders.

Idris Walsh.

The man he had dreamed of. Whom Pierce had tried to neutralise in a Moroccan city, almost a year ago now. Rabat, was it?

It was Walsh who had incarcerated and tortured Pierce for many months...

Naked. Bound. Beaten.

Was the woman he kept seeing not a woman, but himself?

But Walsh had also performed a far worse act—

Shaking his head to clear away a memory he couldn't accurately retrieve, he asked himself, was Walsh the reason Pierce had journeyed to South America? The two men loathed each other, and Pierce had no qualms about killing the former spymaster when they next met. Walsh was both dangerous and a threat to innocent people everywhere. He didn't deserve to live, and Pierce was more than happy to complete the gruesome task of eradicating him permanently.

Then Pierce asked himself, why was he remembering details about Walsh now, when many other memories from his recent past remained elusive?

At least, he thought, his memories were returning to him, so his head injury seemed not to be as permanent as he had earlier feared.

"Mark, you know we have no choice but to trust each other and work together."

Pierce remained silent. He struggled to piece together all the nagging elements of this mystery dancing around in his still foggy mind, still not crystallising into intelligence he could action. Walsh must be only one of many reasons as to why he was in South America—

"Mark! Amelia is certainly alive, and I have a means to find her."

Alerted, Pierce turned to face her. Savannah's skin flickering in the orange firelight gave her a ghost-like quality. "How?"

"I regularly feed her tracking devices just in case something like this happens, where we became separated. I fed her one yesterday morning. If I can break into this cell phone, I can download the application that will track it, provided she and the tracker inside her is near a cell phone network. She did parachute near to us. I watched them jump out of the aircraft. And Maceo Parra, the SEBIN operative who took her, will want to escape the jungle too. Like us, they'll head north. We have to stop him before my girlfriend disappears forever inside a SEBIN torture camp."

"You really felt something for her? She wasn't just a mission for you?"

Savannah frowned. "At first, yes, she was. But not later when I got to know her. Don't tell me you never fell for someone you shouldn't have?"

Pondering her words, Pierce suspected he had, but no names or faces came to him, and this infuriated him. Then, recognising the plan was a good one, and with no options of his own to put forward, he nodded. "Sure."

Savannah snorted. "Don't act like you don't care about Amelia. You'll do anything to save her from those Venezuelan butchers. I saw you in action, remember? You were ready to give your life for her in the stadium."

Pierce stood and slipped on his dried pants. As he gathered up his socks to dry them, he said, "Are you saying you love Amelia?"

"Yes, I am," Savannah said without hesitation and without breaking eye contact. "She's vulnerable. Very fragile. I have a soft spot for those traits. I want to heal her. But healing her first requires saving her."

The definitiveness in her response was enough for Pierce to trust her. "Good. Then we hunt them at first light."

25

Mexico City, Mexico

After a long flight from Caracas to Mexico City, SEBIN's fuming director, Juan Garcia, sat motionlessly at his taco restaurant table overlooking the historic streets of the city's Centro district, where tourists, businesspeople, and residents alike enjoyed a late evening out. Only Garcia couldn't enjoy this moment, for he fought to control the rage burning inside him. Turmoil that had festered since this morning's warehouse discovery and the disturbing phone conversation with a man who had hijacked his wife's cell phone number. A man who had no right to challenge him.

At least this man hadn't taken Marcela's physical cell phone. He'd checked that straight away, and now felt a modicum of relief at this knowledge.

Garcia's other problems were many, and they deserved his attention more than this upstart did. He'd just learned the aircraft bringing Amelia Reyes into Venezuela had crashed into the Amazon jungle, and it seemed no one had survived, a failure he had yet to bring to the attention of the president. And yesterday when he'd called on his house's landline, he'd argued over the phone with his fifteen-year-old daughter after learning of her disobedience, told her she must practice her piano because he paid good money for the lessons she didn't appreciate. Sofia had screamed at him in response and told him he was an awful father.

But what worried Garcia more than either of these failings were the four warehouse massacres, which had become the only reason Garcia was here in Mexico. The meeting today was to ensure similar incidents didn't happen again.

The SEBIN director sipped his tonic water and watched the crowd. Eight FAES special forces operatives, who had flown with him at great expense, spread themselves throughout the restaurant, and a dozen more patrolled rooftops and the streets, armed with weapons they had quickly procured from Garcia's contacts with the local narco cartel, ready to take out the man who wished to meet Garcia to "negotiate terms". Garcia wished only to shoot the asshole first through the balls and then in the gut and finally in his mouth. He might do that if the Italian man's contingency plans to walk away from this meeting weren't airtight.

When the man showed, he was unimposing, of medium height with a shaved scalp. He wore a cotton shirt, slacks, and polished shoes. He sat opposite Garcia without waiting for permission, laid a napkin across his lap and called over the waiter. When he spoke, it was in English. "Two bean tacos, please, and your best beer for myself and my friend."

"Very good, sir," said the waiter before he disappeared.

The man grinned and looked up over the table at Garcia. "I wasn't sure you were brave enough to meet."

Garcia clenched his teeth and spoke more with a growl than a proper voice. "Me, not brave enough? It's you whose respect is misplaced!"

The man shrugged. "How is that lovely wife of yours, Marcela, and that beautiful daughter you've raised so daintily together? Sofia, right? How are her piano lessons coming along?"

Garcia almost leaped across the table to strangle this man with his own hands.

"Don't fume, Mr Garcia. I'm not here to make your life uncomfortable. I'm here to improve it." He passed over a smart phone, which showed a video of Sofia practising piano in Garcia's supposedly secure mansion in the heart of Caracas. "Children, they are so beautiful. They are the future, no?"

The head of SEBIN gripped the table until his knuckles turned white. "What the fuck is it you want, Real?"

The man tensed as his face reddened, and for a moment Garcia thought the individual was about to lose his cool. "No! My name is *Mr Real*. It is the only name I go by." Then, just as suddenly, he regained his composure and grinned. "Seems your intelligence apparatus isn't a complete failure, then."

SEBIN had requested assistance from the Russians, Cubans and Chinese, and it was the latter who had returned a name. Mr Real was a fixer, a money man and a go-between representing various shady Mediterranean and Middle Eastern arms traffickers and terrorist groups, who had a reputation for appearing in more places than any one man should respectively find time to be in. Garcia also learnt that Mr Real could speak Arabic fluently and could easily pass himself off as a native from the many nations in the Arabian

Peninsula. But that was about the sum of what the Chinese knew. "Well? What the fuck do you want?"

Mr Real shrugged. "It's simple, really, a partnership. We want to work with Venezuela, make your oil industry profitable again, and get the Chinese off your back once and for all."

"What makes you think we need your help?"

Mr Real leaned too comfortably into his chair. "With all due respect, Director, you've fucked your country. Your nationalised economy has collapsed, and so has your only profitable money-earner, oil. When you run out of gold in those mines you exploit in the Orinoco, and when the Colombian drug lords realise there are more profitable routes to move their cocaine up into the United States other than through Venezuela, you'll lose everything. With your stupidly out-of-control inflation, you'll soon have no money to pay for your secret police or the Army, Navy and Air Force, and then the revolt really will happen, and it will be you and the president and every other corrupt official up against the wall, facing the firing squad of the people. And let's not forget our little stunt yesterday and the day before and the weeks before that. If we do it again and publicise it—"

"How dare you! You pig... whore!"

Mr Real raised a hand. "If you choose not to comply with my demands today, Mr Garcia, I'm sure we will convince the National Bolivarian Armed Forces to revolt against their government. You saw what happened to those poor, unfortunate men and women who got very sick? We can do that again, without breaking a sweat. And make it much, much worse."

Garcia shuddered with rage. "One day, I will fucking skin

you alive and feed you to my alligators, starting with your tiny, tiny testicles. I keep several penned at my personal ranch, but I'm sure with your immaculate intelligence apparatus behind you, you know that already. But remember this, I will watch every moment and enjoy every fucking second of your excruciating pain in the alligator pit until your gruesome drawn-out end. They don't kill you straight away. It's in their nature not to. Can you imagine, being eaten alive?"

The beers arrived, and Mr Real took his with a smile, sipped its frothy head and made a gesture of admiration for its taste. "No, you won't, Mr Garcia, because you will soon appreciate how pervasive my organisation is, and how we can come for you and the people you care about at any time. That video should be proof enough. But, more importantly, you should listen to me because of what we can do so easily to decimate your armed forces and turn them against you. Nobody wants to die like those men in those warehouses did. Not even the most hardened soldiers."

It brought Garcia no solace that FAES snipers lined Mr Real up in their sights even now, and with a single raise of his hand, the man's head would explode in a rapture of high-velocity bullets.

Mr Real spoke again. "Do you really think you can stop us, Mr Garcia? You think if you delay me long enough, you'll find means to penetrate and destroy my organisation and thus take back control of your country again? If you really believe this is possible, then let your snipers and killers spread through this establishment butcher me now. But if you have the slightest lingering doubt that you might not be in control here, you should listen to my next words very carefully."

The anger welling up inside Garcia prevented him from speaking.

"I am your biggest threat, Mr Garcia. But I am also your only solution. Are you ready to talk? Are you ready to embrace your only path out of this mess?"

Again, Garcia couldn't speak, but like a chess player who could see the inevitable checkmate about to be played out against him, the SEBIN director understood he had no choice but to hear what this man offered.

If for no other reason than to play for time.

26

Azaz, Syria

The lingering scent permanent in the dust clouds was death.

Six armoured Toyota Land Cruisers snaked through the haze, cutting its stillness like a hot knife dissecting camel lard. Rubble-strewn streets slowed their progress. Debris fallen from shelled buildings marked where humans had once lived peacefully, but not anymore. Collapsed by several levels from their original heights, the ruins did little to shade heat radiating from a sun poised high in the cloudless sky.

From the back seat of the second Land Cruiser, Charles Chu gripped his bulletproof briefcase tight against his chest. He watched with unblinking eyes the apocalyptic scenes passing them by, witnessed the aftermath of a city that had only a few years ago endured horrific killings, sustained urban warfare and endless bombing raids by Syrian and Russian fighter jets.

Ahead, a rusted T-90A tank, pivoted at an odd angle, remained half-buried in the city rubble. Men brewed coffee under tarpaulins or in the few standing buildings without walls, which they sold to wandering, listless residents. Other men smelted metal trash in burning oil drums that expunged acrid black smoke. Littered bone fragments spied in rubbish could have been yesterday's lamb dinner or human casualties dating back many years. Chu had seen no birds since they'd crossed over from the Turkish border. What secrets about this hellish world did the winged animals know that he did not?

Azaz, and Aleppo like it situated only thirty kilometres to the south, had endured the worst of the Islamic State's barbarity and still wore its many scars. Today the town's key players were Turkish military and paramilitary forces, displaced Kurds, the ineffective Syrian interim government and a dozen other ideological and fanatical groups Chu couldn't name and didn't want to. But not Islamic State. They remained pariahs here, even amongst the most fanatical rebels active in the city, and Chu was grateful for the new status quo.

"Stop worrying!" Morat Kozan grinned from the passenger seat next to Chu. He was a rotund Turk, with mere wisps of white hair dangling over his ears, and where the tuffs did grow out, it remained messy at the back of his head. His cashmere suit, linen shirt and leather shoes counted amongst the most expensive brands offered in the European market, but nothing ever looked good on the oil trader. Kozan always had been and always would be uglier than an old pig.

But Kozan didn't care for looks and never allowed his ugliness to define him, doing whatever the fuck he felt like whenever he felt like it, including this spontaneous excursion into Syria across from the Turkish border. He'd not bothered to explain to Chu the purpose of their visit.

"Tell me, Chu, what the fuck is wrong?"

"Syria!" said Chu with a grimace. "This country is fucked up. I thought it would be obvious?"

Kozan chuckled. "Azaz is completely safe for us."

"Seriously, sir, why do you and I need to be here at all? This is a fucking war zone and dangerous."

Kozan patted Chu on the knee, presumably an affectionate signal of friendship, but Chu always sensed gay undertones every time the pig-man touched him, despite Kozan's insatiable need to fuck expensive female prostitutes almost every night. "Relax, my very competent chief financial officer. I told you, I own this part of Syria. Every last fucking inch of it. No one would dare touch us."

Chu nodded despite his lacking confidence. The ease of the border crossing from Türkiye into Syria, the fifteen soldiers armed with the latest model HK416 assault rifles and state-of-the-art body armour who rode with them, and the surveillance drone that hovered above on the constant lookout for advance threats should have offered some comfort. But this was a wild, lawless land of warlords and caliphates, where Westernised Asians like himself wouldn't last long if kidnapped by a group that didn't care for ransom money or maintaining the farce of peace. Islamic State might suffer diminished power and membership in these still lawless lands, but there were plenty here who fought to reignite similar outdated and barbaric societal ideals and cared nothing for modern alliances. They were the enemy Chu feared the most.

Kozan snorted. "If you don't trust me, trust the organisation we work for. This mission today, it's for them."

The organisation Kozan spoke of held tangible and frightening power in this part of the world, even amidst the chaos of war-torn Syria. Suddenly, Chu felt confident that today would not be his last day on Earth, and he could finally relax. Kozan should have informed him of this fact earlier.

Chu spotted a checkpoint ahead, armed by turbaned men, with thick greasy beards and dirty desert clothes, bandoliers and AK-47 assault rifles. Two guards behind a makeshift wall constructed of concrete rubble watched them along the sights of a DShK heavy machine gun and aimed the business end at the convoy. Despite their Land Cruisers' armour, Chu didn't believe they would survive sustained machine-gun firepower should their presence displease the gunners.

"We've arrived!" Kozan flung open his door and, eyeing Chu, thumbed his hand that his financial officer should follow. Chu reluctantly obeyed, despite the dozen paramilitary soldiers already out of their vehicles securing defensive positions, with their eyes lined up along the sights of their Heckler & Koch HK416 assault rifles.

The largest of the turbaned men who armed the checkpoint stepped forward. He smiled without expressing pleasure, revealing two missing teeth. Chu felt he knew this man from a past encounter but couldn't place the time or location.

"Muhammad ibn Musa al-Khwarizmi," said the leader of the checkpoint guards.

"Abu'l-Hasan al-Uqlidisi." Kozan gave the correct response codeword.

The two men sized each other up. With a nod, each man unbuttoned their shirts. Kozan took an ultraviolet torch from his pocket, shined it upon the fat wobbling over his pectoral muscle, to illuminate a tattoo of a circle within a circle, each dissected by the same straight line drawn in their middles. Kozan then shined the light upon the turbaned man's chest, revealing the same symbol. The two men grinned, then embraced three times, kissing each other on the cheeks.

Chu watched with interest, knowing that he too carried the circle within a circle symbol tattooed upon his chest. His branding, unfortunately, was not marked with invisible ink, and he understood both its dangerous and protective powers.

"Mr Real sends his greeting," said the bearded insurgent.

"You are Sami Ghazaleh?"

The man nodded.

Chu remembered now where he'd heard the name before and seen this man's photograph. Ghazaleh was a former Islamic State intelligence officer, and before that, had been a high-ranking officer with Egypt's General Intelligence Service, or Mukhabarat. He been reported killed during a bombing raid on Raqqa several years earlier. Back when Kozan wanted to build pipelines deep within these lands, when they were controlled by the caliphates of Islamic State at the height of their power.

Ghazaleh said, "Did you bring what we requested?"

Kozan nodded and clicked his fingers. Two black-clad soldiers opened the trunk of a Land Cruiser and brought forth a young, unconscious Asian woman tied to a stretcher. The fat oil executive ran his fingers through her hair, leaving his sweat on her scalp like an unwanted stain. Chu noticed her attractiveness and guessed her age to be late twenties or early thirties, the same age as a woman rather dear to him, whom he often feared would one day face a similar fate if he didn't keep protecting her.

Kozan said, "Her name is Li Chyou. Her husband, Li Hu, is a network security expert in the Chinese petrochemical company poised to take control of Venezuela's oil networks, should the country's president default on his Chinese loans. Hu is distraught, of course. He believes Chyou died during a diving accident last week while they vacationed in the Red Sea." He laughed from his belly. "They never found her body."

Ghazaleh's grin grew wider. "Mr Real will be pleased. I shall deliver this gift to the Fortress myself, where she will remain an honoured guest."

Kozan coughed up phlegm. "I was careful, Ghazaleh, to ensure the world is convinced she is dead."

The intelligence officer nodded. "Your efforts shall bring rewards for us all, Mr Kozan. Through her, we'll secure backdoors into the petrochemical company's IT networks." Ghazaleh laughed.

27

The conversation between Morat and Ghazaleh dredged up old memories from Charles Chu's past, physically manifested as a shiver that ran the length of his spine.

Chu's first steps into this corrupt world populated by terrorists, spies, criminals and murderers had begun simply enough, via innocently accepting an occasional bribe here and there. Later came requests for the erasure of minor but questionable transactions from the Kozan ledgers, or to disguise immoral purchases as mundane items. Before he knew it, many years had passed, and those discretions had grown larger and more daring. These days, laws he broke on a daily basis would have seen him on trial at the Hague should the authorities ever catch up with him, and would have caused his younger, more innocent self to become repulsed by his lack of morals and human decency.

Unfortunately, Chu's indiscretions also meant that Kozan now "owned" him, and by extension, so did the shadowy global organisation they were both beholden to. Little criminal acts were now massive criminal acts and the sole reason why Chu found himself playing assistant to a corrupt and ruthless oil trader, brokering deals with sadistic terrorists in the world's worst hellholes. A far cry from the penthouse mansions and luxury yachts he'd once enjoyed in New York and Hong Kong, from a time when his indiscretions were minor and innocent in comparison to the horrendous crimes he committed now. A time when he had both enjoyed the villas, mansions, sexy prostitutes, tailored clothes, exotic meals and fast cars that his position of power granted him, but without the cost to his freedom, indebted to Morat for the rest of his life, however long that turned out to be.

His choice for this life had cost him more than his freedom and had led to his wife committing suicide, and his adult daughter detesting him, rating him as less than a dog turd smeared on a street corner.

At first, Chu had thought himself justified in his actions. As his indiscretions had come to light in his relationship, Chu's wife had turned against him, disrespected the financial security and the indulgences he had provided her. He'd at first despised her when she started denying him her body, which had led him to cheating on her for more than a decade before she took her life. Whatever love they'd once shared, it had died emotionally long before her physical departure from the world.

His daughter had drawn away from him in that time too and eventually wanted nothing to do with him after his wife's death. He had tried to control his only child, make her respect him, but all that had done was to completely shut him out of her life. He wondered where she was now.

Now when she was gone, he had grown to realise she was the only person in his world other than himself that he cared about. If he could change anything, it would be to have his daughter accept and love him again.

In the distance, they heard gunfire. The drone above turned and focused its camera lens on the threat. Kozan and Ghazaleh ignored it, figuring the skirmish to be too distant to bother them.

Sweat beading on his forehead, Chu looked to their head of security. The former Belgian commando shook his head as if to say the distant conflict would not concern them.

Kozan asked Ghazaleh, "Is the plan still proceeding as expected. Or has it changed?"

The Egyptian ran his fingers through his thick, oily beard. "We have struck at the heart of the Venezuelan military, GNB, SEBIN, and FAES. They are scared, no doubt, but not convinced. I would say we need to strike two, maybe three more times before their soldiers can't stand it anymore and revolt against their leaders."

"This is good news, but what about Amelia Reyes?"

"What about her?"

The Turk shrugged. "Well, the intel you fed her did turn the president's inner circle into a pack of rabid dogs, as you said it would. I was impressed. I enjoyed watching them attack each other each time she released uncomfortable truths out into the world."

"This side scheme works well, yes."

Kozan snorted. "Or used to work well, Ghazaleh. Now I hear she is dead!"

Ghazaleh nodded and shrugged. "That seems to be the case, but unconfirmed. We have two of our top operatives on her trail, who should confirm soon enough if she lives or not. If so, we'll capture her and return her to hiding and get her back to doing what she is good at. Bringing down the Venezuelan government."

"Well, I hope so!" Kozan licked his lips. "I've made too many uncomfortable deals getting every piece of this complex game into position, ready for this last decisive strike. I don't want it all fucked up now because your side isn't playing with a full contingent of pieces."

"Don't worry," snarled the Egyptian. "Our organisation knows what it is doing. You will get rich from this. Venezuela's oil will soon be yours and, by proxy, ours to control. No one wants to lose this opportunity. Finally, we can strike an actual blow against the established geopolitical order. China, Russia, the United Kingdom *and* the United States."

Kozan nodded, but Chu could see his boss didn't believe the former fundamentalist. Their plan was daring — no one doubted that — and if they pulled it off, all of them would soon possess more money than lined all the treasure vaults of the Royal House of Saud. Chu could buy anything then, including watertight protection for the one individual close to him. The risks were worth it, and their plan arranged so if some elements failed, overall, they would achieve the coup they strived for. Venezuela sat on the largest untapped oil reserves in the world, and soon it would be theirs to control.

"I hope you are right, Ghazaleh. If this fails, we all fail, and there is no coming back for any of us."

"Then we don't fail, Kozan. We are all committed to this cause. We will all see this through to its end." He patted Kozan on the back, but Chu sensed he was not happy. "Relax. Now that we have Li Hu, we are another step closer to success."

"We'd better be!"

The giant of a man gripped Kozan by the back of his neck and pulled him close enough so there was nowhere else to stare but into each other's cold, calculating eyes. "Don't question me again, Kozan! When you question me, you question our organisation, and there are plenty more powerful individuals higher up the chain of command who won't respond well to your lack of faith. Do you understand what I am saying, my friend?"

Chu witnessed an emotion he had never seen Kozan express, despite their many years together.

Fear.

Kozan hiccupped. "You are correct, Ghazaleh, I was wrong to question. The inner circle knows what they are doing."

Ghazaleh pushed Kozan backwards, causing the fat man to stumble. "Hurry back to Türkiye, my friend. When the time comes, we will call upon you to play your part. In this late stage of the game, you also can't afford to fail us either."

28

Miami International Airport, Florida, United States

Miami proved stormy and muggy, which Rachel Zang could have interpreted as a foreboding sign of what was to come. Knowing that no other choice was open to her, she advanced through to the customs counter with her US passport at hand and noticed her sweat had stained the pages. When called forward, she sensed someone had already "red-flashed" her credentials. The young hipster customs officer who gripped her passport bit his lower lip. His blue eyes stared through his flatscreen monitor, angled so she couldn't see the message he'd read that troubled him.

Moments later, two security guards approached. "Follow us, please, ma'am."

Instinctively, Zang prepared for combat and to make her escape. Airports, and particularly customs checkpoints, were chokepoints every field operative feared. It was a location where control didn't exist. But this was the United States and her home, the nation she had sworn to protect with her life, twice, first as an officer and pilot of the United States Air Force, and second as an operator within the CIA. She told herself their request was a formality, nothing sinister, so why did her skin prickle and her senses heighten?

With no realistic alternative choices or viable lines of action available, Zang followed the man and the woman as they took possession of her carry-on luggage, cell phone, credit cards, passport and other forms of identification. They led her through an unmarked and keypad-locked door. One guard stood at an angle so she could not see as he punched in the code.

On the other side, away from arriving passenger scrutiny, the female guard patted her down, finding no weapons. Satisfied she was no threat, the guards led her along several white-wall corridors with many doors marked only by numbers, then asked her to step inside one designated 314. Zang figured her best option was to comply.

It surprised her the guards didn't follow her in.

With the door locked behind her, she felt both relief and a chill when she recognised the two men waiting for her. Their backdrop was the bare room with only a table, several plastic chairs, CCTV cameras in the corners, and a mirrored glass partition on the far wall, but they weren't interesting like the men. Kenneth Karcher and Deep Ranjan, two off-the-books CIA assets, who, rumour had it, worked directly for the ambitious and often duplicitous chief of the CIA's Special Operations Group, Abdul Ibrahim.

Their presence here spoke volumes to the seriousness of her predicament.

Karcher was bald and bearded, bulked with muscles and today dressed in a black T-shirt, matching jeans and sturdy lace-up boots, so he resembled a biker. Ranjan was his opposite, of medium height, brown skin and thick black hair and a wisp of a beard. He favoured conservative suits and ties and was never without his black-rimmed glasses.

Despite their conflicting appearances, both men were proficient operatives and had garnished a fearsome reputation in the halls of Langley. They eliminated threats posed against CIA officers while inside the United States' borders, performed local surveillance, transported intelligence officers between safe houses and meet sites, and cleaned kill scenes so they never reached the attention of federal and local law enforcement agencies. And they always worked as a team, never alone.

Karcher's and Ranjan's presence here could mean anything, but one aspect was clear. Ibrahim must be behind the glass partition, scrutinising Zang through the two-way mirror.

Zang stared back at her reflection, unblinking, but her eyes were not for her.

"Take a seat, Ms Zang," said Karcher, as Ranjan scraped a chair across the floor towards her.

"No thanks, boys. I'd rather stand."

"Suit yourself." Releasing his grip on the chair, Ranjan gave a slight bow.

The door opened, and in stepped Patricia Knight, with a laptop under her arm and dark circles under her eyes, suggestive she had forgone sleep again for too many recent and consecutive nights. She glared at the two assets, and they both exited without making a sound.

Zang crossed her arms and leaned against the mirrored glass, so that whoever watched her could only see her back. They could still observe her through the CCTV cameras via grainy images, but with lessened abilities in reading her emotional state than gained by staring at her directly.

"You trying to scare me, Patricia, with these goons?"

"For God's sake, Rachel, take a seat." Knight rubbed her nose. "Yes, we're trying to scare you, and for good reason."

"We?" Zang didn't move but glanced again at the mirror. "You mean you and the C/SOG?"

Zang's comment caused Knight to pause for a moment; then she regained her composure. "This is about Mark Pierce, aka the Trigger Man. You told me he was dead."

Zang felt a chill, and not from the temperature, for the interrogation room was pleasantly air-conditioned. She was not expecting this conversation to turn towards the rogue operative she hadn't seen in three months. Without wanting to, her mind stretched back through time as she remembered the defining moment standing on the deck of a ship during a night-time storm. She'd fired her weapon at Pierce before he fell and disappeared into the swelling ocean, but her bullet hadn't hit him.

Deliberately hadn't hit him.

"Are you in love with Mark Pierce?"

At first, Zang thought she had misheard the question. Then she shuddered and failed to hide her emotional-laden reaction, and her superior saw she had stung Zang with this revelation. What was wrong with her to so easily lose all her training in subterfuge and wear her heart on her sleeve, as the expression went?

"I take it from your silence, I'm correct."

"I hardly knew him."

Knight raised an eyebrow. "'Knew', Zang? Pierce still lives. You already 'know' this. Until four days ago, you were the only one who did. I ask because your actions in helping him only make sense if you are infatuated with him."

The night in question was as vivid as if it had happened yesterday. Pierce had asked Zang to shoot over him, so to the CIA's watching surveillance drones, Pierce *had* died. He'd asked her to fake his death so he could disappear. He hadn't explained why. In that moment, Zang had obliged, and still didn't completely understand the reasoning behind his, and her, choices.

It was true, she'd been intimate with Pierce, and there was no doubt she felt a strong sexual and, dare she say it, emotional attraction to him, even now three months later. But she had also seen the pain screaming from behind his always troubled eyes, speaking of the prolonged tortures his body had endured that had come close to destroying him, even if Pierce couldn't see it himself. She understood that pain and respected his need for time to heal, alone. She certainly respected and valued him. But when Knight had asked if Zang was in love with Mark Pierce, she realised she was not.

Maybe, in time.

Or maybe not.

"Zang?"

Tensing her back, Zang stuck with her established lie fabricated three months earlier. "I shot him, yes. I can't confirm if I hit Pierce as I reported, but I watched him fall into the Atlantic Ocean, and he did not resurface."

Knight snorted as she sat at the table, then opened her laptop. "For the record, you missed! The Trigger Man *is* alive. Four days ago, he showed up in a shoot-out in Rio de Janeiro." Knight's screen opened to a satellite image of an eight-metre-long wooden boat with an outboard motor cruising downriver, deep within a jungle environment. Two people sat in the boat, a man and woman. "One of our Blackjack satellites captured this image three hours ago, on a tributary of the Orinoco River in Venezuela. We're five hundred per cent certain this man is Mark Pierce, and he's travelled with this woman downriver for two days now."

Zang examined her thoughts and feelings that this news now dredged up in her, but without context to what the former CIA operative was doing in South America or his mission objectives, there was nothing of value she could add. Much to her ire, she noticed the tiniest flutter in her stomach in anticipation that she might soon reunite with her enigmatic fling. She didn't dwell on that and asked her next question. "Who is the woman?"

Knight glared at Zang for several moments. "We'll come to that. For fuck's sake, sit down, Zang, and let's talk like normal people."

Zang slid her long, slender body catlike into the seat opposite Knight, planted her elbows on the table and clasped her hands together. "We're not normal people, Patricia. We never were. Never will be."

The two women stared at each other for a long moment as Zang tried to understand what this meet was all about. It was obvious Knight expected an actionable response from Zang, or the admission of a secret, but Zang couldn't imagine exactly what such a revelation would resemble.

"Why are we talking like this, ma'am? And why am I back in the States, when you and I agreed it wasn't safe for me to be here?"

Zang wasn't certain if Knight was about to answer her in a meaningful way. She would never know, however, because the room's only door flung open, and a man stepped in. The first aspect Zang noticed about him was his thick, dark hair and beard. The second was his expensive grey suit, shiny dress shoes and a crisp white business shirt with an open collar.

As he stepped forward, he smiled warmly and held out his hand for Zang to shake. He didn't appear sinister in the slightest. "We haven't met face-to-face before, Rachel Zang, but I feel I already know a lot about you."

The hand waited, and so did Abdul Ibrahim's eyes, for Zang to shake it.

She did what he expected of her.

"Good. We have a problem with the Trigger Man, Zang, and we want you to bring him in. The question is, can I trust you to do it?"

29

"Of course you can trust me." Rachel Zang almost spat her words so they wouldn't feel trapped in her throat.

Abdul Ibrahim pulled down on his grey suit jacket, straightening it, and returned a smile. "That's all I wanted to hear, Zang."

"My loyalty never wavered."

"Maybe." He shrugged. "The Port-au-Prince operation is stood down for the moment. Pierce is our immediate priority. Now, please allow Knight to update you on recent developments."

Ibrahim and Zang watched as Patricia Knight opened several files, images and data feeds on her laptop as she briefed Zang on Trigger Man's recent and multiple violent encounters in Rio de Janeiro against SEBIN. She told of the two women he'd teamed up with, their eventual capture and transportation by aircraft to Venezuela, and how the flight had never made it to its planned destination, the capital, Caracas.

"Early this morning, we identified the Hawker 800 wreckage deep in the jungle of Venezuela's Amazonas region, broken into at least fourteen major pieces. At first, we believed everyone on board died, including Pierce. Later satellite surveillance identified two groups of two people each, both trekking and boating out of the Amazon as we speak. All four must have parachuted to safety before impact."

Knight clicked open several satellite images taken from low orbit. The first was of Pierce and a woman on a motorboat almost identical to the original image Knight had shown Zang earlier.

Zang studied the image, not recognising Pierce's companion. Zang had initially suspected the woman to be Pierce's former case officer and friend, Mackenzie Summerfield, but the two women looked nothing alike. Pierce had been busy since Zang's last encounter with him in Angola three months ago. "I'll ask again, ma'am, have you identified this woman?"

Ibrahim answered, "She's Juliana Munoz. Former DNI, Colombian intelligence. Her superiors supposedly discharged her from active duty three years ago because of embezzlement charges against the government they could never prove. Munoz soon disappeared off the radar until four days ago when she showed up in Rio de Janeiro, aiding Pierce. We thought she'd turned mercenary somewhere. Or worked as an enforcer for one of the many Mexican drug cartels. Both options now seem unlikely, as I'll explain."

Knight brought up file pictures of the woman, the first during her service with the DNI in a military uniform, and more recent shots caught on CCTV cameras in Rio. Gone was the black hair tied in a tight bun and her patriotic and serious stare, replaced by anti-establishment purple streaks, shaved portions of her scalp, and nose and ear studs. "We now believe the DNI fabricated her expulsion. A ruse to place Munoz into a deep cover operation under the fake identity of Savannah Fonseca, an anti-establishment and anarchist hacker — and the lover of this woman."

Knight opened a second image of a young and pretty twenty-something Latin woman with large brown eyes that expressed both intense defiance and equally intense pain. Zang sensed this woman had endured the worst brutalities the world could inflict upon her but had come out the other side a stronger and determined woman. "This is Amelia Reyes. A popular YouTuber with billions of channel views and millions of supporters. She regularly criticises and exposes the corruption of the Venezuelan government, their army, the secret police, including SEBIN and FAES, the oil companies, the drug cartels and gangs that operate there with impunity. Basically, everyone with power and a subpar moral base, she calls out and shames mercilessly."

"Why?" Zang felt surprised that she knew nothing of this woman, but suspected she would soon hear an intriguing tale. Zang had never operated in Latin America, so her regional geopolitical understanding of this part of the world remained limited.

"Reyes has good reason to hate the powers that are systematically destroying her country. Five years ago, SEBIN arrested her father, a factory worker, for organising peaceful protests against the government. Weeks later, after vanishing, he turned up dead. His naked, decapitated body hung from a bridge near Reyes's home, and his head in a cardboard box was left nearby for wild dogs to sniff out and chew up." Knight sniffled before she continued, "Reyes's mother died six months later, shot on a street corner in front of Amelia while they were both out. Purchasing groceries they couldn't afford because of the out-of-control inflation Venezuela still endures. Not hard to imagine how both tragedies destroyed this poor woman."

Zang flinched. It wasn't the first time she'd encountered victims with similar tragic pasts, but it still maddened her that other individuals with power and absent morals could still be this cruel to decent people like Amelia Reyes.

Realising her emotions were getting the better of her, Zang tensed and buried her feelings because she didn't want Knight or Ibrahim further questioning her ability to remain impartial in the field — if that was their plan for her. "So Amelia turned activist. I'm not surprised. You can cower or fight back. There is no middle ground for someone with her traumas."

"Yes, indeed." Ibrahim nodded. "Knight and I believe it was Munoz who smuggled Reyes out of the country shortly after the mother's execution and established them with new identities, allowing them to hide out in Rio de Janeiro. It's no secret the Colombians endure the brunt of refugees escaping Venezuela. Currently one-point-five million displaced men, women and children barely survive in multiple refugee camps lined up along the border regions between both nations. Refugee numbers like that strain Colombia's economy and internal stability. The DNI has a vested interest in instigating a regime change in their neighbour."

Knight touched her temple with her forefinger. "We believe Munoz, under the deep cover legend of Savannah Fonseca, still works for the DNI and, through her employer, provides Amelia Reyes with accurate intelligence on the various actions and crimes of the Venezuelan government. So accurate, in fact, Amelia's videos have forced the president to take drastic action against his inner circle because Reyes keeps calling out their internal deceptions and power plays against the very man they are supposedly supporting in power."

"Ouch!"

"Yes, indeed. Reyes's YouTube channel is forcing those closest to the president to turn against each other. Some of it might be lies to instigate unwarranted mistrust, but there is enough truth in Reyes's accusations that nothing she says they can readily dismiss. She also has the power of popular opinion, and no one in the Caracas elite likes it."

Zang nodded. "So, four days ago, Pierce and SEBIN turn up in Rio. Conflict happens, which forces Reyes and Fonseca out of hiding, and now Pierce, Reyes and Fonseca are unwittingly back in Venezuela. I take it the second team you are tracking in the jungle includes Amelia Reyes?"

With a few keystrokes on her laptop, Knight bought up a satellite image of a man and a woman in a second boat. The woman was unmistakably the YouTube activist, hog-tied and prone on the floor of the boat. The face of the man controlling the outboard motor was not visible because of the angle of the satellite image, but the Russian-made AKM assault rifle in his lap was unmistakable and spoke of the man's intensions and capabilities.

Knight cleared her throat and rubbed her red nose. "This is Maceo Parra, a FAES paramilitary operator and sometimes SEBIN operative. He also regularly moonlights as a freelance assassin, so a man with no moral compass. Also known for his comic-book-style art he likes to draw, mostly of men being violent to other men and women. The usual fucked-up personality type we too often encounter in this business. The weapons you see in his possession, he gained from drug smugglers he has established relationships with. Killers who operate with impunity in the region."

"The kind of people we always end up dealing with. So what?"

Knight tensed. "Let me just be clear on one thing, Zang. The Trigger Man had no problem in almost taking out the entire SEBIN team sent to extract Amelia Reyes in Rio, but this one individual, Pierce has not yet been able to incapacitate. Parra has since bested Pierce multiple times in the last few days, and Pierce is lucky to still be alive and in one piece. Don't underestimate Parra."

More keystrokes allowed Knight to enlarge a SEBIN file image of Maceo Parra.

Like lots of killers Zang had taken down in her time, Parra's stare was intense and his eyes dark. He exuded every element that defined an apex predator in that single image. Zang recognised Knight was correct to warn about the dangers posed by this deadly killer. If, or when, she encountered this foe, she would engage with him carefully.

"What is happening here, in the jungle?" Zang asked. "How does it all connect?"

Ibrahim took a step forward. "We believe Parra is completing SEBIN's mission and returning Reyes to Caracas, which, if he is successful, will result in her torture and murder as revenge against the humiliation she has brought against the Venezuelan government. We believe Pierce and Munoz — let's just call her Savannah Fonseca — are tracking Parra and Amelia, and our analysis suggests the two groups will converge at this location in two days." Ibrahim pointed to coordinates on a digital map now on Knight's laptop. "On the Orinoco River, near the Colombian border. Pierce's mission seems likely to be a rescue attempt."

Knight zoomed in on the satellite image until a riverside trading post, interlinked by multiple jetties and motorboats, emerged. The wild land encroaching on the settlement was jungles, hills and boulder-strewn waterways. Zang noticed the many fuel tanks.

"This is a known area for cocaine production and trafficking. Smuggler seaplanes often pass through here on their way to Mexico, Guatemala and Florida. The Venezuelan government looks the other way because they receive a cut of the profits. Hard US-dollar payoffs when their own currency is now effectively worth nothing."

"So Parra is heading here, because the local smugglers do business with SEBIN, and he can leverage their resources?"

"Exactly, Zang," said Ibrahim with a grin. "When Pierce, Fonseca, Reyes and Parra converge, I'm certain it will be a bloodbath, unless..."

Zang gritted her teeth. "You want me there to aid Pierce and Fonseca in their rescue and bring all three back to the US?"

Knight scratched the back of her head and couldn't look Zang in the eyes when she said, "No one knows Pierce like you do, Rachel. I don't think he trusts anyone, but you come closest. You're best positioned to convince him to return home willingly so we can extract exactly what he has been up to."

Rachel Zang shook her head and crossed her arms. "This is more important than Haiti?"

Knight and Ibrahim both nodded.

"You've got the wrong person. The only person Pierce

trusts is his former handler, Mackenzie Summerfield. They operated together for years in the Middle East, then West Africa. I've seen what they are both like, in person, and I've witnessed firsthand the respect and bonds of friendship they have for each other. If you really want to convince Pierce it's safe for him to come in, she is who we need. That said, I'll happily accompany Summerfield to this meet, providing protection duty."

Ibrahim and Knight exchanged glances and grim expressions and still said nothing.

Zang leaned forward as she tensed her muscles and clenched her teeth. "What am I missing here?"

The C/SOG answered her. "Summerfield is missing in action. MIA for some time. No one has seen her in three months."

"In fact," said Knight, "Rachel, you were the last known contact with Summerfield."

Zang slumped back in her chair and let out a long sigh. She was not responsible for Mackenzie's vanishing, hadn't even known about it until this meeting, so why did she experience a sudden pang of guilt?

Everything about this new mission suddenly sat uneasily with her and likely contained many potential risks she couldn't predict or was not being told about. But she owed it to Mark Pierce and Mackenzie Summerfield and the brave woman Amelia Reyes she knew little about but already respected, to do everything she could to save them all.

Zang nodded. She would do this, whatever the cost, despite her sense that Knight and particularly Ibrahim weren't telling her everything she needed to know to complete this mission safely.

"I'm glad you're on the team, Zang," said Ibrahim.

"We covered this." Zang glared at the senior CIA chief like he was scum, recognising that she could never have imagined herself ever disrespecting a senior officer of the CIA until today, and didn't like what it said about any of them. "I was never off the team, sir!"

"I know. But you lied to us, Zang. This is your opportunity to prove you understand what being a team player actually means."

30

Orinoco River, Venezuela-Colombia Border

On the third day of downstream travel along the fast-flowing Orinoco River, Pierce's mind fog finally vanished. His thoughts cleared, and his muscles didn't ache so much. Yet despite his recovery, he still couldn't remember much of his recent past.

Memories had formed of missions in Yemen, Ethiopia, Mali and Algeria, and of a prolonged period incarcerated in a rebel camp in the jungles of Central Africa. Somehow, he had escaped that last predicament without enduring serious injury, but after that event, more recent recollections remained hazy or altogether absent.

Often in the last couple of days, he'd experienced fleeting flashbacks of recent experiences in Southern Africa, Central Asia and South America, but no specific memories formed a narrative that made sense. As for the naked and beaten woman tied to a chair, he had no luck in remembering who she was, but felt certain she was the sole reason as to why Pierce now faced his current predicament. He also felt immense guilt, for perhaps he had been responsible, directly or indirectly, for her capture and incarceration.

The mind fog loomed, so he turned his mind back to their current situation.

Two days ago, Savannah had purchased a motorboat and a simple knife from a local Yanomami indigenous family, costing them all their cash and the Glock pistol. This left them defenceless and needing to fish with makeshift lines for nourishment because they had no other food. But without a boat, there was no chance of reaching Amelia in time and staging a rescue mission here in the jungle. If Parra returned Amelia to Caracas, their chances of saving her diminished significantly.

While Pierce steered the motor and guided them downstream, with Colombia on the left and Venezuela on the right, Savannah worked the cell phone, attempting multiple strategies to unlock it.

Over the last few days, Pierce had observed her tradecraft and wilderness survival skills, which today left no doubt in his mind as to her intelligence training and professionalism.

Savannah pumped her fists in the air and said in Spanish, "Fantastic! I'm in. I've cracked the phone."

"Great," Pierce responded in the same language, speaking it like a native.

Animated, the Colombian operative went to work installing the apps she required to track Amelia. "I hope we are not too late."

"We'll find her, Savannah. Parra is marching out of the same patch of jungle. It's logical he'll too end up on this stretch of river."

"Mark, the Orinoco is huge! It's the fourth-largest river in the world by discharge volume of water... Okay, reception isn't great. The app will take a while to download, then to configure for tracking."

"How much battery do we have?"

She grimaced. "Enough."

Over the last three days, Pierce had noticed Savannah's ongoing and rising agitation. Jittery legs, bitten nails, clenched teeth and mumbles during her sleep. In Pierce's experience, these were behaviours difficult to fake over a prolonged period. He now believed the woman had actual feelings for Amelia. And it was forefront in both Savannah's and his minds that the longer Amelia remained in Maceo Parra's custody, the worse her traumas would become.

"Do you know this territory?" he asked while she waited for the software to download.

Savannah nodded. "This is cocaine cartel territory. With the Venezuelan bolivar worth nothing, the government needs hard US dollars and euros to pay off crippling foreign loans, the military, the police, enforcers, etcetera. An easy cash injection is through the provision of safe havens for drug traffickers moving product from Colombia, Peru and Bolivia to up north. Cartel seaplanes stop here to refuel, and since fuel costs almost nothing in Venezuela, everyone wins."

"Except for twenty million Venezuelans living in poverty."

She sighed. "Yes, except for them. The president fucked this country well and good."

Pierce nodded and surveyed their environment. The water course was wide and flowed with speed, creating an illusion the river was at an angle to the horizon, while enormous boulders and wide sandbanks broke up the jungle foliage. He felt a breeze on his skin, and the constant heat and humidity. Biting insects were a constant problem, and it concerned Pierce that he couldn't remember if his vaccinations were up to date, and neither of them were on anti-malarials.

Savannah returned her attention to her cell phone.

Now that he no longer experienced mind fog, Pierce again focused on his memories, to analyse what he knew and what gaps needed filling.

He suspected he was in South America hunting his nemesis, Idris Walsh, the former CIA operative who had betrayed and tortured Pierce for many months in Central Africa. With Pierce naked and tied to a chair, Walsh had beaten and tortured him for months on end. The same experience the unknown woman had suffered, which had left Pierce wondering if Walsh was behind those tortures.

During Pierce's incarceration, Walsh had framed him as the scapegoat involving a conspiracy to secure nuclear waste, which had also turned the CIA against him. The man bound inside the crashed car in Rio's slums had likely been Walsh. Pierce had let him live when he should have just killed him. But he hadn't, which left Pierce suspicious that Walsh knew a secret he'd used to bargain for his life. He suspected that secret was the identity and location of the bound and beaten woman plaguing his waking and sleeping mind, and Pierce had come to believe the woman in question was his friend and former case officer, Mackenzie Summerfield. The only person on this earth whom he trusted and truly cared for.

What also bothered him was that rather than leading a rescue mission to save Mackenzie, Pierce was instead deep inside the Amazon rainforest, aiding two women he didn't know and had no emotional connection with, and that he was embroiled in a deadly fight that wasn't his.

Why?

Other than the last six months, a period of time that remained mostly unknown to him still, it had been half a decade since Pierce knew he had last operated in Latin America, and never during his "official" time with the CIA under the identity of Mark Pierce. This had led Pierce to believe he acted now to protect these women because they were an integral element of Idris Walsh's scheme, and because — if he were honest with himself — it was the right thing to do. Amelia and Savannah certainly needed his help with the enemies they faced. He hoped by following this "mission" through to conclusion, he might learn more about where his missing friend was imprisoned and who held her captive. Then he would find and rescue her, whatever collateral damage he caused along the way.

"Brilliant!" came an excited voice from the front of the boat. "App has downloaded and works."

Pierce turned to Savannah, her face alive with a large, beaming smile.

"And I've found Amelia!"

"That's positive."

Now Savannah frowned. "Except the location isn't good."

"Why?"

"You know how I told you this jungle is thick with drug lords?"

"Yes?"

"Well, Amelia's tracker places her smack in a territory controlled by one of the worst of them. A psychopathic drug smuggler who operates an island on this river and moves vast quantities cocaine in and out of the country."

31

Port-au-Prince, Haiti

M r Real powered the Jeep through the streets of Haiti's capital, Port-au-Prince, as rain pelted down in the tropical heat. Idris Walsh, tense and gripping his cramping stomach in the car seat next to his captor, had endured constant nausea during the trip through the windy, narrow streets that led them up the side of the southern mountain overlooking the city on their drive into Petion-Ville, the upper-class neighbourhood of this otherwise impoverished city. He listened as heavy raindrops exploded on the cabin roof because nothing else could distract him from his pain.

He'd thought many times of yanking on the steering wheel, causing them to crash, perhaps allowing Walsh an opportunity to escape. Walsh's hesitation, however, stemmed from his weakened physical state, the two large muscular paramilitary soldiers in the back seat with their American M4 assault rifles, and the alarming reality that Walsh had not taken his liver anti-rejection drugs in three days. He sweated constantly and feared he might have a fever or, worse, an infection in his organs. If Walsh somehow survived a crash that may or may not incapacitate his three minders, he would likely die from organ failure a few days later anyway. Mr Real was the only source of Walsh's life-saving drugs in this Caribbean nation, and he might not have those drugs on his person.

He focused instead on the raindrops.

"What's our destination?" Walsh scratched at his pectoral muscle, raw with the itchy tattoo of a circle within a circle dissected by a line. Again, he wondered what it symbolised to this unusual secret organisation he was now an unwilling member of.

Walsh turned to Mr Real and frowned. This was the first time the short, Italian man had deemed to answer him since their arrival in Haiti. "A compound, Mr Walsh, that the rest of the world believes is an NGO-funded scientific research facility."

Walsh nodded. "What is this organisation that you work for—?"

"That we work for, Mr Walsh," Mr Real corrected him. "You are one of us now."

The former CIA spymaster snorted, not hiding his contempt at his situation. "Fine." He gestured to the two soldiers in the back, one of whom was West Coast American and the other Korean, judging by their accents when Walsh had overheard them talking earlier. "You're not nationalistic or of one particular ideological or religious belief. Your team is too diverse for that."

"Very astute of you. We are international and secular. We have been growing our power behind the scenes for years now, but only recently have we begun to flex our muscles and enact our grand schemes."

"To do what?"

Mr Real chuckled as he took a corner fast, forcing a young man and his pregnant wife riding on a scooter to get off the road quickly before Mr Real caused them to crash. "Our objective is the control of power and wealth, the same as everyone else on this planet. But you don't need to know any more than that just yet. But I will tell you that our first objective is economic and political control of Venezuela. You need to know this because you are now a part of that first objective's process."

"Control? Of Venezuela? The entire country is a tinderbox ready to explode into civil war. Why would you want to own a mess like that?"

"What you forget, Mr Walsh, are the potential and vast fossil fuel reserves the country has access to. When I say we will control the country, we only need to control the oil, and the rest of the poor excuse of a nation — how do you say it — then flows into our palms naturally. Without oil, Venezuela has nothing. Is nothing."

Mr Real bounced them through a large pile of garbage that had collected on the road. He increased the speed of the windscreen wipers to push aside the rainfall running as streams off the glass. "The Venezuelan president's biggest fear is losing control of his military. If the Army, Navy and Air Force turn against him, if they feel they can't trust him or sense that he has lost control, then it is all over for him. They will lead a coup and execute him as they take power. Our plan is to turn the military against the president, but not actually unleash them. In his fear of what we can instigate, he will sign over all the country's oil rights to us, and only then do we take away the military threat."

"When you say 'us', you mean your 'circle' organisation."

"Yes, but that is not our name."

"Then what is it?" With a name, Walsh knew he had a starting point to learn more about this mysterious group, and knowledge would be the first step of many to eventually regain his freedom.

The Italian laughed. "All in good time, Mr Walsh. Ah, we have arrived."

They were in Petion-Ville now, on a street lined with large and well-maintained houses all adorned behind high stone walled fences. Cotton and seagrape trees grew everywhere, interspersed with occasional banana trees and tall palms. A gate on automatic rollers opened, and they drove into a large walled estate prominent with a gingerbread-style house that was common in Haiti, and several more utilitarian steel-framed buildings that had been erected recently. Multiple modern SUVs and vans parked in the gravel driveway. Of more interest were the many paramilitary soldiers guarding the facility, armed with M4s and dressed in black fatigues under chest rigs and plate carriers.

Walsh performed several quick calculations in his head to estimate the expenditure required to establish and maintain this operation, which he counted in the tens of millions of dollars, if not significantly more. But what was the purpose of this place? What about it made Mr Real so certain it could produce an actual change in Venezuela and turn a profit for them?

Mr Real parked the Jeep, and the four clambered out to stretch their limbs after the long drive from Toussaint Louverture International Airport. The heavy rain drenched them now, so they moved onto the veranda of the ginger-bread house. Walsh admired the structure with its fancy millwork, scroll designs, steep pitched rooflines and lace-like cut-outs and patterns. He guessed this building dated back to the Victorian era.

A tall, muscular man with a shaved head and a recent, brutal scar on his scalp approached. He wore a paramilitary uniform with a SIG Sauer P320 semi-automatic pistol holstered at his hip. Dark eyes seemed to vanish into the shadows cast by his brows. He stepped close to Mr Real, and the two shook hands. "Greetings, Mr Real, it has been a while."

"Greetings, Mr Mansaray. I've brought you a fresh addition to your team." Mr Real pushed Walsh forward like he was cattle for sale at a meat market. "Mr Walsh, Mr Alpha Mansaray manages security at this research facility, and he is your new boss."

"He doesn't look like much," said Mansaray as his lids pinched close around his eyes.

"Mr Walsh is a disgraced and former CIA operator, but he's highly proficient at strategising and executing successful covert operations. He will help you plan your next series of infiltration missions."

"I don't need him. We are doing fine already, Mr Real."

"Are you?" the Italian man said with a sneer. "We're not moving anywhere near fast enough with what we need to achieve. And you have failed to achieve a real impact on our enemy."

Mansaray snarled, as his head wound spotted with tiny dots of fresh blood.

"Don't let emotions rule you, Mr Mansaray. You know

how our organisation deals with failure, so you don't want to fail here."

Walsh watched the security manager shudder. "Very well, if you think this American is what we need."

"He is what *you* need, Mr Mansaray. Especially after that CIA extraction squad almost snatched you here, in Port-au-Prince, four days ago. This has my organisation suspicious that you are not as cautious as you led us to believe you are."

Mansaray tensed. "How did you know about that?"

Mr Real laughed. "Because our high-level asset inside the CIA told us, that's why. You should have informed us straight away. Failing to do so lessens our trust in you. And without trust..."

The bald, muscular man sneered again.

Walsh noticed Mansaray had grown increasingly agitated as the conversation had progressed. It struck Walsh that the secret organisation Mr Real had hinted at induced actual fear in their followers, but how did they achieve that? Mr Real wasn't imposing, had never spoken with aggression or anger. Was he a high-ranking fixer or mouthpiece for the top-ranking, shadowy members of this secretive group Walsh knew nothing about, or was he one of those senior members who knew far more than he let on? Whatever his position, Mr Real was not a man to be underestimated.

But Mansaray... this man might be a different story...

"The next incursion you must complete in a few days, Mr Mansaray. We want the Venezuelan president fearing for his life." The rain eased up. Mr Real turned his attention to Walsh and said, "For you to be useful, it's time for you to understand the purpose of this facility."

As they wandered the facility, Walsh took in further details, and each detail unsettled him further. First were the research laboratories inside the steel-framed buildings. Their interiors contained laboratory spaces, refrigeration areas with multiple test tube samples kept inside, and a portion of one building they were not allowed to enter, but it had men and women coming in and out dressed in full biohazard gear, which included air particulate filter masks and negative-pressure suits.

Another building featured a morgue, with corpses of men, women and children wrapped and tagged in yellow biohazard bags. They all looked to be local people judging by the colour of the skins. In the same building, they passed a wall with glass partitions, which looked into what resembled a medical ward, with more Haitians handcuffed to beds. Many thrashed and snarled in their agitated states, while others lay unmoving because of their exhaustion. Some had saline drips in their arms, while others did not. Walsh watched as two men in biohazard suits entered, then proceeded to take blood samples from each of the chained patients.

But it was the last steel-framed facility that unsettled Walsh the most, containing multiple pens each housing mixed-breed dogs known locally as potcakes. Some dogs lay on their sides, breathing fast and panting. Others salivated excessively and barked aggressively. One dog was so far gone, it had been gnawing at its own legs so that the muscles showed.

Mr Real came up beside Walsh and watched the dog chew on its own leg. "Worked it out yet?"

Walsh nodded, both impressed and terrified by what he saw. "Those dogs, rabies infects them."

"Exactly," said Mr Real, still smiling. He threw Walsh a pill, his anti-rejection medication.

Walsh snatched it from its trajectory and swallowed it.

"The world once feared COVID-19 coronavirus, Mr Walsh, but its horror is nothing compared to what our bioengineered strain of rabies will bring to Venezuela."

"What do you mean?"

"Our front is a French NGO here to help eradicate rabies in the local dog population. But the truth is, we've weaponised it. We've turned it into an airborne virus, able to spread from human to human, and reduced its incubation period from weeks to months down to days. If Venezuela doesn't capitulate to our demands, we could completely destroy their country."

Walsh shuddered, realising that everything he had tried to achieve in his life was amateurish compared to what this organisation could, or already had, accomplished.

32

Orinoco River, Venezuela-Colombia Border

Pierce and Savannah hung low in the water, their aching hands gripping the large log as it floated them downstream. An hour since abandoning their boat, El Pirana's island appeared on the horizon.

They kicked to guide the log inwards to stage their assault. Their plan was daring, as they were without weapons other than the knife, which Savannah pocketed. They had also gambled on abandoning their motorboat several kilometres upriver, beyond their reach now, and denying them its option as a getaway vehicle should they need it. Their mission would succeed only if they could achieve a stealthy insertion onto the island, and they only had a single opportunity for success. If they floated past, the current was too strong to swim back and try again.

"Ready for this?" Savannah spoke in his ear, reminding Pierce of their physical closeness during their tiring swim.

"What do you mean?"

"I mean, Mark, you weren't so well a few days ago."

Pierce tensed. He felt guilt and an underlying disgust with himself, but had no understanding why these emotions troubled him. "I'm fine, Savannah. Besides, what choice do we have? We strike now, or we lose Amelia forever."

He watched her frown, then shudder. With her emotional investment in their target, she had more to lose than he did.

The muddy flows made underwater visibility impossible, so they kept their nostrils just above water and their heads behind the log. They kicked regularly to ensure they drifted towards the island.

As they drew closer, Pierce noticed the inhabited island comprised many wooden houses built on stilts, surrounded by multiple raised walkways, which extended as a maze of jetties out across the flowing water.

Moored to the jetties were many motorised boats and seaplanes. Guards walked the floating platforms, armed with AK, AKM and M16 assault rifles, or old Israeli Uzi 9mm submachine guns. Other men were labourers who hauled bags of cocaine from boats into a seaplane. The few women Pierce spotted were prostitutes, all young and skinny. Each dressed in jean shorts or skirts cut high to show off their asses and string bikini tops displaying ample bosoms. Also prominent were large, elevated fuel tanks, connected to pier-supported pipelines that stretched out across the water and disappeared into the jungle on the Venezuelan side. When nothing else functioned in Venezuela, oil did, even in these remote Amazonian jungle backwaters.

Concealed by the leafy branches, he spotted that several of the smugglers with assault rifles now watched the floating log with interest. So far, they had not reacted as if the log might be a threat...

Savannah said, "See that clump of trees; let's regroup there."

"Affirmative."

The current seemed to speed up the closer they came to the island.

"We're almost there. In three... two... one..."

Together, only metres from the closest jetty, they both dived and swam fast underwater. Pierce held his breath, not wanting to release bubbles giving away his position, and hoped Savannah achieved the same. Then he remembered she had proved herself a competent operative. He should trust that his concerns about her were unfounded.

Without warning, Pierce hit a submerged wire fence, which knocked the wind out of him and forced him to surface. He sucked in a lungful of air, producing gurgling noises. Luck had him emerge under a wooden jetty and far from anyone who might notice his arrival.

When he felt certain he was alone, he rested a minute, oxygenated his lungs, and recovered his strength. Small marine animals behind the wire fence thrashed and smacked against the fence. Was this a fish farm? There seemed to be hundreds, if not thousands, of the marine vertebrates trapped in the wire cage. Their numbers seemed to increase the longer he watched the splashing water on the opposite side of the wire netting, as if they sensed his presence and hunted him.

Before Pierce could reflect further on this anomaly, a guard with a slung AK-47 walked past and hummed a tune to himself.

Pierce exploded out of the water, grabbed the man by the

belt and pulled him back down into the murky depths. With rapid motions, Pierce locked his arms around the man's neck and held him under. The man thrashed in his panic to breathe and escape Pierce's vice-like grip. The fish thrashed too, muffling any noise the men made in their battle to the death. Within a minute, without the strength to match Pierce's grip, the foe ceased struggling and turned into a corpse.

After regathering his breath, Pierce unslung the AK and wrapped it around his own shoulders. He searched the dead body for spare banana clips, finding two, and pocketed them as well, all performed underwater and with only his sense of touch. Further searching revealed nothing other than a small knife, but that suited Pierce's needs. So that the corpse wouldn't float away and surface downstream for easy identification, Pierce tied the man's belt around his neck and secured it to a pier positioned just below the waterline.

Ducking low, he swam perpendicular to the wire netting. The thrashing fish were disconcerting because they followed him.

After crossing between several jetties, he surfaced again and identified the collection of lush trees that Savannah and he had agreed to meet at, less than twenty metres from his current position. Taking a breath, he dived low and swam again. When he resurfaced, he was at the jetty, overhung with vines and other jungle creepers. He waited a moment, ensured no one approached or watched him, then surfaced and lay low on the wooden planks.

A minute later Savannah slinked onto the deck like a snake and lay next to him. She had secured herself an Uzi submachine gun.

"Want to swap?"

Pierce couldn't guess if she was genuine in her request or making a quip. "I'm good. Me and AKs, we have a history together."

"A good one?"

"Never cheated on me, if that's what you mean."

Savannah laughed.

Under their cover of tropical foliage, they had little chance of being observed, but they kept their attention focused on the island and the many soldiers, labourers, and prostitutes acting like today was no different from any other day. She pointed her gun towards the largest building, with a sign out the front that said La Cantina de las Piranas.

With a sinking feeling in his gut, Pierce now understood what species of marine animals lay on the other side of the wire net. "Don't fall in the water, Savannah. Particularly not beyond that wire fence line." He pointed out the underwater cage held taut by the many inner pylons distributed through the multiple jetty lattices.

"Why?"

"These cocaine cowboys, they also breed the fish they eat. Carnivorous fish."

"Oh, I see." Savannah shuddered momentarily, then recovered her composure. "I count at least twenty armed men. Labourers outnumber them two to one, and the prostitutes in a similar number. Weapons are AKs, AKMs, M16s and Uzis, and some pistols. The latter are mostly old semi-automatics and revolvers. If Amelia is still here, my bet is she's in that cantina. See the congregation of guards loitering outside, peering in? And that seaplane, they will fly her out on that."

Pierce nodded. "Copy that." Her assessment matched his, and he suspected Maceo Parra also lurked inside the cantina, and he was the one foe neither of them could afford to underestimate. "And remember, if Amelia is here, Maceo Parra will also be close by."

"Yes, true." She pointed to the seaplane. "The turboprop is almost loaded with cocaine. I'm guessing we don't have long to act."

Licking his lips, tasting the sweat on his skin now that the river water no longer cooled him, Pierce said, "You have a tactical plan you'd like to share?"

"I do, and our weapons dictate it."

Pierce smirked. "Fair enough. What is the plan?"

"You're sniper. I'm infiltrator. I swim down, and when I emerge at that jetty there, you take out the external guards and cover me while I go in."

Pierce pointed to the fuel tanks. "They'd cause a fine distraction."

She smirked. "They would, but only when we know where Amelia is. We can't risk catching her in the blast radius."

He reflected on the plan but couldn't imagine a better option. The locals heavily outgunned them, and their only advantages were their ability to surprise the enemy and their military training, which these drug smugglers seemed to lack. Then he identified a second option. "What if I sneak up to that side of the cantina? There is plenty of thick foliage there, and I can take out the guards from that position, as well as aid you from a flanked position when you assault from the front? Also allows me to get in close to Amelia and protect her, assuming she's in there."

Her eyes reassessed the battlefield, and soon she nodded in agreement. "Yes, that could work. Let's do your plan."

She seemed overly eager to get moving, which

concerned Pierce that she might be too impulsive to properly focus on the difficult engagement ahead. "Savannah, wait; be careful."

"I will, but what choice do I have but to take risks? Give up on Amelia and allow her torture and execution? I don't think so."

Pierce gritted his teeth and found himself only able to say, "Copy that."

Savannah shuffled forward, then silently lowered herself into the water. When she was only a head and an arm, she reached forward and gently squeezed Pierce's shoulder. "Thank you."

"For what?"

"For risking your life. Helping to save a woman you barely know. A girl who means the world to me."

He waited until she disappeared and had swum some distance before he assessed how her last words made him feel. Savannah could be genuine in her affection for Amelia Reyes, but he also felt she'd oversold it.

With the iron sight of his Russian assault rifle lined up with his vision, Pierce shuffled forward along the rickety jetty and over the wire cage of hungry piranhas. Then he shuffled low along the ground until he was under the foliage adjacent to the cantina and mentally prepared himself for the carnage they were about to unleash.

Then he heard voices, of two people talking, just on the other side of the cantina wall.

Maceo Parra and Amelia Reyes.

33

"Eat. Drink. You need the energy," said Parra.

From his hiding spot under the cover of thick jungle scrub, Pierce found a tiny crack in the wooden wall only just large enough for a single eye to peer through, seeing Maceo Parra seated at a cantina table only a few metres from him. He had his Raging Bull laid on the table but kept his hand over the revolver's grip. The weapon, Pierce knew, was a Brazilian revolver that fired .44 Magnum rounds at 580 metres per second, delivering a mighty 2,700 joules of life-stopping force. Certainly, an overstatement of a weapon, and most brands of body armour on the market would be ineffective against its lethality.

Parra looked up over the weapon, past two bottles of Monserrate Red Beer and two plates of fried piranha dripping with freshly squeezed lemon juice arranged on the table he sat at, until his eyes rested on Amelia Reyes, who Pierce only now noticed sat opposite him. She stared back at Parra through dark, sunken eyes, and Pierce felt shock at how much more battered and bruised she appeared since he had last seen her. Further inside the cantina, Pierce noticed at least four other smugglers drinking beers, but with AKs and Uzis nearby and ready to use.

Pierce turned his attention to the two individuals he and Savannah had tracked to this location. He watched as Parra gulped down half of the first beer. He said to Amelia, "You won't get the chance to eat again."

Amelia answered, "Why bother? You will soon kill me."

He laughed as he bit into strips of grilled piranha flesh. "Not me, Amelia. I'm just the courier. Caracas is where we go next."

She breathed sharply through flaring nostrils. "That is a mistake. You should kill me while you have the chance."

He chuckled again.

"If you don't, it will be I who kills you. Or Mark Pierce..."

Parra raised an eyebrow. "Is that the name of the man who tried to rescue you?"

Amelia swallowed and expressed guilt that she had let slip a key piece of information regarding Pierce.

"He won't defeat me because he's dead. And neither will you." Parra swallowed his mouthful and smiled with amusement at her threat, which he would likely think of only as a joke. "But your threats are amusing. Given up being a pacifist, have you?"

She didn't answer. Her breath raged like a flaming dragon. Then, distracted, her eyes scanned the cantina, to linger on the many art pieces that decorated the walls that Pierce too was only now noticing.

One canvas depicted a bikini-clad girl seen from a submerged point of view, kicking in the water, her head not visible above the surface. A dozen piranhas savaged her flesh as blood streams gushed around her.

Another showed a Peruvian Indian wearing a Panama hat. He gushed tears as a revolver in an unseen assassin's grip blew out brain matter from a hole in his skull on his opposite temple.

A third showed an emaciated young man tied naked to a chair, with his feet in a metal bucket and wires pinching his nipples. His body tensed as electric volts surged through his flesh and muscles.

But Pierce noticed that the painting Amelia's stare lingered longest on was an attractive woman in a summer dress, sprawled broken in a mound of slum rubbish. Her corpse carried many bullet holes, and blood saturated her chest. A dog curled up next to her mourned the passing of its owner.

When Amelia caught Parra watching her, her bloodshot eyes shot back to his and held his gaze. "Is that my mother?"

The SEBIN killer said nothing.

"That is your art, right, hanging on these walls? Why? Do you sell your art to all the crims? Glorify violence for the very men who instigated the violence in the first place?"

Parra shrugged.

"Tell me! Is that one of my mother?"

Shaking his head, Parra didn't appear to be bothered by her question and said, "I honestly can't remember." She spat at him.

Pierce thought to fire through the room right now, to execute Parra with a single shot. He deserved it, and it would have been easy enough to do, but there were too many armed guards in the cantina with him. In response they would shoot without thought, killing Amelia in the crossfire. Pierce knew he just needed to bide his time until Savannah got into position, when they could engage the enemy from two directions and be ready to snatch Amelia back when the time was right.

He focused on Parra again, who, snarling, reached over and took Amelia's beer and plate of grilled piranha. "Somebody's going hungry." He took a paper napkin and wiped her spit off his shoulder where it had landed, then waved over a waiter with an Uzi slung over his shoulder.

"Yes, sir?"

"When will the seaplane be ready?"

The man's answer came as a spray of blood as his chest exploded with a volley of bullets bursting out of him.

Savannah had engaged, so it was time for Pierce to act. He fired his AK through the wall, blind but knowing where his target was. Two bursts. Centred on Parra's head.

But when Pierce peered again through the crack in the wood, he noticed Parra and Amelia were gone, and there were no corpses on the floor. Parra had reacted too fast, just as Pierce would have, and gotten himself and his prisoner out of the line of fire immediately.

Soon there was gunfire in all directions. Pierce could no longer see Parra, but he saw smugglers firing their Uzis and AKs in Savannah's direction.

Pierce fired off several short bursts, splintering the wall now between him and his targets, and saw through the shattered wood that he had killed three men.

But two other smugglers now turned towards where Pierce hid himself, and fired.

Pierce ducked as the wood above him disintegrated further with a volley of bullets firing indiscriminately over the top of him.

Pierce moved as he reloaded his AK-47, ducked low and

searched for another position of cover to engage the enemy from.

But over the foliage at his back, he spotted Parra running for the seaplane, with a tight grip on Amelia, dragging her behind him. When he reached the jetty mooring the aircraft, he turned, and Pierce saw he had a handheld grenade launcher in his free hand.

Pierce's heart thumped madly inside his chest. Nearby sat the tank of aviation fuel containing at least a thousand litres of volatile hydrocarbons.

Pierce was in the blast radius.

Parra was readying the launcher.

He couldn't shoot him because Amelia was now in front position as a human shield.

So Pierce took off at a sprint and ran for the closest jetty over the water and dived.

34

The explosion erupting behind him was sudden and shocking in its ferocity. Pierce had only seconds to dive into the murky water before flames consumed the air above him. If he'd hesitated, the burning fuel oils would have incinerated him into cinders.

No sooner had Pierce submerged than he felt a sharp pain in his calf and then one in his elbow. The pain then grew in intensity.

He realised he'd dived into the net of piranhas.

Fighting his rising panic, and still submerged, Pierce emptied thirty rounds from his AK-47 into the murky water in a broad sweep, hoping to kill a few of the carnivorous fish. His goal was to direct their siblings towards the newly created piscine corpses rather than savage Pierce.

Still holding his breath, he looked up to see the fireball disperse.

Knowing that to remain underwater was perilous, Pierce abandoned the Russian assault rifle and swam for the surface, coming up next to a blackened and charred jetty, where he propelled himself with speed from the churning water. Several dead piranhas floated to the surface with him. Many more alive specimens now tore their brothers and sisters to pieces, seeking cannibalistic nourishment.

With the jetty burning around him, Pierce checked his calf and elbow on his left side. He grimaced at the needle-like teeth marks that had punctured and torn his flesh. The pain wasn't so bad with the adrenalin surging through his body, and they were injuries far preferable to the burns he would have suffered had he not jumped into the water. But when he faced the inevitable adrenalin come-down, these injuries would hurt like hell.

He glanced around. Most of the jetties and almost all the buildings, including the cantina, were no more. The entire island was similar to the aftermath of ground zero from a fuel-air explosive detonation, resembling many devastated towns he'd witnessed too often in Yemen. Several blackened corpses of men and women, little more than cooked morsels of flesh and bone, littered the burning causeways. One surviving soldier screamed and paddled pointlessly in the caged netting where piranhas churned and turned the waters red. The guard was too far from a structurally stable jetty to save himself.

The path back towards the cantina where he had jumped from was now a wall of hot flames, blocking that exit for him.

In the opposite direction, a section of the burning jetty near Pierce disintegrated and splashed into the water. The entire structure would collapse under him soon if he didn't get away using that route. Pierce sprinted, danced and jumped along the failing timbers as they both charcoaled with flames and broke apart and dropped into the piranha-infested water. Pressure from every footstep didn't help, and much of the decking collapsed behind him as he propelled forward. His right leg disappeared into the water, and he only just climbed back out in time before the vicious fish converged upon him.

Eventually, he found a route that took him back to the island proper and threw himself onto the singed grassy earth.

Another explosion, not as large as the last, erupted behind him.

With a sharp turn of his head, he looked back as a burning electrical generator succumbed to the heat and flames and tore itself into pieces. Luckily, none of those pieces flew in his direction.

The carnage across the island was absolute and extensive.

He wondered if Savannah had instigated the earlier fuel tank explosion but guessed she wouldn't take such risks when her actions would likely hurt or kill Amelia.

He searched for Parra and Amelia, to determine if they had survived the blast, only guessing their fate when he spotted the Quest Kodiak seaplane moving out into the fast-flowing river. With the distance separating them, he couldn't tell who was inside the cockpit, but one passenger was a woman with dark hair.

It had to be Amelia.

Pierce turned in a circle and searched for fallen weapons.

Instead, his gaze lined up with the barrel of a Browning Hi-Power pistol pointed at him from close quarters.

The man behind the weapon suffered horrific burns, his skin red and blistering and his purple shirt and black pants destroyed. The only part of him not ruined and disfigured was his gold belt buckle stylised as a piranha.

"You fucker, coming into my place like this—"

He didn't finish his sentence. The side of his head exploded with brain, blood, and bone matter.

With his ears ringing from the supersonic bullet that had passed near him, Pierce dropped to the scorched earth, knowing the kill of a sniper when he saw one. Had Savannah survived the carnage, and was she the sniper protecting him from afar?

He hoped so. But he couldn't risk the chance that she was his saviour. Getting back up on his feet would make him an easy target should the sniper be a surviving drug smuggler, or Parra himself, waiting to take him out.

Instead, Pierce crawled around the blackened earth, using fallen debris and corpses as cover while ignoring the radiating heat on his hands and knees. He knew soot got inside his piranha wounds, but there was nothing he could do about that right now. When he reached the corpse of a soldier, he clawed a blackened AK from the dead man's brittle-boned fingers.

In the distance, the seaplane's turboprops spun faster. It now moved through the water, gaining speed.

Pierce first heard, then spied, bullets pinging off its hull and floats. The sniper no longer shot at him, but at the aircraft.

Someone else was trying to prevent the aircraft from taking off.

Was this Savannah?

Taking the risk that he wasn't the sniper's target, Pierce came up in a low crouch and sprinted towards the intact jetty where the seaplane had moored earlier.

When he reached the end of the jetty, he crouched on one knee and emptied the clip of the assault rifle at the far-off seaplane. His aim centred on the engine block and turbo-prop, so as not to hit Amelia. But with the distance that now separated them, his and the sniper's efforts were in vain. The aircraft soon gained speed and was quickly airborne and out of range. Pierce gritted his teeth and cursed as it grew smaller by the second, disappearing to the north, no doubt with Parra and Amelia on board.

They had failed in their rescue mission.

He checked the banana-shaped clip of his weapon and found it empty.

Then he saw across the water a modern speedboat a hundred metres from his position, anchored so it wouldn't drift, but bobbing in the current.

A tall Asian woman stared along the sights of a M40A5 sniper rifle aimed at him.

Pierce could have run for cover, but he knew if her intention was to kill him, she would have done so already.

Instead, she lowered the weapon and waved to him, like they were friends.

In his confusion, he didn't respond, not recognising her.

Expressing frustration, she shouted, but her voice got lost over the rushing water. He detected her accent was American, but nothing more.

When he shrugged and shook his head, she pulled up anchor and powered the speedboat to the jetty where Pierce stood.

Knowing he had time before she arrived, Pierce scooped up the fallen Browning 9mm from the corpse with the gold piranha belt buckle. He checked that it contained an almost full clip before he tucked the weapon into his belt at the small of his back.

With his heart rate slowing and the immediate dangers behind him, Pierce's bite wounds soon stung. He explored the ruined cantina until he unearthed an intact bottle of tequila. Screwing off the lid, he splashed the alcohol over his wounds. The sting intensified the pain he already felt, but at least he'd cleaned them of soot and other debris.

With the speedboat slowing as it reached the intact jetty, Pierce gathered up two spare thirty-round AK-47 clips from further fallen smugglers and waited.

As the Asian woman moored her boat, he recognised her.

Naked... Bound... Beaten...

It wasn't Mackenzie he had remembered. This was the woman he kept imagining, trapped in the chair, begging for him to come find her.

35

"**M**ark?" The woman brushed her long dark hair from her eyes, where it had escaped her ponytail.

Every muscle in her face expressed puzzlement, but he kept his expression impassive in response. Her arms, legs and neck were all long and slim, yet defined with muscle and devoid of recent wounds. Emerald eyes shone with an intensity Pierce had never encountered or could ever remember encountering in his life. Every aspect of her caused him to pause with fascination.

"What's up?"

The inflections in her words and the recognition in her stare implied she knew him, and she knew him well.

"Hi..." Pierce knew he knew her, but he could recall nothing about her.

"Are you okay?" She stepped close, expressing familiarity. Her hand touched his elbow.

He flinched because her fingers brushed his bite wound.

"What happened to you?"

"It's nothing."

She pouted. "With you, it's never nothing." With the same hand, she turned over his arm and flinched when she discovered the bite wound. "What the hell happened to you?"

He studied her, noticed how beautiful she was. Her attractiveness stirred a memory he couldn't grasp or hold on to, but one that stirred desire within him.

"Mark? You going to talk to me?"

"Sorry. Piranha bites."

"Seriously?" Shaking her head, she gestured with her thumb to the speedboat. "I've got a first aid kit back there and penicillin. Don't go anywhere."

He nodded, then held up his hand. "Wait. My friend..."

"Friend?"

"Yes. She and I... stormed this place."

"You made quite the mess."

Pierce nodded. "Her name is Savannah. I doubt she survived this... carnage. But I must look."

The woman stared at him. Her frown suggested that she required a better explanation.

"Savannah's Colombian intelligence. She saved my life more than once these last few days. I need to find her even if I only find her corpse. I owe her that much." Pierce didn't know why he was providing this stranger with information she didn't need to know, but his instincts screamed at him that she was on his side.

The Asian woman nodded, then gently bit her lower lip. "Okay, but your injuries need dressing. I'll get the kit. You look for her. But don't take too long. If that wound becomes infected..."

"Yeah, yeah. I know."

He watched her leave, observed how comfortable she was, being in his presence. There was no fear that he might turn against her.

Knowing that the Asian woman could wait, Pierce set off, ignoring the bite in his calf that caused intense stabs of pain each time he took a step. He circumnavigated the ruins of the tiny island where spot fires still burned, and the acrid stench of melted plastic and human flesh filled his nostrils. Many of the bodies were obviously men, but a few he could not guess their sex. What he searched for was a woman holding an Uzi or an assault rifle, close to where the cantina still burned with intense flames. He discovered many bodies, but nothing definitive.

"Mark?"

The Asian woman had returned and had prepared her field kit on the jetty where the seaplane had previously moored. It was the only space on the island that didn't burn.

He joined her.

She pointed to his calf. Blood and tequila stained his cargo pants. When she instructed him to take a seat on a step on the jetty, he obeyed. She went to work. First, she cleaned the wounds, then bathed them with antiseptic. Pierce tensed against the agony and tried not to show it on his face. His subconscious was clear that he liked this woman, wanted to impress her. His instincts told him he trusted her, which was an odd feeling, because for as long as he could remember, Pierce had only trusted one woman. That woman was Mackenzie Summerfield, and this Asian-American woman was not her.

As she bandaged his wounds, he took a risk with his next question.

"The CIA sent you?"

She halted with her bandaging and looked him in the eyes. "I thought you wanted to disappear. Hell, I even helped you fake your own death. I didn't think I'd ever see you again, but then you had to go shoot up a bunch of SEBIN operatives in Rio in a very public display of not being dead. You deliberately wanted to announce to the entire world you're back again?"

Her response answered many questions. They asked many more.

He nodded and licked his lips, tasting the salt of his perspiration. "I guess I did. But coming back out of the shadows wasn't intentional." He almost asked if the CIA were the second group to ambush him in Rio, and if so, why the CIA were helping him now. Instead, he held his tongue, knowing that to say less in this moment would allow him time to remember her, and his past, so as not to give away that his memory currently crippled him.

Finished with his dressing, she stood and placed her hands on her slender hips. He expected her to speak her mind. She certainly opened her mouth to speak several times, but remained silent.

"If the CIA really wanted me dead, we wouldn't be talking, right?"

She frowned again. "What the hell is up with you, Mark?"

He wanted to tell her he suffered short-term memory loss but couldn't trust that she was one hundred per cent on his side. If she wasn't, she could use the knowledge of his limitation against him, and he wouldn't know that she was. Why was he so confused with his intentions with this woman?

"Mark?"

He shrugged again and grinned. "You know, the past is the same as the present, with terrorists and assassins everywhere trying to torture and kill me. Sometimes you just want a vacation and get away from it all."

Once again, she shook her head. "You don't look well. Worse than when I saved your sorry ass in the Central African Republic. And yes, I know you are not very subtly dancing around the subject of why I'm here. Let me put your mind at ease. I'm bringing you in for debriefing at Langley."

"But—"

"No. You've been in the wilderness for too long, Mark. And I can't cover for you anymore. And don't worry, I know why you didn't want to come back to the CIA the first time. It was because you don't want to be an outside contractor. You want to be a salaried employee of the CIA again. I'm right, aren't I?"

She kept using his name, and he couldn't remember hers.

He imagined her again tied and bound and beaten in the chair, begging him to come rescue her. But that scenario seemed all wrong now. He knew he'd seen her naked before, because memories of her body were easy to imagine, and those memories were intimate. Perhaps she wasn't the woman he sought. Perhaps it was Mackenzie he imagined in that scenario, but didn't want to.

He wanted to ask why he'd gone dark, turned against his superiors and acted as if no one in the Central Intelligence Agency were trustworthy anymore, or if they ever had been. Pierce guessed she knew the answer to this question, but to ask would reveal his faulty memory.

"You're not in trouble, Mark, if that's what's got you all

worked up. We all know what happened. We know how Walsh betrayed and framed you."

Pierce risked voicing an assumption. "Then why send a kill team for me in Rio?"

She laughed. "I was told they were amateurs. Foes you could have easily defeated, which you did."

He frowned.

"Don't look at me like that. You're still alive. You still have friends in Langley."

When she spoke that last sentence, he knew there was a lie buried in there somewhere.

She glanced at her speedboat. "We should leave."

"No!"

"No?"

He stood, feeling the pain in his muscles and bite wounds now that he was moving again. With the bandages, the pain wasn't as intense. Still, he took painkillers from the field kit and popped them in his mouth. "No. I made a promise to rescue a young woman who is probably now halfway to Caracas. We finish that mission first before we come in."

"We?"

"Yes!" Pierce nodded, not yet certain that bringing this Asian woman with him was a sound strategy, but was doing so anyway. "You're coming with me."

36

The speedboat made good time as it powered northwards and downstream, always in the centre of the wide and muddy Orinoco River, with Colombia on the left and Venezuela on the right. There were few travellers or settlements this deep within the Amazonian jungle, comprised only of occasional fishermen in canoes, poor village communities, and old resorts or schools now long abandoned and falling into ruin.

The Asian woman directed the outboard motor while Pierce sat up front, with the loaded M40A5 sniper rifle in his grip, and its sights set for three hundred metres in anticipation of future threats. She showed no fear that he was armed. This spoke volumes regarding their past relationship, suggestive that they trusted and cared for each other deeply, but he still couldn't recall any past time spent with her.

He wondered why he hadn't yet told her he had short-term amnesia and couldn't remember. His instincts told him he should, but his rational mind fought against that idea. In the end, he settled on keeping this information to himself in the hope that something about her would come back to him so broaching the subject would be easier.

After an hour of downstream travel, they had barely talked. Mostly this was because the engine noises made conversation difficult, another good reason not to tell her his secret yet. Silence, however, gave him time to mentally prepare answers should she start asking difficult questions again.

Eventually Pierce identified a sight that caused him to tense that didn't involve his personal mental state.

"Hey!" He pointed to sandbanks on the Colombian coast surrounded by the thick rainforest foliage. "Over there, can you take us in?"

She turned the motor as she yelled over the noisy engine, "I have a name, or have you forgotten?"

Pierce laughed. This was one difficult question he had no answer for. "Of course not."

"Jennifer!" She frowned and pouted. "Sleep with a man once and he pretends he doesn't know you anymore. It's Jennifer. I can't believe you forgot."

He nodded. The name suited her. "I didn't think you liked me using your real name during an operation?"

She killed the engine and stormed towards him. "For fuck's sake, Mark Pierce! My name isn't Jennifer!" she snarled; then her eyes expressed concern. For the first time, she seemed to examine the many bruises and cuts prominent all over his body. "Wait a minute...? You seriously can't remember? I mean, you really can't remember my name?"

Pierce hesitated, mentally balancing whether to stick with his ruse or come clean. But this was an intelligent and perceptive woman, and she obviously knew him well. She would see through his lie soon enough if he kept up the pretence.

"No."

"No?"

He looked back at the sandbank and the shape he had spotted. They were drifting past and would soon lose sight of it if they kept with their current trajectory. "Pull up here. This is important, and I'll explain when we weigh anchor."

"You'd better."

It took several minutes to cross from the centre of the wide river to the sandbank, where they moored the boat. Pierce clambered out and marched to the body. There was no mistaking its identity as Savannah Fonseca. Her lifeless eyes lay open and unblinking. Half her face had blistered and peeled and was peppered with metal and wood fragments. He guessed she'd died instantly from her wounds, and the force of the blast had thrown her into the current, washing her downstream to this location. He looked away as his eyes lost focus and reddened. He didn't wish for his companion to guess at his distraught emotional state.

He forced himself to speak. "She was a good person."

The woman nodded.

"And I hardly knew her."

"Her name isn't Savannah, by the way. It's Juliana Munoz. She's DNI. Direccion Nacional de Inteligencia."

Pierce nodded, not surprised that his companion knew far more about this dead woman than he did. "I knew that, except for the name." He crouched down and closed Savannah's eyelids. He hoped the gesture would make her appear more peaceful. It didn't.

The Asian woman tensed. "What's my name?"

He stood and held her stare. It was time to come clean, and she had guessed already. "I don't know."

"Amnesia?"

He nodded. "It was a car crash."

"But you seem to know who you are? You answer to your name, and you know you are an operator with the CIA. You know a lot, but not everything?"

Pierce felt his hands tremble. "Yes. Seems I can remember everything until up to somewhere between three months and a year or thereabouts. It's fuzzy, trying to remember the sequence of events too, what happened when. I'm presuming you and I... we haven't known each other that long?"

She crossed her arms as her back stiffened. "You could say that."

"Well?"

"Well, what?"

"What is your name? I seriously can't recall it."

Her teeth bit upon her lower lip, and she stared through him like he was momentarily not there. Five seconds passed before she answered, looking him in the eye when she spoke. "It's Rachel Zang."

Pierce nodded again. The name brought no further clarity to his confused mind. "I like Rachel more than I like Jennifer."

"Liar!"

Pierce sighed, recognised that in the balance of all possibilities, coming clean would likely serve him better than keeping his guard up. He'd worn armour all his adult life, shielding him from really feeling anything, because he'd had to. But locking out his friends from ever really knowing him came with a cost, and it was only now, when Pierce felt like he was losing everything because he couldn't remember what he had in his life to lose, that he realised he wanted, desperately, to connect back into the world somewhere and somehow. Perhaps Rachel Zang was his path back to salvation.

"Six days ago, in Rio de Janeiro, I experienced a car accident. I think it knocked me out, but I can't remember. All I know is for the last few days no memories in my immediate past have stuck, but recently some have started sticking, and only snippets are seeping back in. Bizarrely, really old memories remain intact. I'm sorry if I can't remember you, Rachel Zang. I want to. I really do. I feel like our relationship... was..." He didn't finish the sentence because he had been about to say "intimate". If he was wrong...

She wiped her hands across her eyes, then looked away.

Perhaps he wasn't wrong, remembering her quip about sleeping with a man one time.

He felt wetness on his own cheeks. Then he quickly wiped it away. What was wrong with him, to react with such overt, weak emotions?

She stepped up to him, hesitated, then opened her arms, and hesitated again.

Pierce stepped forward and hesitated too.

Then they hugged and held each other close until he felt her heartbeat race with his.

He thought the hug would be brief, but she didn't let go, and neither did he.

Pierce wanted to remember her. He knew it was important for them both to embrace her back into his life, but how could he achieve this when his mind fought a war against him?

After a minute of just holding, sensing, feeling the presence of each other, they released. Rachel wiped her eyes again, and Pierce found he had to do the same. Emotions were welling up inside him, exploding outwards. He couldn't control it, and he didn't like it.

"We need to get you back stateside, Mark. You can't operate like this. You need medical attention."

"No."

"Bullshit."

"No! We must save Amelia Reyes first. You know who she is, I take it?"

Rachel nodded. "She'll be in a white torture cell by now, inside La Tumba, where we'll never reach her."

It frustrated Pierce this was a detail learned in his past that he did recall. La Tumba served as the sixteen-story headquarters of SEBIN, with five basement levels lined with concrete cells merely two by three metres wide, located in the heart of Venezuela's capital, Caracas. Each cell remained constantly bathed in white light shone upon white walls, and absent of noise, subjecting political prisoners to prolonged sensory deprivation. Rachel was correct. Rescuing Amelia from that fortress of a building would be near impossible.

"We still have to try."

Rachel stared at him again. She gave no indication that she agreed or disagreed with his proposal.

Then, without answering, she stepped past Pierce and withdrew a torch from her pocket, which Pierce noticed shone with ultraviolet light. Crouching next to Juliana Munoz's body, Rachel tore open her T-shirt to shine the light across the corpse's flaccid skin.

A tattoo appeared, invisible until the ultraviolet rays

shone upon it. The tattoo was a circle within a circle, both dissected by a straight line.

"Do you know what that is?" Rachel asked.

Pierce shook his head, but felt he had seen it before, and more than once.

"She wasn't your friend, and she didn't work for DNI."

"Then who did she work for?"

Rachel stood and dusted beach sand off her cargo pants. "That's what we need to find out, fast, before our ignorance gets us killed."

37

Port-au-Prince, Haiti

I dris Walsh rewatched the hacked satellite footage of an island consumed by fire. His body rigid, and barely blinking or breathing, he waited forty seconds for the destructive flames to dissipate. Then he observed again the man he had watched before the explosion erupted. That man now swam to the surface and pulled himself onto a burning jetty before he sprinted to dry land. Then the satellite moved beyond observable range, and the image turned to static.

It wasn't a lengthy feed, but it was enough. Cross-referenced against other intelligence he'd collated through the night, Walsh felt confident the man he'd just watched was Mark Pierce.

The Trigger Man.

The former CIA spymaster leaned back and allowed his mind to process what he'd seen.

An idea struck. Suddenly Walsh saw how he could draw

Pierce into a trap while still executing Mr Real's rabies-infestation operation. He would end his nemesis's life while keeping good with his new employers.

"What's got you smiling?"

Taisiya Ozerova watched him suspiciously from over the top of her monitor and her mug of black coffee.

He stared at his co-worker and froze his fake smile.

Formerly of the Russian Federal Security Service, or FSB, Ozerova was a forty-something intelligence analyst who spoke English with the same proficiency as Walsh, which was how they conversed because he hadn't let on his Russian was as good as hers. A blonde, she was pale skinned, and skinny like a fitness addict. Her style was tight black jeans, black boots and a chest-hugging black sleeveless T-shirt, which seemed out of place in the tropics where everything else was bright and colourful, but made her unique.

Walsh hadn't asked her what her story was, and how she came to be in Port-au-Prince, employed by a global secret organisation that had their talons clawed deep into them both, but he hadn't wanted to. Her story was likely as convoluted as his own, and asking would only prompt her to ask him similar questions about things he didn't wish to reveal. Nobody got into the business of spying because they wanted to share.

"Tell me!" Her request came across as an order. "You never smiled until now."

Walsh tapped a pencil against his teeth. "I'm not sure I should..."

"Show me!"

She rolled her chair across the wooden floorboards to join him at his monitor. Their air-conditioned steel-framed hut comprised multiple monitors, desktops, laptops, data cables, servers and uplinks, connecting them via backdoors into the databases of various intelligence organisations and Indian, Japanese, Canadian and French spy satellite networks. Ozerova's specialty was hacking data without leaving a trail. Walsh's expertise was compiling data into cohesive intelligence reports to support ongoing ground operations. Together, they prepared for the organisation's next genetically modified rabies assault on Venezuela, and what they had achieved in a short period had impressed Walsh.

"That explosion... It happened yesterday. A refuelling station for drug traffickers. Why is that of interest?"

"Let me show you." Walsh flicked screens to a French satellite feed that had tracked the unregistered flight of a Quest Kodiak seaplane across Venezuela. Walsh's interest in it was because it had departed the island during the destruction and had flown directly to a private airfield on the outskirts of Caracas. Two passengers departed, a man and a woman, before the seaplane continued north across the Caribbean Sea, headed for Florida. "I'll tell you why I'm interested, Ozerova, when you identify these two individuals."

She crossed her arms and leaned back in her chair. "I could do that if I wanted to. Why do you want to know? And why should I?"

Walsh shrugged. "Forget it. It's probably nothing. Like you said, just drug smugglers." He wanted the Russian to believe he was far less competent than he was. But he also wished to understand how many risks she would take to help him, and therefore determine how easily he could manipulate her.

Ozerova stared at him for many seconds, projected an air

of ambivalence, then switched her posture when she leaned forward and uncrossed her arms. "Are you certain it's nothing?" She pushed him aside and went to work on his screen. Within minutes, she zoomed in on the image, improved its resolution using software and techniques he had never mastered.

"A pack of cigarettes, Ozerova, says you can't identify these characters before I do."

"Challenge accepted." She emailed a data pack of Walsh's satellite grabs to her desktop and got to work.

Walsh suspected the woman was Amelia Reyes, and the man was one of the SEBIN operatives he'd fought off in Rio de Janeiro just before Pierce had kidnapped him in the favela. To test his hypothesis, he ran facial recognition against known images of Reyes and narrowed his search on the man against known SEBIN or FAES operatives.

Thirty-eight seconds later, he had hits on both. Amelia Reyes told him nothing he did not already know. The man, however, was a ninety-five per cent match to Sergeant Maceo Parra, a FAES-trained sniper and soldier and an occasional freelance assassin who also went by the name "Comic Book Killer". Walsh soon found out why, discovering several uploaded illustrations he'd posted on an Instagram account under the name "Carl Seltz". All his posted illustrations depicted men inflicting tortures or executions of other men and women. Walsh admitted to himself that Parra was talented. He particularly enjoyed one illustration of a shadowed government man torturing a muscular bound and naked man sweating under a lamp shade with electric cables attached to his nipples. Walsh liked it because he saw himself and Pierce as the torturer and the tortured respectively.

Walsh turned his thoughts back to the mission and guessed that Pierce would follow both Parra and Reyes to the ends of the earth, driven by his skewered sense of justice to both rescue the agitator and to exact revenge against SEBIN operative.

The Trigger Man was so predictable.

Walsh pretended to continue with his search, expressing occasional groans of frustration, until Ozerova let out a squeal and raised her fisted hands high over her head. "I did it!"

Now Walsh leaned back and crossed his arms. "Prove it."

"He's Maceo Parra. A real BAMF. A badass motherfucker assassin working for SEBIN."

Walsh resisted a smile. Her finds confirmed his own research was solid. "What about the woman?"

"Give me a minute." Ozerova pounded her thin fingers over the keyboard. Seconds later, her jaw dropped. Her face turned paler than Walsh thought possible for an already pasty Russian. "Shit!"

"What's the problem?"

She stared both at him and through him. "How did you know, Walsh?"

"How did I know what?"

Ignoring him, she radioed Mr Real and spoke to him in Russian. She asked him to come to her immediately.

Minutes later, Mr Real and Alpha Mansaray joined them, and they all pinned their stares on Walsh's monitor.

It was the Nigerian who leaned over Walsh and snarled his question. "Walsh! How the fuck could you find Amelia Reyes so easily, when the rest of us couldn't?"

38

Walsh turned in his chair and stared down at the gazes of the three sets of eyes staring at him. Alpha Mansaray was the most physically impressive of the three, but his intelligence wasn't in the same league as the Italian, Mr Real, nor did either man possess the technical or analytical skills that Taisiya Ozerova commanded. Together, the three were a formidable opponent, but individually, Walsh knew he was better than all of them. They didn't know it, but he was in control here.

"Let me run a scenario past you. Interrupt me if I get any of the details wrong." Walsh paused, daring them with his stare to interrupt him, but no one said a word. "I see how in Rio I disrupted your scheme. You wanted Amelia Reyes in play because when you release the modified rabies virus to infect the Venezuelan military, you were ready with fake intelligence your activist could use to 'prove' this was all the president's doing. With her popularity, she was to be the catalyst that would push the country into a civil war."

Mr Real was calm when he said, "Is that right, Mr Walsh?"

The American spymaster shrugged. "You said it yourself, Mr Real. I'm good at what I do. I put puzzle pieces together, and I see the reality of any situation."

The Italian scratched his neck. "Reyes would still be in play in Rio if you hadn't tried to sell her to SEBIN. She wouldn't be a problem now."

Walsh opened his arms wide in a peace-making gesture. "I didn't know you people existed back then. If I had, I would have acted differently, but that's all in the past. I know where SEBIN will take her, and how we can remove her from the picture once and for all."

"But we don't want her dead," said Ozerova, revealing that she was privy to more information regarding this operation than Walsh had given her credit for. "How does 'removing her from the picture' help?"

"If she is dead, she can't contradict you, and SEBIN will use her to do just that. Besides, I know you'll already have deep-fake videos of her ready to upload, spouting all the false-flag tales of woe you want the world to believe about public enemy number one. *El Presidente Incompetente.*"

Mr Real rubbed his close-cropped beard as he studied Walsh. "You are a slippery snake, aren't you, Mr Walsh? You've worked it all out."

He grinned. "Tell me I'm wrong."

Mr Real returned the grin. "You're not wrong. What is your plan? Prove to me that keeping you alive and working for us is worth all the trouble you caused."

Walsh turned to his screen, then pulled up a file on La Tumba. "You all know about SEBIN's headquarters and their five basement levels where they torture dissidents. Reyes will end up here, if she hasn't already."

Mansaray flexed his muscles. "That's not so hard to guess. How do you plan to take her out now that she is effectively unreachable inside this fortress?"

"You must have a list of SEBIN officers working in that building."

"The plan, Mr Walsh?"

"I'm presuming the rabies virus can be spread just through the use of aerosol cans?"

Mr Real and Mansaray nodded.

"Well, we establish your people outside La Tumba, about a block out. When they spot any known SEBIN operatives returning to the building, and particularly if they are bringing in arrest individuals, they subtly spray and infect them. Before SEBIN knows it, first their dungeons, then their command centre will come under infection, spreading the rabies virus everywhere. In no time, we decimate Venezuela's only effective intelligence organisation. Everyone inside that building, including Reyes, dies, and the only force that might have seriously challenged this operation to take control of Venezuela's oil, we will have crippled, if not destroyed, at its very heart."

Walsh watched Mr Real as he processed the plan, and he was soon nodding. "Okay, Mr Walsh, I'm listening. But we need more. Taking out SEBIN is a good next step, but what if we still cannot convince the president his oil is our oil? What is the next step after that?"

Returning to his monitor, Walsh pulled up a Google Maps image of western Venezuela where it bordered Colombia. "If you wish to instigate real chaos in the country, you strike here, here and here." He pointed to three major border-crossing points into Colombia at Maracaibo near the Caribbean Sea, San Cristobal deep inland but within the Cordillera de Merida range, and Puerto Paez near the Amazon rainforests in the south. "GHB and the Army are thick on the ground in all three locations, preventing Venezuelans from fleeing their country and preventing Colombian aid from getting in. Riots and violence are constant in all three locations, and if rabies starts spreading here, the world's media will know about it pretty damn quickly, because they can easily witness it unfold across the border. The Colombians watch everything that goes on down here closely."

Alpha Mansaray grinned.

So did Mr Real.

Ozerova expressed shock. Then she quickly masked her emotions before anyone other than Walsh noticed.

"It won't be difficult," Walsh said. "You operate small teams in each location, armed with the aerosols and with rabies vaticinations already administered, and perhaps additional vaccine as backup should we need it. That's all we have to do to infect thousands. The virus will do the rest. The world's media will learn about it pretty damn fast, and therefore the Venezuelans will have a hard time covering up as it gets out of control."

Mr Real patted Walsh on the shoulder. "I'm impressed." He turned to Mansaray. "See, much better than your ideas." As the Nigerian mercenary smarted, the Italian turned his attention back to Walsh. "We hold off infecting the borders until after the attack on SEBIN headquarters. La Tumba should be enough for the president to capitulate to our demands, and contains the outbreak to a single building. If we can help it, we take Venezuela without causing a pandemic."

Walsh resisted his urge to grin. Mr Real and his underlings had played into his scheme exactly as he had hoped they would.

"Mr Mansaray, I want you on the ground coordinating the La Tumba attack. Mr Walsh, you and Ms Ozerova can coordinate the San Cristobal strike. I have people who can coordinate the other two border assaults."

"What?" Walsh's jaw dropped. He had not expected that he would be operational in the field again, in the direct firing line and potentially in direct engagement with Mark Pierce. An encounter Walsh did not have the physical or combat skills to survive. His gut twinged, reminding him of his wound and another man's liver that kept him alive, and how he was not the man he had once been.

Mr Real grinned. "You thought you'd stay here, nice and safe and cosy, did you? No, Mr Walsh, we all do what our organisation asks of us, and this is what we ask of you."

Walsh felt sweat run down the side of his temples as he felt the raw tattoo itch where it had been forged onto his chest. "What about the rabies? How do I protect myself, with my already weakened constitution?"

The three others in the room all smiled. Mr Real threw him a jet injector syringe, designed to deliver high-pressure liquids just under the skin rather than by penetration with a needle. "You didn't think we'd play with this enhanced version of rabies without protecting ourselves first?"

The former CIA spymaster turned the jet injector over in his hand. "You mean...?"

"Yes, Mr Walsh. We have vaccinations against the

enhanced airborne strain we created. Our organisation is that good. Normal rabies vaccinations, if taken in the last six months, will prevent you catching our souped-up version only fifty per cent of the time. And those odds drop off pretty fast after that the longer since your last shots. But don't worry, if you have contact with the virus, shoot this into your body within twelve to twenty-four hours of exposure, and you'll be fine. We have noticed that victims often get fevers in that period, but again, shoot the vaccine into you during that period, and you'll recover quickly enough with no lasting damage. After that period though, the virus is one hundred per cent fatal, with or without the vaccine."

Walsh shuddered. "Your organisation really has thought this all through."

"Yes. Venezuelan oil is worth billions to us. Hundreds of billions. So we want to do this right the first time. We can't have anyone else controlling a virus we can threaten to spread like wildfire, do we, and risk our overall plan? The threat of airborne rabies also stops anyone else from taking Venezuela's oil back from us once we have it."

Walsh nodded. His last rabies injection had been years ago, so this vaccination significantly increased his surviv-ability on this mission, presuming this was not a deceit designed to lure Walsh into a false sense of security.

Then Walsh smiled, this time with a genuine expression of his emotions. What Walsh had told no one, but was at the core of his scheme, was that this was a trap for Mark Pierce. Even if Pierce survived his attempt to rescue Amelia Reyes from La Tumba, which was unlikely, the assassin would then head west to cross over the border, attempting to make their escape into Colombia. That gave Walsh two opportunities to take Pierce out, using a deadly virus his enemy would not see coming. It all seemed too easy now.

Perhaps it was worth the risk of travelling to South America again, just to see the Trigger Man die.

"Fine, Mr Real. When do we leave?"

"Immediately!"

39

Caracas, Venezuela

Another hot day in Caracas, with clouds gathering across the sky, hinting at another downpour to saturate the already humid metropolis. In the rubbish dump overlooking the city and festering on the edge of the barrio, the place stank of sewer waters and sweet garbage. Dog packs roamed the compacted dirt and trash mounds, sniffing for morsels. Faded billboards pronounced the president's good deeds and presented his smiling face with the paper torn away from his eyes. A thin, dirt-smeared woman in her twenties huddled under a cardboard box as a shelter, shared with two younger boys who could have been her siblings or her children. It was impossible to know.

Director Garcia's convoy of five white Toyota Prados sped through the muck and refuge without their occupants giving the scene much thought. When the all-wheel drives reached Sergeant Maceo Parra, in chinos, desert boots and a light rain jacket to conceal his weapons, their tires squealed in the mud and churned a circle until they surrounded him like he was cattle being rustled. Parra didn't move from where he rested against his Ford sedan and just watched. Garcia realised he knew no one was about to kill him, at least not until he proved he'd delivered the goods, so acted casual.

FAES soldiers in their black suits, bulletproof vests, bala-clavas, with AR-15 assault rifles and Heckler & Koch MP5 submachine guns, soon surrounded Parra and menaced from behind their sun visors.

With the scene secure, Director Juan Garcia stepped from his vehicle, the first in the convoy. Today he wore khaki chinos, tan loafers and a long-sleeve white shirt with flowery vine patterns. He too wore sunglasses and swaggered over to Parra while still deciding what to do with this potentially volatile asset he supposedly had under his command.

"Sergeant Maceo Parra, back from the dead, I see."

They shook hands. Soon their grips turned competitive to see who could crush whose fingers. It was no competition, and soon Garcia released his hand as he smarted from the pain Parra had caused him.

"I'm not dead, Director."

"You cost me a lot, you son of a bitch. An entire team. I hope you came bearing gifts, as you promised."

Parra remained motionless for the count of several seconds, then pushed himself off his sedan, and opened the trunk. Two timid eyes blinked up at him as they adjusted to the sunlight. A frail Amelia Reyes still wore the same yellow dress, but with its many stains and tears, it barely clung to her and presented as an off-brown colour. Parra had hog-tied and gagged her, which would have cramped her muscles. The dyke moaned, then struggled when she caught sight of the half dozen FAES soldiers in her line of sight.

"Fuck your mother!" Garcia's mouth dropped. "Parra, that's Songbird! You fucking did it!"

Parra didn't answer as he drew his black tactical fighting knife and cut the rope until only Reyes's wrists remained bound. He pulled her to her feet, then steadied her because she'd grown weak in his captivity. He pushed her over to Garcia, and he caught her when she staggered into his embrace. Garcia looked Reyes over until he felt satisfied that she was the woman he had invested too much time and money to capture, all on the whim of their egotistical and narcissistic president.

"Good job. All is forgiven. You can rejoin FAES."

Parra shook his head.

"What the fuck? It's not like there are options for you, my friend."

Parra examined the FAES soldiers surrounding him, as if the fool thought he could calculate his odds of surviving a gunfight here. Because of Parra's questionable actions over the last week, Garcia had prepped his men to shoot Parra down like a dog if he gave the word or displayed a prearranged hand signal, but for the moment, he didn't feel the need to do so. He wanted to understand why Parra thought he held any power here.

"Sergeant!"

"No, Director. I quit. I'm going solo."

Garcia frowned, then grinned, then broke out in laughter, not believing what he was hearing from this upstart. "What the fuck are you talking about?"

"I've learned much this last week. I've learned I'm fucking good at what I do."

Laughter brought tears to Garcia's eyes. "What the fuck?

Think you will make it big time as a comic artist? You're not that good."

"No. I'm talking about going it solo as a freelance contract killer."

Garcia paused, then handed off an almost unconscious Amelia to the nearest soldier. The younger man bagged her and forced her into the cabin of the third Prado.

Then a thought occurred to the director. "Is this about the American assassin the Chinese will pay good money for?"

Parra nodded. "I've given you Amelia Reyes. My reward is that you don't send anyone after me, and we part on good terms."

Garcia eyeballed Parra for many seconds, his facial muscles tensing now that he no longer saw the humour in their conversation. "I don't think so. Returning Reyes was your job. It's what I fucking pay you to do."

"No!"

"No?" Garcia almost raised his hand in the signal for his men to gun Parra down, but his curiosity got the better of him. "Why the fuck should I listen to this shit?"

With every muscle tensed, Parra stepped forward.

Garcia flinched as if the sergeant had struck him, and stepped back. Then he recovered and stood tall to mask his embarrassed moment of expressed terror. How had that happened?

But true to their loyalty to him and not Parra, several of his FAES soldiers raised their weapons, warning Parra to stand down.

But Parra ignored them and instead focused only on Garcia. "You should listen, Director, because what I do next also serves you and will save your life."

"Donkey's balls!"

"Listen to me. The assassin who took out the rest of my team in Rio, he is good, but he's not as good as me. If I don't stop him, no one else will, and he will come for you. He knows you now have Amelia Reyes, and that is his ultimate prize, regardless of who gets in his way."

Garcia still couldn't believe what he was hearing. "My men can take out this assassin."

"If you believe that, Director, then kill me now."

Another lengthy silence stretched out between them.

Garcia stared off across the horizon, where a Boeing 747 passenger airliner trailed across the sky. It wouldn't land in Venezuela. It was merely transiting their once fine nation, because there was nothing here for visitors to see or experience except death and misery. Eventually, Garcia took in a deep breath, gritted his teeth and turned again to his supposed subordinate. "Give me the assassin's name."

Parra shook his head.

"Playing this one close to the chest, Sergeant?"

Again, he gave no answer.

"I'll tell you what, I might as well fucking make a deal with you because it's no loss to me how all this fucking mess works out, now I have Songbird again. I don't know why, but the Chinese want this man alive, and they'll pay ten million US dollars for the privilege. So I'll agree to this. You bring him in. I'll set up the exchange. That seems fair, so you and I split the reward down the middle. Only then will I allow you to go your separate way."

"No!"

Garcia's face reddened as he tried not to unleash his fury as physical aggression. "You're not in a position to negotiate, Parra, no matter how fucking 'cool' you think you are. One word, and my men — your former buddies — will gun you down where you stand. Their loyalty is to me, not you. Not for the only survivor of a massacre where all their other buddies died."

Parra kept his nerve, and this both impressed and troubled Garcia. He spoke his next words calmly and slowly, without any emotional inflection. "And you'll be dead days later, Director, when the assassin tracks you down. You know what he was capable of in Rio. Do you want to take that risk now, when he is already here in Caracas, profiling you as we speak?"

Garcia tightened his fists as a vein pulsed in his left temple. He knew Parra was likely correct in this assumption, but could Parra's offer really be the way to solve this problem?

Parra stretched his back to stand taller. "Two million."

"What?"

"If you set up the deal with the Chinese, then your split is two million. That seems fair to me."

Garcia paced. "What if you don't bring him in?"

"Then the assassin will have killed me, and I'll never be a problem for you ever again."

"And then he comes for me?"

Parra shrugged. "I can't help you if I'm dead. In anything."

"Then you'd better fucking kill him." Now Garcia stood taller, smirked, then took a white handkerchief from his pocket to dab at the sweat forming across his brow. "Three million!"

Parra consider the offer for a moment. "Very well. We have a deal."

The two men stared at each other for a count of ten

seconds. Then Garcia, bored of this conversation and remembering that he had Reyes now, felt keen to get her back to La Tumba and ready her for humiliation. He put his hand forward, and they shook. No unfriendly vice-like grips this time.

"You really want to go freelance, Parra?"

The sergeant nodded. "If everyone around me can be false and profit from it, why shouldn't I? I'm just choosing a new identity that suits me."

"That of a freelance assassin?"

Parra shrugged. "Why not?"

Garcia chuckled. "You already have a code name. The comic book killer is what I hear everyone already calls you."

Parra expressed emotion for the first time, and in this instance it was disgust. "No."

Garcia broke into further laughter, finding Parra's intense seriousness unnerving and wanting to hide how he actually felt. But his laughter soon became infectious, and his men also laughed at Parra. "We'll see, 'Comic Book Killer', we'll see. Who the fuck do you think you are? Some Rubicon want-to-be?"

"Who?" Parra asked, not understanding the reference.

"You don't know?" Garcia frowned, remembering the assassin he had hired once for a very delicate assignment that the Rubicon operative had pulled off rather spectacularly. "Just the scariest, highest-fucking-paid assassin the world has ever seen, Parra. If you want to play with big boys like him, and you don't know who he is, then you won't last long in this world."

Parra seemed to consider this for a moment.

Garcia, however, was growing more and more bored with the conversation now he had what he wanted. "If we meet again, you'd better have the fucking American assassin bound and gagged like you did Reyes. The reward is only worthwhile to me if you bring him back alive."

"I will."

Garcia turned his finger in a circle. The FAES soldiers stepped back and climbed into the five Toyota Prados, with Garcia joining them in the vehicle they had locked Amelia Reyes in. He felt he might torment her on the long drive back to SEBIN headquarters, because that would be fun.

40

After a night and day of driving, Zang and Pierce
crossed nearly four hundred miles of central
Venezuela to reach Caracas's outskirts by late
afternoon. Three further hours of navigation through the
congested and National Guard–patrolled road networks of
Venezuela's capital brought them to the residential district of
Los Palos Grande. The wealthy city sector featured streets
lined with trees, palms and ferns. Those same streets
featured potholes, walled houses and secure residential
towers, overlooked by the jungle-clad mountainous peaks of
Parque Nacional El Avila. Many people walked the pavements, most of them elderly couples. Many cars rusted on
the roadsides, vehicles too expensive to maintain, even for
the well-off and educated citizens who lived here.

As the sun dipped on the horizon, Zang pulled them into
the driveway of the CIA safe house Patricia Knight had
briefed her on before departing Miami. She keyed in the
eight-digit PIN code and drove them into the semi-under-
ground car park. The rusted and near-decrepit Toyota

hatchback Pierce had stolen in Cabruta upon the Orinoco River didn't look out of place, but it was prudent to hide such vehicles from public view.

With the garage door closed behind them, Pierce turned to Zang and grinned. His eyes were bloodshot, and his pupils dilated. The bruises and cuts on his face, hands and arms, visible where he had rolled up his shirtsleeves, were many, and most of them were fresh. He didn't look to be in a good way.

"We made it," he said.

"Yeah. Lots of fun, that was."

Together they explored the safe house to ensure they were alone and that the three-storey facility was secure. Zang noted the bulletproof glass, steel-reinforced doors and rushed paint job on one wall that probably had an interesting story behind it that they would never know. Such was the nature of working for the intelligence services.

She found the false floorboards Knight had directed her to, pulled them aside and opened the large safe embedded in the concrete foundation. Inside were many pistols, assault rifles, explosives, field kits, radios, laptops, surveillance gear, climbing equipment, military-grade medical kits and a host of additional tools — more than enough resources any operator could reasonably need. Zang collected a Glock 19 for Pierce and a SIG Sauer P320 semi-automatic for herself and three spare magazines for both. She threw the Glock at Pierce, who caught it nimbly but with a shaky left hand.

"You okay?" Zang had noticed the body shakes the previous time the two had operated together in Central Africa and Angola. Now he also suffered with amnesia, and she asked herself how far beyond operational capacity he actually was. Was helping him to continue with his personal mission worth the risks to her own safety and ongoing career with the CIA?

Pierce shrugged. "Memories are sticking, Zang, but I still can't remember much about the recent past or you. Sorry."

"What do you remember?"

He looked away, and Zang detected an embarrassed stare.

"Tell me?"

"We've... been together? Shared... intimate moments?"

Zang nodded as her heart fluttered. It had both worried and annoyed her that Pierce could not remember the physical couplings they had enjoyed. Sexual intimacy with Pierce had scratched a need she otherwise could not fulfil in her secretive and lonely profession as a clandestine operative of the CIA. She wasn't certain she wanted more than casual hook-ups with Pierce in the future, but she didn't wish for a platonic relationship with this man either, which seemed to be their current status with his head injury.

"Rachel... were you... tied up and beaten recently? Naked?"

Zang stood and crossed her arms. Not the question she expected, and she felt a little insulted, even though she guessed this was not Pierce's intention. "It's how we first met. Why?"

Pierce massaged his forehead. "I'm sorry. I keep having these images of a woman tied to a chair, naked and beaten, asking me to come find and rescue her."

Zang reflected on their last twenty-four hours together. During the drive north, she had witnessed a man who was confused, physically exhausted and badly beaten. She didn't dismiss the possibility Pierce faked his illness, but her instincts and careful observations of his actions told her he wasn't. Regardless, she remained wary of Pierce and his motives, because his short-term amnesia might have resulted in other mental impairments that could compromise their time together. Whatever the truth, no option seemed a good one.

"Zang, is it you I'm remembering?"

"No. Different circumstances."

Pierce nodded. "I'm sorry. It's the one memory that keeps coming back to me, but I can't hold it. Can't solidify in my mind who the captured woman is."

"Let's hydrate and talk about it."

They entered the kitchen. Zang boiled the kettle and made two black teas. She added sugar to perk them both up after a lack of decent sleep during last night's long drive. Each had snatched naps while the other had driven, but that was all they had been, snatched moments.

Zang noticed the bag of fresh groceries resting on the counter, which Pierce had purchased on their trip north. The food had cost them the equivalent of over five hundred US dollars because of the out-of-control inflation Venezuela suffered, and the only people making money were racketeers overcharging on any goods still worth buying, such as fresh edible food. She was glad of the provisions now because the house stocked only MREs, military meals-ready-to-eat, and she could do with a supplement of fresh fruit and vegetables into her diet.

They sat in the lounge and sipped their teas.

"Have you thought, Pierce, that your amnesia might be psychological rather than neurological?"

"What do you mean?"

She paused, knew that what she was about to tell Pierce, he might not be ready to hear, but it was information he needed to know. "Mark, do you remember Mackenzie Summerfield?"

"Yes!" The mention of Summerfield brought a smile to his face. "She's my case officer and friend. We worked together in Yemen and West Africa."

Without realising she had, Zang had rested her hand on Pierce's knee. He didn't seem bothered by the affectionate gesture, so she left it there. "She *was* your case officer. The CIA forced her out close to a year ago now, when you disappeared."

"Disappeared?"

"You've been on the run from the CIA for nearly twelve months, Mark. Do you remember any of that?"

Pierce gripped his head, as if experiencing intense pain inside his skull. "Flashes... Bits and pieces... I remember imprisonment in a warlord's camp in the African jungle."

"That happened, yes. Your enemies, who held you hostage, also framed you as a terrorist, but Langley now knows all that was a lie. It's safe for you to come back in."

"Then why was a kill team sent to take me out in Rio?"

Zang shuddered. "That was... a misunderstanding." She cleared her thoughts and focused her mind. "Look, Pierce, three months ago, I helped you fake your death in Angola because the CIA wanted to use you as a double agent, non-official cover operative against this organisation we keep coming up against. But now, knowing what we didn't know then, and seeing you in your deteriorated operational state —" The comment caused Pierce to raise a questioning eyebrow, but she ignored it and kept talking. "Well, everyone has realised it's better for all of us if you are back working on the inside again. A fully instated SOG Ground Branch operator, like me."

Pierce nodded, as if this statement was simple and easy for him to accept, yet everything else they had discussed distressed him. "Well, we can discuss all that later, once we have secured Amelia. But what were you saying about Mackenzie Summerfield?"

Zang moved her hand from his leg to his back and rubbed it. "I'm saying, Mark, that Mackenzie disappeared three months ago. The same time you and I last saw each other. No one has seen her since. But I'm wondering if you have. If this organisation we came across has snatched her and shown you images of what they are doing to her."

Pierce's gaze intensified.

"I'm sorry. I'm saying the naked and beaten woman you keep remembering, it's a strong possibility that she is Mackenzie."

"You mean...?"

"Yes, Mark, your friend is likely a hostage of the people we are fighting here in Venezuela. And they are using her captivity against you."

Pierce nodded. "Only, I can't remember why or how."

41

P ierce sat for a minute, not speaking or moving.

Zang studied him. He looked to be in shock.

Their previous time together, Pierce had always acted as a consummate professional, a special forces trained CIA operator with honed situational awareness, physical fortitude and a calculating and quick mind, despite the physical and mental injuries he had suffered at the time. She didn't see that competence now. She worried Pierce was a broken man who couldn't be put back together.

Then, before her eyes, he composed himself. His back straightened. His eyes gained their focus. Every muscle in his body tightened, ready for action. In an instant, he was the man she had once known.

"It must be a lot to take in, Mark. You need time to process, and I need time to report in."

"Thanks, Rachel," said Pierce with a forced grin. "But I'm okay. Let's see this through, and please ensure Langley provides you with everything we need, as we discussed earlier."

Zang smiled, then headed into a bedroom, securing the door behind her.

Reassembling the satellite phone she'd purchased in the Dominican Republic during her transit from the States to Venezuela, she dialled the private cell phone number of Patricia Knight. A burner phone only known to the two of them. With the encryption software running on this and Knight's phone, Zang felt comfortable in using actual names rather than code words.

"Where are you?" Knight asked as soon as the line connected.

"Caracas."

"Is Trigger Man with you?"

"Yes."

"Then get yourself to the States, immediately."

"I can't do that."

The pause that followed was longer than Zang would have liked. Eventually Knight said, "Why is that?"

"Because Savannah Fonseca, who we know as Juliana Munoz, wasn't actually working for Colombia's DNI. That's why."

"What? Who was she working for?"

"The same organisation that provides intelligence to Morat Kozan."

"Bullshit?"

"No, it's true." Zang described the last twenty-four hours with Pierce, his short-term amnesia explaining his actions in Rio, and his call into Langley because he thought he was still on their payroll. She next described the circle within a circle tattoo discovered on Savannah's corpse. The same tattoo Zang had seen on Alpha Mansaray in Port-au-Prince and on the chest of a senior enforcer who operated within Morat's inner circle, witnessed from a time long ago.

Knight sniffled. "So Mansaray, Walsh, SEBIN and Amelia Reyes are all connected? How?"

Zang's eyes drifted to the door as she imagined Pierce behind it, eavesdropping on this conversation. Then she remembered safe houses included noise-dampening materials built into all walls and doors, allowing for privacy. It was unlikely Pierce was privy to what Zang and Knight discussed, despite her paranoia that suggested otherwise. "I don't know yet."

"Bring Pierce in. We'll work this out together."

"No. With all due respect, ma'am, we still don't know who the mole inside the CIA is. And I feel much more comfortable remaining outside the States, considering what happened to my peers."

Knight sniffled again, and Zang remembered Knight suffered ongoing hay fever. A year earlier, Zang had even hacked Knight's medical records to confirm this was true and not some ruse. Zang had learned long ago that it was always a mistake to take anything at face value. She worried she might be doing exactly that with Pierce.

"Ma'am, I'm presuming you still don't know who the mole is?"

"No, we don't. But getting back to matters at hand, because this *is* a secure line and the conversation goes no further, what do you hope to achieve by remaining in Caracas?"

Zang took in a deep breath. "Pierce has a plan. He still wants to rescue Amelia Reyes. Only then will he agree to bring her and himself in. He seems happy to return if he's back on the payroll, and not as an outside contractor, but only once we are done here."

Knight scoffed. "That's ridiculous. CIA intel suggests Reyes is already in SEBIN custody."

"Pierce's plan is sound. Risky, but it might just work."

"Tell me!"

Zang sighed. "Sorry, ma'am, but with the mole still in play, I can't. However, I need some audio files." She described her requirements.

"That seems doable. I'll talk to my senior intelligence analyst. Give me forty-eight hours."

"Twenty-four. We don't know what our window of opportunity will be, and the longer we wait, the more damage SEBIN will inflict on Reyes. SEBIN might have commenced torturing her already."

"Tell me, is Reyes worth it?"

Zang pondered the question, but the answer had been clear to her since teaming again with the Trigger Man. "You want to win Pierce over? This is how you do it. He feels he made a promise to her, which he intends to keep. And yes, I believe Reyes can help us piece together this conspiracy, which you and I have spent too many years failing to unravel. Finally we are starting to understand who they are and their reach. This is an opportunity for us, too. One we've never had before."

Knight was silent for a moment, then said, "Very well. I don't like it, but I know I can't stop you. I'll set up an extraction point for you in Cucuta, on the Colombian-Venezuela border."

Zang remembered Cucuta was a Colombian town, some six hundred miles west of her current location. "That's a lot of distance to cover on our own."

"With the Russians, Cubans and Chinese providing an arsenal of intelligence resources to the Bolivarian president, there is no way we can helo in discreetly and get you out. We'd be shot out of the air in minutes. But the Colombians, hell, they beg us to build secret bases in their country now, so extracting you from Cucuta is no problem. So if you want to attempt this hare-brained scheme to rescue Reyes, then this is the consequence."

Zang nodded, not that anyone other than herself noticed the gesture. Subconsciously, was she trying to convince herself that Pierce's scheme wouldn't get them both killed? Because that seemed likely in the balance of all possibilities.

"Thanks, ma'am. I'll wait to hear from you."

She was about to end the call when Knight said, "Wait..."

"Yes, ma'am?"

"You're an excellent operator, Zang. Good luck, but you don't need it. You know what you are doing."

With the call ended, Zang asked herself if she should be second-guessing her every action when her superior had faith in her? Perhaps she really did know what she was doing?

A minute later, Zang returned to the kitchen, where Pierce was at the stove, boiling rice and stirring beef and vegetables in a wok. Aromas were chilli, pepper, and garlic. It smelled wonderful, reminding her of dinners her now dead mother had often cooked up for her as a child. Those memories brought a tear to her eye.

Before Pierce noticed, she wiped away the physical manifestation of a memory she didn't wish to relive. "So, you know how to cook a girl a decent meal?"

He grinned. "I'm a man of many hidden talents."

She didn't doubt it, imagining that Pierce had found a

means to hear every word she had just discussed with
Patricia Knight.

"What did Langley say?"

"We're a go. Everything we need, Mark, we'll have in
twenty-four hours."

42

Guarico State, Venezuela

The Beechcraft King Air 250 turboprop shuddered and rattled as it managed a bumpy landing along the grass airstrip.

The rapid touchdown proved uneventful, much like the two-hour flight from Port-au-Prince into Venezuela had been. But for Idris Walsh, the journey included continuous nausea, vomiting, loss of appetite and abdominal pains like a knife continuously cut through the linings of his gut. It was Pierce's fault Walsh endured constant agony. Therefore, it was imperative the Trigger Man would pay for the former spymaster's discomfort with his life. At least Walsh now had a plan to make this happen.

When the aircraft taxied and halted, Walsh couldn't clamber outside fast enough.

With freedom of movement, he noticed the airfield was little more than a shack, with a navigation beacon in a remote and rural location surrounded by flat grassland dotted only with palm trees. Warm air carried humidity like it did in most of Venezuela, yet here in the vast wilderness, the air remained absent of human scents, diesel or garbage odours he often associated with Latin America nations.

What caught Walsh's attention were the many pickup trucks, all-wheel drives, and men in bright clothes with assault rifles and pistols. They weren't military. Walsh knew criminals when he saw them, their lack of discipline and disregard for situational awareness giving it away. This was a drug cartel-controlled airfield, a halfway point in the transportation of Colombian-, Peruvian- and Bolivian-cultivated cocaine, flown north into the United States. Mr Real's "business relationship" established with the cartels to ship cocaine into the Middle East offered the additional benefit of impunity for his organisation's flights to, from and within the country. Walsh had to credit the man. Mr Real thought of everything.

Taisiya Ozerova joined Walsh and offered him a Russian brand of cigarette. He shook his head and looked away. She shrugged and lit up while Walsh secretly enjoyed the taste of second-hand smoke that drifted to his nostrils. If he relented and enjoyed the high a cigarette would bring, Walsh knew he would lessen his life expectancy significantly. He wasn't ready to go there yet.

The Russian hacker pointed to flecks of vomit on his shirt. "I thought American men were tougher than that. Can't handle a little air turbulence?"

Walsh smirked as he brushed the dried bile off his clothes. "Yes, I embarrassed myself."

"It's not an attractive feature in a man."

The former spymaster lifted his shirt, showed Ozerova the bullet wound and the lengthy scar where skilled surgeons had cut open his gut and saved his life. "I lost my liver. The one I have now belonged to another man... or a woman. I don't know. I don't care who they were. But it fucked me up."

She dragged on her cigarette as her eyes looked him up and down. She pointed to the puckered bullet wound with her cigarette. "You get the man, or woman, who gave you that scar?"

"Not yet."

"Let me know when you do. I want to see what kind of man you'll become afterwards."

Walsh licked his lips. Did she just flirt with him?

She gestured toward Mr Real with the cigarette before drawing on it. "He's a 'real' man." Then she laughed, realising that, speaking English, she had made an unintentional joke. "They say he is everywhere. Can be in multiple locations at once. No one knows how he does it."

"It's all bullshit." Walsh's eyebrows pinched together. "Men like him love to cultivate legends around themselves. They believe it makes them more feared."

"What is it that you do, Mr Walsh, to make men, and women, fear you?"

"My actions," he said without hesitation. "Words, feelings, thoughts, and intentions mean nothing. Only your actions define you."

She nodded, as he appreciated the deeper meaning behind his words at the same time she failed to comprehend their significance.

Ozerova and Walsh turned and watched Mr Real negotiate with the cartel enforcers, which included the provision of five four-wheel drives of various makes, models, dents and scratches. The Italian fixer handed over bags loaded with cash, exchanged for larger bags of cocaine, which disappeared inside the King Air 250. The cartel had no comprehension as to the purpose of their real mission here. They cared only that they were getting paid.

With the transfers complete, Mr Real joined Walsh, Ozerova, Mansaray and five other paramilitary soldiers dressed in civilian gear. He cleared his throat, then addressed them. "You'll operate as four groups of two. You know your destinations. Keys are in the ignitions. Kit in each truck includes AN-94s, M16s and Makarov pistols, food and provisions, more vaccine and jet injector syringes, plenty of cash, and passports to get yourself out of the country. Don't fuck this up."

Walsh expected complaints or further questions, but everyone in the team kept silent. Walsh didn't know if he sensed professionalism or fear that held their tongues. Then he realised he sensed an equal mixture of both.

"This is for you." Mr Real handed Walsh a tiny bottle with seven tablets. Seven days' worth of anti-rejection medication.

Walsh took the bottle without comment.

Mr Real gave a salute. "This is where I leave you." He turned and returned to his aircraft, which would soon lift into the skies and disappear as if it had never been here.

Walsh didn't know why but suspected the two men would never again cross paths. The feeling was so strong, it felt like a premonition, which was odd because Walsh had no beliefs in higher powers, luck or fate.

43

"Come on." Ozerova pressed Walsh gently in the back to lead him to the closest four-wheel drive, distracting him from his morose thoughts. "You want to drive, or me?"

Walsh smirked. "I'll drive. With all this macho culture prevalent south of the border, you'll look out of place behind the wheel."

Ozerova smirked. "Spoken like a true, sexist man."

"Then I'll fit right in, won't I?"

Before they departed the cartel-controlled airfield, Walsh found their assigned pistols, which were Czechoslovak Cz 83s, variants of the Makarov with twelve 9×18mm rounds in the magazine. A Soviet Union–era weapon, the Cz 83 had an effective firing range of fifty metres. Not ideal, but Walsh mused it was better than nothing. If their mission went to plan, they wouldn't need firepower, but Walsh still tucked the weapon into his pants pocket, where it would remain within easy reach. He also checked that they had plenty of the aerosol cans loaded with the airborne rabies virus, and plenty of vaccine injectors should they need them. Everyone on the team had been injected with the vaccine that would supposedly protect them from the genetically modified virus, so in theory they had no chance of contracting it. But that was only what Walsh had been told, and it was not necessarily the truth. Either way, he was committed to this mission, because he had no other choice, not with an organisation as large and powerful as Mr Real's group "owning" him now.

As they drove out, Walsh noticed the cartel thugs paid them no attention.

Minutes later, Walsh found a paved but potholed road headed east. He calculated a five-hundred-mile journey ahead of them, which, in a country as devastated as Venezuela, would take twelve to twenty-four hours to cover. They would drive in shifts rather than stopping somewhere for the night, and take routes that avoided likely police checkpoints.

After an hour of driving, and the sun dropping on the horizon, Walsh noticed Ozerova's hand resting on his thigh. He didn't ask her to remove her palm.

A few minutes later, she rubbed his crotch, and soon he grew hard.

The country road remained empty of traffic, so Walsh pulled over and parked. She pulled off her pants and knickers, opened his belt and trousers, and crawled on top of him. Their bodies gyrated and pounded against each other. Her mouth sucked on his face; then they kissed with wet and wild adventure. His hand disappeared under her shirt, pulled a breast from her bra and tugged on a nipple. This brought her extra excitement, and soon, they both climaxed.

Panting and with a wet face, Walsh hadn't expected their coupling to end so quickly, but he wasn't a young man anymore.

She stayed on top of him for several minutes, hugging him.

"What was that for?" The pain in his abdomen stung again, but for a few minutes during their spontaneous fuck, his mind had ignored the sharp discomforts completely. He should fuck her again before the mission ended.

Ozerova ran her fingers through her hair, dragging its wet clumps off her face, then climbed off him. "Got any tissues?"

He found a roll of toilet paper and handed it to her. She wiped herself clean while he tucked himself back inside his pants and buckled his belt again.

Ozerova searched around for her knickers. "I sensed you wanted it. And I haven't had a good fuck in months." She found her knickers still inside her pants and pulled both back up along her slim legs until she covered herself again. "You're a man, right? You enjoyed it?"

"Of course." This was not a lie. It had been years since he had enjoyed the pleasures of a woman.

"Well?"

He raised an eyebrow.

She smirked. "Back to the mission?"

"Right."

After they'd driven for twenty minutes, Walsh suddenly understood Taisiya Ozerova's actions. She was terrified of Mr Real and his secret organisation as much as Walsh was. This was her attempt at building an alliance, to make him like her and feel emotionally responsible for her.

Walsh allowed himself the tiniest of grins. Ozerova could

not comprehend how futile her actions had been. There was only one woman in his life he would give up everything to protect, and it wasn't her.

44

Caracas, Venezuela

Three days after securing Amelia Reyes into his custody, SEBIN director Juan Garcia decided he needed a good fuck.

He'd wanted to torture and humiliate the lesbian, but word had come down from the president himself that no one was to touch her but him. His excellency had ordered Garcia to incarcerate Reyes in a white sensory deprivation cell, mentally break her before he found an opening in his schedule to have his way with her. The president would probably fuck Reyes against her will, because that was how men with power destroyed women who humiliated them. That had been Garcia's intention as well, to make her pay for the trouble she had caused him, but that choice was beyond him now. Still needing a good fuck, and to avoid negotiating with his wife for boring sex, he sought solace with his mistress.

There was no need for Garcia to negotiate his perversions with Daniela. She needed his money to both survive and to enjoy the lifestyle she had grown accustomed to under his protection. He gained pleasure knowing she pretended his perversions excited her as much as they did him. Power over women was the best of all aphrodisiacs.

For three years, Garcia had kept Daniela in a spacious apartment on the eleventh floor of a twelve-story residential tower in Las Mercedes, the capital's former district once renowned for its shopping and leisure activities. With the failed Bolivarian Revolution, most shops had permanently closed, and all the international brands once for sale in its many elegant shops had divested offshore. These days, the streets were quiet and empty except for occasional police and GHB patrols. A perfect location to hide away a mistress.

When Garcia's convoy of five white Toyota Prados reached Daniela's tower, two vehicles entered the underground car park while three parked outside to watch all points of entry.

In the car park, eight FAES soldiers in their black jeans and T-shirts, body armour, balaclavas, tactical gloves and baseball caps secured the building's interior. The eight comprised Garcia's most trusted men, armed with Heckler & Koch MP5 submachine guns and a variety of 9mm semi-automatic pistols, who fanned out in practised motions to assess for threats, then spread throughout the building to secure all entry and potential assault points.

Garcia's most trusted operator, Leopold Colmenares, alone accompanied the director during the one minute it took the elevator to ascend from the car park basement to the eleventh floor. At Daniela's door, Colmenares handed Garcia a bouquet of seven red roses, then stood to attention, his Beretta Px4 Storm pistol now in hand. The FAES operator was in for a long night.

After he knocked, a young woman with a pixie haircut and bright, doe-like eyes opened the door. Her eyes lit up when she identified Garcia and lit further when she spied the roses. She embraced the bouquet as her kiss on Garcia's open mouth lingered.

When they separated thirty seconds later, Garcia studied Daniela as he licked his lips. His twenty-two-year-old mistress was not overly tall, but her slim, toned figure was a piece of art. She wore a blood red dress with noodle straps across her bare shoulders. Her feet remained bare, as they should be.

"Juan, darling. Come in."

With a nod to Colmenares, Garcia stepped inside and locked the door behind him. "Daniela."

The apartment was modern, with sharp angular designs, olive green and beach sand-coloured textured walls, spherical low-hanging clusters of lights, and a mixture of slate floors and soft wool carpet. He had chosen well.

Daniela rushed to him, pressed her delicate hand to his heart as she kissed him again. "The flowers are beautiful, my love. You shouldn't have."

He smirked. "I think you are wearing too many clothes."

She smiled, turned so her back faced him, then shimmied out of her dress to discard it on the carpet. Underneath, she wore a red lacy teddy, cut to maximise the exposure of sensual flesh. Her bare bottom was both firm and soft, inviting a touch.

Before he could reach out, she turned so he could face her. Free of her dress, Daniela's breasts seemed larger, barely held in the flimsy fabric, and her dark nipples, visible through the transparent material, seemed to watch him with as much interest as her large brown eyes expressed.

Seeing her exposed and comfortable in her near nudity, Garcia remembered again why he spent so much of his money keeping her locked away in this private retreat, accessible whenever he felt the need to spoil himself.

"I'll just put these in a vase. Then I'll make us a drink. Diplomatico rum with ice, just as you like it?"

Garcia nodded. An evening with Daniela and her sensual ways was what he needed after the stressful week he'd experienced. He watched her dainty legs as she moved around the kitchen, and asked himself how long he could hold out before he forced her down over the kitchen bench and fucked her from behind. He would take her roughly, and she would scream for his mercy, and she would enjoy it.

With the roses in a vase, Daniela poured them both shot glasses of rum. With tongs, she removed shards of iced from a bowl, which she first rubbed against the flesh of her breast before dropping them into Garcia's glass. He felt himself grow hard just watching her.

Daniela returned the ice to the freezer, turned and was about to smile when her face contorted into an expression of chilling terror.

Garcia was about to ask her what was wrong when he felt the cold metal of a gun muzzle press against the back of his neck.

"Director," said the intruder with an accent that sounded American but wasn't. "I don't believe we've met."

45

D ressed in the uniform of the FAES operator Pierce had incapacitated in the corridor, he stood with his suppressed Glock 19 aimed at the back of Juan Garcia's head. In Spanish, he said, "Raise your hands where I can see them, Director."

Garcia obeyed with slow movements so as not to provoke Pierce, but his voice rose when he responded, "You mother-fucker! Twenty of my men guard this building. They will fucking kill you when they inevitably find you."

The young woman in the skimpy lingerie whimpered at the kitchen bench, distracting Pierce. She shifted her weight from one leg to the other as tears rolled down her cheeks. Fear had nearly paralysed her.

"Grab your dress and hide in the bathroom." Pierce motioned with his pistol. "Lock the door, get down low, and don't come out."

It took the woman a moment to comprehend what he had said. Then she sprinted to the bathroom and disappeared.

Pierce waited until he heard the door lock before he patted down Garcia, finding a Beretta Px4 Storm, a two-way radio and a cell phone, all of which he pocketed. "On your knees, Director. Keep your hands raised."

Again, Garcia complied without argument, but Pierce sensed the rage boiling within the middle-aged man. This was not an individual accustomed to being threatened, whose ego couldn't accept any foe besting him. "How the fuck did you bypass my men?"

Pierce tightened a cable tie around Garcia's wrists. Then he stepped back and walked around the SEBIN director, kept his pistol pointed at his foe while he maintained a good three metres distance between them. "I knew you'd come see Daniela soon enough. Two days hiding out on the roof hardly taxed me. Honestly, I thought you'd hold out much longer with everything going down right now."

"I don't know who you are, American, but let me tell you this, you will not survive. And when my men incarcerate you, which is inevitable, your death will be slow and gruesomely painful. Plasma cutters, to melt away first your feet, then hands, then testicles, is how I shall do it... This is not a threat, but a promise."

Pierce grinned behind his mask. "You think I'd come here without leverage?"

Garcia tensed, expressing concern that until now he had not experienced, or had hidden. "You're bullshitting?"

With his pistol in one hand still aimed at Garcia, Pierce removed his cell phone from his pocket with his other and dialled a number. "Someone close wants to talk."

The colour drained from Garcia's smug features. "Who?"

The cell phone answered. Pierce put the caller on speaker.

The soft voice of a timid woman answered. "Juan?"

The director's face turned white, then red, as he clenched his teeth and the blood vessels in his temples pulsed. "Marcela! What have they done to you?" The quiver in his voice he could not conceal, and his hands trembled.

There was a pause that dragged across seconds before Marcela said, "Juan. Oh my God! I'm so scared. They have Sofia... and me..." She broke into sobs.

"I'm coming for you, darling. I'm coming for you both—"

She spoke over him. "They said... they said they'd hurt our daughter first if you don't cooperate—"

Pierce ended the call.

Garcia raced to his feet before Pierce kicked him and sent him back down onto his knees. Even from his disadvantaged position, the SEBIN director looked ready to tear Pierce to pieces. "You asshole. I'll skin you alive for this! I'll fry your balls in oil while they are still attached to your body. You should shoot yourself now, American, because when my men—"

"Keep it under control, Director."

"Or you'll fucking... what?"

Several silent seconds passed, without either man moving or speaking, before Garcia's full appreciation of his situation slowly showed in his red, inflamed eyes.

"You already know the answer to that question. You already know what I'll do if you don't cooperate. Keep calm if you want your family to survive this."

"You... fucking..."

"Garcia! Understand, I'll be sending code words to my team every thirty minutes. If they don't receive the correct code every half hour until we finish what I need to be done, they'll begin with the torture, starting with your daughter."

The concealed radio earpiece in his canal chirped twice, an acknowledgement from Rachel Zang that she listened to everything they said, and agreed that the ploy was so far proceeding as they had planned.

Garcia growled like a cornered dog. "You asshole!"

"Cooperate, and we'll return Marcela and Sofia unharmed. Is that so hard to understand?"

"You fucking asshole!"

Pierce raised an eyebrow and said nothing while his suppressed Glock never wavered.

Eventually, Garcia's face softened, and his eyes dropped as he realised Pierce had defeated him. "Very well, American. What do I have to do to keep your barbarity in check?"

"First off, lie down, face on the floor."

"Why?"

"It doesn't matter why. We can do what I need you to do with a bullet in your leg, or not. Either option works for me, so you choose."

With every muscle tensed, Garcia obeyed and lay with his face pressed upon the carpet.

Pierce secured a second set of cable ties around Garcia's feet. Then, noticing Daniela's red dress discarded on the floor, he used it to tie a blindfold around the director's eyes. Next, he pressed the muzzle of his weapon into Garcia's calf. "Move a centimetre, and I pull the trigger."

Garcia nodded.

With his target incapacitated and deprived of sight, Pierce felt confident to complete the next stage of his deception. He took a USB stick from his pocket, provided to him by Rachel Zang, and inserted it into Garcia's cell phone. Its red light blinked as it loaded software that cloned the phone's contents while simultaneously installing surveillance and tracking apps, and transmitted the captured data to Zang's cell phone, who waited in a car a block from the apartment.

Thirty seconds passed before the USB light turned green. The download was complete, and it had cracked the cell phone's passcode. Zang sent two chirps to show she had the data.

Pierce chirped back twice, then opened the phone app and noted the most prominent call history was to a National Guard officer, Colonel Jesus Alvarez. He memorised the number. It surprised Pierce that Garcia was deluded enough to believe his encryption was so good he didn't need to conceal the identity of his contacts. This oversight would aid Langley analysts to no end when they trawled the phone's data, which Zang no doubt had already forwarded on.

Further searches identified the cell phone number of Leopold Colmenares, the FAES operator Pierce now impersonated, and noted his rank as sergeant.

Pierce disconnected the two tech devices and slipped the cell phone back in his pocket.

In an act of defiance, Garcia rolled onto his back and shook the dress off his eyes. He fumed again, tensed every muscle in his body to control his anger, which he seemed unable to keep in check for any length of time. "If you lay a single finger on my daughter—"

Pierce refocused his pistol on the director's chest. "Garcia, focus on what is important. Getting Sofia and Marcela back unharmed when I have Amelia Reyes."

"Reyes?" The SEBIN director's brows pinched. "Wait a second! You're the fucking assassin Parra chased in Rio, aren't you?"

Pierce kept silent.

"You're the asshole the Chinese have offered a ten-million bounty for?"

"The Chinese have the wrong guy."

"Sure they do. What the fuck did you do to upset them so much?"

Without warning, Pierce kicked Garcia hard enough in the back to startle, but not enough to leave any lasting damage. The man groaned, and while distracted by the pain, Pierce cut the man's bindings. "Get to your feet."

The director did as he was instructed while his eyes searched the room, perhaps seeking a weapon to use against Pierce.

"Shall I make a call?" Pierce kept his distance from the anger-fuelled man, and his muscles limber should he need to subdue his foe quickly. "Kill one hostage now, to show you how serious I am? Your wife, perhaps?"

Garcia froze. "No, please don't."

"Then act like they matter to you." Pierce again removed the director's cell phone from his own pocket. "Time to rally your men and return to base."

"What? You want to enter La Tumba? With me?"

Pierce nodded. He had thought of convincing Garcia to order Amelia's removal from the SEBIN headquarters and to bring her to another location, but he hadn't been able to devise a scenario where it wouldn't alert too many officials that something was not right, and for them to set a trap for him. "That *is* where you have Amelia held?"

Garcia nodded. "You have bigger balls than I imagined, American. Whatever you did to piss off the Chinese, it would have required enormous balls too. Better use them now, while they still remain attached to your body."

46

P ierce barely moved, seated rigid in the back seat of the second Prado, but he watched everything.

Garcia, next to Pierce, sweated and fidgeted, but remained silent, as Pierce had instructed him.

The driver and the second guard in the front watched the road and focused on external threats.

Outside, ragged, weakened men and women slept rough, but otherwise the streets remained empty, and cars were few. Rats darted across the roads. Garbage gathered in building alcoves. They heard occasional gunfire in the distance, but no one reacted as if this were anything unusual. Caracas was not a city to be out and about late at night.

The radio in Pierce's ear chirped. Zang spoke so only he could hear.

"Everything okay?"

Pierce did not want Garcia to know he had a teammate watching over him, so he said nothing. He instead twice pressed the speech pod he'd secured to his wrist, chirping a "yes". Not that Zang or he could take on nineteen heavily armed and trained soldiers, but her presence would provide him an edge in this risky plan they had concocted should they face unexpected complications.

"Good." Zang spoke softly. "I presume your talking is not an option?"

He chirped twice. One chirp would have been a "no".

"Okay then. A white van follows you. It's keeping beyond your visible range. Driver seems to know your destination."

Pierce chirped twice to acknowledge. The appearance of a third interested party complicated matters and escalated the risks, but he didn't want to ask who this might be when his SEBIN companion would overhear.

Without prompting, Zang spoke on, guessing what Pierce wanted to know. "Occupant is male, Latin, buzzed hair, wearing dark clothes. I spotted him before he drove off. He carried a large sports bag heavy enough to contain a weapon. Sniper or assault rifle, perhaps. My guess is he was watching Daniela's apartment, waiting for you to show so he could take you out with a sniper bullet. I presume he didn't because you naturally kept yourself out of any potential sniper lines of sight while inside?"

Once more, Pierce chirped twice.

"Could this be Parra? The FAES and sometimes SEBIN assassin?"

The description matched Maceo Parra, so Pierce chirped an acknowledgement. This revelation asked many more questions than it answered. Why was Amelia's kidnapper acting independently from the FAES operators in the five Prados? Had Parra tipped off Garcia to Pierce's intentions, and this was a trap? A bluff of Garcia's making? Or was Parra out for the Chinese reward on Pierce's head and had turned rogue against his own organisation? That latter option made a weird kind of sense in Pierce's mind.

"Abort mission?" Zang asked.

Pierce chirped once.

"Shall I take out this foe?"

He quickly chirped once. Securing himself inside La Tumba was a near suicidal mission, and any enemy engagement now would ruin any chance of success. Despite knowing how insane his position was, a part of him, drawn deep from his dark and troubled subconscious, pushed him on and to ignore the Parra element for now. Rescuing Amelia was paramount. Every other consideration was secondary.

And he didn't know why.

"You'll be at La Tumba in two minutes. You sure you don't want to abort?"

He gave a single chirp.

"Very well... Be careful, Mark. I'll be outside, parked in the agreed spot. Don't get yourself killed or captured. And don't put yourself in any position where this sniper could take you out when you leave again."

He chirped twice and smiled behind his balaclava. Despite his continued failure to recall Rachel Zang from before the car crash in Rio, his instincts still told him to trust her. He did worry that his instincts to trust Savannah had been unfounded when her later deceit had come to light, so why did this feel different? He didn't have a good answer for that question just yet.

He hoped his instincts were correct, because if this infiltration failed, Pierce could end up incarcerated inside La

Tumba for the rest of — what would be — his ultimately brief life. If she was his enemy, this was the perfect opportunity to trap him.

Sooner than he expected, the dark building loomed. Pierce realised he was now committed to his plan.

He made a prearranged hand signal from behind the driver's seat, so only Garcia would see. The sweating director noticed, then said to the FAES operative in the front passenger seat as they had agreed, "Radio ahead. Get Amelia Reyes prepped in interrogation room eight, now!"

"Sir," answered the soldier, who relayed the order over the radio back to headquarters.

Pierce listened to the conversation closely, but picked up nothing in either man's tone that concerned him. He turned to Garcia, who glared at him with dark, pinched eyes.

Pierce said nothing. His primary concern tonight was Garcia's temper, which could unleash at any moment and cause him to act irrationally and childlike. If that happened, his deceit would quickly collapse, and Pierce didn't feel confident he could shoot his way out of La Tumba, but he would do his best if it came to that. And with Amelia by his side.

On the outside, La Tumba was a modern-style office complex in a commercial district, lit up like any other office high-rise on a normal night. Nothing about it appeared ominous or foreboding, despite the late hour. It did, however, hold a fearsome reputation as the headquarters of SEBIN, the Bolivian Intelligence Services, and as a detention centre where political prisoners remained incarcerated indefinitely and were tortured daily.

Pierce wished he could rescue every prisoner suffering in the white-walled cells, but his resources and capability extended only to one person. Amelia Reyes. A young, driven woman whom, for reasons he could not yet recall, he had promised to protect with his life. And this man before him was the originator of all the pain she had suffered this last week.

The convoy drove into the underground car park. As the roller doors shut behind them, Garcia's vehicle parked before the lift. Pierce and Garcia stepped out.

Inside the building now, Pierce had no choice but to proceed.

Alone together, Garcia pressed the elevator call button. They waited for the first lift to descend.

Garcia looked at Pierce, still with his balaclava, cap, and sunglasses disguising his features. "No one hides their faces inside this building."

Pierce turned to stare down his foe. "My next coded call is in twelve minutes. Better ensure we have Amelia by then..."

Garcia's face reddened, and his fists clenched tight. "When I get my wife and daughter back, which I will, then I will come for you. I will see to it personally that your suffering is extreme."

The elevator arrived.

It opened, and no one stepped out.

After checking for CCTV cameras and finding none, Pierce pushed Garcia inside. The door closed, and Garcia pressed the button to the fifth floor.

With a sudden motion, Pierce punched Garcia hard in the gut.

The director didn't see it coming. The pain shocked him, and bent over, he winced as tears streamed from his eyes.

It was an effort of wills not to beat Juan Garcia to death.

"I promised if you cooperated, Garcia, your wife and daughter would be fine. But I promised you nothing regarding your long-term fate. Be nice to me, and I might just let you live through this night."

47

Rachel Zang had never believed Pierce's plan was viable. The risks were many, and, if any became a reality, they each carried serious consequences. Pierce's memory remained faulty — he still claimed not to remember their time together in Central Asia and Africa. Physically, he was way below operational capacity, with the many cuts and abrasions his body had endured, and perhaps a cracked rib or two. Two days ago, she'd witnessed him shirtless in their shared bathroom. His athletic physique was a network of purple and yellow bruising worse than she had imagined. His sunken eyes were most telling because often they were unfocused.

Despite these concerns, Pierce's sole motivation was not on recovery, but on rescuing Amelia Reyes from SEBIN's torture cells.

With any other operator, Zang would have talked them down. But she'd witnessed Pierce in action and knew of his incredible strategic and tactical skills and admirable ability to endure pain. He was intelligent and self-aware compared to most men. If anyone could pull off this deception, it was Pierce, even in his debilitated state.

But she still worried he might fail.

From the shadows that hid her car, parked with a direct line of sight to La Tumba's front entrance, Zang watched patiently. An alternative vehicle to the one they had driven into Caracas in would have been preferable for tonight's operation. Unfortunately, functional cars were a rarity in Venezuela. Those that would have suited her purposes remained locked in owners' caged garages beyond the reach of even the most cunning thieves.

Inventory for tonight's mission included M4 assault carbines; flashbang, smoke and fragmentation grenades; body armour; night-vision goggles; radio comms; trauma kits; cash; and meals-ready-to-eat to last them weeks. Once they had Reyes, Pierce and Zang had everything they needed for a quick sprint and an illegal crossing into Colombia, where Patricia Knight had a team of 7th Special Forces Group operators prepped to bring them home.

But getting home first required Pierce completing his mission inside the Tomb.

Pierce had entered SEBIN's headquarters fifteen minutes earlier. There had been no sign of any action since. Because of the various electronic counter-surveillance measures within the building, their radio communications remained useless until he stepped outside again.

If he ever did.

She reminisced about their brief but passion-fuelled encounter in another safe house in Namibia. There had been a string of men in Zang's life since joining the CIA, and all had been casual acquaintances. Men she could pass the time with and share intimacy. Brief releases from the tension

of her work and providers of temporary endorphin highs
before she and her partners went on their separate missions
across the globe. Pierce had been the same.

But was this true?

He was the only casual partner she reminisced about.

Since their last encounter in the Atlantic Ocean three
months earlier, she'd turned down an opportunity to spend
the night with another of her casual partners. She never did
that.

Her annoyance seemed to stem from a single thought.
Mark Pierce remembered nothing about their time together,
while she constantly questioned how much attraction she
felt towards him. That was just wrong in her mind.

She didn't want emotional. Didn't do emotional. But here
she was, deeply worried that Mark was about to get himself
killed, and she could have stopped him, but hadn't. Worse,
she wasn't ready to lose him from her life, even when she
had bigger emotional issues to deal with, tied closely to this
operation but on a continent far from where she operated
now. Perhaps, Zang realised, she saw Pierce not so much as a
lover, but as a potential friend, and that was why he was
important to her?

A man walked past, not noticing Zang or the car she sat
in, as the night's shadows concealed her.

He was tall, muscular, dark-skinned, and walked with
purpose.

A bandage covered a long wound on his scalp.

And then he was gone.

It took Zang a moment to realise who he was.

Alpha Mansaray.

The realisation caused an involuntary shudder.

What was Mansaray doing in Caracas? His presence

must connect to everything Pierce was involved with here in South America, as she had suggested to Patricia Knight.

With her suppressed SIG Sauer P320 semi-automatic in hand, Zang exited her car and followed him.

He crossed three hundred feet of road, then tapped on the door of a shop in the Mercado La Gran Manzana with steel bars across the window. Another man unlocked the door, and they both disappeared into the darkness. The shop looked directly across the road at the SEBIN building. She didn't know why, but figured Mansaray's interest in the secret police headquarters coinciding with Pierce's attempted prison rescue wasn't a random occurrence.

Zang knew better than to approach from the same entrance. Mansaray no doubt had La Tumba under observation and would see her approach. From inside the market, however, which was closed for the night, other entrances to the shops would be easier to access and unlikely to be under observation.

Zang snuck around the back of the market, sought a downpipe, and climbed it onto the roof. From there, she shimmied in the darkness across the metal sheeting until she was positioned over Mansaray's hideout. Part of the roof near the hideout was loose, so she quietly removed the tin sheet and slipped inside the rafters. Then, shimming through an access hole, Zang dropped herself inside the empty market, making barely any noise.

She listened until she heard two men speaking English, until there was no doubt that the target was Alpha Mansaray. The Nigerian killer who had brutally murdered her entire team in Port-au-Prince.

With clenched teeth and her temperature on the rise, Zang removed her lock picks and stealthily unlocked the market entrance to the shop. Then she slipped silently inside.

Mansaray and the second man watched SEBIN head-quarters through binoculars and didn't notice her.

The suppressor made a noise like a sneeze as Zang shot the unknown man through the back of his skull, ending his life abruptly with a sudden splash of red.

A second later, her weapon turned on Mansaray. She fired a bullet through the hand that held the binoculars. Further blood sprayed in the darkness.

"Fuck off!" Mansaray turned with his intact hand to bring his own pistol to bear on Zang.

She was faster and shot the weapon out of his other hand, destroying the bones and muscles.

Fuelled with adrenaline, Mansaray rushed her until he saw Zang's steady pistol, ready to blow his brains into mist, too far from him to easily knock it from her grip. Now he stood motionless and breathed heavily as sweat poured down his face.

"No hands." Zang spoke softly. "You're fucked, Alpha Mansaray."

"Fuck you!" He looked at his ruined appendages and saw both were now nothing more than mangled, meaty clubs. "Bitch!" He gritted his teeth to stifle a scream against the agony he surely experienced. Handless, he couldn't fight.

"It's over for you, Mansaray. I promise I'll make it quick... No more pain, but only if you explain what the fuck you are doing here."

48

Pierce and Garcia shared space in an empty interrogation room. With the CCTV cameras disabled, no pretence to their troubled mental states was required, yet they both felt no need to talk. Sweat built on Pierce's temples, hidden by his balaclava. Garcia was correct in that no one inside La Tumba concealed their identity, but no one had questioned Pierce's mask either, as they'd passed through the corridors of La Tumba to reach this sterile room. And yet he still felt he'd walked into a trap.

He glanced at his wristwatch. Eighteen minutes had passed since they had entered the building. No one had brought Amelia Reyes to them. He speculated on options to speed up the process, but no suitable solutions came to him other than to keep waiting. The longer they waited, however, the greater the chance he would get caught.

Garcia paced and sweated more than Pierce. "What about my wife and daughter? You should have coded in by now?"

Pierce shrugged. "That's right. Bad news for you."

"I've done everything you've asked."

"Then where is Amelia?"

"For fuck's sake!"

"Garcia, this building's countermeasures prevent me from radioing out."

"Then use my phone. Call!"

Garcia's anger had grown more pronounced as the minutes passed. Pierce sensed he was close to losing control, and Pierce did not wish to deal with this complication, which would no doubt limit his ability to walk out of here alive.

"Are they torturing my Sofia? Marcela?"

Pierce was deliberate in his long seconds of silence before he answered. "We'll find out only when we're out of here, won't we?"

The SEBIN director hit the intercom button on the desk phone and dialled a number.

"Yes, sir?" answered a nervous voice.

"Reyes. You have one minute to bring her to me, or I cut your balls off."

The man on the phone made an audible swallowing noise. "Yes, sir. This was an unusual request. Normally, the rules stipulate prisoners aren't to be removed from the basement. It takes time—"

"It takes no fucking time, if you just obey your superior and get the fucking job done!"

Garcia ended the call, then paced again. Every footstep felt heavy, as if he wore lead boots.

"What's the obsession with testicles?"

Garcia halted, then turned and expressed surprise at Pierce's question. "What the fuck do you mean?"

"Testicles? Balls? Nuts? It seems to be all you talk about."

Garcia grinned, like he'd just experienced an epiphany. "You North Americans, you wouldn't understand, with your politically correct bullshit and pathetic new age sensibilities. Our balls make us real men. Real Latin men who are virile Latin lovers. To cut off a man's balls is to take away his masculinity. No other threat holds quite the same gravitas. You homos wouldn't understand."

Pierce shrugged. "Or is it you're all trying to prove none of you are gay?"

Garcia grinned again, but there was a wildness in his eyes Pierce didn't like. "Homosexuality is ungodly. A sin of the worst order. Are you gay, American?"

"A close friend of mine is gay."

"Well, I reckon you are a homo."

Pierce laughed. "Is that why you and your president are so threatened by Amelia? She's a lesbian, and she is far more popular and loved than either of you will ever be. I'd say that's the real threat to your masculinity."

Garcia raised his fist as his face reddened. "I swear, American, when this is over, I will serve up your balls to my dogs for breakfast."

"See, you're at it again. For a straight man, you're obsessed with other men's genitals." Pierce knew he was baiting Garcia because of the rage burning inside him, making him speak emotionally and without a strategy, but he found he couldn't stop himself. Garcia was the kind of man Pierce had no qualms about killing because a world without him could only be a better place. "Do you even know who you are? Know what your identity is?"

Before Garcia could answer, the door to the interview room sprang open. Two uniformed men stepped in, dragged in a semi-conscious Amelia Reyes and dropped her onto an interview chair. She was so weak they hadn't bothered to cuff her.

Pierce felt shock at seeing her physical state. Her blood-shot eyes couldn't focus, and her bare arms and legs sported many bruises. Amelia shivered yet burned with a fever. The white T-shirt she wore was her only clothing, saturated with her own sweat. She had also lost weight and looked in need of immediate hospitalisation.

Pierce fought his instincts not to strangle Garcia to death for the tortures he had inflicted upon this woman. He also fought his instincts not to run to her and offer words of comfort, for he still had a role to play before this mission ended, and his mission required maintaining his current disguise as Sergeant Leopold Colmenares to remain in play.

"Leave us," Garcia instructed the guards.

"Sir," said the older of the two men, "we have a problem."

"I don't fucking care. Get out of my sight."

"Sir," the guard insisted, "every prisoner is very sick. I mean really sick. The worst are the three we processed yesterday."

The hairs on Pierce's arms tingled. He felt his stomach churn. He couldn't stop himself as he asked in Spanish, "What do you mean?"

"All the prisoners in the white cells. They have fevers and are acting crazy."

Pierce studied the two guards. Both men sweated and panted, just like Amelia. An infection was spreading through the building, and no one had yet realised the seriousness of their situation.

Pierce's attention turned to Amelia. She could barely hold herself upright in her chair. The sweat pouring off her was pervasive, and she seemed unable to concentrate on anything around her. Whatever infected her and the two guards was a serious disease. Pierce couldn't help but speculate this was some biological attack on the SEBIN headquarters.

In the space of two seconds, Pierce shot the two guards with his suppressed pistol. Then put two more bullets in their skulls as they lay twitching on the floor, lying in expanding pools of their own tainted blood.

Garcia recoiled. "What the fuck did you do that for?"

Pierce took handcuffs from the closest guard, then forcibly restrained Garcia by securing him to the interview table. There was no use protecting himself. He was exposed to the infection now, along with everyone else inside La Tumba.

"Fuck you. You never intended to release my wife and daughter."

Pierce took Garcia's cell phone from his pocket. "You know anything about biological weapon attacks, Garcia? Here, recently, in Venezuela?"

The change in the director's facial expression was sudden and telling. He lost all colour as his eyes lost their focus. "What do you mean?"

"What I said." Pierce flicked through Garcia's call history, then his emails. A quick examination of correspondence between Colonel Jesus Alvarez of the GNB and Garcia concerned several infectious outbreaks occurring within various Venezuelan military outfits over the last weeks.

Pierce glanced at his hand. It shook with tremors he could not control. His stomach tightened against a fear he could not understand. "What is it you and Colonel Alvarez know that I don't?"

Garcia whispered a name Pierce couldn't discern. He, too, looked to be experiencing a debilitating shock.

"What did you say?"

"Mr Real."

"Who?"

Then, from nowhere, Pierce's body shook as if someone had just struck him.

Mr Real. He knew that name... He didn't know why or how, but the thought of this man chilled him...

"Mr Real. He's trying to fuck us all. He wants to bring down this country and take the oil for himself. Now let me the fuck out of here! You have Reyes. I want my wife and daughter back, unharmed."

Pierce went to Amelia and brushed her soaked hair from her eyes. "Amelia, it's me, Mark. I'm getting you out of here."

She didn't recognise him, didn't respond. It was as if she could not perceive him at all.

"American? Answer me!"

"Your wife and daughter are fine, Garcia. I never had them."

"What the fuck?"

"Audio software has advanced significantly in the last few years. The voices you heard were AI-generated simulations based on years of surveillance tapes the CIA and NSA gathered on you and your family. Recordings you never guessed we had."

Garcia pulled at the handcuffs binding him to the table. "You. Fucking. Asshole!" His muscles flexed, and his face throbbed as he struggled to breathe at a normal pace. "Guards!"

Pierce lifted his Glock semi-automatic and shot Garcia through the mouth. The director's spine opened behind him as bone and fleshy lumps bounced across the far wall. Then he slumped dead against the interview table. Pierce put another bullet through his chest, just to make sure.

Even though the radio didn't work, Garcia's cell phone did, likely connected to a SEBIN Wi-Fi network spread throughout the building. Pierce sent text messages to all the senior SEBIN officers on Garcia's phone list, told them that Leopold Colmenares was taking Amelia Reyes to another secure, undisclosed location, and no one was to stop him from exiting the building.

He lifted the barely conscious Amelia in a fireman's embrace, positioned over his shoulder, then exited the interview room and locked the door behind him. He also had to presume the sniper who was likely Parra would be outside waiting for Pierce, so he needed a plan to deal with that possibility too. But whatever the situation actually was, he needed to get out of La Tumba immediately.

"Amelia, I promise you, I'm getting us out of here."

What he didn't want to escape this facility was the biological weapon that infected them both, but for the moment, he felt he had no choice on this matter.

49

Blood flowed from Alpha Mansaray's butchered palms, fastest from his left hand where Zang's bullet must have ruptured a major artery. The man who'd murdered three of her teammates now dropped to his knees as the pace of his shallow breaths increased. With his hands now ruined slabs of meat, the former detective made no effort to save himself, because he couldn't. Zang guessed she had minutes at most before he bled out, and he likely knew it too.

"Why are you here?"

Mansaray grinned, his mouth wide, resembling a predator displaying his carnivorous teeth, while his eyes expressed a cruelty that caused Zang to tense. When she had first encountered this killer in Port-au-Prince, he had terrified her with his raw physical power and the clinical skills he'd employed to dispatch Olivia, Jarrad and Peter. It was difficult not to relive that same fear now, despite his crippling wounds. She kept her distance should he try to subdue her.

"Tell me, Mansaray?"

He laughed as he glanced at each ruined paw. "Why the fuck not? I'm dead anyway."

She straightened her arm to draw attention to her SIG Sauer. "I'm listening."

Sweat ran off his bald and bandaged head. "We're talking genetically modified rabies. One that spreads through the air and kills in days or weeks rather than months."

"What?" Zang wasn't certain she'd heard him correctly. "What did you say?"

Mansaray nodded to the corpse sprawled next to him. "Me and the man you killed, we've been spraying known SEBIN operators as they return to their headquarters." He glanced through the window at La Tumba across the darkened road. "We included prisoners they were taking inside as well. Now, everyone inside is infected."

Zang's jaw dropped, and her skin itched. She *had* heard him correctly. "How are you not getting caught?"

"It's not like we are acting threateningly. We just spray into the air, and a few seconds later, the SEBIN idiots walk straight through the mist."

Zang knew this was an act of terrorism, but why attack a country that was already crippled by failed economics and authoritarian military rule? She wondered why they hadn't struck in Europe or North America, where the impact would have generated greater global fear of their organisation — if terror was their aim.

"There'll be more attacks... on the borders with Colombia, where SEBIN can't hide it, and the world will soon know all about it."

"Again, why?"

Mansaray winced against his pain and weakening state. "What it's always about. Money and power."

"Not terrorism?"

He shook his head.

She pointed her weapon at his foot, knowing that a third injury would enhance the pain he already experienced. "Be specific?"

"Oil, you bitch. Venezuela signs over control of the oil to my people. Only then do we halt the surgical rabies attacks on their military and intelligence services. This was their last warning, and it's as simple as that. Amelia Reyes, she was to be the one to tell the world the lie that it was the Venezuelan president infecting his own people. He was to be the scapegoat."

Zang paused. The connections between SEBIN, Kozan Petroleum and the secret organisation Mansaray worked for now made perfect sense, and their scheme was so much more elaborate and forward-thinking than she had imagined possible. If she kept Mansaray talking, she might learn their operational structure or the names of key members of their group. Actual targets she could go after for real, and perhaps even cripple their capabilities and reach. "The symbol on your chest, the circle within a circle dissected by a line, it represents the organisation you work for. The mastermind behind all this. Tell me about them?"

Mansaray laughed again, but when he spoke, his voice was barely a whisper. She saw he could barely keep himself upright. "They're more dangerous than you might think. They're everywhere, even inside your CIA. How do you think we got to your friends inside the United States and deep-sixed them? You thought you'd infiltrate us. No, you bitch, we infiltrated you!"

Zang experienced physical illness. She'd expected Mansaray's group to be a sizable force, but she had underestimated how extensive their influence extended, which must be global. They must know everything about her, and she knew nothing about them.

Mansaray said, "I likely carry the enhanced rabies virus myself, but I'm vaccinated. Yes, our organisation developed the vaccine first before we unleashed it on the world. The strain we collect has an onset of twelve to twenty-four hours. After that, it's a rapid deterioration for you. Fevers, headaches, anxiety, confusion, and weirdly hydrophobia, fear of water of all things. Eventually it ends with brain swelling and comas, which ultimately leads to death. Normally it takes months to kill you, but we've cut that time down to days or a week at most."

He moved again, with a speed she never imagined possible with his blood loss, and threw his arms towards her. Blood sprayed from his shattered hands, splashed on her face, her mouth, and her eyes.

Before she registered it, she blinked Mansaray's crimson fluids from her eyelashes.

"Bitch. You're infected too."

She shot him twice in the chest.

For a single second, Mansaray danced like a maniac, then fell forward, as his muscular frame bounced on the oil-stained concrete floor, and he didn't move again.

Zang put another bullet in his head to ensure he was dead.

Then she collapsed on the floor as the shock of what she had learned washed over her. Her face and hands numbed. Her body trembled.

SAC/SOG operators often faced the risk of death in the

field. Zang expected this, but she never imagined her end would be this gruesome. Rabies, she presumed, was a painful and protracted killer. She imagined the symptoms Mansaray had described working their way into her cells even now. In twenty-four hours... forty-eight hours at the most, it would all be over for her.

And Pierce too. He was inside SEBIN headquarters, so infected like her. If he'd rescued Amelia, she too would carry the virus.

What could Zang do? Was any course of action worthwhile with the time they had left to them? Even if Pierce escaped La Tumba with Amelia Reyes, there was no chance they could make it to safety in time. Even if they did, they would only die a short time later.

She thought of calling her father, her only living relative, someone she could spend her last moments with, and a man whom she was supposed to love. But she didn't know how to reach him or what to say. The situation was fucked up. It would have been better to die suddenly and have no time to contemplate her brief mortality.

Then, recognising her moment of self-pity was just that, she sprang into action. Zang might die, but she could stop the spread, prevent others from contracting the deadly virus. Her desire to do good in the world was why she'd joined the CIA in the first place. She could still achieve good, even now.

Zang called Patricia Knight.

50

Baltimore, Maryland, United States

K night sat up straight and forced open her eyes. A moment passed before she disengaged from confused dreams and their decontextualised reality and focused on her burner cell phone, which rang with shrill tones. Again, Knight had fallen asleep sprawled upon her lounge without remembering that she had, and her head ached.

The television still played CNN news reports from across the globe.

Rubbing her eyes, she answered the call. "Yes?"

"It's me!" There was a desperation in Zang's tone Knight had never heard before.

"Where are you?"

"Caracas. It's not good."

Zang relayed the genetically modified airborne rabies scheme instigated by the secretive organisation the two women had failed to track for years now. Then she described

Pierce's current engagement inside SEBIN's headquarters, firmly centred on the outbreak's ground zero. Zang concluded her brief with Alpha Mansaray's warnings concerning the impending and uncontrolled rabies outbreaks the secretive organisation planned for the Venezuela-Colombia border.

When the briefing ended, Knight didn't know what to say or how to respond. This information now aligned with other intelligence Knight had gathered from other sources related to this secretive organisation they couldn't yet fully understand or define, related to NGOs and pharmaceutical companies working on virus vaccines with tenuous links to this group. Information she had not yet shared with Zang, but now felt like the missing puzzle piece that revealed what one part of the overall puzzle represented. This was a threat much larger and more complicated than she was equipped or trained to cope with. She just wanted to sleep some more and forget the rest of the world had problems too.

"Ma'am?"

"Zang, what is your situation?"

Her operative almost choked up when she answered, "I'm infected." Zang described her encounter with Alpha Mansaray, ending with the moment before she neutralised him when he sprayed his blood into her eyes. But she'd likely breathed in the virus long before that anyway, if what Mansary had reported was true.

Knight gritted her teeth. If Zang had read the situation correctly, then she was a goner. "I'm sorry to hear that."

Zang coughed. "Well, it is what it is. I might not have rabies."

Again, Knight wasn't certain how to respond because she didn't believe luck was on Zang's side. Another operative lost. Knight should offer words of comfort and encouragement. She decided to stick with facts. "Are you operational?"

"Yes, for twelve, maybe twenty-four hours. Then it's quickly downhill. But I'm also a carrier. I must be careful who I come into contact with."

"We need to control this outbreak."

"I know." Zang drew in a deep breath. "And I think I know how, ma'am. Pierce and I hacked into Director Juan Garcia's cell phone. You have access to it, too, as I uploaded it onto Langley's servers. Use it to fake message all SEBIN operatives, ordering them to return to headquarters. That controls the flow of infected persons to one location."

Knight had enjoyed herself too much last night, overindulging her suppressed emotional needs. She stood, realised that she needed to pee, while her dry mouth told her to rehydrate. Instead of doing either, she consumed the dregs of her whisky with the ice cubes now turned to water.

"Ma'am?"

"That's a good idea. Thanks, Zang, looking now."

Knight logged in to her laptop. She opened a CIA app that allowed her to remotely access hacked cell phones, found Garcia's call history and checked his message logs. "Oh, that's interesting..."

"What's interesting?"

"Director Garcia has already done that. Ordered all operatives to return to HQ."

"That must be Pierce." There was excitement in Zang's voice, but it didn't last. "He thought of it first, which means he's alive and hopefully on his way out."

"But also infected."

Zang didn't answer immediately, but Knight could hear her top operative's shallow breathing as her mind processed the unfolding situation. Knight sensed there was much on Zang's mind she was not sharing. "Yes, ma'am. Infected, as well."

"You two get somewhere isolated. I have that 7th Special Forces Group contingent on standby in the Caribbean Sea. They'll exfiltrate you." This was a lie, but Knight figured false hope was better than no hope for Zang after all she had accomplished in her years as a top Ground Branch operator, because Knight would not risk the lives of American soldiers on dead operatives. Zang should have just brought Pierce in when she first found him, and none of them would now face this insurmountable threat. This orchestrated rabies outbreak might have occurred regardless, but no one would have implicated Knight as responsible. Now every executive officer on Langley's seventh floor would turn on Knight and make her their scapegoat because it was her operative on the ground at the outbreak's epicentre.

"Ma'am, I thought you said you can't get forces inside Venezuela without the Chinese or Russians pinging us?"

Knight felt her throat tighten as she prepared another lie. "I'll figure something out, Zang."

Further silence followed before Zang spoke again. "What about the attacks on the Colombian border? We must try to stop them."

"Others will do that. Like you said, you and Pierce moving there will just cause the spread of the virus, defeating any good you could do."

"Maybe..." Another pause followed as Zang's mind went to work. "There can't be too many flights between Haiti and Venezuela. Ma'am, can you work backwards, track any air movements in the last five days between both locales, and see if you can connect them to ground-vehicle movements headed for major Colombian-Venezuelan border crossings? That might give us actionable targets to neutralise."

Knight nodded. Zang was way ahead of her. It might be intel Knight could use to lessen the political fallout when this turned into another global pandemic disaster. This could be the COVID-19 pandemic all over again, but much, much worse. "I'll see what I can do. Call me in six hours."

Another delay, and this time Zang did not respond.

"Zang?"

"Ma'am... are you okay?"

"Of course I am. Why do you ask?"

"It's just, you sound... out of it. If you aren't up to this, you'd let me know, right?"

Knight felt offended. She was a highly competent CIA operations officer and a senior government servant. Zang had no right to question her abilities. "If what you are telling me is true, and from everything we've learnt so far, I believe it means you're infected with a serious, fatal virus, Zang. I know that is as scary as fuck. I promise you I'll do everything I can to extract you and bring the vaccine if I can."

"Yes, ma'am." Zang fumbled with her phone, making crackling sounds, as if on the move. "Activity outside SEBIN headquarters. I'll call you back."

The call ended.

Knight staggered to the bathroom and recoiled at the tired woman with dishevelled hair and dark rings around her eyes who stared back at her.

After peeing and drinking from the tap, Knight stood under a cold shower and shocked herself into alertness. Draped in a threadbare dressing gown, she made herself a strong coffee, drank it fast while she glanced at an old-fashioned clock on the wall that had been there for years. It was

1:12 in the morning, and Venezuela ran in the same time zone.

Could she save Zang and Pierce?

Knight doubted it, but she had to control the infection if she wanted to save her career.

She recalled a highly classified mission plan the CIA considered during the 2014 to 2016 West Africa Ebola outbreak and imagined how it could apply in these circumstances. A B-2 Spirit stealth bomber deployed from Barksdale Air Force Base in Louisiana could deliver the destruction required to raze La Tumba to the ground. The flight time would be a little under five hours to Caracas, and therefore the B-2 could engage under the cover of darkness before morning light, or sooner if one was already airborne and near Venezuelan airspace. But it would require deception of the highest magnitude to keep the US involvement deniable and to blame the destruction on the Venezuelans themselves.

There was her access to Garcia's cell phone. She could fake-message the Bolivarian National Guard of Venezuela, the GNB, order them to bring down the building with their armoured personnel carriers, to contain the outbreak. The perfect cover while the B-2 dropped a massive ordnance airblast bomb into the battle zone, disintegrating everything in a fireball called up from the pits of hell itself. Nothing would survive, including this rabies virus, and the Venezuela intelligence community would also suffer a severe setback.

This, however, was not a strike she could authorise.

She speed-dialled Abdul Ibrahim.

51

Caracas, Venezuela

After choke-holding another FEAS operative to death that Pierce and Amelia had encountered in the corridors during their exfiltration from SEBIN headquarters, Pierce found a storeroom, dragged the body inside and dressed Amelia in the soldier's clothes. He covered her head with sunglasses and a balaclava like the one he wore. Even though the clothes were slightly too large on her, they now resembled the hundreds of other FEAS killers who entered and exited this building every day. He needed the disguise so the sniper didn't pick them as identified targets.

Walking out of SEBIN headquarters disguised as masked FAES operators, even with the feverish and near unconscious Amelia Reyes hanging off his left shoulder, proved easier than Pierce had expected. Several text messages from Garcia's cell phone authorised his departure while ordering all other SEBIN and FAES operatives to return to base. No one challenged him, and hopefully, Pierce's deception would contain the outbreak to within this building.

Once outside La Tumba, immersed in the late-night heat of downtown Caracas, he walked north towards the closed and silent Mercado La Gran Manzana, near his planned meet with Zang. No bullets came for him, and he knew his deception had worked.

He was about to call Zang when she appeared, a dark shadow in the poorly lit streets. A hot tropical breeze blew rubbish around her feet.

"Zang?"

"Pierce."

Her tone concerned him, so he walked faster. When five metres separated them, he halted. Tingling at the back of his neck told him something was wrong. Amelia fainted in his arms, so he tore off the balaclava now they were under cover, because the mask would heat her unnecessarily with her fever.

Zang forced a grin. "You rescued Amelia. I'm impressed."

"Yes, but she's sick. Infected with a biological weapon. Don't come close, Zang; otherwise you'll contract it too."

"I know." Zang wiped tears from her eyes. "It's rabies."

"What?"

"I've caught it too. So don't worry about infecting me."

"Shit! I'm sorry to hear that!"

"Feel sorry for all of us. We all have it now."

"How?"

She shook her head. "We need to exfiltrate, immediately."

An explosion detonated inside a shop in the nearby markets, startling Pierce. Zang didn't react.

"Was that you?"

"Yes, I'm cleaning up an infection site. Now, are you ready to go?"

"Okay." Pierce wasn't certain what recent experiences had drawn Zang to her conclusions, but its revelation shocked her. It should have shocked him too, but his mind focused on getting them away safely.

She took them to her car. Within two minutes, she'd driven their Toyota sedan west through the near-empty streets. Amelia lay on the back seat, conscious but still not aware of her surroundings, her fever burning every centimetre of her skin. Pierce rummaged through Mansaray's and his companion's backpacks, which Zang had collected. While he searched, the two American CIA operators relayed to each other the intelligence they had gathered since their last communication. Soon there was no doubt in Pierce's mind that the biological weapon was a modified strain of rabies, and it had infected all three of them.

"It's fucked up!" Zang exclaimed.

"You said Mansaray told you he was immune?"

"Yeah." Zang nodded as she turned down a dark, narrow street. Military roadblocks everywhere in the city would restrict their movements and their ability to escape into the countryside. Backstreets were the best tactic to avoid GNB and other military forces, which would soon no doubt be searching for them. Backstreets, however, made it slow going. "But how does Mansaray's immunity help us?"

"With these."

Pierce showed her over a half dozen single-use jet injector syringes he'd discovered in Mansaray's pack. "They used these five, and recently. These two are ready to go."

Zang drew in a deep breath and sat straighter. Finally, there was a glimmer of hope in her eyes. "You mean...?"

"Yeah... These must be vaccines. They would only have them should they get exposed to the virus and develop symptoms and need to take it post-infection. Just like us."

Zang turned another corner only to find the road ahead obstructed by a wrecked car missing all its wheels. She shifted gears and reversed out. Stopping even momentarily to change direction increased the chance of an ambush or a carjacking from criminal elements that operated across the city at night. She spoke between gear crunches. "That's enough for you and me."

Pierce shook his head. "If we do that, Amelia dies!"

Zang sighed. "One of us will die, Pierce. She's likely too far gone to save already, even with a vaccine."

He didn't answer her.

Her brow pinched. "Pierce! You know I'm right."

"Very well." He held forth the first jet injector syringe. "You first?"

"Sure."

She parked the car in an open stretch of road where no one could sneak up on them unobserved, but left the engine running. He fired the vaccine into her neck. After a count of ten seconds, after which Zang had experienced no adverse effects, he grinned, and she drove again. "How do you feel?"

"Fine."

"Good, keep driving."

Zang pushed up the gears and sped them through the streets. In the distance, they heard police sirens and a helicopter circling in the dark skies above. "Now your turn, Pierce. Inject yourself."

He reached over into the back seat and fired the gun into Amelia Reyes's neck. She barely registered his actions.

Zang swerved momentarily, almost crashed their car into a parked food delivery van. "Mark! What the hell!"

He shrugged. "I made a promise."

"What? Why?"

He shrugged again. "I don't know how to answer that, Rachel. So much to unpack. Right now, Amelia will die without the vaccine. But me, I could last until we make it to the border."

Tears streamed down Zang's cheeks. "I don't understand you, Mark. With the roadblocks, the GNB patrols, and the fucked-up state of this country's infrastructure, we'll never make it to the Colombian border in time. You'll be dead long before we get there."

Pierce shrugged and forced a grin. "Mansaray said they planned three more attacks at three border crossings."

"Yeah... How does that help?"

"The San Cristobal to Cucuta crossing is the closest and easiest for us to reach. It's also a major chokepoint for refugees fleeing Venezuela, in their clashes with the GNB and *Colectivo* paramilitary gangs, so a perfect target for a terror strike. One of the three teams with the rabies virus will be there."

"You think they'll have more vaccine?"

Pierce nodded. He knew this was his only chance of surviving the infection growing in his body. Their likelihood of obtaining the vaccine was slim, but it was a chance worth chasing.

"How do we even recognise this terror cell? Or stop them? And they may not have any vaccines if we find them. That's a lot of 'ifs' you're betting your life on, Mark."

"You asked your CIA superiors to track the threats at the

border crossings. We use that intelligence when we receive it."

Zang made a growling noise. "I don't understand you. Is this some kind of death wish, to make up for whatever it is you did in your secret past that makes you hate yourself?"

"No!" Pierce answered with a firm tone that surprised them both, even though Zang had guessed his motives perfectly. "No. I..."

"Then what, Mark? You have to make the world a better place, even at the cost of your own life?"

He shrugged, not liking her insightful perception concerning his character. She was one of only two people who knew him better than he knew himself. "Maybe."

"How do we get to San Cristobal by morning? No way we can drive six hundred odd miles in this fucked-up country and get there in time."

"Not driving." Pierce held up Juan Garcia's cell phone. "In a helicopter, which I know you know how to fly. We can be there by morning."

Ahead, they heard the helicopter again power through the night skies, slowing its descent for a landing.

"I texted one Colonel Jesus Alvarez of the Bolivarian National Guard of Venezuela. The GNB. I demanded one of their Bell JetRanger helicopters collect us from Aristides Rojas Park, which you'll see just up ahead."

Zang sighed. She looked ready to berate Pierce further when Amelia stirred in the back seat. "Wh... What...?" the young Venezuelan activist mumbled.

"See," Pierce said with a smirk. "Amelia's better already. The vaccine works. And we'll find more."

Zang turned a corner fast, deliberately so, which forced

Pierce to press his hand against the dashboard so as not to bang his head on the windscreen. "I suppose, Pierce, you also planned that I'd fly that helicopter out?"

"Of course, as I said earlier. You are ex-USAF, and I've seen you fly a helicopter. Remember?"

"You forget I crashed it?" she said with a smirk.

"Didn't forget. And you crashed it very well, by the way. So I have faith you know what you're doing."

The garden park they drove into, like most of Caracas, was run-down and dirty. Its centrepiece was a basketball court with cracked pavements and trash strewn everywhere, rusting play equipment for children, and metal fences with barbed tips. Only the many trees looked healthy.

The Bell 206 Jet Ranger with GNB logos painted on its sides touched down on the basketball court, causing trash and dead leaves to flutter everywhere in the air.

"Leave this to me," Pierce said as he covered his face with the balaclava, recreating his disguise as an FAES operator, then stepped up to the pilot and co-pilot with his Heckler & Koch MP5 raised. They wouldn't hear him over the engine noises if he yelled instructions at them, but it didn't take long to recognise the threatening pose of his weapon. Pierce motioned they should get out. The pilots quickly obeyed and sprinted off into the night.

Zang carried a still barely conscious Amelia to the helicopter and strapped her into a chair in the back. With the blades still whipping above them, she yelled at Pierce even though they stood less than a metre apart. "Okay, you proved that was easy enough. I'll fly. You see what weapons we have!"

Pierce nodded. Of course, SEBIN and the GNB would

come after them when they realised Pierce and Zang had stolen one of their helicopters. They would need to defend themselves with every weapon in their arsenal if they planned to live through the long night still ahead of them.

52

M aceo Parra fumed as he sped from the GNB checkpoint that had detained him and searched his van, discovering an array of small arms and surveillance gear. They had him cuffed and left him supine on the ground for half an hour before someone checked his identification. When they discovered he was FAES, the apologies were numerous and unending. Parra still punched the lead sergeant in the throat, not hard enough to kill but with enough force that he thought he might die. Every minute Parra was delayed was a minute that Pierce might escape his clutches, and the Chinese reward would be lost.

When Parra arrived at SEBIN headquarters, Parra discovered numerous VN-4 Rhinoceros armoured personnel carriers releasing heavy firepower and explosive ordnance into the various exit points of the building. No one was getting out, and no one was getting in. It was like watching an enraged man offload a machine gun into a wall just to kill a single mosquito that had bitten him.

Parra spotted Colonel Jesus Alvarez twirling his moustache as he directed his men. He'd already shown his FAES pass to the soldiers maintaining the perimeter, so no one stopped him as he approached the high-ranking military officer.

"Sir." Parra snapped off a salute.

Alvarez turned and, recognising Parra, pinched his brows together. His moustache seemed to make a sad face at the same moment his mouth did. "Sergeant, what are you doing here?"

"Keeping the peace." He pointed to the building. "What's going on?"

"A biological weapon attack. A deadly virus has infected everyone inside. No one is allowed in or out."

Parra couldn't believe what he was hearing. "You're joking?"

"I'm not. I've seen it before. Besides, Director Garcia confirmed it. It was his orders that we bring down the building."

Parra paused and reassembled in his mind all the puzzle pieces he was aware of. Garcia had left Daniela's apartment with Mark Pierce, and the two had entered SEBIN headquarters together. Who had walked out before this disaster had unfolded? Parra would bet high stakes the director was still inside the building the GNB were shelling into rubble. "Tell me, Colonel, did anyone see a man and woman leaving this building just before you unloaded this fury?"

The colonel opened his mouth, ready to argue, then changed his mind. "I'll ask around." He spoke into his radio, communicating with his soldiers. A minute later a reply returned, as one conscript reported a FAES operator aiding another, short-statured FEAs operative who seemed to be unsteady on his feet, but no women. That event had occurred at least half an hour ago.

"That's got to be Pierce."

Another rocket was fired into the entrance hallway of La Tumba and, as it exploded loudly, erased the next words out of the colonel's mouth. Both men turned and saw a fire had started. Perhaps that was the intent, Parra mused, to burn this facility to the ground.

The colonel repeated his words. "This 'Pierce' character, is he behind this biological weapons attack?"

"He must be." Parra considered what he would do if he were in Pierce's position. The obvious answer was to flee the city and make a run for the Colombian border. The quickest means of achieving that was by air. "Lost any helicopters recently, Colonel?"

"No, why do you ask?"

Parra kept his expression stone-like, even though every muscle in his face tensed. "Check."

Then, from nowhere, the SEBIN building disintegrated. The roof seemed to explode downward, forcing the upper floors to implode and collapse sequential floors below them. The noise was like nothing Parra had ever heard, and the light of the flames ignited his eyeballs with blinding images. He had enough sense left in him to wrestle Alvarez to the ground, using the colonel as a shield against shrapnel as they fell behind a VN-4 Rhinoceros. The action momentarily saved both their lives as rubble exploded through the air around them.

Then it began to rain, not with water, but with debris and falling embers.

Parra and Alvarez rolled under the destroyed VN-4, a second action that saved their lives a second time, as falling concrete and steel support structures pinged and clanged as they fell upon the armoured personnel carrier.

They lay still until their eyesight normalised after the blinding light, and they watched between the huge tires of the VN-4 as La Tumba dropped into a cloud of smoke and carnage. Anyone inside could not have survived. The same could be said for almost all the GNB soldiers assaulting the building.

Parra always found it weird that in these moments of extreme violence, his mind quickly turned to how he could capture its awfulness in an illustration. He was mentally composing the picture of this moment in his mind even now.

Then dust billowed under the carrier, bringing Parra back to the moment. Soon both Parra and Alvarez were choking and spluttering, wondering if they would ever breathe again.

Soon the pounding of falling debris ceased, so Parra scrambled from the blast centre until the air cleared enough to breathe normally again. A coughing and wheezing Alvarez followed after him.

"What. The. Fuck. Happened?" Alvarez exclaimed.

"Air strike." Parra spat out the concrete dust in his mouth. "Your men couldn't have achieved that level of destruction."

The GNB colonel bent over and vomited up the dregs of an earlier dinner. Then he stood and wiped his mouth with his sleeve. "No, you're right there. Only the Americans are that precise with their missiles."

Parra remembered that Pierce was American. Perhaps his connections with the United States military and intelligence services were far stronger than he had originally anticipated. He turned to the colonel and said, "Yes, and your assault on the building gave the gringos a perfect cover to take SEBIN out."

"My orders came from Director Garcia himself."

"No, Colonel. They came from an American operative and his accomplice. Check on the status of your missing aircraft, helicopters in particular. You're a helo pilot, right?"

Alvarez nodded. "Yes. Why?"

"We're going after them."

"How can you be certain that is their course of action?"

Parra paused, asked himself why he felt confident in his assumptions. "I identify with this man. He is the same as me."

53

Sierra Nevada de Merida, Venezuela

Dawn spilled over the horizon, lighting the snow-capped mountain range in brilliant hues of yellows, oranges and purples. The cloudless, crisp air of this pristine land presented Venezuela's highest peaks as serene, but Pierce knew the risks they faced were many. They flew the length of the Sierra Nevada de Merida range, partially to hide behind peaks, lessening their chances of military aircraft spotting them, but also because it was the fastest route.

Rachel Zang, in the pilot's seat, kept their flight path steady and smooth. Amelia progressively recovered in the Bell 206 JetRanger's passenger bay. With her fever dropping, awareness of her surrounds grew with each passing minute. There was no doubt in Pierce's mind the vaccine had worked, because Zang showed no symptoms, while he experienced headaches, sweats, a fever and an inability to concentrate.

Earlier he'd checked the GNB helo's pintle-mounted 7.62mm machine guns, positioned at each side door. Many nations across the globe, including Venezuela, incorporated Bell 206s into their military fleets. Its main purpose was as a training helicopter, intelligence gatherer, for transportation of key personnel, or for battlefield observation. This was not a fighting aircraft, hence its light armaments.

Amelia yelled at him, but he couldn't hear her over the engines.

He passed her headphones, which she slipped over her ears and positioned the mic near her mouth.

"Can you hear me now?"

She gave the thumbs up. "Mark, you came back for me. How...?"

"How did I bust you from incarceration? It's a long story I'll save for later. How are you feeling?"

"Better... Defiled... What happened to me?"

Pierce hesitated. There was much Amelia did not yet know, and every revelation could drive her into shock if not handled carefully. "SEBIN held you inside La Tumba. I don't know what awful experiences they subjected you to, but you're safe now."

"Safe?"

Pierce pointed to the cockpit. "My friend Rachel is flying us to Colombia."

Amelia's eyes grew wide. "We're still in Venezuela?"

"Yes, but not for much longer."

She touched her short face-framing bob and noted the many knotted strands. "I remember I was sick. A fever. Everyone inside was getting terribly ill! Fevers, headaches..."

Pierce nodded and glanced out across the ragged mountain range they passed over. He sweated profusely, and his exhaustion was worse than immediately after his car crash in Rio de Janeiro. He reflected it had been less than two weeks since his memory-loss incident, and much had happened since then.

His thoughts turned to Mackenzie in this moment, and he reflected on what Zang had said about the naked and beaten woman he kept remembering as being his friend and co-worker.

Then he understood why he thought of her now, because he was about to die from an aggressive rabies virus, which meant he wouldn't find and rescue her, also dooming her to a short and unpleasant existence. That thought brought up feelings of failure and a lack of self-worth, even though Pierce was normally never burdened by moments of self-doubt as strong as this one felt.

"Mark?"

He glanced back at Amelia. She had called his name several times without him registering.

"You're sick, Mark. Look at the sweat pouring off you, and the shakes in your hands. Why am I okay, and you're not?"

Pierce smiled only with his mouth. "Only enough vaccine for the two of you."

Amelia glanced at Zang.

"Yes, Rachel Zang and you, Amelia. We'll secure additional vaccine in Colombia."

The young woman glanced around the cockpit and passenger bay. Her mouth was open, and her hands moved to cover her gaping expression. "Where... Where is Savannah?"

Pierce hesitated for several seconds, then said, "I'm sorry, Amelia. Savannah didn't make it."

"What? How?" She wailed uncontrollably as tears

gushed from her eyes. "Oh my God! I don't know... I don't know if I can keep going, losing another person dear to me."

Not knowing what to say, Pierce massaged her shoulder.

"Was it Maceo Parra?"

He nodded again. "I'm sorry. He killed her while we tried to rescue you from the piranha island. Savannah fought bravely. Her sole focus was to rescue you."

Amelia sobbed further as her face contorted into unnatural angles.

Pierce pulled her close and held her. She sobbed into his T-shirt, drenching him.

Zang spoke through the headphones. "Sorry to break this up, but we have company."

"Roger that." Pierce released Amelia and looked through the starboard, then port side of the helicopter. Pierce spotted another Bell 206 JetRanger hugging the side of a snow-capped mountain, chasing them. It could have been far worse, considering the variety of jet fighters and attack helicopters active in Venezuela's air force that could have come for them. In this dogfight, their aircraft were equally matched. Better odds than he could have hoped for.

Pierce turned to Amelia. "Get harnessed. I'll need to open these doors, and I don't want you tumbling out."

"Why?"

Pierce fitted a harness and hooked himself to the bay's railing. "Our enemies pursue us."

"Pierce?"

"Yes, Zang?"

"Look again."

Pierce opened the port side door, as the chill of icy winds filled the cabin. He swung out the 7.62mm machine gun on its pintle-mount. The enemy JetRanger was not concerned about fuel and closed in on them at maximum speed.

"I've got this, Zang."

"No. Behind it. Look again!"

Pierce did.

A second helicopter appeared, hidden behind the first.

"Shit! That's a Mil Mi-17!"

"Exactly."

Amelia locked her harness to the railing inside the bay as Pierce had. "What's a Mi-17?"

"Soviet-era attack helicopter. Not only will it have machine guns and rockets, but its cruise speed also easily outperforms our top speed!"

"We're in trouble?"

Pierce grimaced. It seemed his concern about dying from rabies would soon no longer bother him. "That's one way of putting it, yes."

54

Pierce glanced through the opening in the JetRanger, his eyes transfixed on the two enemy helicopters about to blast them from the skies. With the icy winds chilling him and bringing some reprieve from the virus slowly killing him, he thought to spray the skies with hundreds of 7.62mm rounds from the pintle-mounted machine gun. Such a course of action, however, would be pointless. The Mil Mi-17 could take them out with a single rocket. If Pierce, Amelia and Zang were to survive this encounter, it would only be through negotiation.

Zang chirped through the radio, "My only option is to fly close to the mountain peaks, but that is only a marginal protection from rockets. I mean very marginal."

"Roger that." He knew, as Zang knew, this was a futile option. "Can you open up radio comms?"

"Sure. How will that help?"

Pierce stared at the distant enemy JetRanger, barely made out a man behind the machine gun mounted on that helicopter. From this distance, it was impossible to tell who the individual was, but Pierce was betting his life this was Maceo Parra. "The man in that helo chasing us, I've already met."

"Worth a shot. Give me a minute."

While he waited, Pierce directed his gaze towards Amelia. "I need your help."

Her black hair danced madly around her head as the chilly winds blew through the bay. She shivered, and so did he, but for very different reasons. "Whatever you need, Mark."

"Search the cabin. See what you can find."

"What am I looking for, exactly?"

"Weapons, ideally. Explosive weaponry, more ideally."

"Channel eight," Zang chirped through the radio as she sent their helo in a sweeping arc, forcing Pierce to grip a handrail to avoid falling from the bay. His harness would secure him, but he'd make a terrible impression upon the enemy if he ended up dangling from the JetRanger.

As soon as Pierce switched channels, he heard a voice.

"Mark Pierce, I knew it was you."

The American operator chuckled. "Finally worked out who I am, Maceo Parra?"

"Your friend Amelia Reyes told me. Let it slip while I was bringing her out of the jungle."

Pierce recalled the conversation he had overheard at the island of piranhas, then paused and weighed his next words. He and his companions were one wrong phrase away from annihilation. He knew Zang now executed her own evasive strategies, most of which would involve dangerous manoeuvres through the towering, rugged peaks. Pierce hoped it wouldn't come to that.

He cleared his throat and replied to the FAES sniper. "So, you've worked out why we're worth keeping alive?"

"Are you, though? I hear a viral weapon of mass destruction has infected the three of you. Even if I captured you alive, you still wouldn't live long enough for me to collect my reward with the Chinese."

Pierce looked down, through the wind and the thousand metres of nothing that separated him and the helo from the rugged, black rock interspersed with desolate Andean grasslands. There was no flat ground down there for emergency landings. His mind absorbed what he heard and quickly planned an elaborate lie.

"My job, Pierce, is to blow you fuckers out of the sky so you can't infect anyone else."

"You're wrong, Parra, on both counts."

No response came across the radio frequencies, but then Parra had proved to be a man of few words. Pierce figured, however, that if Parra truly believed there was no option but to kill Pierce, he wouldn't have bothered with conversation.

"Explain?"

Pierced realised he had held his breath for several seconds, so he sucked in a lungful of chilled air. "First, we've always known about the modified rabies virus, even before we left Langley, and that means we're all vaccinated here and uninfected."

"You lie."

"No, not even Amelia. We gave her a vaccine as soon as we escaped La Tumba, and she's fine now."

"I still don't believe you."

"Yeah?" Pierce tensed as he questioned if his bluff would succeed, yet projected confidence in his next words. "A smart man like you, Parra, should have put all the pieces together already. You already know what's going down."

This time, when Parra responded, he had lost a little of the confidence he had always projected until now. "Tell me, then? Presume I know nothing."

"Why do you think the CIA sent me to Rio de Janeiro in the first place? Why do you think the Chinese have put out a ten-million-dollar reward for my capture?" Pierce's heart rate and breathing increased as the lies flowed effortlessly from his tongue. "It's all connected. It was the Chinese who weaponised the rabies strain now infecting your country. It was me and Walsh in Wuhan who sabotaged China's biological weapons research facility there, shortly after we stole their only virus samples and all their vaccine. Intel we gathered in Wuhan led us to Amelia Reyes and SEBIN's interest in her. Of course the Chinese want me dead, because Walsh and me, we cost them their leverage. US pharma companies are mass-producing vaccine even as we speak. China's biological threat, which they planned to let loose in Venezuela, is a non-starter now."

Pierce waited for a response.

None came.

The Mi-17 turned as a bright yellow-orange streak flared from a side-mounted hard point.

"Fuck!"

Proximity sensors activated, filling the cabin and cockpit with high-pitched warning alarms.

"Incoming. Brace for impact!"

The rocket tore through the thin air, headed straight at them.

And there was no time for evasive manoeuvres.

The rocket passed close enough for Pierce to feel the

heat of its propellant flames before it shot past and exploded into the side of the massif. Rock and snow thundered outwards. As the JetRanger buffeted and rocked from the blast wave, and Zang fought to keep them steady and not crash into the mountains, debris fell, collected on an outcrop of collected snow and ice. The outcrop then crumpled, and soon an avalanche of snow, rock and ice rapidly dropped down the side of the mountain. The sheer enormity of the destruction left Pierce in awe, as he realised their helo could have been part of that accelerating downward propagation of obliteration.

"That's a warning." Parra spoke again over the radio. "Fly to Merida, and land there. If you deviate from your flight path... Well, you've already seen how easily we can end your lives suddenly."

Pierce hesitated only a moment, realising he had merely postponed their deaths, not prevented it. But he had bought them time to formulate another plan. "Very well, Parra."

"When you land, we will talk, but it will be on my terms."

The radio went dead.

Pierce moved to close the cabin, and noticed how much sweat was pouring off him despite the alpine chill in the air.

It was Amelia who closed the cabin door and helped Pierce to a seat. "You look awful."

He laughed, feeling his face and chest burn, with his fever now sweating his skin with the wind no longer chilling him, and his body shaking. "I'm okay. What... did you find?"

She passed him a box.

He opened it, finding casing for twelve high-explosive grenades, with one missing.

"Can you use them?"

"Without a doubt." Pierce shuddered and tried to ignore the nausea gripping him. "Zang, you heard all that?"

"Every word."

"How far to Merida?" he said, remembering from his research this was a city within the Sierra Nevada de Merida, but still a long way from San Cristobal, the Venezuela-Colombia border, and any chance of Pierce getting his hands on a vaccine.

Amelia asked, "What happens when we land?"

Zang spoke from the cockpit, using a radio channel only the three of them had access to. "They'll execute you and me, Amelia, and then Pierce when they realise he's infected."

"Then why did we agree to that crazy plan?"

Pierce wiped more sweat from his overly hot forehead. "Because it buys us time. Zang, we have grenades. Do you have a plan?"

"Yes, but you're not going to like it."

55

Parra watched from his JetRanger as Pierce, Reyes and whoever it was piloting the enemy helicopter stayed steady on their flight path as agreed. He had believed little of what Pierce had told him, yet greed motivated him enough to at least check if the American's story held some truth. If Pierce had told no lies, Parra could hand him over to the Chinese and collect the reward. If Pierce had samples of this modified rabies virus and its vaccine that he spoke of, Parra could sell them on the black market to multiple fanatical terrorist groups across the globe, who would pay a small fortune for such a weapon. If neither of these options were true, Parra would simply execute the three and collect on the lesser reward for Pierce's corpse. None of these options were viable if he simply vaporised them over a mountain range where their bodies would never be found.

After confirming with the Mi-17 crew not to shoot Pierce's helo out of the sky unless he gave the order, Parra moved to the cockpit and sat next to Jesus Alvarez. The Venezuelan

National Guard colonel had proved a competent pilot, but nothing special. Parra felt glad there had been no need to go one-to-one with Pierce's mysterious and highly competent pilot, judging by the manoeuvres he had witnessed them pull off.

"Whatever happens, Alvarez, no one in that helicopter leaves my sight alive. Understood?"

"Of course I understand, Sergeant."

Parra controlled his breathing until he felt calm again. "We're going to fix this."

"We'd better; otherwise you and I are fucked."

Parra didn't say it would only be Alvarez facing the firing squad, as Parra would disappear if circumstances today turned against him. But he didn't think it would come to that. At least Garcia was out of the picture now, so he wouldn't have to worry about sharing the reward with the director any longer.

Soon the landscape below them, while still mountainous, became cloud forests, with palms and thick vegetation growing everywhere, interspersed with several sugar cane plantations. The city of Merida, while tiny compared to Caracas, was a similar unplanned sprawl with terracotta-roofed houses, Spanish Colonial architecture, multiple churches, and slums lining the city outskirts and steeper slopes. The airport came into view in the city's centre, where the Mi-17 would force Pierce's helicopter to land.

Then Parra watched as the JetRanger deviated from its course. It turned sharply, almost perpendicular to the direction it had been following, and picked up speed.

Parra realised if they opened fire here, it would be over the houses of the city's most wealthy citizens, and collateral casualties could later be problematic. Whatever this day brought, he needed to ensure he could disappear from Venezuela without SEBIN or FAES having a reason to come after him. Distraught and grieving families with money would find a way to race him to the top of Venezuela's most wanted list if he accidentally killed someone important during the crossfire.

"Do we shoot him down?" asked the Mil Mi-17 pilot.

"No. Force him to land. Anywhere that is practical!"

"Affirmative."

The Mi-17 sped after Pierce's JetRanger and buffered the enemy aircraft with the downward pressure of the Russian attack helicopter's more powerful rotary engines. The JetRanger shook and had no choice but to drop.

"What's it doing?"

Parra sensed panic in the colonel's voice. Then he noticed sweat on the moustached man's grip on the cyclic control.

"Let the Mi-17 engage, Parra! Force them to land with over-the-bow missile strikes!"

It was then that Parra realised their mistake.

The JetRanger had flown under a string of high-voltage electric transmission lines passing through rocky cloud forest terrain, and the Mi-17 had followed, maintaining its higher elevation and position of power. Parra watched as his brows pinched, as a series of explosions rocked the base of one transmission tower. The structure buckled, then toppled.

The high-voltage lines snapped and shot through the air like cracking whips.

One cable caught in the rotor blades of the Mi-17. Electric arcs surged between the helo and the earth before the attack helicopter dropped like a stone and exploded on impact when it smashed into a rocky, vegetation-clad outcrop.

"Pull up!" Parra yelled over the noise and destruction. Alvarez was flying them straight into the collapsing transmission lines. Of all the places in Venezuela that experienced ongoing power failures for days and weeks on end, why wasn't Merida one of those places right now? "Pull up, or an electrical arc will destroy our electronics too!"

The air crackled around them. Parra felt the hairs on his head and arms tingle. He imagined dying, until Alvarez regained his composure and turned them away from the carnage Pierce and his friends had caused. Parra realised he wasn't getting out of Venezuela now without a target on his back.

When they were far enough from the disaster, he searched the skies. The enemy JetRanger was nowhere to be found.

"What do we do now?" Alvarez asked. The colonel had lost all ability to take command in this situation. But that was what dictatorships did. They forced everyone to relinquish their abilities to make decisive decisions because they left all important choices to only one man. The big man. *El Presidente Incompetente.* Another reason Sergeant Maceo Parra needed to escape Venezuela soon, so he didn't become just another incompetent cog in the incompetent machinery that was his nation's failed government and military. A country without a true purpose or identity that mattered.

"We know their destination, Colonel. San Cristobal. Get us there as fast as you can."

56

San Cristobal, Venezuela

Rachel Zang fought a losing battle. During their engagement with the Mi-17, the JetRanger had taken a hit. She didn't know the exact extent of the damage, but she knew the flight controls fought her their entire journey from the mountains to San Cristobal while the engine steadily lost its power. No longer able to ascend, they gradually lost altitude, and she was not able to regain it. When the ground was a mere one hundred metres below them, she knew now was the time to land.

She'd overflown the city of San Cristobal, much larger than Merida but of a similar appearance when seen from the sky. Continuing west, she crossed into the border region between Venezuela and Colombia, separated by the Rio Tachira. The township of San Antonio del Tachira lay between San Cristobal and Cucuta in Colombia, visible now on the horizon. Zang knew she could have flown them into Colombia and safety, even with the damage sustained by the helo, but that would kill Pierce. He needed the rabies vaccine in the next few hours, and the only place they might find it was here, on the border and on the Venezuelan side.

"Pierce?" she yelled through the radio comms.

No answer.

"For fuck's sake, Pierce, talk to me!"

Again, silence.

She was about to swear again when Amelia Reyes answered, speaking Spanish.

Not even close to having any fluency in the local language, Zang missed everything that she had said. "Do you speak English?"

"Some. Small words."

"Sounds better than my Spanish. What did you say?"

"Pierce. He's... what is the word...?"

"He's what?" Now the helicopter started to rattle unnaturally, and the controls started to fight her.

"Sleep...?"

"Then wake him."

"I can't. He is..."

Zang suddenly understood. The situation was worse than she imagined. "He's unconscious?"

"Yes. Correct word."

Zang looked down on the streets. She noticed people everywhere, and many raised sticks, rifles and machetes in threatening poses. Some wore makeshift gas masks made from plastic bottles and cotton wool. She guessed this was a protection against tear gas. Then she identified Bolivarian National Guard Rhino armoured personnel carriers, paramilitary soldiers clad in black uniforms wielding batons, shields, riot gear and more lethal weapons, and all of them featuring the GNB logo. The same logo plastered all over their helicopter.

Zang swore again. "Find my medical kit. We'll need it as soon as we land."

"Yes. I understand."

"And strap in. The landing will be... bad."

Zang shook her head and asked herself why she cared for Mark as much as she did, when he was so reckless with his life and the lives of those around him. She should just keep flying. As soon as they landed, the rioters would swarm them. They would have to fight their way out, but they could only do that if Pierce remained lucid and operational.

She heard and felt bullets ping off the helo's hull. The ground was only a dozen metres below them now, comprising an old, tired-looking road surrounded by barely held together houses constructed of red brick, cement and corrugated iron roofing. Green vegetation grew in the cracks in the concrete, and residential power lines spread like spiderwebs between every structure and concrete power pole.

Zang spied a soccer pitch and immediately felt something was finally working in her favour. Delicately adjusting the collective pitch control, she brought them in for a smooth landing.

Soon rioters flung rocks at the helo. The glass in the cockpit frosted white; then as a second rock hit, webs of cracks sprang up everywhere. The angry men and women outside would be upon them in seconds.

Zang clambered from the cockpit into the bay, to find Pierce drenched in his own sweat and unconscious, as Amelia had said. The Venezuelan woman handed over the CIA-supplied military-grade trauma kit. Zang found the adrenalin injector and stabbed it hard into Pierce's outer thigh.

It had the immediate effect she desired, of waking him and bringing alertness.

She forced an M4 assault carbine into his hands. "Pierce! We're on the wrong side of the Colombia-Venezuela border, surrounded by scores of angry locals who think we are GNB and therefore desperately wish to kill us. We need to fight our way out. You up for it?"

He nodded as he stared unfocused, with bloodshot eyes.

"Good. Fire in the hole."

Zang dropped a flashbang, then smoke grenades outside both side windows of the helo. They detonated within seconds, dispersing the already aggravated and aggressive crowd. "Move!"

Amelia gripped Zang's forearm and locked eyes. "They are civilians out there. You won't kill them!" Her words were statements of defiance, not requests.

Zang returned a stony stare. "No, Amelia. Pierce and I are more professional than you give us credit for."

Pierce was already out of the helicopter and laid covering fire to discourage the crowd from returning to fight them.

Zang pushed Amelia out, and the three sprinted for the cover of buildings.

Suddenly, they had found themselves in a midst of violent civil rioting.

57

San Antonio del Tachira, Venezuela

Idris Walsh drove into the town centre of San Antonio del Tachira and realised they had stumbled upon a battlefield. Taisiya Ozerova in the passenger seat tied her blonde hair into a ponytail and pulled her Czechoslovak Cz 83 because she now saw what he saw. Civilian men and women, mostly young people, throwing stones, Molotov cocktails and concrete blocks at the Bolivarian National Guard blockading the Puente Internacional Simon Bolivar bridge crossing the tiny Rio Tachira dividing Venezuela from Colombia. Trucks loaded with international food and medical aid waited to cross into the failed state, but the GNB would not allow it. Venezuela could not appear weak and in need of international support, not here where the world's media watched from across the tiny river shallow enough to wade across, but impossible to bring a truck through.

"It's on all the Colombian news sites," said Ozerova. "We chose the wrong time to be here."

A rock bounced off their bonnet. Then another cracked the windscreen.

"Or the right time."

Walsh collected all their aerosol cans, vaccines and jet injector syringes in a backpack he slung over his shoulder. He thought about grabbing an AN-94 assault rifle, but that would only draw attention. Instead, he pulled back the slide on the Cz 83, chambering a round, and checked that his pockets had enough spare magazines.

Ozerova watched him closely without comment.

"It's time. Let's get out there and start spraying this virus into the crowds, and then watch as it spreads like wildfire."

"You say so."

Because Walsh was not a man to take unnecessary risks, he popped an anti-rejection pill, then fired the jet injector syringe into his neck. He might die a hundred ways today, but death by rabies infection wouldn't be one of them. Walsh handed Ozerova their second-last injector.

She hesitated for a moment, then forced the vaccine into her own neck muscles.

Another projectile hit the truck. Then flames spread across the bonnet as the Molotov cocktail ignited.

Walsh leaped from their four-wheel drive and fired four shots in the attackers' general direction. Mostly they were young men who fled at the sound of gunfire.

Ignoring the flames gathering on the truck, Walsh raced to the back of the vehicle for better cover.

Then Walsh heard gunfire before he registered it as controlled bursts fired from professional soldiers, and it was coming from behind them now. Another group were aiming at Ozerova and him specifically, firing from an alley wedge between two buildings to his left.

Walsh knew he was a dead man if he didn't act immediately, and in the next second he had Ozerova in front of him, acting as a shield.

In seconds, her body filled with bullets, and her death was instant.

Walsh dragged Ozerova's corpse with him as he shuffled backwards, reaching his own side street providing cover. Then he dropped the Russian and sprinted deeper into the city streets.

When he'd covered a half dozen blocks, with cramps in his gut and a burning throat, the spymaster stopped to gather his breath. He wasn't a young man anymore, and his liver transplant had aged him by decades.

He checked to see if he still had one of the aerosol cans with the virus, but he did not. They were all back at the four-wheel drive he had sprinted from.

Walsh swore under his breath. If he escaped today, he had to hide, go deep and hope no one ever found him. It would mean living off the grid as much as possible, but Walsh didn't believe he had an option anymore, because he'd now failed to complete the operation his mysterious organisation demanded of him, and they would kill him for his failure. He no longer possessed the health or stamina to fight and scheme in this world of deceit, death, and deception. Hiding was the only option.

A GNB JetRanger flew low overhead.

For a second, Walsh thought the helo crew had spotted him. Then he watched the helicopter race onwards towards the Simon Bolivar bridge, where a major battle between civilians and the guard soldiers progressed at full force. He smelled residual tear gas and noticed rubber bullets discarded on the earth, but it wouldn't take long for the fighting to turn lethal.

Deciding he'd wasted enough time, and guessing that the men who had attacked him were likely US Special Forces and probably his old crew from the CIA's Special Operations Group, Walsh headed west. He was in search of a strip of the Rio Tachira that didn't flow too fast and wouldn't leave him too exposed to random shooters, precise snipers or overzealous border guards as he crossed it.

Then he saw a sight that he'd expected, but hoped he wouldn't, under these trying circumstances.

Rachel Zang and Mark Pierce.

They hadn't seen him yet, which gave him the advantage.

58

Pierce moved fast, checking all corners, pausing while he covered Zang and Amelia when they moved, and sprinting when Zang covered him.

The adrenalin shot provided alertness and strength, but he knew it wouldn't last. Fever was rampant in his system, and it might already be too late for the vaccine. He sweated profusely; his head screamed with a migraine. He'd read somewhere once that over fifty thousand people died of rabies each year, so if this airborne version got out, it could kill a hundred times that. This was a number on par with the worldwide death total to date from the COVID-19 coronavirus, and the world wasn't ready to face another threat like that. They had to contain it, here and now.

As they moved, Pierce ensured he never came close to any other human other than Zang and Amelia, not wishing to infect anyone else.

When he almost fainted, Zang came up behind him. Her M4 assault carbine provided cover and scared off the few rioters who thought to give them trouble. He fell onto his haunches and couldn't move.

"Walsh is here," Zang reported as she caught her breath. "I contacted Langley, and they told me."

Pierce nodded. He didn't remember Zang calling in, but she must have done so some time after they had landed. "How do they know Walsh is here?"

"Because a 7th Special Forces Group unit just engaged with Walsh. They killed his team member, but said he got away, for now. Exactly what similar 7th SFG units accomplished in Maracaibo and Puerto Paez against similar targets. The only rabies threat vectors left now, Pierce, are you and our old nemesis."

Pierce grinned through his bloodstained teeth. His hands shook, and his legs didn't feel that they would support him for much longer. "What did you tell Langley?"

Zang frowned. "That we're all vaccinated."

"That's only true if we find Walsh."

"Then we'd better find him."

Pierce reached into his combat webbing and searched for the last of the high-explosive grenades Amelia had found for him on the helo. Most he'd used to bring down the high-voltage transmission line, but he'd kept one... just in case he didn't make it. Blowing himself to pieces if there was no escape seemed the preferable option, and its incinerating heat would hopefully prevent the virus from spreading beyond his explosive ending.

He said, "This Special Forces unit won't discriminate, Zang. If they think we carry infection, they won't hesitate to take us out."

"I know!"

They heard gunfire in the distance.

Pierce couldn't be certain, but it didn't sound to be rubber bullets anymore. He grabbed Zang's shirt. "Give me another adrenalin shot."

"It could kill you."

He laughed as what felt to be buckets worth of sweat poured off him. "Hilarious, Zang."

She nodded, then plunged an injector into his thigh.

The alertness, buzzing and paranoia was sudden and overwhelming. He felt his heart crash against his ribcage, and when, a few seconds later, he was surprised to discover he wasn't dead, Pierce recognised he was ready to go again.

He stood, then searched for Amelia.

Still in her FAES outfit, minus the weapons, armour and balaclava, she cowered behind a ruined concrete wall and covered her ears with her hands and rocked back and forth like a terrified child. Pierce helped her to her feet. "It's almost over. Colombia is just over there."

She nodded, and he noticed how pale she was. The constant fear was beating her, and Pierce worried she might become catatonic at any moment. Then her eyes widened, and she whispered, "I saw him."

"Who?"

"Maceo Parra. It was him. He's with the GNB forces."

Pierce nodded, but the action hurt. His brain felt to be pressing hard against the inside of his skull. "He's not our problem. Your safety is, and the vaccine for me is the secondary priority."

Massaging his forehead, Pierce glanced between his fingers only to see a man he recognised turn the corner and face him.

Idris Walsh was a ghost of his former self. Boney and rake-like, with ashen skin and hollow eyes, but his stares were alert and revealed his still-cunning nature, just as he had been at the car crash in the Rio favela.

Both men raised their weapons and fired simultaneously.

Neither aimed accurately, and both men soon emptied their magazines.

"It's Walsh!" Pierce said as he chased after the one man on this planet who could save his life.

59

P ierce pursued Walsh westwards, knowing the man would make a break across the shallow Rio Tachira into Colombia despite the risks that a GNB soldier would shoot him as a defector trying to escape Venezuela. But Walsh would know Pierce was a far more dangerous threat, and risk the crossing anyway.

As sweat poured off Pierce, he fumbled with his M4 as he ran.

Then, deciding the weapon was useless to him in his shaky hands and fevered state, he dropped the assault carbine and pulled his Glock semi-automatic. He fired off a few poorly aimed shots, all missing Walsh and all failing to convince him to stop running.

Pierce gained on the spymaster until a coughing fit caused him to double over and lose the distance he had closed between them.

Walsh disappeared into the low-lying green foliage that separated San Antonio del Tachira from Cucuta on the Colombian side of the river. Knowing that his only hope was pursuit, Pierce pushed through his pain and gave chase.

He came through the other side of the greenery, into a pebbly field, to discover Walsh knee-deep in fast-flowing water.

"Walsh!" Pierce bellowed. "Stop, or I'll fucking shoot you dead!"

When the spymaster turned, he discovered Pierce only a dozen metres from him and the pistol lined up with Walsh's gut.

In Walsh's left hand, he held a jet injector gun. "You're infected, Pierce. I can tell just by looking at you."

Pierce advanced, pistol held high, ready to shoot his nemesis.

"Keep advancing, Pierce, and I break it."

The threat caused Pierce to pause.

"Throw your weapon away. Now!"

Pierce didn't hesitate. He felt ready to pass out. He had to solve this problem in the next few minutes, or he was a dead man.

When the Glock vanished into the fast-flowing water, Walsh grinned. "Smart man." He also threw the jet injector gun into the water, then turned and sprinted into Colombia.

Knowing that Walsh was getting away, Pierce dived into the Rio Tachira where he saw the injector go under, and felt around in the murky waters, searching for it.

He hoped it hadn't floated away, because if it had, there was no chance he would find it.

As his fever burned, he splashed cold water on his face. He crawled low in the fast flow as his fingers fumbled between hundreds of pebbles worn smooth by the millennia.

Then his hands felt it.

He gripped it, then lifted it carefully so it didn't snap if lodged in the rocks. When the jet injector gun was firm in his hands and seemingly undamaged, Pierce fired the vaccine into his neck.

He didn't feel any different. The fever still burned. His limbs shook, and his exhaustion now seemed too much to bear.

Pierce crawled from the river up onto the pebbly edge, then into the undergrowth on the opposite, Colombian side until he fell into a patch of concealing green vegetation.

As he passed into unconsciousness, he had only one thought. He would wake cured, or he would never wake again.

60

Z ang had intended to chase after Pierce, until a panicked crowd of protestors flooded the street, creating a wall of bodies between them. She soon understood why. GNB soldiers advanced, firing AK-190 and FN Herstal FAL assault rifles, and they didn't use rubber bullets. Tear gas flowed as dispersing clouds around her. A few panicked citizens carried or dragged bleeding men and women from the carnage. One victim, shot in the back, fell near Zang. She was only a young girl, perhaps fifteen. Her eyes lay open and stared at nothing.

When an elderly fleeing woman spotted Zang with her M4, she screamed and pointed, alerting the crowd and the GNB to their position.

"We've got to move."

Zang grabbed Amelia, and the two raced from the panicked crowd, which took them further from Pierce. Mixed feelings overcame Zang. She worried that Pierce was her friend, and he was dying and needed her help. She also felt frustration and annoyance that the man was reckless and unpredictable, had caused his own problems and had dragged her into a mess not of her making. Then she remembered they were a team. She would come back for him, but would do so on a circumventive route. Zang's duty also extended to Amelia Reyes, who followed starry-eyed behind Zang and barely spoke. It was Zang's duty to protect them both at all costs.

Once they'd covered a few blocks and increased their distance from the GNB assaults, the crowds dispersed, and they paused. She found cover, the protection of a corner between two buildings where Zang had a full view of all approach angles.

"What about Mark?"

Zang listened to Amelia's words carefully. She heard stress and fear in the Venezuelan. Zang had encountered victims like her before, one fright away from losing it completely, to either act out in rage and uncontrolled violence, or to mentally shut down and turn catatonic. It was difficult to tell which way Amelia would swing, but she carried too much internally repressed momentum to remain calm for much longer.

"Listen to me, Amelia. Pierce's best chance for survival was going after Walsh and the vaccine. We're going after him now, but not through this fighting. We'll find him, help him, and then cross into Colombia, where you'll be safe. We all will."

"What if I don't want to be safe?"

Zang's brows pinched. "What does that mean?"

"I saw him."

"Who?"

"Parra."

Zang growled. "That asshole is the least of your problems right now, and mine, too!" She grabbed Amelia, and they advanced again through the claustrophobic streets that stank of tear gas, cordite and piss. Everywhere, from all directions, she heard sporadic gunfire, screams, and other indiscernible noises that humans only expressed when they were both angry and afraid.

Then it occurred to Zang to ask Amelia where she had seen Parra.

But she didn't have to ask because they walked right into him.

Parra and a colonel with a prominent moustache, flanked by a dozen armed GNB soldiers, turned a corner at the same time Zang did.

She squeezed the trigger of her M4, flooding the street with dozens of 5.56x45mm NATO rounds into three GNB soldiers, who went down fast before surprise or shock could alert them that they were already dead. She pushed Amelia back at the same moment AK and FN assault rifles barked back, filling the air with muzzle flashes, high-speed projectiles, and more burned gunpowder.

They raced down a street between half-built houses with dirty concrete walls, corrugated roofs, and weeds everywhere. A dog slinked past, then gaited when a bullet nipped its already mangy ear. The GNB were close behind and firing again.

Zang pulled Amelia close as she ran at speed at a house door. The force had the desired effect, and it collapsed under impact. They landed hard, but Zang had sense enough to roll on her back, M4 raised and ready. She'd timed her manoeuvre well. As she emptied the magazine of her M4 into the door, soldiers burst in and died instantly as her slugs tore their insides into mincemeat.

No one followed after, so she reloaded in less than three seconds and fired a second controlled burst through the door. Then she pulled an incendiary grenade she'd secured from the Caracas safe house and threw it through the open door. It detonated loudly and with much light. She heard men scream while she spotted flames licking the air near the edge of her line of sight.

"Find an exit!" Zang exclaimed.

Amelia stood, appearing unnaturally pale and unblinking. "There is no exit, and I heard soldiers behind us."

Zang didn't want to speak the words she feared out loud, but she thought them. This was it. There was no escape for either of them. She climbed to her feet anyway, M4 raised, ready to take out as many of the fuckers as she could before she went down.

Amelia stared through the open door. "I'm not doing this anymore!" she said in her clumsy English.

"What do you mean?"

"Tell the world what you saw today."

And without looking back, Amelia stepped out into the sunlight.

61

Sergeant Maceo Parra knew victory would soon be his, but he didn't expect it to be easy. He never did. Careful planning, dedicated training and constant vigilance had kept him alive until now and would keep him alive for decades to come.

He watched Amelia Reyes, the dyke, step into the carnage and ignore the half dozen maimed, charred or dead men littering the battlefield she had become the centre of. Fires burned nearby, lighting up her coffee-coloured skin in an unreal vibrance. Parra wanted to remember this scene so he could draw it later. He didn't understand why, but in his retelling of this moment, he wanted her to feature angel wings, but they would be cut and broken, smouldering in places, and covered in soot.

Wearing only the tattered and dirty remains of a FAES outfit many sizes too big for her, she locked eyes with his and walked towards him.

Colonel Jesus Alvarez, looking like someone had dragged him through a burning pig pen, pulled his Makarov pistol and aimed the muzzle for a clean shot between the dyke's eyes.

Parra lifted his arm to force down the colonel's aim. The former FAES sniper then raised his other arm, instructing the soldiers not to shoot her. "Cover that entrance, though. Shoot the other woman dead if she sticks her nose out."

Amelia walked without fear or concern and took the shortest route to reach Parra. Her stare was both unfocused and coldly intense, and she projected an air of equal parts defiance and defeat. Whatever her game was, Parra couldn't guess. But he knew this woman and knew she would be weak and malleable in his presence.

When she was a metre from him, she halted, and their eyes locked.

"You must know I'll take you back to Caracas, where they'll torture you again."

She looked him up and down, as if seeing the real him for the first time, or understanding his depths that she had never previously appreciated. What concerned him was that she wasn't afraid.

She held his stare. "Do you remember anything?"

"Remember anything about what?"

She snorted a laugh. "My mother, Parra. You butchered my mother. You remembered enough to draw a picture of her! It was her, in that cantina in the jungle, and even when I pointed it out, you still couldn't remember!"

He shrugged, enjoying her pain. "I don't remember. Why would I?"

Amelia stepped closer, close enough to kiss if he felt that way inclined. The colonel, mere metres from the two of them, kept his pistol trained on Amelia's head, but she didn't notice him. She noticed nothing about the world except

Parra. Her hand reached up and gently stroked his chin. "It's sad that you and I are the same."

He laughed. "We are not the same."

"We are, only you can't see it. This country of ours, this cage of traitors, where we all have to create false identities to mask how we all feel, just to survive... It exhausts me just as much as it exhausts you."

"I'm not tired."

She smiled with pity. "But you are, Maceo. I hurt. You hurt. I've seen it in your art. I will not pretend anymore. And you won't have to, either."

Parra sniggered as he scratched the back of his neck where it itched. He thought to order the colonel to shoot the bitch, just to shut her up. But the president wouldn't like it. Parra had to bring her back, alive, and for a second time, to lessen the chances of FAES or SEBIN coming after him when he disappeared to begin his new life as a contract assassin. It was so tiring, dealing with the idiots who ran this country, and the pointless errands they all made him endlessly perform.

He looked back at Amelia. "It's time."

"It is."

She opened her hand.

In it, she carried a grenade.

"I pulled the pin two seconds ago."

62

Zang recoiled, watching through a bullet hole in the concrete wall as Amelia Reyes sacrificed herself with the detonation that obliterated her and the colonel and shredded the skin and flesh from one half of Maceo Parra's body. He staggered for a moment, but only a moment, before he toppled dead onto the charred and blood-soaked earth.

Zang didn't understand what she had witnessed, but she saw an opportunity. The soldiers, seeking cover from the blast, looked away as Zang burst from the building as she laid covering fire and made her escape. She obliterated two soldiers, then fled.

Sprinting with burning muscles and rasping lungs, Zang dropped her M4 because it made her a target, and blended with the rioting crowds. The city was a storm of chaos, and more people would die tonight in the fighting that seemed unable to be quelled.

She moved towards the Puente Internacional Simon Bolivar bridge, crossing the tiny Rio Tachira, and spotted the GNB Unimog UR-416 armoured personnel carrier blocking the crossing so the lines of food aid trucks couldn't drive over. The anger burning inside her forced her jaw to tighten and her fists to clench. A migraine was building, and if she didn't act decisively, it would soon cripple her. It was Mark Pierce's and Amelia Reyes's pointless sacrifices that infuriated her. She had to make their gestures mean something.

With a rigid gait, she walked through the line of GNB soldiers, with none of them seeing her, or seeing through her because she was an unarmed woman in their eyes, and dropped the last of her incendiary grenades into the cabin. She ducked back as the heat and flames ravaged the surrounding air and burned the soldiers and the cabin interior to cinders in seconds.

The crowds quietened for a second, shocked at first, then grew elated. Then they gained a newfound confidence and beat at the remaining GNB soldiers with clubs and gardening implements.

No one seemed to have noticed it was Zang who had dropped the grenade, so she kept walking, unmolested, across the river into Colombia. By the time she reached the opposite side, the blackened hull of the Unimog had been rolled off the road onto the vegetated banks of the Rio Tachira. The aid trucks started up their engines and drove into Venezuela. The crowds cheered, and the last remaining GNB soldiers fled before the emboldened crowds turned on them.

On the outskirts of Cucuta, Zang turned south and followed the low vegetation line that separated the slum dwellings from the shallow-flowing river. She looked for tracks and soon found them. Zang followed the path into the greenery, where she spotted a corpse lying face down on the earth.

She raced to Pierce, turned him over and listened for breaths.

She heard it and breathed herself.

Then she wiped the tears streaming down her face when she spotted the used vaccine injector gun.

"Mark, you asshole."

She hugged him tight, felt his heartbeat to remind herself he lived. Zang had convinced herself that when Pierce had gone after Walsh, she would never see him alive again. She realised there would have been a hole in her life if Pierce had not survived through this day. Zang needed a friend like Pierce in her life.

Soldiers materialised around them, dressed in jungle fatigues and equipped with modern US military weaponry and kit and, perhaps more telling, biohazard gear. These were 7th Special Forces Group operators, and their assortment of assault rifles aimed at Pierce and her.

"We're no longer infected," she cried out, hugging the unconscious body of Mark Pierce close to her chest.

One soldier called back, "We know that, ma'am."

PART III

RESPONSE

63

Eglin Air Force Base, Florida, United States

Pierce woke to bright fluorescent lights, the dripping sounds from a saline solution connected to a cannula inserted into his left forearm, a breathing tube in his nose, and multiple electrocardiogram tabs adhered to his chest.

A pretty nurse in an Air Force uniform checked his chart. She looked up when she sensed him staring at her. "Ah, you're awake." She took his pulse with her icy hands and counted as she checked her watch. Then she felt his forehead. "It seems you are recovering well, Corporal Kaplan."

Pierce looked up, noticed she wore a face shield, a face mask, and disposable gloves. Plastic lined the walls, and someone had installed negative-air-pressure units, but they weren't operational now. His false identity, in comparison, seemed perfectly normal. Pierce couldn't remember a time spent in an American military hospital under his real name, or even under the name Mark Pierce.

"The... rabies?" he asked with a dry throat.

"All gone. You're a lucky man, Corporal. Blood samples show you were only a few hours away from not making it at all."

He nodded, figuring that the modified vaccine for the modified virus and not his constitution had everything to do with his survival.

Sensing his discomfort, she said, "Let me get you some water."

Pierce sat as she poured a glass of chilled liquid from the jug waiting by his bedside. She handed it to him and smiled. Her ID said her name was Sarah Tilby. "I'll get a doctor to check in on you."

He gulped the water and felt more alive now he had hydrated. "Where am I?"

"Eglin Air Force Base. The Eglin AFB Hospital, to be precise."

Pierce nodded again and tried to remember how long it had been since he had stepped foot inside the United States. It was over twelve months and possibly longer. His memories were improving, but they weren't yet perfect.

"Don't worry, Corporal. It's natural to feel disorientated."

He worried that Tilby seemed able to read his thoughts, but before he could say anything else, she disappeared. He lay for a moment, his eyes closed, until he heard the distinctive roar of an F-35A Lightning combat aircraft overshoot the base. The noise allowed him to relax because the setup could be a ruse, and he might be back in Venezuela and a prisoner of SEBIN again for all he knew. But like the aircraft, the power sockets, the detail in the furnishings and fittings, and the small print on the medical equipment to keep him alive should he need it, all spoke American.

A doctor checked in and spent more time examining his charts than she did examining him. "Your bloods are all cleared. Your vitals are all normal. Headache? Nausea?"

Pierce shook his head.

"We should have you cleared by this afternoon. Rest until then."

His next visitor was Rachel Zang, tall and slim as he remembered her. Memories came to him of making love with her in a remote ranch in southern Africa, and how he had sunk into her embrace, seeking a comfort and connection that had been absent in his life for too long. He desired her now, dressed in loose tracksuit pants, a tight running singlet and runners. Her shoulder-length dark hair she'd tied in a ponytail, and he thought her to be the most attractive woman he had ever laid eyes on.

He smiled at her.

She smiled back and hugged him. "You've been asleep for two days."

He shrugged and grinned. "After what you put me through, I needed it."

Zang play punched him in the arm. "Get dressed. My SOO wants a word."

Senior operations officer. Zang must have referred to her direct line manager. "This SOO has a name?"

"Patricia Knight. Apparently, you're already acquainted."

"I don't remember."

"Oh, she remembers you. Now get dressed and get moving, soldier."

Pierce looked around for privacy curtains.

Zang poked out her tongue. "Don't be like that. There is no one else here, and I've already seen all your equipment. Or do you still not remember?"

An image of her lying on a bed, naked, while he massaged her bare hips filled his mind.

Then he paused, and another memory came to him, of another woman who was also naked. But that memory only caused him to tense and for his feelings to shrink deep inside, where they could not hurt.

There was no doubt or confusion in his mind any longer. The woman, naked, beaten and tied to a chair, was Mackenzie Summerfield.

"Oh, I remember," he said as he pulled the cannula from his arm and climbed out of bed while he stripped from his flimsy hospital gown. But there was no fun left in his voice.

64

Two minutes later, when Pierce had dressed in jeans, a white-collared shirt whose sleeves he rolled up to just below his elbows, and blue and white canvas shoes, they discharged Pierce from the hospital and walked to Rachel Zang's grey Honda Civic. She motioned he get in, and before he closed the door, she took off, exiting the base, and they drove until she found a Cuban bar and grill in neighbouring Ocean City. She ordered them both burgers, fries, and large glasses of orange juice. The establishment was a hive of activity, but not overwhelming. Most patrons were young families. It was just as hot and muggy inside this establishment as it was standing on the bright Florida streets.

"I bet you haven't eaten a decent meal for weeks?"

Pierce laughed. "I can't remember."

"Talking about memories, are they improving?"

He held her stare. He found that when he reflected on his recent past, very little felt blocked or confusing to him now. He hoped this meant he had made a full recovery or was well on the way to doing so. "I remember you, Rachel, and what we... did together in Namibia."

She smiled and looked away. "That's something, I guess." Then she turned back and took his hand in his. "I have some bad news."

Pierce tensed, not sure what constituted bad news in Zang's mind. Then he guessed what she was about to tell him, and a sudden pain gripped his chest. "Amelia Reyes didn't make it?"

Zang shook her head as she now gripped his hand with both of hers. "I'm sorry, Mark. If it makes a difference, she sacrificed her life to save mine. She blew herself to pieces with a grenade, taking out Maceo Parra in the process."

For half a minute, Pierce couldn't speak. He felt that he was a failure, and that he'd let Amelia down.

The next words out of his mouth sounded awful and uncaring, but he didn't know how to express the multitude of emotions he felt all at once, so he focused only on the facts. "That explains the missing grenade."

"What do you mean?"

Pierce cleared his throat until he felt ready to speak again. "In the helo flight from Caracas, I asked her to find me weapons. She did. A box of grenades, and one was missing."

Now Zang tensed. "You think she planned on killing herself even then?"

After considering this possibility, he shook his head. "No. I don't think so. But I think she wouldn't allow herself to be tortured again, so that was her way out if she had no other choice."

They squeezed hands.

Pierce said, "It's fitting that she took out Parra. He did butcher her mother, after all."

"Oh." Zang looked away, and like Pierce, she too had trouble speaking.

Pierce thought it might have been better if they'd both cried, released the emotions overwhelming them both. But that was not the way the CIA trained them. They would suppress their emotions every time situations became difficult, so their pain had to eventually express itself in other, less healthy ways. Gambling, drinking, drugs, reckless risk-taking, wife beating...

He held up his hand, remembering that grenade blast in Yemen a couple of years back, which he had put down to his body's occasional uncontrolled tremors that came on at random times. A nurse had once told him the condition was more likely to be suppressed emotions than neurological, and he believed her now because the tremors were obvious to anyone who watched his fingers shake.

A waitress arrived with their meals and beverages. Pierce drank his orange juice in a single gulp, then hoed into his food. Rachel had been correct that they needed to eat, and he immediately felt better with a burger in his stomach.

They ate in silence for a while until Zang said, "There was no sign of Walsh anywhere, dead or alive."

"I know. He escaped. I'll find him, eventually."

"And kill him?"

He caught her stare. "You want him dead as much as I do."

"Not quite like you, but I take your point."

Pierce bit into his burger. "He can wait, though. He's not the danger that he once was."

Further silence followed as they ate some more. Pierce could never remember fries ever tasting this good.

"Mark, we stopped the rabies outbreak in Venezuela and severely crippled SEBIN, if that counts for anything."

Pierce swallowed his mouthful while he nodded. "It does."

Her eyes lost their focus when she said, "It's not over yet. We still need to shut down the research facility in Port-au-Prince where the virus was manufactured."

He stopped eating, watched her closely as he tried to understand what she was thinking, because it didn't seem to align with what she was saying. "You already have a plan on that?"

Zang nodded.

He squeezed her hand. He liked these moments of public intimacy that they shared, which gave their relationship a realism he hadn't been certain was there before. "My head's clearer now. Some rest, food and forty-eight hours of a saline drip have brought my senses back to me."

"You still look awful, with all those bruises and cuts. And you've lost a lot of weight."

Pierce leaned forward. "What I'm saying, Rachel, is that I sense... No! I *know* something else is bothering you. Something big, and something that hurts you deep. I didn't recognise it when we were south of the border, but I do now. Everything we did in South America was secondary to whatever's eating you up now!"

They stayed motionless for a moment, and Zang bit on her lower lip.

Then she pulled her hand away and consumed more fries. Her face became a mask.

"Eat up, Pierce." She glanced at her watch, a functional

brand but not an exorbitant timepiece that most other operators opted for. "Knight wants to brief us in thirty minutes."

He wasn't getting the truth out of her now, so he dug into his food and tried not to think about Amelia Reyes and her last moments on this Earth.

65

G etting inside the unmarked 7th Special Forces Group building within Eglin Air Force Base proved far more complicated than Zang or Pierce expected. Zang had no problem with her identity, as many of the operators here knew her personally, but Pierce was an outsider and always had been. It took several calls to CIA headquarters in Langley, Virginia, and a direct request from Patricia Knight before the gate security detail let him inside.

Behind the gates, Zang shook her head and frowned. "No one knows you. I mean, no one anywhere knows you."

Pierce shrugged. He knew exactly why this was so, but he couldn't easily explain it away to Zang without compromising hundreds of secrets he'd sworn to take with him to the grave. "It's not that interesting."

She showed him which door he should pass through. "You know, Pierce, every time you say something like that, I can only imagine the opposite."

The meeting room was large, with no windows, plastic chairs and fold-out tables, a whiteboard on rollers, and two individuals seated at opposite ends of the table so neither could see the other's laptop screens.

The first individual was a fit officer wearing a khaki US Army combat uniform featuring operational camouflage pattern, coyote brown boots, and the 1st Special Forces Command (Airborne) shoulder sleeve of a yellow dagger on a teal blue background interspersed with three yellow lightning bolts. The lieutenant stood and saluted Pierce and Zang. "Captain Ross Sidor, ma'am, sir, reporting to duty."

They both returned the salute. "At ease, Captain."

Pierce remembered Zang had reached the rank of second lieutenant when she had served with the United States Air Force, and Pierce's rank was no better, so why was this senior officer reporting to them?

The other individual was an African American woman in her fifties, slim and attractive for her age, with her hair cut short and her pant suit of the expensive variety. When she identified Zang, the two embraced as friends. Pierce guessed this was Zang's immediate superior.

"Mark Pierce, I'd like to introduce Senior Operations Officer Patricia Knight."

Pierce took her hand and shook it firmly. "Pleased to meet you, ma'am."

As they came close, she sniffled, and Pierce noticed her dilated pupils.

"Likewise, Pierce. That was quite an outcome you and Zang accomplished in Venezuela. My hat goes off to you both."

"Thank you, ma'am, but we didn't bring Amelia Reyes back safely."

Knight studied him. Her expression suggested that she believed she could read his mind, and that she didn't like his unhelpful thoughts. "No. Your mission was to prevent a weaponised rabies outbreak, which you accomplished admirably."

He nodded and didn't say that Zang and he had been well-entrenched in Venezuela long before anyone knew about the pandemic threat. Pierce glanced at Zang, who seemed at ease with Knight, so Pierce guessed they might be friends outside of the job. But something about the SOO didn't sit right with Pierce, and he had an inkling what that might be.

Knight said, "I'm sorry, Zang, that you are back in the States, again, when we agreed home territory isn't safe for you. But in the circumstances, I had nowhere else to bring you." She looked to Pierce and then back to Zang. "We'll have you both on the move again soon enough."

Zang nodded but wouldn't hold Knight's stare. "Thank you, ma'am."

Knight gestured to the Special Operations officer. "Captain Sidor led the operational team that extracted you back to the States. He's with the 7th SFG."

Pierce nodded to the man and grinned. "Would I be right in saying, Captain, you would have neutralised me without question if you thought I carried the weaponised virus?"

Sidor smirked. "Without hesitation, sir." They shook hands. "But I'm glad to see it didn't come to that."

Knight said, "Captain Sidor and his unit are on standby, ready to take down the enemy biological weapons production site once we identify its exact location."

Pierce sensed everyone in the room knew far more than he regarding the details of the operation they discussed. The only way he could catch up was by asking questions. "I take it from your smirk, ma'am, that you already have a plan to obtain this intel?"

Knight crossed her arms and looked at Zang.

When Zang registered three sets of eyes watching her, Pierce couldn't believe that she blushed. This hardened woman, who'd fought bloody battles at his side on three continents in some of the most hostile countries on the planet, was now embarrassed.

"Yes..." Zang cleared her throat. "It relates to one part of the equation, Pierce, that no one has yet filled you in on."

"Why this secret organisation wanted to infect Venezuela with this virus in the first place?"

Zang nodded, and together with Knight, they briefed him on Kozan Petroleum, its owner Morat Kozan and his connection to a secretive, global intelligence organisation whose symbol was the two circles each bisected by a single line. How Kozan Petroleum was poised to take over operations of Venezuela's oil production when the Bolivarian government collapsed and the country fell into true anarchy. Then she told him that a contingent of 7th SFG operators already maintained close-quarter surveillance on Morat Kozan in his penthouse villa in coastal resort town of Marmaris, Türkiye, ready to sweep in and extract anyone Knight and Zang considered worthy of taking alive.

Pierce explained that he had seen this symbol twice before, first on an insurgent he'd neutralised in Mali twelve months earlier, and again on the DNI officer Juliana Munoz operating under the cover of Savannah Fonseca. He didn't mention his third encounter with this symbol he had seen in Baku, Azerbaijan, but its frequency in showing up in seemingly random locations did talk to how pervasive and dangerous this organisation likely was.

When everyone stopped speaking, Pierce said, "You think Kozan will tell you where this secret facility is?"

Knight shook her head. "Not Kozan."

Pierce looked at the three military and intelligence professionals all staring at him. Despite the detailed briefing, he was still ignorant to an important piece of intelligence none of them had yet shared. "Then who?"

Sidor and Knight again turned to Zang, who crossed her arms and stepped backwards. "Our target is Kozan's chief financial officer, Charles Chu. He's hiding out in the same Marmaris villa."

"And what makes you think he'll talk the fastest?"

Zang croaked. "Because Charles Chu is my estranged father."

66

Pierce barely kept his cool through the rest of the briefing. He instead felt constant fury, which, for the next hour, he barely managed to keep on a controlled simmer. The meeting ended when Knight decided Zang, Pierce and Sidor would take the next available military flight to Europe and meet up with the 7th Special Forces Group unit in Marmaris, ready to extract Chu.

When Knight dismissed them to pack and get themselves to their flight, Pierce was the first to exit, and he marched outside. It was a balmy night, warm enough to feel comfortable in single layers. He glanced up into the night sky but could only pick out a few of the brightest stars because of light pollution. Sirius, Arcturus, Rigel, Betelgeuse and Aldebaran were stars he knew well, and he found them quickly. Staring at the stars often helped calm his mind when troubled thoughts plagued him, because it reminded him of the good times he'd had with his dad, on the rare occasions when they were in the United States, when camping trips in the national parks of Arizona and New Mexico were permitted. His father had once told Pierce that Arab astronomers named most of the brightest stars, from a time in the past when Arabs commanded the most civilised nations on earth and were the leading scientists of their time. This had struck Pierce as unexpected, because all he'd heard from other kids his age and their parents was how backwards and violent the people in the Middle East were. They were Arab stars, Pierce had realised, that gave him peace in his darkest moments, and he had always thought there was something profound about this revelation.

He heard Zang approach, but didn't turn to greet her. He felt anger towards her too.

"Mark, what's up with you?"

"Your father? He works for the people we are trying to bring down. Can't you see how fucked up this is?"

"Fucked up!" She almost screamed her words. "That's rich, coming from you. I don't know what happened between you and your parents, but knowing you as I do, I know whatever it was, they fucked you up too, just as bad as my dad fucked me up. All that propelled you on a self-imposed mission of saving your soul. Well, guess what? So am I."

Pierce turned and stared Zang down. Since their arrival in Florida, more of his memories had returned, of the intimate conversations they had once shared, and the little secrets they had previously revealed to each other. Not every detail, but enough to fill in some missing puzzle pieces in each other's covert and guarded lives. He nodded towards the building where Knight had just briefed them. "They're using you, or can't you see it?"

"Who's using me, Mark? Walsh? He's long out of the picture."

"Not Walsh. I'm talking about Knight. She's a coke addict, and drug users can never be trusted!"

"What?" Zang expressed genuine surprise.

"Dilated pupils, and all that sniffling—"

"She has allergies. I checked."

"Really, Rachel? How many times did Knight become excitable during that briefing? How many times was she recklessly confident, and did you notice the erratic switches in her speaking speeds? They aren't symptoms of someone with just allergies."

Zang didn't answer immediately, and Pierce saw he had gotten through to her, at least enough to give her suspicion that her boss might not be as on her side as she might claim to be.

"Rachel, drug addicts take unnecessary risks, and in our profession, those risks could needlessly cost us our lives."

"You think she's being reckless with my father? I took this to her."

Pierce clenched his fists. "Is this why you joined the CIA, just to get back at your dad?"

He'd raised his voice, and she'd raised hers. But the answer she gave was not the answer he expected.

"Yes!"

"What?"

"Yes! My asshole of a father is a sociopath. When he no longer had a need for her, he destroyed her mentally and emotionally until she took her own life."

"Who are we talking about?" Then a memory returned of a story about her life that Rachel had previously shared, and Pierce felt strong emotions of guilt and insensitivity for not remembering this earlier.

"Yes, Mark. I'm talking about my mother. Daddy dearest drove her to suicide. I just know it. Have always known it, even when I didn't want to admit it to myself." Tears streamed down her cheeks. "Don't just fucking stare at me like that and act like this is news to you! You would have worked this all out long ago."

She stood motionless, tense all over, clenching and unclenching her fists. Rachel Zang's story was very different to his own and so much worse. In this moment, with this revelation, he admired her even more than he already had, that despite the hurdles she'd confronted, Rachel had emerged from the other side of her childhood as a decent, ethical person. She might believe in extrajudicial justice as Pierce did, ridding the world of sociopaths, warlords and despots who didn't deserve to live because they inflicted unnecessary pain and suffering on others for personal gains, but despite her means, she was a good person.

"I'm sorry," he said, feeling the tension leave his body.

"For what? You have nothing to do with any of this."

"For momentarily not trusting you, and forgetting that you know exactly what you are doing, and why you are doing it."

Further tears welled in her eyes, and Pierce recognised that she fought against herself from expressing her hurt.

He saved her the indignity of losing control, as he pulled her close and hugged her tight. She was almost his height, so she nuzzled his neck rather than his chest.

"You can be such an idiot, sometimes, Mark Pierce."

He wanted to tell her, in that moment, that Pierce wasn't his real name. He wanted to tell her who he really was.

But he didn't.

67

Marmaris, Türkiye

C harles Chu woke suddenly, not because he heard a noise, but because he heard nothing.

He lay in his opulent bed, naked upon silken sheets, with two equally unclad prostitutes asleep at each side. Without moving, he listened. Distant waves of the Mediterranean lapped upon the shore, and the low rumble of late-night traffic was audible only if he strained to hear it. He glanced at his Omega Seamaster wristwatch. It was quarter past four in the morning.

Untangling himself from the two slumbering beauties, Chu found his cotton pants and slipped them on, then a silken shirt, which he buttoned quickly before slipping on his loafers. He dressed without making a noise.

He moved to the window to look outside. In the moonlight, everything was as he knew it should be. He overlooked the villa's marble-lined pool, with a million-dollar view over the Mediterranean Sea. Scenery included pine-forested mountains, pristine sandy beaches, and clear ocean waters mooring hundreds of yachts that spoke of the quality of tourists who flocked here every year. His home was a luxurious villa, complete with state-of-the-art security systems and discreet, military-trained guards, which commanded a prime real estate position within the Turkish resort town of Marmaris. So why were the hairs on the back of his neck prickly?

He heard a barely audible knock on the door.

"It's me," whispered Morat Kozan from the other side.

Chu opened the door. His employer greeted him, wearing a silken dressing gown and slippers. In the near darkness, Kozan's features took on devilish proportions. "People are in the house."

With a nod, Chu found his Italian-made Beretta 92, pulled back the slide to ensure a chambered 9mm round was ready for firing, then followed Kozan into the corridor. Chu knew better than to expect their highly trained guard detail to hold full responsibility in the protection of the villa when under assault. Kozan demanded everyone must fight, and those who didn't would later suffer the pig-man's wrath, which could be worse than being shot.

"The power is out. Three of my men are already dead."

Chu flinched. They'd come under physical attack before, but no one had died in those past confrontations. At least, no one fighting on Kozan's side had lost their lives. Tonight, however, was already different. "Who is the enemy?"

Kozan grinned. "Let's find out, shall we?"

Moving with stealth, they reached the marble staircase that led to the lower floor. Chu identified a guard laid out on his back, in a circular pool of his own blood centred on his chest. Chu must have paused involuntarily, for Kozan hissed for Chu to keep moving. The accountant feared he was walking to his death, but staying was as equally suicidal. He just had to hope they could escape.

At one window overlooking the swimming pool, they noticed a symbol drawn on the glass in blood. A circle within a circle, each bisected by the same straight line.

"Did we fuck up?"

Kozan snorted like a swine. "Keep your cool, Chu."

On the opposite side of the swimming pool, Chu noticed two of their guards with their pistols drawn, advancing through the property. Then he heard two muffled gunshots, and both men's heads snapped backwards at unnatural angles. One corpse bounced on the marble pavers. The other dropped into the pool. Soon the low-lit underwater lights turned black, submerged in the inky cloud of blood billowing from his fatal head wound.

"Snipers?" whispered Chu.

"Fuckers! How dare our masters turn against me after everything we have done to make them great!" Kozan fired his revolver through the glass door into the pool area. The glass shattered, creating a screeching noise that caused Chu to cower involuntarily.

Then three muffled shots filled the air.

Chu thought a bullet had hit him, but the pain was merely his erratic heart beating violently against his ribcage. He looked up to see Kozan pivot towards him, smoke billowing from three holes in his chest and his eyes wide open but dead, like the rest of him. The body crumpled at Chu's feet.

Chu turned and fled.

He remembered the servants' entrance, downstairs and

past the cellars, that led into a quiet side street the intruders might not know about.

As he ran, he heard the unmistakable noise of automatic gunfire. Kozan and he must have fucked up this deal, but by doing what? Or something had gone wrong on the Venezuelan side of the operation, and they were seen as responsible, but how exactly?

Outside, in the narrow street, Chu saw no one. He'd gotten lucky, so he walked fast towards the beach. He was rational enough to know that running would only draw attention to him, and a sniper's bullet. All the streetlights were out, and he was grateful for this.

When he'd covered three blocks of the tourist town, he sensed someone following him.

Chu entered a plaza, with pavers, closed shopfronts boarded up with metal roller doors for the night, and over-looked by apartment and office buildings, two to four stories in height. Three figures stood unmoving in the centre of the plaza until Chu remembered these were life-sized bronze statues representing tourists. He was alone at this late hour.

A cloud of smoke shattered the pavement next to Chu. Then he heard the muffled sound of a silenced bullet.

"Drop the weapon." A man spoke from the shadows.

Chu threw his Beretta far from him and held his hands high above his head. If he were smart, he would have fought and died. To be taken prisoner by these people was to expect a short future anyway, and one comprised entirely of crip-pling and maiming tortures. But he was too much the coward to take his own life.

The man stepped into the starlight. Dressed entirely in black, he wore a balaclava, disguising his identity. He scooped up Chu's fallen pistol and pocketed it before he approached with his own semi-automatic pistol at the ready. "Turn around. Keep your arms raised."

Chu obeyed.

The assailant patted him down, finding no further weapons. "Hands behind your back."

Again, Chu obeyed, feeling the cable ties, two of them, tighten around his wrists.

A second figure appeared, tall and also dressed entirely in black, her face covered. She, too, carried a pistol at the ready.

The man gripped Chu by his hair and shone a torch on his face. "This him?" he asked the woman.

She nodded.

The man whispered in Chu's ear, "We're taking a walk to the beach. Try anything stupid and I'll start putting bullets inside you. Not to kill, but to create excruciating pain. Do you understand?"

Chu noticed that his heartbeat and his breathing had become rapid again. "Yes!"

They walked him to the shorefront, then to a jetty until they reached a speedboat. Once on board, the woman started up the engine while the man forced Chu down onto the deck, then hog-tied him with further cable ties.

"Tonight is your lucky night, Charles Chu."

"How is that?" he asked, dreading the answer.

"The right people got to you first."

68

Rhodes, Greece

Maintaining her disguise, Zang powered the speedboat through the night, using her PVS-7 night-vision goggles to enhance her vision. The Greek island of Rhodes lay to the south, their destination, forty miles from Marmaris Bay. She spent the time fretting that she had made an awful mistake. The man she and Pierce had just extracted was her father, Charles Chu. A man Zang had not seen in ten years, when Zang was eighteen and had enlisted with the United States Air Force for officer training. She had told herself that, despite how much she despised her father, kidnapping and bringing him into the custody of the CIA was the best option for protecting him, both from himself and the unsavoury characters he now dealt with.

With the wind cooling them as they bounced across the choppy waters, she glanced at Pierce. She noticed he kept his attention split equally on her bound father and on the waters behind them, should anyone follow.

It had been Pierce's idea to false flag their attack, make it appear orchestrated by the secret organisation still operating in the shadows of this convoluted conspiracy. Captain Ross's team had pulled it off spectacularly, even allowing some of the minor underlings to escape to spread news of the assault. The 7th Special Forces Group team had radioed her that they were already outside Türkiye and in international waters, and that his team were unharmed. Ross had wished her luck with their new "guest".

Eighty minutes after leaving Marmaris, Zang navigated the speedboat into a secluded bay on the west side of the island of Rhodes. With the sun dipping above the inland mountainous peaks, she identified the island's thick Mediterranean scrub, white craggy cliff edges, and the pristine sandy beach. Zang laid anchor while Pierce walked her father through the waves up onto the sandy shore. Then Zang followed.

In a car park, approximately one hundred feet from them, waited two black sport utility vehicles. Six figures, silhouetted against the rising morning sun, stood motionless. Zang knew they were the CIA extraction team selected for this mission, tasked with delivering Chu to an undisclosed location for weeks and months of relentless interrogation. Zang had insisted they go gently on him, and Knight had agreed.

Zang whispered into Pierce's ear, "What are they waiting for?"

He turned to her, but she could not read his expression because they both still wore their concealing balaclavas. "They're waiting for you."

"What do you mean?"

Pierce shrugged. "This is your only opportunity... If you want to say anything."

Zang nodded. The agreement with the higher powers on the seventh floor of Langley was that Zang could supervise her father's extraction, but she couldn't become part of the interrogation team. She shuddered, realising that regardless of how this event turned out, word would still spread through the CIA that she was a tainted operative. Her blood relative was a high-ranking officer of an enemy and hostile organisation working against the interests of the United States and her allies. This was not a reputation that would aid her in any way, and could easily destroy her career.

But Charles Chu was still her father. She still loved him even though she detested him. They hadn't spoken in ten years. After tonight, it might be another ten years or more before they spoke again.

She nodded to Pierce.

He returned the nod, then lifted Chu to his feet, because in his fear and exhaustion Chu had fallen on his knees, burying them in the sand. His look was one Zang had seen a hundred times, a man defeated, who had surrendered fully to whatever fate awaited him, knowing that fate would not be pleasant.

He watched with fear as she removed her mask.

As she swung out her long dark hair, allowing the emerging sunlight to light up her face, Charles's expression transformed. First to elation, then confusion. "Rachel?"

"Yes, Dad."

She choked up as her fists tightened, and her legs locked rigid. She didn't want this confrontation, even though she had planned it in her mind for a decade now.

"Rachel!" He raced forward to hug her.

She reacted instinctively, raised her SIG Sauer P320 semi-automatic and aimed the lethal end between his eyeballs.

"I...? I don't understand?"

Tears welled in Zang's eyes. "Neither do I." She wiped the wet streaks away, knowing that Pierce covered Charles should he try anything stupid, and she didn't need to concern herself with self-protection. Her laughter was manic. "You know, Dad, I've planned this conversation over and over in my head for years, and now I'm here, I don't know what to say."

"Why am I here? I don't understand what you're involved with."

"Yeah?" Zang felt anger consume her. "With all your meddling in my life, I thought you kept better tabs on me. I mean, you used your connections in the federal government to get me forced out of the USAF. Couldn't have your daughter trained in the use of guns and able to defend herself, could you?"

"What?"

"I'm with the CIA now, but I guess you wouldn't know that because that is a tightly guarded secret."

"Why?" He looked genuinely confused by everything she said. "What is going on?"

She motioned with her pistol to the two parked SUVs. "The people up there, they are CIA interrogators. I've asked them to go easy on you, being my dad and all."

"Are you crazy, Rachel? You should have studied law or economics, like I told you to. Then you wouldn't be embroiled in this dangerous, covert world like I am."

Zang snorted another laugh. She had hoped for contrition from Charles, at least some level of guilt felt for destroying her life and driving her mother, his wife, to suicide. But Zang saw it now. Her father hadn't changed in the slightest. "I joined the CIA, Dad, so I could bring down narcissistic assholes like you, who believe it's their god-given right to take whatever the hell it is they please regardless of the consequences for others."

"What are you talking about? It was you who wanted nothing to do with me. It was you who closed me off from your life."

"Just say it!" Zang snapped. She realised she had almost accidentally shot her father in that moment, and if she had, it would have been in anger. Her superiors were right to keep them apart.

"Say what?"

"You destroyed Mum! It was your fault she killed herself. Say it!"

"What? No! Rachel, honey, you've got it all wrong. You're deluded. You're sick, and I can help you—"

Suddenly, she had her gun up at his forehead, ready to pull the trigger.

Charles squeezed his eyes tight and tensed. She saw the fear in him then that she had seen in her mother's eyes for years before her end. As a pre-teen, Rachel's life had been good, but as a teenager, something had changed in her parents, and everything fell apart.

She lowered her weapon and threw it onto the sand. "Dad, listen to me."

Shuddering, with tears welling in his eyes, he opened them and held her stare.

"Dad, these men are going to take you away. It won't be pleasant, but it won't be horrible, like some of the black prisons Langley operates across the globe. It's the only solution I know that stops you from hurting other people while keeping you safe. I hate that I'm doing this to you, but I am."

"Why? Honey, can't you just let me go? I'll disappear. You'll never hear from me again."

Zang shook her head as she tasted acid at the back of her throat. "Isn't that what you did ten years ago? And look where you ended up, the financier for a corrupt oil crime lord willing to destroy a country and its people just so you can both get rich."

Charles shook and barely held himself upright, and he didn't answer her.

"You're right, Dad. We won't see each other again, ever. But before we part our ways, I just want to ask one question. How you answer it determines what I tell those men, concerning how gentle they will be regarding your interrogations."

"You've got it all wrong. I've done nothing—"

"ONE QUESTION!" she screamed over him. "The weaponised rabies manufacturing facility in Haiti. Where is it? I need exact coordinates."

69

Ten seconds later, Rachel Zang had her answer.

She nodded for Pierce to approach. He did so while keeping his weapon trained on Charles Chu. The man behaved as if he were weak and a victim, but that could be a ruse. Regardless, Pierce trusted Zang to know what she was doing, so he hadn't interfered when Chu was in positions where he could have attacked her.

She wiped her red eyes. "Take him away, please. Tell them... to go gently on him."

Pierce nodded. He checked over Chu's bindings and patted him down again on the off chance he might have secured a makeshift weapon during the speedboat ride between islands. Then the two walked up to the car park while Zang stared out to the sea, her arms folded with the wind blowing her long dark hair around her face.

The figures were four men and two women. While they dressed as tourists, Pierce sensed their honed situational awareness and military prowess. The lead operative was a muscular man in his mid-fifties, with a crewcut grey head of hair and beard. "After the last season, don't you think the New York Yankees should give up baseball and switch to lawn bowls?"

Pierce grinned. That was the correct password. "I'm more of a World Cup man myself, but my real talent lies in backgammon."

The grey-haired operator laughed, then pumped Pierce's hand with a generous handshake. "I'm Bob Adamcik, one of Langley's top BAMF interrogators. You probably don't know me, but I know you well enough to know your handle is Trigger Man."

Pierce kept his expression neutral. "Nice to meet you, Bob." He tilted his head towards Zang on the beach. "I was told to inform you to go easy on him." He pushed Chu forward. Two operatives stepped close to place a hood over the man's head and bind him with more secure handcuffs than the cable ties Pierce had used. Then they placed him in the back of one SUV.

Adamcik said, "Thank you, Trigger Man. Did he say anything I should be made aware of?"

Pierce passed on the precise location of the Haiti facility, in Petion-Ville on the outskirts of Port-au-Prince.

"That's all I need to know regarding immediate actions. Now it's my turn to pass on a message."

"What message is that?"

"You and the lady are to get yourself to Ramstein Air Base and await further instructions."

Pierce gave a salute, turned, and walked back down to the beach as the two vehicles disappeared over the rocky horizon.

Zang only turned to look at him when he stood next to her. "Did I do the right thing?"

Pierce shrugged. "I'm more fucked up than you are, Rachel, so I don't know if I can answer that. But you did good today. You got the intel we needed. You'll save lives, potentially millions of them. Hold on to that, if nothing else."

She turned and hugged him. "Is that why you do what you do? Always trying to outweigh all the bad you've done with good deeds?"

He hugged her back. "Of course. What other option in life do we have?"

70

Ramstein Air Base, Germany

A nother air base, another world away. Eighteen hours after handing off Charles Chu, Pierce and Zang stood side by side in a dark operations room deep within the United States' Ramstein Air Base. On the generous wall screen ran multiple green and black camera feeds from 7th SFG helmet cams, and satellite imagery of the operators materialising from the alleyways and thick foliage as they advanced stealthily into the Port-au-Prince facility, exactly where Zang's father had promised it would be, but it only took a few minutes to identify its thorough emptiness. The gingerbread house and the man stainless-steel buildings remained, and the gruesome discoveries included pyres of men, women and children, now nothing more than charred corpses still smoking and barbecuing in the night. Someone had stripped the facilities of computers, hard drives, equipment stores, weapons and provisions.

Pierce looked across at Patricia Knight and Captain

Sidor, both returning the stare. Pierce said, "Zang tells me you have a mole inside the CIA?"

Knight grimaced. "That's true. It would explain the current situation."

"Let's not be too hasty," said Sidor, today in his full-dress military uniform. "After our successes in Venezuela and Türkiye, they must have known we were coming for them."

"That doesn't fix the mole problem," said Zang, massaging her forehead. Pierce guessed she fought an internal war against a looming migraine. He had his shakes and now a faulty memory that hopefully wasn't permanent. She had crippling headaches. Their own bodies fought them whenever they had important work to do.

"No, it doesn't," said Knight. "But it is why I compartmentalised who in the CIA knew about the operation, and utilised the 7th SFG rather than SAC/SOG Ground Branch teams."

Pierce watched Knight closely as she sniffled and wiped her sleeve with the back of her hand. His instincts told him not to trust her in the slightest. Drug addicts let everyone down, including themselves. But it was a long stretch to connect a cocaine habit to a traitor and mole.

"We're at a dead end unless Matchstick delivers—"

"Who?"

Knight paled. "Sorry, Zang. Matchstick is the code name we randomly assigned to your father."

Zang nodded and looked away. Pierce knew the signs of guilt, and he saw those signs written all over her.

"You two can take a week off. You both look goddamn awful, so take the time to rest and recuperate. And, Pierce?"

"Yes, ma'am?"

"You're reinstated with the CIA, effective immediately,

and reporting to me. When you return, we'll look into what happened to Mackenzie Summerfield. I promise."

Pierce almost believed her until she spoke her last two words. "Yes, ma'am."

Everyone stood for a moment, no one talking and no one moving.

"You're both dismissed. You can stay in Europe, but you don't go east anywhere past the old Iron Curtain."

Pierce nodded, then grabbed Zang by the arm because she seemed mildly traumatised and unable to focus, and led them outside the base to his rented Volkswagen Eos six-speed coupe. She climbed into the passenger seat, secured her seat belt and allowed him to drive them with speed from the base to Frankfurt. He'd chosen the Eos partially because it blended in with local traffic in Germany, but also because it afforded him enough manoeuvrability and speed should anyone come after them.

He entered the Bahnhofsviertel neighbourhood, passing Hauptbahnhof, Frankfurt's main train station. The region featured many and varied bars, and after parking in an easy-to-exit space, he led Zang inside a bar lit in red neon lights and ordered them a beer each. After a moment of sitting and just staring into space, Zang noticed the patrons. They were an equal mix of men and women, some dressed in common fashion, but there were drag queens and girls in tight leather dresses. The men only had eyes for the men, and the women only had eyes for the women.

"I didn't know you swung both ways, Mark?"

"I don't. Here's to Amelia Reyes. May she finally find peace."

Zang chinked his bottle with hers, and they both drank.

"And besides, if anyone is looking for us, the last place they'll expect to find us is in an LGBTQ bar."

The crowd's rumblings and techno music were loud enough so there was no risk of anyone overhearing them, but not loud enough they couldn't talk.

"Did I do the right thing, Mark?"

He nodded and drank. "I can't see what else you could have done. I'm assuming you also worked out that, if your father is working with the enemy, they can use him against you. Compromise you, with threats to his safety."

"He's going to spend the rest of his life in a black prison."

Pierce shrugged. "He may not. If he talks, they might retire him away somewhere nice and harmless. He might even end up working for the CIA, eventually."

She reached over and kissed him quickly. "Why is it, when I need you to, you always know how to say the right things?"

He laughed, pointed to the bruises and cuts on his face still healing from their ordeal in South America. "The woman who gave me these might disagree with you."

She laughed and drank more beer. "You're not going back... To the CIA, I mean? Are you?"

He looked away and down into his now half-empty glass. "The woman I kept imagining, naked and beaten and tied to a chair. I'm one hundred per cent convinced it's Mackenzie, like you said back in Caracas. We communicate through various websites, leaving coded messages for each other, checking in from time to time so we know each other is okay. She's posted nothing since I last spoke to her while we were in Angola, three months ago."

"You think this hostile organisation we keep crossing paths with is behind her disappearance?"

Pierce shrugged again. "It's a theory I'll work until proven otherwise."

Two men sat close to Pierce, and for a moment he felt concern that they might have tailed him. He watched the men kiss each other, then disappear into the throngs of dancers, and Pierce then gave them no thought.

"Walsh might know?"

"True, Rachel, but he's also gone to ground. We might both detest him, but his skills as a spymaster are second to none. Finding him won't be easy."

Zang finished her beer and ordered another round for them both. They chinked glasses again, and Pierce watched Zang smile. He still believed she was the most gorgeous woman he had ever laid eyes on. Just being with her, he felt he could be himself, as much as his new cover would allow him to be, and that made him feel good.

"Mark, I could come with you? Help you find her."

He shook his head.

"You trying to protect me? That's ludicrous."

"No. I need someone on the inside who can feed me intel when I need it. That's how Mackenzie and I once operated. I need you to be that person now, at least until I get Mackenzie back. And this circle organisation we know almost nothing about is a serious threat. To almost pull off that scheme in Venezuela required significant resources and funding. We have to take them seriously, and we can only do that by working inside the CIA."

"So you'll come back? Eventually?"

He nodded. "Once I have Mackenzie, or if I learn definitively that she no longer lives."

Zang nodded but looked away.

"Besides, you have your father to deal with now. You can't

be away from all that, even if you are kept at arm's length from him. The intel he provides will result in operations against this enemy. It would kill you not to be part of that."

"True." Zang shrugged as she looked down at their half-finished second beers. "You had enough to drink?"

"Sure."

She seemed to hesitate for a moment, as if making up her mind about something. Then she reached over and kissed him again. "I need some company tonight, and I have a sneaking suspicion you already know the best hotel in town."

71

H alf an hour later, they booked into a hotel, stripped each other and dived under the covers of the room's queen-sized bed.

Their night of lovemaking was gentle compared to their first and only other coupling. Zang and Pierce took their time to explore, cuddle, kiss, touch and whisper before coming together in the final act. They climaxed close together, then fell hard upon the covers, and both were asleep in minutes.

Pierce woke later in the night but didn't move when he heard Zang going about the bedroom without making a sound. He pretended to sleep as she dressed, packed her bag, and wrote him a note. She disappeared through the hotel room's door with equal efficiency in silence, and was gone.

He waited two minutes. Then climbed from the bed and checked the time. Four in the morning. Zang had not wanted a difficult last goodbye.

He read the note:

LAST NIGHT WAS GREAT
LET'S KEEP THIS CASUAL AND NON-EXCLUSIVE
X.

Pierce felt a taste of regret. He liked Rachel more than he had any other lover in his life. Her not feeling the same way about him hurt. But if he examined their situation dispassionately, what other choice did they have?

He was about to crumple the note and burn it in an ashtray when a thought occurred.

Holding the note to the bedside lamp, he saw additional words imprinted on the paper.

Pierce took a pencil and created a rubbing over the indentations. A new message appeared.

OUR MUTUAL ENEMY...
TRY GERMIGNAGA, LAKE MAGGIORE

Grinning, Pierce crumpled the note and burned it. He dressed, checked over his quickly assembled field kit, which included a KAMPO fighting knife and Glock 19 pistol, raced downstairs to his Volkswagen Eos, and drove off into the night. It was a seven-hour drive to Italy from Frankfurt via Switzerland and the Alps. Enough time to reach his destination by mid-morning.

72

Lake Maggiore, Italy

With a cautious swagger, Idris Walsh approached the exclusive medical clinic on the shore of Lake Maggiore and checked that he had everything he needed. Flowers, his favourite novel, morphine, syringes, and a Browning HP semi-automatic he'd purchased two days earlier from a Tunisian fixer in Rome. The view over the vast clear blue Lake Maggiore, with tree- and snow-capped mountains gripping its edges, was postcard perfect. The town itself carried old-world charm, with quaint cobbled streets, balustraded two- and three-storey houses hundreds of years old, bygone-era shuttered windows, and gabled rooftops. If Walsh could pick any part of the world to retire to, it would have been here in Germignaga, an idyllic community nestled deep in the Italian Alps.

But Walsh's gut twinged, reminding him of the seriousness of his deteriorating condition. Last night, after showering in his hotel room in Milan, he'd studied his frail, ageing body in the mirror. He'd lost so much weight he resembled a cross between a zombie and a Holocaust victim. His skin carried a yellow tinge, suggesting he had contracted hepatitis in South America, and he sensed the anti-rejection drugs no longer worked. Even if he never laid eyes on Pierce again, his enemy had won. His knife wound in the Moroccan medina almost a year ago was the wound that would eventually kill him.

The medical clinic, while modern, featured intricate and old-style bas-reliefs that hinted at architectural designs from centuries past. The ground floor was white and the upper two floors a creamy yellow. A garden protected by wrought-iron fences and brick posts encircled the building and featured trimmed hedges and neatly manicured palm trees.

Walsh stepped inside.

The young lady behind the reception desk, prim in a tight skirt and shirt like she was an airline steward, smiled from behind her bright red lips. Her raven black hair, pulled into a bun tied at the back of her head, made her far more attractive in Walsh's mind than if she'd let her hair down.

"Ah, Mr Chase," she said in perfect English. "We weren't expecting you."

Walsh grinned. Alarm bells would have sounded in his mind if she had said the opposite. "Sorry, last-minute opportunity to drop by."

"I'll just check if your sister is available. If you wouldn't mind signing in, Mr Chase?"

Walsh almost laughed. There was no opportunity for his sister not to see him. He signed his name "F.U. Pierce", then looked up at the pretty woman.

She smiled with a curve of her lip that Walsh interpreted

as sexy. "Clementine is ready, if you wish to make your way up to her room."

He nodded, then looked at both the marble stairs and the elevator. As a trained field operative and former soldier, Walsh knew the risks of elevators and how easy it was to become trapped in them if the enemy was closing in. But stairs brought him mental pain on parity with the pain of his failing liver.

He pressed the elevator button, rode the death trap to the second floor, and found Clementine seated in her usual chair, sipping a gin and tonic through a straw. Mozart played lightly in the background. Just like every other time he had visited, he found her admiring the view over Lake Maggiore that she had stared at now for close to forty years. Her limbs were more wasted than his own, and she looked much older than he did despite their nearness in age and his rapidly deteriorating condition.

"Hello, brother."

Walsh smiled and placed the flowers in a vase that a nurse had obviously brought in ahead of him.

"You've been away a long time this time. I was thinking you were finally dead."

He grinned and didn't answer. Walsh rarely felt guilt about anything, but with Clementine, guilt was all he felt. For what he had done to her, and how she had lied for him her entire adult life.

"What brings you here today? The guilt finally got to you?"

Adolescent memories returned of them playing together in their parents' mansion in Long Island. How, when he was sixteen, and she was fourteen, Walsh had flown into a rage and pushed his sister down the hallway stairs, breaking her back in three places. Walsh had never lost control since, and Clementine had lost permanent control of everything from the neck down.

To her credit, she had told no one it was Walsh who had pushed her, sticking with the story that she had tripped. Walsh could no longer remember what they had fought about that day, but hindsight suggested it must have been over trivial matters.

Since the accident, he'd left home at eighteen and joined the US Army. Later, he turned mercenary, to fight brutal battles in the world's worst war zones. He'd spent too much time chasing dictator gold in Libya and Iraq when both countries collapsed into civil war, but finally struck it rich when he "liberated" a diamond mine with his mercenary buddies in the Congo. Those diamonds had paid for all this and kept his sister in the best possible life it was feasible to live as a quadriplegic.

After establishing the required trust funds to ensure Clementine's future prosperity, he found himself to be penniless again. So he bluffed his way into the CIA, fast-tracked himself up the chain of command, and picked operations where he could always trade in dirty money, drugs, diamonds and gold on the side. After decades of deceit, embezzlement and hard work, he'd become moderately wealthy once more, or had been until Pierce had come into his life and ruined everything. The plan had always been to retire in comfort and obscurity. Now the only retirement plan left for him was a shallow grave.

He reached over and kissed Clementine on the cheek. "It's good to see you again, sis. I thought I'd stay a while and read you a story."

She frowned the same moment she smiled. "It'd better not be one of those god-awful romances you think I like."

"Don't be silly." He removed the novel from his jacket pocket. *Use of Weapons*, by Iain M. Banks. A science fiction novel set in a far-future utopia, where the main character was an operator like him and both a good and an evil man. "This is my favourite novel. I don't think I've ever read it to you."

She looked at the cover. It was an old edition from the 1990s, with silver-plated lettering and a spaceship resembling a fighter jet being shot at by a laser from a canyon city. He'd found it in a second-hand English-language bookstore in Rome two days earlier.

Stepping behind her, he injected several capsules of morphine into her saline drip, connected to a cannula conveniently present in her arm. The morphine was enough to guarantee she would be dead by evening, so he had time.

Walsh sat on the chair next to her and opened the book.

"Let's see, where to begin, hey? What about this quote? *The bomb lives only as it is falling.*"

73

Pierce waited until Walsh's BMW entered the highway tunnel hugging Lake Maggiore, seen through arches cut on the river side of the underpass. He pulled up close, overtook, then emptied the magazine of his Glock 19 into Walsh's engine block and front tire.

Walsh smashed his coupe against the brick walls multiple times before they both sped out of the tunnel, and then Walsh's vehicle hit a ditch and spun in a full circle before coming to a complete stop. It was late, almost night, and the road was empty. Pierce screeched to a halt, pulled the dazed and confused Walsh from his wreckage, removed all his weapons and possessions other than clothes, then threw him in the trunk of his Eos, and sped off.

No one had seen the attack, for which Pierce was grateful.

In the town of Brenna, he took a road into the forest-clad mountains and drove until they were far into the fern and pine tree forest. He parked as night settled in, dragged the still dazed Walsh from the trunk, and with his pistol jabbed in the spymaster's back, forced the old man to march up a trail leading deep into the night-clad wilderness. When they were far enough not to be seen, and positioned with a view from a natural rocky ledge overlooking the lake lit up by a sliver of the moon, Pierce halted and forced Walsh down on his knees.

Walsh cackled madly. "I would have preferred if you'd just shot me on sight."

"Cut the bullshit. Just tell me where she is!" Pierce would have gladly eliminated Walsh suddenly and from afar, given the choice, but as always, Walsh had information Pierce needed. Secrets were the currency Walsh had traded in for decades and what had kept him alive. Not tonight, however.

"Who are we talking about, Pierce?"

"Don't insult my intelligence, or yours."

Walsh winced from a sudden pain erupting in his gut.

Pierce watched, suspecting an act, but the man looked much sicker than he had even four days ago in Venezuela. And the point where Walsh gripped his gut was where Pierce had shot him in Morocco.

"I don't know where Summerfield is, and that's the truth of it."

Pierce licked his lips and thought through the logic. Either Walsh knew, or he didn't, but in either case, he should have convinced Pierce he knew her location, as a bargaining chip to keep himself alive.

Despite himself, and knowing that it was a wasted effort, Pierce asked, "Then what do you know?"

"Seriously? Pierce? I'm done. If you don't kill me now, infection will kill me in the coming days. Just fucking get it over with!" He snatched up a rock and prepared to throw it at Pierce.

With his Glock already raised, and the action instinctive, Pierce fired a single bullet into Walsh's forehead. The blast caused the back of the spymaster's head to explode outwards in a shower of gore and blood. Walsh's attack had been a worthless gesture unless his intention had been for Pierce to kill him quickly, in which case he'd gotten his wish.

The spymaster crumpled into a pile of skin and parched bones held together by deteriorated muscles and almost no fat. Out of habit more than to be sure the man was dead, Pierce put two further bullets into Walsh's heart despite it not beating anymore. Then he kicked the body off the ledge into thick bushes, where it might not be found for days.

Pierce returned to his Volkswagen Eos, swapped the number plates and altered it to its open-top convertible mode. Having disabled the GPS tracker earlier, he felt he had covered his tracks as well as he could have expected, so he drove into the night, headed for Switzerland.

He wished he felt something, but he felt nothing.

74

Paris, France

It was a sunny day in Paris, but not warm. Rachel Zang sat outside anyway and admired the charming Boulevard St Germain, with its stylish cafés, white Parisian apartment architecture, and a decent line of sight to observe anyone who might have tailed her. She ordered a coffee and a croissant and waited.

Naomi Berenson showed exactly at the agreed time, kissed Zang on the cheeks like they were old friends, and ordered her own coffee. The woman was about the same age as Zang, late twenties with Middle Eastern features, almond-shaped eyes, thick black hair cut short in a pageboy style, and muscle definition even in her neck, which, apart from her hands and face, was the only skin she showed. She wore jeans, a blouse, knee-high boots and a three-quarter coat, all of which looked expensive. Zang in comparison also wore jeans, but her boots only came to her ankles, and on her top half she wore a light sweater and a leather jacket.

Neither woman looked out of place in Paris. They impressed to the world this was their territory.

"Thanks for coming," said Zang.

Naomi nodded. "I owe you, after Iran."

Zang sipped her café latte. "Well, I appreciate you showing today, regardless."

Naomi nodded again and didn't speak for many seconds as she savoured her coffee. "Why did you come to me, and Mossad, with this request? Your own people could have answered this query easily enough."

Forcing a smile at the overt mention of Israel's foreign intelligence services who employed Naomi, Zang said, "If you feel compelled to repay the favour, then I'd appreciate you keeping this request just between you and me."

"You and me and Mossad?"

"I was using the plural version of 'you'. I'd be naive to believe you won't later tell your superiors what we discuss today."

"Of course. You don't want anyone in the CIA knowing, right?"

Zang nodded and sipped more of her coffee. Mossad were Israeli's fearsome and highly effective foreign intelligence service, and if any organisation outside the English-speaking Five Eyes network of intelligence-gathering agencies could help her, that organisation would be Naomi's people.

Naomi passed over a French edition of *Vogue* with Brazilian model Raquel Zimmermann on the cover. "There is an article in there I think you should read."

Zang opened the magazine to find several loose photos of a man, captured by what was presumably drone footage with Chinese characters, which she could easily read but told her nothing. The latitude and longitude, however, revealed the location to be somewhere in the Himalayan Mountain range, if her calculations were correct. The date and time stamps were erased. She studied the man closely, and while the resolution wasn't perfect, he looked a lot like Mark Pierce. Only his features were blunter, less defined. Then Zang realised this was a picture of Pierce before he had undergone facial-reconstruction surgery.

This was a photo from a time before Pierce officially joined the CIA.

She flipped through the two other photos, both similar, but they told her nothing else other than he'd dressed for a cold-weather mission, carried a Chinese-manufactured QBZ-95 assault rifle, and that he looked to have taken a recent beating.

Some things never changed with Pierce.

Naomi reached out her hand. "They aren't for keeping."

Zang handed back the magazine with the photos still safely tucked inside.

Naomi asked, "You know this man?"

"Some details, yes."

"What can you tell me about him?"

"What can you tell *me*, Naomi? This is my favour you're repaying."

The Mossad operator's face softened. "The Chinese don't know who he is, but they are offering a substantial reward... The equivalent of ten million US if handed over alive to the MSS. The Chinese Secret Service. They only offer half a million for his corpse, so they really want him ready to talk."

Zang tried to hide her shock. It had been Pierce who had bluffed — and not Maceo Parra — and told lies, in the frantic flight through the Venezuelan mountains. She hoped her micro-expressions gave nothing away regarding her troubled state of mind with this revelation, but Naomi was a professional operator and would have guessed she was onto something here, just as Zang had.

"Anything else?"

Naomi shook her head. "The Chinese have clammed up tight. Word in the whisper networks is that this man really embarrassed a high-ranking member of the Chinese Communist Party who holds significant political influence."

Zang nodded, not sure what to make of this information and what it said about her peer, lover, and perhaps friend. She had her secrets. Everyone in the game of spying and covert action did. But Zang suspected Pierce's secrets stood many heads and shoulders above everyone else.

"Can you tell me anything, Rachel?"

The way Naomi asked suggested it was not a friend asking, but Mossad itself. "Naomi, a man who looked very much like the man in the photo died recently during an operation in Venezuela. There were rumours that the Chinese had a significant reward offered for his capture."

"Did he have a name?"

Zang kept her expression neutral. "We had a code name for him, but nothing about his true identity."

"I see." Naomi finished her coffee, and Zang copied her. A signal that their meeting was drawing to a close. "What about a body? Other photographs? Fingerprints? DNA samples? Anything?"

"He died in a grenade blast near San Cristobal, Venezuela. There was nothing left. The only intel that we had was he had infiltrated himself inside FAES, operating as a sniper, if that helps?"

Naomi nodded and pinched her teeth together. "Well, it's

good seeing you again, Rachel. Until next time." She threw money on the table and stood. "Give our regards to Matchstick."

Rigid and furious, Zang waited two minutes for Naomi to disappear. Mossad had just sent a very unsubtle message, but was it for her ears only, or to share with the CIA?

What it did tell her was that she was far more compromised than she had suspected. Perhaps Pierce's approach was the right one, that it was always better to operate alone. But then she remembered the mess he had found himself in this last year. She had no desire to find herself in similar turmoil, and Zang could use the CIA as much as it used her.

There was only one answer that made sense. Mossad, like the mole that had infiltrated the CIA, was merely a layer in a bigger mystery. The secret circles-within-circles organisation pulled at many strings, and some of those strings could easily be tied to her.

She stood and walked away. It was time to follow those strings all the way to their puppet master.

75

Baltimore, Maryland, United States

Abdul Ibrahim stepped into the darkened apartment, with an overhead lamp still swinging from the violence someone had recently subjected it to. In the shadow-heavy lounge area, he witnessed two bodies. One alive and one dead.

The alive body was Patricia Knight, passed out and snoring upon the single lounge. Several lines of un-snorted cocaine decorated the glass-topped coffee table, and several smears showed where she had snorted more than once this night.

The body next to her was very dead, terminated only minutes earlier by Ibrahim's covert team. A wound in his chest showed where a knife had expertly pierced his heart, and he'd bled out. The bruises on the assailant's face showed that he'd fought well before receiving the killing strike. A laptop, smashed on the floor, seemed to have featured as a makeshift weapon during his battle to live.

Ibrahim's trusted odd-jobs operatives, Kenneth Karcher in his black biker outfit and Deep Ranjan in his nerdy glasses and tailor-made suit, pulled out books and over-turned drawers, conducting a thorough search of the apart-ment. They had done well to take out this man without breaking a sweat.

"What happened?"

Ranjan answered, "As far as we can tell, sir, the assailant waited for the drugs in the cocaine to render Ms Knight unconscious before he broke into the apartment and began downloading the contents of her laptop."

Ibrahim held his breath. Now the scene made sense to him. "Knight is the mole."

Karcher answered, "We don't believe she willingly passed on the secrets. Not yet anyway, hence the thorough search to confirm that supposition. But her habit made her easily manipulable. We suspect Knight knew the dead man as her dealer, and he mixed the sleeping drugs into the cocaine."

"Knowing that she'd likely take a hit straight away, and while she was passed out cold, he could access her laptop?"

Ranjan nodded. "He could have been doing this for years."

Ibrahim had seen enough. "Right. Search the apartment from top to bottom. Photograph this man and record any distinguishing features, and take blood samples so we can record his DNA. When you are done, clean the flat so it looks as if nothing ever happened tonight, and make the body disappear as if it never existed."

"Yes, sir." Ranjan pointed to Knight. "What about her?"

"Handcuff her, then put her in the trunk of my car."

Five minutes later, with Knight trussed up and secure in

Ibrahim's BMW, he returned to the driver's seat and looked at the woman perched across from him.

A few years older than he was, Karen Dwyer had recently turned fifty, and although her skin was showing wrinkle lines, she had kept herself slim, fit and elegant. She was Chief Eastern Europe, the C/ED, promoted to her senior position at the same time Ibrahim had been promoted to C/SOG, and like him, always disciplined in maintaining her physical and mental health regardless of the stresses their roles demanded of them.

Dwyer raised an eyebrow when he closed the car's door, providing them privacy. "Seems you have a body we need to dispose of. This brings back memories of the old times, Abdul, when you and I were far more starry-eyed."

He straightened his tie and neatened his hair. "This body isn't dead, and I want you to look after her."

"Her? You telling me that's Patricia Knight we have in the trunk of our car?"

"She's the mole. We don't know if she was intentionally passing on secrets or tricked into doing so. The biggest problem you'll face is that Knight is a classic cocaine addict."

Dwyer snorted, not masking her distaste of the situation. "You're asking me to play nursemaid while she detoxes?"

"Yes. I ask, because there is no one else I trust to do this, and no one else who can apply the right pressure in the right measure to understand what we are dealing with here."

She snorted again. "You know, when we were younger, all your flirting did charm me. The things I did for you... But not anymore."

"Please, Karen. This is important."

"You used to say that too, when we were younger." Dwyer

shook her head and appeared exhausted. Half a lifetime of playing spies was catching up with her.

"Two weeks, three max. Take Knight to the Montana facility, where it will be impossible for her to flee or relapse. Find out everything you can."

Slumped in her seat, Dwyer let out a long and frustrated-sounding breath. "Very well. But this'd better help me. Personally and career-wise."

"It will," Ibrahim said with a smile, and drove them into the Baltimore night.

Ten minutes later, when they were on the outskirts of the city and traversing a neon-lit motorway, Dwyer spoke again. "Rumour is you approved Mark Pierce's reinstatement into the Agency?"

Ibrahim bit his lip. His decision was an uncomfortable one, but like the previous time, he felt he had no choice. "The man is reckless. He keeps throwing himself into crazy-dangerous scenarios. I thought he'd have killed himself by now."

Dwyer leaned her elbow on the passenger window and rubbed her forehead with her fingers. "It's what you hoped would happen back the first time. It's what I had hoped would happen, too."

"It still might." Ibrahim spoke with a lightness in his voice that surprised him.

"What do you mean?"

"Trigger Man isn't coming in. He's gone rogue again, and he's going after Mackenzie Summerfield."

"Do we know where she is? Does he?"

Ibrahim shook his head. "Nobody does. In all likelihood, she's long dead, and Pierce will probably soon join her."

Dwyer tuned the radio until she found a jazz station. Music they both enjoyed, and its many improvised solos helped lift their moods when moroseness threatened. "If it happens like you say, it solves many problems."

"That it will, Karen. That it will."

76

Swiss Alps, Switzerland

After changing cars, switching number plates again, and disabling the GPS tracker on the stolen Toyota Yaris hatchback he had commandeered earlier, Pierce drove at a safe, legal speed, taking a scenic rather than direct route through the Swiss Alps. He needed to place as much distance as possible between himself, Walsh's corpse and the wrecked car, figuring that someone must have found the body by now and the police were already investigating.

With any luck, when the CIA learned that the body was a person of interest and formerly one of their own, they would shut down the investigation and sweep the entire event into Langley's dusty and forgotten filing rooms of obscurity and old news. But Pierce couldn't take that chance. He had to act like he was a hunted man.

His plan was to take an unconventional route into Spain, then disappear into North Africa, where he had contacts, from where he would base himself until he learned more on the fate of his friend. Mackenzie Summerfield could be anywhere in the world, and needless travel wouldn't serve him until he gathered more intelligence. Marrakesh seemed an ideal location to set himself up to do just that.

The Swiss mountains he drove through were vast and, in the distance, snow-capped. There were snow patches on the roadside and upon the closer mountain folds where the grass was thick, yet clung close to the earth. The road was constantly turning and twisting, and the continual climbing forced him to stay in the lower gears.

As evening settled in, Pierce noticed the fuel gauge was low. He found a remote gas station and parked at the bowser. After filling the tank, he stepped inside with cash in hand, ready to pay. He wore a cap, sunglasses despite the evening hour, and a face mask in a pretence that he had a cold and didn't wish to infect anyone else. If there were security cameras in the gas station, he didn't want any later facial-recognition software to identify him.

Only one other car was parked outside, a Volkswagen Mini that, judging by its many dents and rust patches, had achieved much mileage in its time. Near the entrance was a cage of dozens of gas cylinders for purchase. There were also racks and racks of firewood for sale.

Inside the service station, which also doubled as a convenience store, a young man with dark skin and African features waited, bored behind the cash register and electronic funds transfer machine.

The Mini occupants were a young couple in their early twenties. He was tall and scraggly, with a thick ginger beard, and she was a curvaceous blonde. They both dressed in designer camping jackets, beanies and tight jeans. Pierce watched them both disappear into the toilets.

From nowhere, the interior filled with bullet fire. The server died instantly as high-velocity bullets disintegrated the top of his torso and mangled his shoulder.

Pierce ducked down below the rows of confectionary and potato crisps where he'd been standing, only just in time to save himself from death, and drew his Glock.

Eight men stormed the service station, each of them armed with a variety of assault rifles, machine pistols and semi-automatics. Three men quickly had Pierce lined up in their sights, but they didn't shoot him. Pierce let the Glock fall from his hand as he raised his arms into the air. From the corner of his eyes, he noticed one assailant lock the toilets from the outside by forcing a broom through the door handle.

"On your feet," said one assailant, speaking in a German or Swiss-German accent. "Fail to cooperate, and we execute the young couple now terrorised in the toilets."

Pierce stood.

One man punched him hard in the gut, causing him to double over in pain while another checked him over for weapons. They found his knife and removed it. As Pierce stood tall again, he pocketed the cigarette lighter he'd lifted from the shelf during the earlier gut punch.

After removing his hat, sunglasses and face mask, they led him to where several chairs and tables offered themselves to patrons who snacked here before undertaking the next leg of their journey.

"Sit!" said the German or Swiss man.

Pierce obeyed. There were too many foes, and they all brandished lethal weapons.

They hadn't killed him yet, which meant the shooting he had ducked for wasn't aimed at him, because someone wanted information from him. That meant he had time to plan how he could walk away from this situation alive and intact.

"You don't talk much, for a man living on borrowed time."

Pierce ignored the German or Swiss foe. He wasn't in charge here. The man, or woman, who was would reveal themselves soon enough.

The individual who eventually stepped forward was not impressive in any particular feature, neither good-looking nor ugly, and not tall or short. He kept himself fit, and his scalp and beard he kept closely shaven. Pierce felt certain the man's ancestry was Mediterranean.

He knew this because they had met before, under similar stressful circumstances and forced duress. But that was all Pierce could remember, because it was obvious now not all his memories had yet returned.

"Hello, Mr Trigger Man. Remember me?"

Pierce snorted. "Should I?"

"You should. I'm Mr Real. Or did that car crash in Rio de Janeiro make you forget?"

77

Pierce felt his hands shake and his legs shudder. There was an aspect to this man, this Mr Real, that terrified him, and he couldn't place why.

Mr Real examined Pierce with clinical interest. "You know, I still can't figure out if this was a ruse or genuine memory loss."

It was real physiological memory loss, Pierce had been about to say, but instead he replied with, "Why does it matter?"

"Because you still completed the mission we agreed you would, and I want to know why."

"*What?*" Pierce's voice felt strained in his throat. What was it he still needed to remember, but hadn't, because the memory he fought to retrieve had occurred too close to his accident, or was it because he didn't want to?

"The mission to rescue Amelia Reyes from SEBIN, of course, as we agreed. When your old friend Idris Walsh stumbled into our little scheme, he fucked it right up. You almost fixed it."

Straightening his jacket, Pierce said, "Why the hell would I help you?"

Mr Real smiled but didn't answer immediately. "You know, we believed you were still working for us, right until the moment your special forces took out Morat Kozan and his people in Marmaris. That was a surprise, I tell you."

"I would never work for you." He felt the fog fill his mind again. He'd thought he was behind all this confusion, cured of his head injury despite the faulty memories from the previous weeks, but now he couldn't be certain of anything.

"It's a pity she died. Reyes would have been a powerful voice for our cause."

Then it hit Pierce, with the same force the accident had when he drove into that wall in the Rio slums. "It's you, Mr Real, who has Mackenzie Summerfield?"

Mr Real took out his smart phone, then played a video of a naked Mackenzie bound and beaten and pleading from a chair where she was restrained. What made it worse this time was seeing how thin and pasty Mackenzie had become. They had held her captive for some time. Months, at least.

"You fuckers!"

"Calm yourself, Mr Trigger Man. You still work for us. We need you again. A different mission this time, back in a land familiar to you. The Middle East. Keep doing as we say, and she won't come to any further harm."

Pierce lost it. With strength he didn't know he possessed, he lifted and flung the table into the centre of the congregating assailants, then rising to his feet, pulled Mr Real in front of him as a shield while bullets bored bloody holes into the fixer's chest.

Dropping the dead weight, Pierce dived over the service counter as more full automatic fire filled the air where he had just stood. Behind the counter, he found a spray can for killing cockroaches. Igniting the cigarette lighter in his pocket, Pierce turned the spray can into a flamethrower and burned the face of the attacker coming around the counter to shoot him.

As the man screamed, Pierce relieved him of his Heckler & Koch MP5 submachine gun and sprayed bullets into two more approaching assailants. He stood on the burned man's throat, who was now wailing on the floor, until his windpipe crushed.

When the magazine emptied, Pierce ducked back down behind the counter and fumbled through the dying man's gear, searching for a second magazine. Pierce knew he'd killed at least four assailants, including Mr Real, but that left five sneaking up on him now. Not good odds.

Pierce found the public announcement system, switched it on and turned the volume up to max. He waited for a lull in the shooting, then lifted both the MP5 and microphone so that as he fired, the already loud noise of the weapon discharge screamed through the service centre, hurting all their ears.

He'd known it was coming, and despite the pain his eardrums experienced, he pushed through it and sprinted for the closest shelves while his enemies covered their ears. The MP5 was empty, so he needed new tactics.

Pierce toppled the shelf stacked with canned foods and curry pastes over, so it came down on the assailant on the other side, who had been preparing his Steyr AUG assault rifle for action, with its bullpup design featuring the magazine behind the trigger guard. As the man screamed, Pierce threw a can of beans at another approaching man, connecting him in the head and knocking him cold. Pierce then jumped on the fallen shelves, crushing the attacker underneath.

More sprays of bullets zipped through the air around him.

As Pierce rolled for cover behind the next set of shelves, he dislodged the Steyr from the dead assailant's hand. Then he fired through the wall to where the gas cylinders were. He hit one, and they all exploded, sending shockwaves, flames, and projectiles of concrete and steel straight through the wall and into the remaining assailants all standing too close to the blast epicentre.

That was nine.

Pierce searched for and found a Makarov pistol in the pocket of the man he'd knocked out cold with the can. Next, he traversed the room, executing the wounded and unconscious alike. When the bullets ran out in the Makarov pistol, he found another MP5 and used that to complete the job.

Then he collapsed, fell against the front counter full of bullet holes, with his back against it.

He collapsed because the shaking in his hands and legs was beyond control.

He needed a moment.

A cellular phone rang.

78

P ierce bent over the blood-soaked body of Mr Real and snatched up the fallen cell phone. Breathing heavily and recovering from the post-comedown of an intense battle, he answered. He figured he had nothing to lose by taking the call.

"Yes."

The caller didn't answer immediately, but Pierce could hear him breathing. "You are not Mr Real?"

"No. Got me there."

"Then who are you?"

Pierce laughed as his hands still shook. "Someone you'll later regret crossing paths with."

"Put him on, now. Or you'll regret it."

Pierce paused, still slumped amid the carnage, and waited for his shaky hands and legs to work again. He needed to extract himself from this crime scene full of his DNA as rapidly as possible. But until his limbs worked, he wouldn't be able to get himself very far, so he'd ascertain what this mysterious caller could tell him until then. "Have we met? Your voice sounds familiar."

Then the realisation hit Pierce. The caller spoke in an Italian accent and sounded exactly like Mr Real.

"Fuck! You're his brother."

The line fell silent, but Pierce still heard the breathing. He remembered a story he'd heard about Mr Real, now that his memories of their previous encounter in Rio were seeping back to him. Mr Real had a reputation for uncannily being in multiple places at once.

"You're more than brothers. You are twins, pretending to be each other." Pierce laughed manically. "Seems I only got half the job done."

"My brother...? You murdered him?"

Pierce glanced over at the corpse staring glass-eyed towards the ceiling with meaty patches all over his chest. "Yes. I'm looking at him right now. One hundred per cent... not living."

"You fucker! You will suffer for this. And so will Ms Summerfield, whom you know we have in our custody."

"We'll see about that. I'm coming for you, Mr Real Part Two."

The call ended, so Pierce threw away the phone.

He staggered to his feet, and his legs didn't give out on him. There was nothing he could do to protect his friend from whatever tortures they'd already subjected her to. But if this circles-within-circles organisation had no means to reach him, they had no means to manipulate him. He would go dark, again, to find her, just as he had before.

Pierce pulled the broom from the door to the toilet, freeing the young couple, no doubt terrified on the other side. He thought again about snipers, but figured if any other assailants were present, they could have easily taken him out with a well-aimed shot during the intense nine-against-one melee. The service station windows gave ample view of the interior, and the darkness of the night could have concealed an attacker standing a dozen metres away. Pierce knew no one else waited to ambush or kill him this night.

He found the couple cowering together.

"You need to get far away from here. I won't hurt you, but you can't be around, just in case there are more of them."

Pierce walked away, found a first aid kit, and quickly tied a bandage around a minor bullet graze he'd just discovered on his thigh. It bled a little, but now that he was on the comedown from an intense battle, the pain would only worsen.

He watched the blonde woman and the ginger-haired man sprint to their car and drive with speed into the night.

Pierce grinned. Now they were safely away, he could cover his tracks.

After driving his Yaris fifty metres up the road towards Germany and parking it, he used several bowsers to spray gas around the station and into the shop loaded with dead thugs. Then he stepped back, used the lighter to ignite a Molotov cocktail he had built from an emptied Coke bottle, and threw the flaming projectile into the closest puddle of highly flammable hydrocarbons.

Almost instantly, the service station lit up, and the flames burned fast and would hopefully destroy all evidence that Pierce had ever been here.

He turned and vanished into the night.

After too many false starts, he was coming for Mackenzie now, and he would make her captors pay.

Every last one of them.

ACKNOWLEDGMENTS

Special thanks to Leo Iriarte for his incredible insights into Venezuela and first-hand knowledge of his home country discussed over many bottles of wine, Ross Sidor, Bodo Pfündl, Deep Ranjan, Roxy Long and Kashif Hussain for first reviews of the manuscript, Kenneth Karcher for advice on weapons featured in this novel, and Ian and Anne Short for their support.

I'd like to thank everyone at Inkubator for their fantastic support and professionalism in getting this series out into the world, and those I have engaged with directly include Lizzie Bayliss, Shirley Khan, Brian Lynch, Claire Milto, Carol Mulligan-John, Garret Ryan, Stephen Ryan, and my editor Alice Latchford. I thank you all.

And again, as always, Bec Short for her ongoing support and encouragement at every step I've taken with the Trigger Man series.

ABOUT THE AUTHOR

Aiden Bailey is an international bestselling thriller author from Australia. Formerly an engineer, he built a career marketing multi-national technology, engineering, and construction companies. His various roles have included corporate communications with the Australian Submarine Corporation, technical writing for several defence contractors, engineering on an outback petroleum pipeline, a magazine editor and art director, and engineering proposal writer for the Royal Australian Air Force's surveillance and intelligence gathering aircraft and drone enabling works. Aiden has travelled widely in six continents and his experiences are the basis of many of his stories.

Did you enjoy *Cage of Traitors*? Please consider leaving a review to help other readers discover the book.

www.aidenlbailey.com

ALSO BY AIDEN BAILEY

Printed in Great Britain
by Amazon

45146172R00253